Compulsion

A "Poison In My Veins" Novel
Book 1

Cynthia Eden

They wake up hand-cuffed together in a serial killer's lair...hardly the meet-cute of her dreams. But then again, her dreams are usually nightmares so...

Lily Gallo knows killers. She should, after all, because serial killers are her specialty. She's the daughter of a notorious serial killer, and she's made it her life's work to study the brutal predators. And, recently, she's been researching the offspring of serials. She's looking for others who are just like she is. Her research has brought her into the life of reclusive billionaire Atlas Bennett. He'd refused her repeated requests for a meeting. She'd suspected he might be following in his father's brutal footsteps. But now...

They're both trapped, and they have to rely on each other for survival.

Atlas can't believe it when he wakes up handcuffed to the beautiful and infuriating Lily. The woman thinks he's as savage as his twisted father, but she has no clue what dark secrets he really holds. For the moment, though, escape is their priority. But once they get out of that hell, Lily will be his. He'd warned her to stay away. Now, it's too late. Her fate is sealed.

A killer is after them both. To survive, they have to trust each other. They also have to stay very, very close to one another...

Atlas knows that his reaction to Lily isn't normal. The lust he feels is too strong, too consuming, but she calls to the primitive darkness within Atlas that he's tried to hide from the rest of the world. He's going to need that darkness because a killer is hunting him...and Lily. A predator who is intent on taking out the children of serial killers. Innocence and guilt doesn't matter. Only survival does. The killer has uncovered Lily's research, and he's using it to track his prey. As each day passes, he's also growing increasingly obsessed with Lily.

Being prey wasn't on her agenda.

Lily's mother is the most infamous female serial killer of modern times, and her mother passed on more than a few of her dangerous traits to Lily. Lily has no intention of being some helpless victim, but she will trap the killer who is on her trail. She'll also stick close to Atlas because she knows he holds plenty of secrets. Fair enough. She's got secrets, too. Atlas stirs a part of her that she has tried to fight her entire life. Wild, forbidden, and dangerous, he is a lover she can't resist. He may just be the perfect partner for her... unless, of course, she turns out to be dead wrong about him.

Because some people carry darkness, some people carry sins...and there are some monsters that you never see coming, not until it's far too late.

Author's Note: Danger, serious steam, and two lovers who share a passion that will obliterate everything else... He's possessive, dangerous, and willing to kill. She's methodical, controlled, and fighting to hide her true self. When they come together, their worlds will shift, their lust will consume them, and they will either be the perfect team...or the most diabolical couple to walk the earth. Ah, fun times are ahead.

Don't be afraid of the dark.
Make the dark be afraid of you.

Prologue

JULIA TUTWILER PRISON FOR WOMEN
  Wetumpka, Alabama

EIGHT MONTHS AGO...

"PRISON IS BORING. I haven't been given the opportunity to kill anyone in ages." Magnolia Calhoun let out a long and despondent sigh as she sat at the small table, her hands folded in front of her, not a single line appearing on her face.

Lily shifted in her seat. The uneven legs of the chair made it rock forward, then back. "That's not a funny joke, Mother." She cast a quick glance toward the guard who stood to the right, watching every movement. Hearing every single word. And, no doubt, intending to report every single word back to the warden.

"Who's joking?" Magnolia responded.

Lily lifted one eyebrow.

Her mother's gaze darted to the guard. "Oh, right. *I'm joking. Me.*" One hand lifted as she waved toward the guard. "Hi, handsome."

Her mother always took every opportunity to flirt with a handsome man. So what if he was thirty years her junior? Magnolia didn't care about numbers.

She also didn't care very much about life or death.

No one's life mattered to her.

And she truly had gone a long time without killing anyone. Considering that Magnolia was in jail for murdering twelve men, she had to be struggling. Killing to Magnolia was like getting a rush from the very best drug in the world. The hit gave off a high that was euphoric.

She killed at least twelve men. But I know there were more. The cops and the Feds and the DA just couldn't prove it.

"You look pale, Lily," Magnolia suddenly scolded. Sounding like a typical mother. Though there would never, ever be anything typical about her. "Are you getting enough Vitamin D? Spending enough time outdoors? Eating enough protein? Drinking enough water?" She smiled. "I hear all of that is very important. *I* need more of those vital things." A deliberate glance toward the guard. "Make sure the warden understands that, will you, Jesse? Tell him I need more outside time. I'm sure Lawrence will accommodate me. We have such a warm relationship."

Lily sincerely hoped that her mother was not fucking the warden.

Magnolia winked at her.

Crap, she probably is fucking him.

"I received another marriage proposal." Magnolia's hands folded in front of her again. Magnolia had never been one for nervous movements. She was completely contained.

Every small twitch carefully orchestrated. "You know, it's not just women who fall for the bad guys. Not just women who think that something broken can be fixed. Such a cliché to think it's only us."

Now this was interesting. Her mother had never, ever referred to herself as *broken* before. "Since when do you need to be fixed?"

Her mother's warm, slow smile stretched over her face, lighting her dark eyes. Making her look warm and approachable. Beautiful. Charming.

Magnolia had been charming men since she was sixteen years old.

She'd also been killing them for that long.

"Since never, of course," Magnolia demurred. "But it is so fun when people try." Musical laughter. Everything about Magnolia was entrancing. Always had been. Her laughter drew people to her. Her smiles made them want to smile back.

She was a human Venus Flytrap, ready to draw you in. Then slowly kill you.

And she wants me to be just like her.

"I actually receive a marriage proposal every few days. One individual is particularly persistent. A doctor from Louisiana." A slow nod. "Perhaps I will take him up on his offer. I have been so very bored in here... My letters from the outside world are my main form of entertainment. I get so many letters. Did I mention them?"

She was sure her mother received dozens of letters each week. "Does the doctor from Louisiana understand that all of your past lovers wound up murdered, by you?"

"Of course." A wink. "That's part of his attraction to me. Some people love getting close to danger. It excites them. The thrill of evil can be intoxicating."

Goosebumps rose on Lily's skin. "I thought you weren't evil. I thought you said those men all deserved what happened to them." That had been Magnolia's claim at sentencing time. When she'd tried to get life instead of a lethal injection.

For all the good the explanations had done her. In the end, she'd been given the death penalty.

A verdict still on appeal. A very, very long appeal process. Her mother would not be dying anytime soon.

"Are we talking about me?" Magnolia leaned forward. "Or are we talking about you?" Her full lips pressed together. "A mother does like to keep tabs on her daughter's life. It's only natural."

There was nothing natural about their relationship.

Magnolia's features tightened, just the faintest bit. "Have you put your ridiculous research aside?"

"Thank you, Mother," Lily responded. "It's always lovely to have one's life's work called ridiculous."

"*The children of serial killers.*" Magnolia's nostrils flared. "You do not need to find them. You do not need to get close to those monsters—" But she broke off because...

I am one of those monsters. Lily deliberately widened her eyes as she waited for her mother to continue. Only Magnolia did not speak again, so Lily prompted, "You were saying something about monsters?"

"You aren't like them." A sniff.

"You don't know them." Neither did Lily. Neither did anyone. That was the problem. And the potential. She wanted to dive deeper into their lives. To see what made them tick. Wasn't that the big puzzle in the behavioral and psychological world? Nature or nurture? Which would be stronger?

Or, in the case of children born to serial killers...

Nature or nurture...did you know what your parents were? Did they try to make you like them? Or try to turn you into something completely different?

"You're seeking out the dangerous ones," her mother chided. "That will be problematic for you."

She hadn't talked to her mother about who she was seeking. She rarely talked to her mother about her life. Certainly not her work. But, as always, Magnolia knew her well.

"You don't want to talk to the ones with picket fences and happy babies. You're looking for the ones with evil coiled inside of them. For the ones who hear the call. For the ones who like the blood. You're trying to figure out what pushed them over the edge—or that will push them."

The guard shifted a bit closer.

Lily made certain her expression didn't alter. But she could feel sweat sliding down her back, right between her shoulder blades. The small visiting room at the Alabama maximum security prison was very, very warm.

Then again, the whole prison was a hellhole, so it should be hot. Overcrowded, inhumane—there had been so many lawsuits against the place in the past that the Feds had needed to come in and start setting their own management standards.

But instead of being angry when she found out that she would be living her remaining days at the Julia Tutwiler Prison for Women, Magnolia had seemed...pleased.

Like that wasn't problematic.

Mother, what are you planning?

And, nearly right from the start, Magnolia had made it a point to befriend the warden. *Lawrence.*

Now her mother made a *tut-tut-tut* with a few loud clicks of her tongue. "I know you, sweet child."

She was far from being a child. Or from being sweet. Magnolia had made certain of that fact.

"You want to talk to the killers—the ones who are walking in the footsteps of their parents. You want to find the evil. Root it out." Her mother's head tilted to the side. "Is it because you are so tempted to walk in my footsteps? Darling, does the dark call to you?" And she reached out her hand, as if she'd touch Lily.

Lily whipped back in her wobbly chair. "I'm trying to *stop* the monsters. Not become one." This talk was over. She rose to her feet. "Goodbye, Mother." She turned away, aware that her breathing was too hard. Once again, she'd let her mother get beneath her skin. She should have known better. Even though Lily had a fistful of degrees now, Magnolia was still the pro at manipulation. Some people were just born gifted.

Others were cursed.

"You'll come back?" Magnolia inquired, voice warm as sunshine.

Lily glanced over her shoulder. "Don't I always?"

"Yes. Because you're such a good, dutiful daughter."

"So good that you tried to kill me? Isn't that what the stories say?" Sometimes, Lily swore she could still feel the tube being shoved into her mouth and down her throat. It had scraped and burned because there had been no time for numbing.

Her mother's expression almost cracked. *Almost.* What could have been actual emotion flashed in her eyes. "That was a mistake."

Lily released a soft sigh. "Right." A nod. "Until next time." Her head angled for the door. She took a step forward.

"Lily!" Real alarm. *Real* emotion.

Once more, Lily glanced back. She was surprised to see that her mother was on her feet. Magnolia's hands had slapped down against the tabletop.

"They are not going to be like you," her mother warned. "You will not find someone who can put the pieces of you together and who will make you understand what you feel inside."

She shook her head. "That's not what I am looking for." *I want to stop evil before innocent people are hurt.*

"They will hurt you. They will use you. They will destroy any goodness that you have in you."

It was Lily's turn to laugh. "Mother, I thought you were the one who always told me...I have no goodness inside." With that, she left her mother. She walked out of the visiting room. Down the long, narrow corridor. Past the guards. Past the bars. Past the other inmates who yelled and heckled and she just kept going.

One foot in front of the other.

The way she'd always done.

Lily kept going. She had a job to do, after all. Research that waited.

She would meet the adult children of serial killers. She would talk to them. She would understand them. And, if she found those who were slipping too far into the darkness...

Well, she would have to stop them.

One way or another.

After all, I am my mother's daughter.

Chapter One

"WE ARE IN A LIFE-OR-DEATH SITUATION, and it would be incredibly helpful if you would open your eyes."

The feminine voice—low, husky—floated through the darkness that engulfed him. He kinda liked that voice. It was nice. Warm. Sexy.

Something pulled at his wrist. An insistent tug.

"I don't want to watch you get disemboweled in front of me."

Yeah, a really nice voice. Except...a ragged edge had entered her tone. And had she just said *disemboweled*?

"I'm worried you'll get stabbed over and over again. And that I will, too. So, seriously, do me a favor *and open those eyes of yours. Now!*" A sharp command. "Because we do not have time to wait for the cavalry to arrive!"

A groan escaped him first because his head pounded over and over and nausea rolled in his stomach, but, very slowly, he managed to open his eyes.

His gaze locked on her.

Dark hair tumbled over her shoulders. Somewhere between brown and black. Thick hair. A little wavy. High cheekbones. A slightly pointed chin. Dark eyes. Brown. No, brownish gold. He could see them quite clearly even though the lighting was dim. No lipstick on her full lips. Lips that were currently pressed tightly together as she stared at him with those intense eyes of hers. Eyes that were full of—

"So happy you're back in the land of the living. Truly, I am deliriously happy. Now, how about we *both* stay in this living land, and we get out of here? You were too big and far too heavy for me to drag you out while you were unconscious, but now that you're awake, we really need to make a run for it. Especially, you know, if we want to keep on living. Side note, I do want to keep on living. I very much want that. It is my main goal at the moment."

He blinked.

"Shit," she muttered. Her gaze swept over his face. "Do you have any clue what's happening right now?"

No, he did not, in fact, have any clue.

"I saw him knock you out. A very hard hit." Muttered. Almost more to herself than him. Then she added, "That's when I bravely rushed to the rescue. Don't worry, you can thank me later for that. And we won't talk about the fact that I thought *you* were the one doing the serial killing. My bad. We'll save that discussion for later, too."

His head pounded all the harder, and the nausea he felt got worse.

"Do you know *who* you are?" she suddenly demanded.

Of course, he did. "Atlas." He should take stock of his surroundings and not just stare at her gorgeous face. His memory was more than a bit blurry at the edges, and he couldn't quite remember where he was. "Atlas Bennett."

His voice strengthened. Became a touch brisk because... what in the world was happening? His gaze finally tore from her to search the area around him. The place was dimly lit because the only illumination came from what looked to be an old camping lantern tossed on the floor.

As for the floor—dusty, old wood. Dusty, dark walls. Stairs that led up to who knew where and—

She tugged on him. Or rather, on his wrist. Automatically, he glanced down. And the confusion he'd felt before just thickened. "Why the hell am I handcuffed to you?" Because he was. A shiny handcuff circled his wrist. His handcuff's mate circled hers.

"Excellent question. I'll explain fully—truly, I will— once we are out of here. See, he tossed us both down the stairs not too long ago. During the fall down—even though you were just starting to wake up—you valiantly cushioned my body with your own. Thanks so much for that. Very brave. Didn't expect you to do that as groggy as you were."

What? Someone had tossed them down the stairs?

"But the tumble down the stairs, combined with the blow to the head that you'd already taken—well, you were knocked out again once we hit the bottom. I did manage to drag you a bit away from the stairs, and I searched for a weapon for us to use. Uh, spoiler, there is no weapon here. Though I did find the lantern so we could see our surroundings, and I count that as a win. Not like I wanted to be trapped in the darkness while I waited for the killer to come and finish us off."

He realized they were on the floor. Yeah, he probably should have figured that out sooner. But the pounding in his head continued like a jackhammer, and he choked back the bile that rose in his throat. Atlas also became aware of the aches and pains that throbbed throughout his body.

Probably because he'd been pushed down a damn staircase. "I know who I am," he gritted as more of the cobwebs cleared from his head, "and I know who *you* are." As if he could forget that face.

She wet her lips. "You sound angry."

"Lily. Gallo." Each word was bitten out from between clenched teeth.

"Hello, Atlas," she whispered. "Guess we finally got that private meeting I've been wanting, huh?"

His teeth ground together.

"Honestly, I think you should consider me to be your new guardian angel." She crouched next to him and tugged on the cuff that bound them together. "Without me, you'd be down here all alone, at the mercy of the creep who wants to torture you for hours. That's what he's been doing, you know. Abducting his prey in Dallas. Torturing them, disemboweling them. *Killing* them."

He whipped up to a sitting position. The whole room spun, but Atlas clenched his teeth. No damn way was he going out again.

Lily sent him a weak smile. "That's the spirit. No disemboweling for us, am I right?"

She was fucking gorgeous. Not cover model perfect. But real. Sexy. No, sensual, and if they weren't currently in the pit of hell with the threat of apparent *disembowelment* looming over them, he might have enjoyed being cuffed to her.

But...

Pit of hell.

Serial killer.

*And if she says the word "disembowel" to me one more time...*Yeah, he'd lose it.

He shook his head, and that small move just made the

nausea worse. But, dammit, this was Lily Gallo. Lily *fucking* Gallo. He was handcuffed in a basement to the one and only Lily Gallo. The woman who wanted to slice apart his life. The woman who thought she should get some fast pass that would allow her access to every secret he possessed. The woman he had been avoiding like the plague for weeks.

Because she is dangerous to me.

Her non-cuffed hand rose to press to his cheek. "You're with me this time? Because you tried to wake up in bits and spurts before, but you'd go out again too fast."

"I'm with you." Grim. Her touch seemed to send renewed energy through him. There was certainly some kind of jolt that hit him. He'd analyze it later. When he wasn't in danger of being cut into tiny pieces.

I should have found him. Should have eliminated him. Long before the bastard had been able to get killing close to Atlas. But, truth be told, he'd been distracted that night. Distracted by *Lily*. He'd actually been thinking about her when the bastard attacked. Such a clusterfuck. "I'll keep you safe," he vowed.

Soft laughter greeted his words. "I'm the one who has been keeping *you* safe. After he knocked you out in the parking lot, I'm the one who jumped into action. I'm the one who tried to fight him when he was staring at your unconscious body and figuring out where he wanted to start stabbing. *Me.*"

Atlas had zero clue if he could trust this woman or not. His eyes narrowed on her face. That unforgettable face.

Lily. She'd been haunting his dreams far too frequently of late. She'd tried to get private appointments to see him. Been very tenacious about her visits.

He'd had her escorted from his main office building at

least twice. Had even told the security guards there that she was not to be allowed back on the premises under any circumstances.

Lily wanted to destroy him.

He couldn't let that happen.

Except...now she was saying that she'd saved him? What sick joke was that?

"There are no windows down here." Her voice was low. Still oddly sexy. Husky. "So that means we have to go up the stairs together. The door up there is our only way out. I would have tried to go and get help while you were knocked out, but you know, cuffed. You're no lightweight, so I couldn't haul you up on my own. We have to get out together. You and I are partners in this thing."

He rose to his feet.

She did, too.

When Atlas weaved, Lily's free hand flew out to brace him. As if she worried that wasn't going to be enough, she then put her whole body against him. Softness. Sweetness. The warm scent of vanilla.

He hadn't gotten close enough to ever catch her scent before. Now he knew that he would never forget how she smelled. How very good.

Sweetness in hell.

"It was incredibly heroic of you to twist your body to cushion me as we fell down the stairs. I definitely appreciate the gesture. Especially since you did it when you were only semi-aware. Sort of like an instinct. Didn't exactly realize you had a protective instinct carved so deeply into your bones."

"Stop analyzing me." Lily was a shrink. She lived to poke and prod in people's heads. He didn't want her to talk about his instincts, because they were quite the opposite of protective. Good instincts didn't fill him. He was dangerous. A true predator.

He also had zero memory of any fall down the stairs. Or of cushioning her.

"Clearly, you're hero material, and I was very, very wrong about you. My apologies."

Fuck that. He'd never been a hero a day in his life. And when he found the sonofabitch who'd done this to him...

You're a dead man. But, then again, Atlas had intended to kill the bastard all along. As soon as Atlas had realized a serial was hunting in *his* town, he'd been tracking the kills. Gathering evidence. Researching. Hunting his prey.

It was kind of what he did. Not that he intended to tell the lovely lady with him that important fact. Not like he went around broadcasting the fact that he was a monster.

But...what did she mean about being *wrong* about him? "So you no longer think I'm a chip off the old block, huh?" Deliberate words. A taunt.

Lily didn't answer that question. Of course, not. Because despite the fact that they were trapped in a nightmare, maybe she still thought that Atlas was just like his twisted bastard of a father. As savage and sadistic as they came.

She would not be wrong. "Maybe I'm the one you should fear." The words just came out. Dark and rumbling.

"You're trapped with me." Her immediate response. "You are currently my only hope of survival. I figure you and I will live or die together, so how about you save your scary routine for later?"

His scary *routine*? His jaw nearly dropped.

"You're also probably a lot more intimidating when you aren't weaving on your feet," she added.

Dammit. He was weaving. A bit. Fine, a lot.

"We should hurry," she whispered even as she continued to brace him. "Up the stairs, and then, we'll figure out how to get past the door. I am assuming it's locked. Not like I could drag you up there with me to check. But what kind of killer would *not* lock in his prey? So, let's go. Time is ticking and all that. Getting closer to our own grisly deaths."

She was surprisingly calm about the situation. That should worry him. He didn't think a typical person would be calm in this scenario. But from what he'd learned about her, Lily Gallo was far from typical.

She has a darkness in her past to match my own.

Her calmness—and her darkness—they both just intrigued him. He had tried to stay away from her. Truly, he had. He'd warned the woman to keep her distance. Now they were cuffed. Trapped together, just as she'd said.

Fate had such a twisted sense of humor.

Without another word, Lily eased away and began heading for the stairs. Because they were linked, he had no choice but to follow right behind her.

Now that he was upright, Atlas towered over her. He clocked out around six-foot-three, but she stood at five-foot-four. Yes, he knew her exact height. Atlas knew a great deal about Lily. He'd made it a point to know.

A quick scan showed she wore white sneakers, a white sweater, and faded jeans—jeans that fit her curves and her delectable ass very, very well.

Probably shouldn't be noticing her ass right now.

But he was injured, not dead, and she had one helluva fine ass.

As much as he liked that ass...Atlas stilled and tugged on the cuffs.

Lily stopped and looked back over her shoulder at him.

"I'm bigger than you," he rumbled.

"Uh, yes, I noticed. You're quite big."

"Stronger than you."

"Probably so, yes, that would go along with being *bigger*. Your muscle mass is greater so you're stronger."

"So I'm going be the one who goes through the door first and faces the asshole waiting upstairs." He'd just become aware of something wet sliding into his right eye. He brushed away the wetness.

"That's blood," Lily helpfully told him. "Because you're bigger, you're stronger, and you're also *injured*. As in, you were unconscious two minutes ago, and I'm worried you'll pass out on me again at any moment."

Atlas locked his teeth even as he wiped the blood on the thousand-dollar pair of pants that he wore. "I won't." Hopefully. Maybe not.

Lily sighed. "Fine. Lead the way. You take the knife to the heart when the door opens and the attacker lunges at us. Then, when I'm cuffed to your dead body, please know how incredibly unhappy I am going to be because you insisted on going *first*."

He stepped closer to her. She'd actually climbed up two stairs already, so he was a bit more on eye level with her. Their bodies brushed. "A knife to the heart," he repeated, voice low. He and Lily were both keeping their voices hushed.

As he stared at her, Atlas's gaze was drawn to her mouth. He really liked her mouth. Again, he shouldn't be noticing her ass or her mouth—not under these circumstances—but, he did. Maybe it was because of the blow—blows?—to the head. The concussion he probably had. But Atlas was finding that he noticed and liked far too much about Lily. "Sounds like a killer idea." Then he bent low, and he pulled out the knife that had been strapped to his ankle. A press of a small button, and the blade extended. Wickedly sharp.

Instead of a sigh, this time, Lily inhaled sharply. He waited for her fear.

Instead, a delighted smile spread across her lips. "I wish I'd known about your knife sooner! Great, now we have a fighting chance. You won't hesitate to use it, will you?"

"I never hesitate."

She swallowed. "I'll file that away in my *Points to Know About Atlas* book."

"You have a whole book on me? Ah, Lily, now I'm flattered. I had no idea you were such a fan." Though he knew that *fan* wasn't the right word.

Lily was convinced he was evil. Straight to his marrow.

"You're a work in progress for me." Her confession. Lily wet her lips. "Hold on a sec." Then she shimmied around him and grabbed for the lantern. "Not a knife, but it's better than nothing. In a pinch, I can slam it into the jerk's head."

Yes, he supposed that she could. "So you're bloodthirsty, too. I'll file that away in my *Points to Know About Lily* book."

"You don't have a book on me."

"Um, you're right. I have a file. A very thick one." True story. He always researched his adversaries.

Her free hand clutched the lantern as she straightened. "After you."

The stairway was incredibly narrow. When he began to climb up those stairs, she had to practically paste her body against his back because of the cuffs.

"If we fall, you're going to crush me," she warned.

He had no intention of falling. He *was* getting through the door at the top of the stairs. Then he'd be gutting the prick who'd abducted him. Atlas wondered if Lily was squeamish. He highly doubted it, but if the sight of blood did bother her, then she could look away.

Her sweet vanilla scent surrounded him. Tempted him. His left hand held the knife. His right was cuffed to her. The dumbass who'd attacked him had clearly not done his homework. Atlas was a lefty. He could cut a man open in less than two seconds with his left hand. *From groin to—*

"What are the odds that he just left the door unlocked?" Lily's soft voice barely reached him.

They were right in front of the door now. Or, rather, Atlas was. A mix of light and shadows spilled around them. Dammit, the light from the lantern would be slipping beneath the door, potentially warning the bastard waiting that Atlas was coming with an attack of his own. "Kill the light. *Now*."

She did.

Instant darkness.

In the darkness, he was highly aware of her. Her scent. Her quick pants. Her body. A body that pressed closely to his. Feminine. Warm. Tempting.

He reached for the doorknob. Tried to turn it. Surprise, surprise, it was locked.

"The lock and the hinges are on the other side," she breathed. "This is the part where we both need to try really hard and not panic."

He wasn't going to panic. He was going to kick ass. And probably kill. "Go back down the stairs."

"What?"

"Go back down the stairs." Because he was going to need a bit of a running start.

"Why are we going back down?" Lily's words trembled. The first sign of real fear he'd caught from her.

"Because I'm bigger than you, I'm stronger than you, but if I'm going to break down this door, then I'll need some momentum going so...head down the stairs, then we're racing up." He needed more room to work. That narrow area at the top just wasn't enough space.

"You're...breaking down the door?"

He didn't respond to that question. He'd already said as much, hadn't he? What else did she think he was gonna do? As she'd already noted, the hinges were on the other side, so not like he could take those freaking things off. His options were to break the lock or to shatter the wood of the door.

"You were just unconscious."

She kept harping on that point. He was no longer unconscious. He was bleeding, yes, but definitely awake and aware.

"Do you really think slamming into a door is the best plan?" Lily continued.

He turned his head to look back at her. Only saw darkness. "Do you have a better idea?"

A pause. Then, "No. Let's slam you into the door. As hard as we can. You'll be our battering ram."

His lips wanted to twitch. Trapped in hell, and he wanted to smile. Weird.

"You haven't suspected me," she suddenly blurted even as she crept down the stairs. He crept with her, aware of the faint groan of one stair beneath his feet. "Haven't asked if I'm some horrible villain who staged this whole scene with you."

"You're cuffed to me."

"Uh, yes..."

"You aren't strong enough to have gotten me here alone." And the aches in his body told him that he'd definitely hit some stairs as he tumbled and landed in the basement.

"True. But I could be working with a partner. Yet you are showing *zero* suspicion of me."

He figured they were about half-way down the stairs. "Do you want me to be suspicious?"

"No. I want you to get us out of here. As fast as possible, please."

"Working on it, sweets."

A sharp inhale. "I'm not sweet. Please don't make that mistake."

Her scent surrounded him. And her scent was very, very sweet. His chest ached. Not from the fall he'd taken before. A whole different kind of ache. The kind that told him this woman would probably wind up being more trouble than the killer who waited upstairs.

After all, he intended to murder the bastard upstairs. A quick plunge of Atlas's knife should do the trick. But this woman...

This woman...

Lily Gallo...

"I'll run up with you," Lily blurted. "I mean, I have to do it since we're cuffed together, but I'll throw my body against the door, too. With both of us, maybe we can break the lock or the wood or—or something. But we have to be ready for an attack after the door gives way."

He would be ready.

He *should* have always been ready. The fact that the SOB had gotten the jump on him...

Fuck me. That never should have happened.

"You seem to be hesitating," she noted, her voice a breath of sound.

Yeah, maybe he was. Because when he opened that

door, Atlas didn't know what would happen. He didn't know how many enemies he might face or if he'd survive—if they would. "Sure as fuck seems a shame..." he muttered.

"What's a shame?"

"To realize that I could die without tasting you."

Silence. Stunned. Stark.

"Oh, no. You have one serious concussion, don't you?" Lily fretted.

Probably. Didn't change things. "I want to taste you."

"You don't *know* me," she whispered. "Why would tasting me matter?"

Now laughter came from him. Dark laughter. Maybe a bit mocking. "Oh, Lily, I know you pretty well. Ever since you began calling me, pestering for an interview, I made it my mission to learn as much about you as I possibly could." The darkness had closed tightly around them as they stood on those narrow stairs, their bodies sliding together.

"What do you *think* you know?" Lily asked.

"You're the daughter of a serial killer."

She sucked in a sharp breath. "Guilty."

"A mind fucker of the highest caliber," he said, not without a bit of admiration. Because Lily was quite the mind fucker. "A psychiatrist who loves to play with killers because you want to cut all of us apart and see what drives us."

"Us?" A careful pause. "Are you calling yourself a killer?"

He *was* a killer.

"I'm not particularly interested in playing with anyone," she said. "But I do want to know what makes us kill." And there was the faintest emphasis on *us*.

"Are *you* a killer, Lily Gallo?"

Wood groaned overhead. Someone was up there. He

needed to get his ass moving. Instead... "Fucking shame," Atlas whispered. He wanted her mouth. "Dreamed about you."

"You did not."

Oh, but he had. And he didn't typically have dreams about anyone. Nightmares? Sure, he had plenty of those. Sweet dreams were something entirely different. Entirely special. "One taste before dying. Surely that's not too much to ask." What in the world was he doing? He needed to be getting them the hell out of there. Not...not...

"We're not dying. And you get us out of here—both of us—and I'll give you the best kiss of your life."

Well, that was some mighty fine motivation.

The overhead creaking came again. Dust drifted down on them. Dust or dirt or who the hell knew what it was.

"You know what? Scratch that," Lily decided. "I don't want terror to be the last thing I feel." Her cuffed hand rose. He felt the metal slide against him. "Kiss me. Now."

His mouth lowered. It was so dark he couldn't find her, not clearly, and—

A long groan, followed by the creak of...hinges? The door was opening. Light spilled inside. A small beam.

Her breath caught.

He hadn't tasted her. There was no time. "Now," he snarled to her, voice guttural, and then he was lunging up those steps, with Lily pressed tightly to him. Their feet pounded on the stairs, and he grabbed the door and thrust it open fully even as he roared and shot out of that darkness and launched right at the bastard that he *would* be sending to hell.

Atlas's knife flashed as he drove it toward his prey.

And a scream echoed in his ears.

Lily's scream.

Chapter Two

For the second time that night, Lily Gallo found herself jumping onto a man's back as she tried to stop him from committing murder.

The first time she'd jumped onto a male's back, she'd been desperate to try and save a life. Atlas's life. He'd been sprawled on the pavement near his shiny Benz. His attacker had been close, and she'd been sure the creep was reaching for a knife.

She'd rushed up behind the man in the ski mask. She'd grabbed for him. Stopped the perp from stabbing Atlas.

Unfortunately, she'd succeeded in getting herself abducted, too.

Now, though, she was trying to stop Atlas from killing. He was the one with the knife, and if she didn't get him to pull back, *he'd* be the killer.

"No!" Lily launched onto his back. Or she launched as much as she could considering that she was cuffed to him and she'd already been pretty much right on top of him, anyway. But she dropped the lantern she'd gripped so fiercely, and she grabbed for Atlas. "Stop! *Don't!*"

He shook her off.

Correction, he tried to shake her off. She was far too tenacious to be easily shaken off by anyone.

She tightened her hold. "*Atlas, no, he's a cop!*" A desperate cry from her because the man who'd hit the floor moments before—when Atlas had barreled out of the basement and onto the first floor—he was a man that she recognized. Lily should recognize him, after all. She'd called for his help when she first saw the attacker lunge for Atlas in that parking lot.

Detective Benedict Swain. Mid-thirties, brown hair, hazel eyes. Decorated. Dependable. One of those salt-of-the-earth types.

And the man who currently had a knife pressed to his neck, courtesy of Atlas.

One wrong jerk of Atlas's hand, and he'd cut open Benedict's throat. And then what in the world would they do?

Cop killer.

"Stop." She gripped Atlas as desperately as she could. "I called him before we were taken. He's on our side!"

Atlas's body was rock hard. She was sort of half on top of him, half falling off him. The cuff cut into her wrist and made everything five times harder than it needed to be.

And, unfortunately, she'd just realized another important fact.

Atlas had his knife to Benedict's throat, yes, but Benedict had his gun muzzle shoved against Atlas's chest. The overhead lights shining in the room let her see both weapons as she craned her head and tried to figure out what in the world to do next.

"Tell your cop to lower the gun, Lily," Atlas ordered.

Her lips parted.

"Tell *him* to drop the knife, Lily," Benedict barked.

"Listen up! You two aren't the bad guys, so how about you stop fighting each other so we can figure out what is happening—*ah!*" Her words ended in a scream because glass was suddenly breaking.

The windows were exploding inward. Glass was breaking and flying and a door to the far right had just come crashing open. It banged against the wall even as men in black pants and shirts and masks rushed inside. Armed men.

In a flash, Atlas was off the cop. Atlas was on his feet, and he'd shoved her so that she was behind him. It took her a desperate beat of time to realize that Atlas was protecting her. But they were far outnumbered by the men now fanning out, and there was no way his knife could stop this many attackers.

But one guy rushed forward, standing almost toe to toe with Atlas. She peeked around Atlas and saw the mystery man yank the mask off his head. Not a mask, not exactly. One of those balaclavas that covered his head and fell all the way down to his neck. When he pulled it off, she had a fast impression of a clenched jaw. A glaring expression.

"Boss," he snapped at Atlas, "you good?" His dark eyes glittered.

Boss?

"No, I'm not fucking *good*," Atlas snapped back. "What took you so long? Did you stop for drinks? Dinner? A freaking show? I could have been butchered!"

Several of the other armed men surged toward Benedict.

"I'm a cop!" Benedict blasted as he flashed his badge. "Detective Benedict Swain! Now stand the hell down!"

Everyone tensed. There was no standing down, but there was also no attacking, either.

Lily's heart raced in her chest. Her gaze darted around the room—looked like the den of some old cabin. Lots of wood everywhere. A deer head and antlers on the wall. A bear skin rug on the floor.

Old chairs.

Dust.

Cobwebs.

And a mini army that seemed to be following Atlas's every command.

"I need someone to tell me..." Benedict bit out. "What in the hell is going on here?"

But she'd just realized exactly what was happening. "Wow," Lily said, well and truly impressed, and, in this world, it often took quite a bit to impress her. Her focus locked on Atlas. Atlas—in his wrinkled and bloody black suit and white shirt. "You didn't need saving, did you?"

Atlas turned toward her. His electric blue eyes pinned her, and even the blood dripping toward one of those amazing eyes of his did zero to impact the absolute gorgeousness that was Atlas Bennett.

Pitch black hair. Bright blue eyes. Chiseled jaw. Faint cleft in his chin. Cheekbones made of glass. And an expression that was as cold and unrelenting as death itself.

But as she gaped at him and as she realized exactly what was happening, his slightly cruel lips curled into a smile. One that flashed—of all things—deep dimples.

"No, sweets, I didn't need saving. I'm far, far past that point. But I do appreciate you trying."

Her breath shuddered in and out. In and out. Of course, the man did not need saving. He'd just had a small army rush inside, an army under his command.

"Someone needs to tell me what in the hell is happening!" Benedict thundered as he kept his gun up and swinging toward the armed men. *"Now!"*

"Atlas must be lowjacked." Lily's gaze swept around the cabin. There had to be some sort of GPS tracker on him, and that tracker had led the team right to his location. Smart. "His phone was shattered and tossed near his Benz." She remembered seeing it as she rushed to help. "So he wasn't tracked via that route."

"Your phone is how I found you, Lily," Benedict groused at her. "One minute, you're on the phone with me, telling me someone was attacking Atlas, and then I lost you. It's a damn good thing you kept your phone on for a while—I was able to triangulate the signal with some help and find you."

It had been a good thing—a deliberate thing. As soon as she'd realized what was happening to Atlas, she'd called Benedict. Then she'd hidden the phone in her waistband, pulling the sweater low to cover it, and rushed to help Atlas.

Her phone had been smashed into a million pieces when she tumbled down the stairs, though. She knew because her feet had crunched on a few of those pieces in the basement.

"Your phone went dead," Benedict added, "Luckily, I used your last known location to find you. *This* location."

Uh, it hadn't gone dead. It had gone *smash.* But...

But for locating Atlas, something different had been used. *Where is your tracker, Atlas?* Her eyes narrowed as she considered him. "If you go missing, your men have orders to track you, huh, Atlas? Makes sense." Definitely something she should have thought about sooner. "Seeing as how you are worth millions of dollars."

"Billions," Atlas corrected.

He didn't deny the tracking charge. She wondered where the tracker was. On his watch? She could see the gleaming Rolex that circled his wrist. Maybe it was hidden *inside* the Rolex. Or maybe even on the battered silver ring that circled his right, middle finger. It was very wise of Atlas to have a tracker on him. Someone with his wealth and power would often be a potential target but...

But this isn't some situation where Atlas is being held for ransom. This isn't about ransom at all. She knew it with certainty.

Except...

What was it about? And why did she suddenly have even more unease prickling at her nape? Something was very wrong. Well, something beyond the fact that a killer had taken her and Atlas and tossed them down into a dank and dark basement.

"I think we should all get out of here," she said. Goosebumps had risen onto her skin. The scene didn't feel right. Where was the bad guy? He'd thrown them into the basement, and then what...just left?

Why?

"No one is going *anywhere*," Benedict stated, voice full of authority. "Not until I get my answers. I've called for backup. Local units will be responding soon, and we are all staying right the hell here until they arrive. *But you fuckers are going to drop your guns, now.*"

Atlas gave a slight incline of his head. Because she was watching him so closely, Lily caught the movement.

The men in black immediately lowered their weapons. They didn't drop them, though. Just pointed them at the floor.

Her gaze went to the front door that the mini-army had

used when they burst inside. "Did you try the lock?" she asked. Her stare darted to the leader.

Coal-black eyes held her gaze. Dark, buzzed hair. Clenched jaw. He shook his head.

No. No, he'd assumed the front door was locked so he'd busted inside. *But...was it locked?* It should have been. *Should.* And yet...

"Benedict," she addressed the angry detective, "how did you get inside?"

"I came in through the back window. The sonofabitch had left it unlocked. Hell, it was actually open a few inches. Saw it and knew it was my perfect way inside." Gruff, angry. Then, "Lily, are *you* all right? What did he do to you?"

Physically, she was fine. Just a few bruises and bumps. If Atlas hadn't cradled her with his much bigger body during that fall down the stairs, she could have wound up with broken bones...or even a broken *neck*. But...

This is wrong. Everything is wrong. The perp hadn't searched for her phone when he'd taken her and Atlas. Wasn't that an amateur mistake? He hadn't taken her phone. He hadn't taken Atlas's knife. That made *two* amateur mistakes. But she didn't think she was dealing with an amateur and...

The window was unlocked? The detective was just able to sneak right inside?

Sloppy. Unless...

Unless you wanted people to get inside.

Oh, no. She whirled toward Atlas. "We have to get out. *Now.*"

His eyebrows lowered. "Why?"

"Because you do need me to save you." Maybe to save him and his whole army of guards. "Everyone has to get *out!*" Her heart raced even faster. This scene wasn't right. It was...

Too easy.

She hadn't thought about Atlas having an army at his beck and call, but the predator who'd brought them to this cabin—maybe *he* had known. And if he'd known...

"We're all going to die," she told Atlas. "*Come on!*" Lily lurched toward the open door, trying to force Atlas to run with her.

He didn't. He did wrap an arm around her and yank her back against his body. "Didn't you hear the cop?" he said against her ear. His breath blew over her lobe.

A shiver shook Lily's body.

"He said no one leaves."

"Then we all *die*." She elbowed him, hard. Because she wasn't in the mood to die. Atlas let her go. She stepped to the side. "*Out!*" Lily ordered the men—more men who were taking off their balaclavas and frowning. Some showing real fear. "He wouldn't just leave a window open." How absurd would that be? And how could they not all see that this was just wrong? And it was more than just the open window. "Atlas, think about it! He wouldn't just let them all rush inside!" Unless he *wanted* them inside.

A glance at Atlas let her see the unease on his face. Yes, he was getting it. Finally. But they seriously needed to hurry along this scene. "He made it too easy for them to get in. Far too easy. There has to be more." And, unfortunately, she believed that more meant... "*We are going to die!*" How many times did a woman have to make that dramatic pronouncement before men got it?

A muscle flexed along Atlas's clenched jaw.

Come on, Atlas. Come on. "The lantern was the only thing I found downstairs. Conveniently left right next to our landing spot at the bottom of the steps. There were no torture instruments in the basement."

"Then why the fuck were you going on and on about my disembowelment?"

Because that was done to the other prey. Not something she had time to discuss. Her teeth snapped together. "Why did he bring you here? Bring us here? Why didn't he kill me on the way? Why didn't he kill *you* in the parking lot?" She didn't give him a chance to answer. "Because you need bait if you are planning a trap. Guess what we are?" *Tempting, perfect bait.*

Atlas stared into her eyes.

They were losing time. "What does it hurt to wait outside?" she breathed. "*We need to get out.*" Every instinct she had screamed this truth at her.

"No one is going anywhere." Benedict moved toward the front door. "I'm securing the scene. I already said backup will be here soon. We're talking a matter of minutes. Until the cavalry comes, we stay inside, and we *wait.* For all we know, the perp is outside with a rifle, waiting to pick off his prey." He dipped his head toward Atlas. "That would be you."

No, no, no. If the killer had been outside with a rifle, he would have shot the rescue army when they were rushing toward the cabin. "*We have to get outside.*" Desperation clawed at her. "Atlas, listen to me. *This is life or death.* We need to get out of here, right now. *Now.*"

In the distance, she heard the scream of sirens.

"My backup." Benedict was pleased. "Let's just give it just a little longer and—"

"We're going outside." Atlas nodded. "Now." His gaze cut to his army.

Their weapons all immediately came up again.

"What the hell? Lower your weapons, lower them!" Benedict blasted.

"We're getting the fuck out," Atlas said. He marched toward Benedict. "And you'll either shoot me or you'll get the hell out of the way."

The cuffs had her surging behind him, but—forget being behind him. Lily hurriedly lunged in front of Atlas. The man needed a human shield, and it was gonna have to be her. Not like she wanted Benedict getting trigger happy with the guy.

"What are you doing?" Atlas gritted out.

Uh, protecting him. Wasn't that obvious? "I don't think you'll shoot me," Lily said to Benedict. She certainly hoped the detective wouldn't pull the trigger on her.

"Don't tempt me," Benedict muttered right back. His weapon didn't lower.

"This place is a trap. Why was the back window open?" Her free hand flew out and grabbed for the doorknob. Atlas's men hadn't even tried the lock. They'd just assumed the door was locked when they stormed inside. But she reached for the knob, and it turned easily. "Not even locked. *It's a trap.*"

There was cursing from the men in black. They surged forward.

And worry flashed on Benedict's handsome face.

"He wanted everyone here." She could hear the frayed edges in her own voice. "He wanted—"

"Screw this." Atlas grabbed her. Hauled her off her feet and barreled forward. "*Get the hell out of the way, Detective Swain.*"

Benedict got out of the way. Atlas and his men rushed outside. Atlas had a tight, unbreakable grip on her. His men circled around them, physical shields, as they hurried onto a small, wooden porch, then down into an open yard. Stars glittered overhead. A hazy moon. No other houses or cabins nearby. Gravel crunched beneath them. And she could see blue police lights flashing in the distance.

"I need to search the house!" Benedict yelled.

She looked over her shoulder. He stood in the open doorway.

"There could be other vics." He turned away. Ducked back inside. "I have to check downstairs."

What? No! "Benedict!"

Atlas put her on her feet.

She took a step toward the cabin. "Benedict, no one else was in the basement! Get out—"

The explosion had her flying through the air and crashing into the ground.

Flames erupted. Flames devoured the little cabin.

And she kept screaming for Benedict.

Chapter Three

"Benedict!" Lily leapt back to her feet. She lunged toward the flames. "Benedict!"

"The fuck no!" Atlas locked one arm around her and yanked her back against him. Was the woman crazy? No way did she get to run toward the flames. And they weren't staring at some small inferno. The flames were giant. Already eating at the top of the cabin. Burning at the old shingles. Pouring and raging from the windows along the front of the house. The fire raged because it was a full-on inferno.

Anyone inside had to be dead.

I would have been dead without her.

His men would have been dead.

As for the cop...

"Benedict!" Lily yelled again as she clawed at Atlas's grip. She also elbowed him and kicked back against his shins.

Atlas ignored the blows and just held her tighter.

His men fanned toward the engulfed house. Smoke thickened the air. Cop cars came to a screeching halt and, yeah, there was a fire truck with them. Horn blaring. Firefighters leaping off the truck.

But that fire was too strong.

Anyone inside...

Gone.

She kept struggling. Fighting him. He just held her tighter. The firefighters hauled hoses from the truck. Blasted and blasted, but the fire raged ever more powerfully.

Burning and burning.

"He's not coming out," Atlas told her.

Her head turned toward him.

A tear leaked down her cheek.

* * *

"I guess I did need you to save me." Atlas spoke deliberately because he'd wanted to break the silence in the small hospital room. They'd been transported by ambulance, him and Lily. He'd been the one to get poked and prodded the most by the EMTs, but he'd wanted her checked out, too. She'd hit the ground pretty hard after the blast had hurtled them through the air. He'd tried to protect her, an instinct driving him to wrap his body around hers, but she'd slipped from his grip and—

"Benedict is dead."

Unfortunately, she was not wrong on that point. Not like a body had been recovered, not yet, but Atlas didn't see any way the man could have survived that inferno.

"He came to save me." A ragged breath escaped Lily. "To save us. And he died in that blaze."

Atlas was pretty sure the guy had died in some kind of bomb detonation. He wasn't an expert at demolitions, but that explosion had been hard to miss. Not a fire. A detonation. One that had sent fire racing through the cabin and shooting up into the starry night. "You told him that we all had to get out." *Real damn glad you told me about that, sweets. Otherwise, I'd be burned to ashes right now.*

She sat in the chair a few feet away. Not on the exam table. He wasn't on the damn exam table, either. He was up, pacing the room, with a stupid white paper gown covering his body.

Their cuffs had been removed. They were no longer tied together and for some reason...

I don't like that. I want her tied to me. I want her linked to me. She can't get away.

"Benedict was a protector. A cop. He was doing his job. He just wanted to make sure no one else was in the house."

"He could have done that once the rest of his team in blue arrived." Deliberately, Atlas walked toward her. She was staring at the gleaming, white floor. His hand reached out, curled under her chin, and forced her head back. When she looked up at him, tears swirled in her eyes. He did not like tears in her eyes.

One teardrop rolled down her cheek.

Fuck that. "You told him to get out. You told us all." If it hadn't been for Lily, Atlas and all his men could have died.

She swallowed. Wet her lips. "Why was the front door unlocked? I checked it—that door was *unlocked.* Just like the back window that Benedict used. Why leave them unlocked? Unless you wanted others inside."

"But we were locked in the basement." He'd tried the door at the top of those narrow stairs. The prick had locked him and Lily in the basement.

"Yes, we were locked in." A nod. "Because we were the

main target. Or, at least, you were. Anyone who came to help, though, they were going to die, too."

Only his men hadn't died. Because of Lily.

I didn't die. Because of Lily. His hand moved to brush away the teardrop.

"*Don't.*" Her hand flew up, and her fingers curled around his wrist. "He deserves tears. Tears mean that someone cares Benedict is gone." Her grip tightened. "He was a good cop. I met him shortly after coming to Dallas. He...he knew exactly what I was, and he never judged me."

Another tear leaked down her cheek. This time, Atlas didn't make the mistake of trying to wipe away that tear. If she wanted to cry for the detective, then so be it. But in his experience, tears didn't always mean a person cared. Tears could be faked. And you could grieve as if your very heart was being ripped from your chest even as your eyes remained stone dry. He knew that bitter truth because he'd grieved that way before. When he stood at his mother's grave.

When he stood at his father's grave, though, he'd been laughing his ass off.

Because I am a twisted SOB.

His gaze slid down. Over her. Like him, she now wore a white hospital gown. Their clothes had been taken away by cops. Evidence. Bagged and tagged.

He and Lily had been thoroughly examined. Because the doctors had been worried about potential brain injuries, Atlas and Lily had been subjected to CT scans to rule out brain bleeding and fractures.

After the tests were complete, the doctors had wanted to keep Atlas and Lily separated. He'd refused that request. He'd given his own order. *She stays with me.*

Atlas was used to giving orders and used to having them

obeyed unconditionally. Considering that he'd donated a wing to the hospital not too long ago, the doctors had acquiesced to his demands. *Lily stays. She doesn't leave my sight again.*

His attention shifted to the small, delicate hand that curled around his wrist. Darkening bruises could be seen on her skin where the handcuff had bitten into her. One line looked particularly vicious, as if the handcuff had nearly sliced right into her.

"No worries about that," Lily murmured. "I bruise easily."

He was worried. But he filed away the comment about how easily she bruised. "I'll have to be very careful with you in the future."

"I doubt we'll be handcuffed together again." She let go of him.

"One never knows." He reached for her wrist. Careful now, because he understood that Lily needed care, he lifted her hand up.

"What are you doing?" Husky. Uncertain.

He brought her wrist to his mouth. With gentle care, he kissed the darkening bruise.

"That is not going to make it better," she murmured. Her voice had turned huskier.

His gaze collided with hers. Tension. Heat. Need. Desire pulsed between them. He could feel it. Atlas wondered if she did, too. He wondered even more if she would admit that truth.

"That is not gonna make it better," Lily repeated with a little sigh. "And it could make things exponentially worse."

Perhaps. They should be clear, though. "You were stalking me, Lily Gallo."

She winced. "*Stalking* is such a negative word." Tear

tracks were still on her cheeks. "I was simply trying to get you to have a meeting with me. There are things I wanted to discuss with you. I needed your attention."

"Trust me, you have it." *You wanted to meet with me because you suspected I was a killer.* Should he be that brutally honest? Now? Or later?

She tugged on her wrist.

He did not let go. "You didn't have to step in." He'd heard her tale to the cops on scene as she gave her statement. "No need for you to throw yourself on my attacker's back." She could have been seriously hurt when she'd done that. Or killed right then and there. "You could have just called for help. Followed my abductor. You didn't have to jump into action."

"Oh, see, that's where you're wrong. I did have to jump in. Clearly, you don't know me very well."

He knew many things about her, but there was still much to unravel when it came to his new obsession. *Obsession.* The word slithered through him. "Lily Gallo." He liked saying her name. *Lily.* A beautiful flower. A beautiful woman. He had plenty of background intel on her. Facts in stark black and white. But, when it came down to understanding the complicated mind of Lily Gallo, there were plenty of secrets left to be discovered. "The daughter of a serial killer," he said, because there was no point in ignoring the elephant in the room. Yes, he'd just gone for the brutal honesty track. Why not? Especially since it was her.

Lily didn't flinch. Didn't suddenly stop staring him straight in the eye. If anything, her shoulders straightened. Her chin lifted. "Atlas Bennett." The briefest of pauses. "The son of a serial killer."

Not just any serial killer. One of the most brutal and sadistic killers of all time. His father hadn't just murdered his prey. He'd tortured them. Enjoyed their pain and their screams.

I can still hear the screams when I close my eyes at night.

He brushed another very careful kiss over her injured wrist. "I told you to stay away from me."

"I am pretty sure you had me kicked out of your office building. Twice."

He had. "I don't enjoy having my past dug up and thrown at me."

"I can understand that. But I am working on research that is very, very important. And, considering that I did save you—you admitted that—perhaps you can spare me a few hours? As a thank you?"

Oh, he would spare her more than that. "You aren't getting away."

Her long, dark lashes flickered. "Excuse me?"

He thought she'd heard him perfectly.

A quick knock sounded at the door. That door was almost immediately flung open after the knock, and Atlas turned his head to see a slightly harried doctor standing on the threshold. The man's disheveled blond hair poked out from his head, his white lab coat looked a bit too big for his thin shoulders, and a stethoscope dangled around his neck. "You...you have guards in the hallway." The man's eyes were huge.

Atlas kept his hold on Lily. The woman would not slip from his grasp. "A necessary precaution, considering the night I've had so far."

Desmond poked his head inside the exam room. "You good, boss?"

Good didn't apply. Was he alive? Yes. So that meant he was certainly better than the detective. A man Lily mourned. Clearly, she did not know about Atlas's own complicated relationship with the fellow. There was a reason why Atlas hadn't hesitated to shove his knife against the guy's throat.

Or why Detective Benedict Swain had not hesitated to push the muzzle of his gun over Atlas's heart. If Lily hadn't been there, Atlas did wonder...

Would Benedict have pulled the trigger?

Or...

Would I have slit his throat?

Atlas would not mourn for the cop. It was hard to mourn for someone who wanted you either, A, behind bars, or B, dead in the ground.

"Atlas?" Desmond prompted.

"I'll be heading home soon," Atlas told him. Then, because he knew Desmond was looking for reassurance, "I'm fine."

"Uh, you are *not*." The doctor bustled forward. His lab coat flapped behind him. "You have a concussion. I was told by Dr. Gallo that you lost consciousness after the initial attack."

"So did Dr. Gallo." Atlas had learned that she'd only woken up shortly before being tossed down the stairs.

During the police interviews, one very unfortunate fact had come to light.

Lily had never seen the face of their attacker. Atlas had not, either. They had no description of the sonofabitch.

"You *both* need to stay for observation," the doctor insisted. "You are lucky that you didn't have any broken ribs, Mr. Bennett, but the bruising along your torso is quite severe."

He didn't give a flying shit about his bruising. "I think bruises are expected when you tumble down a flight of stairs."

"They are consistent with a fall, yes." A quick nod from the doctor—Dr. Phillip Owen. The man had introduced himself earlier. He was the doctor in charge of the ER. "All the more reason for you to stay here and—"

"We'll be leaving in the next ten minutes," Atlas cut through the doc's words to say. "Thank you for your time and care."

The doc's mouth hung open. Then his attention jumped to Lily. "Surely, you understand the need to stay overnight, Dr. Gallo."

She hadn't introduced herself as a doctor. She'd just said that her name was Lily Gallo. Atlas knew because he'd been with her at the time.

He intended to be with her for the foreseeable future. Lily getting out of his sight again was not an option. He'd told the woman to stay away before. She had not heeded that particular warning so...

You're mine now.

"How the fuck do you know that she's a doctor?" Atlas asked.

Just like that, Phillip Owen was back to gaping at him. "She's..." Phillip cleared his throat. "I recognized the name. And the face. She...she looks a lot like her mother."

And everyone knew Lily's mother.

The woman who had killed a dozen men.

The woman who was currently sitting on death row in an Alabama prison.

Plenty of movies had been made about Magnolia Calhoun. The beautiful and vivacious southern belle who'd been a true monster. A cold, calculating killer. Poison had been her weapon of choice. A sweet poison that she poured from her grandmother's prized teapot.

She'd smiled at her prey even as she killed them.

She'd killed Lily's father. And, if the stories were true, she'd even attempted to kill Lily, once upon a time.

"I recently read your research piece about hybristophilia," Phillip gushed. Seriously, gushed, as he slanted a glance back at Lily. "I did consider becoming a psychiatrist at one point, so I've always had an interest in aberrant behavior, but emergency medicine called to me more and I—"

"Yeah, excuse me," Atlas cut in to say. "But what in the hell is hybristophilia?" His head turned back toward Lily.

Those full lips of hers pressed together. The tear tracks on her cheeks had partially dried, but sorrow lingered in her eyes. Grief. He really wanted to get her out of there. Dr. Phillip Owen should not be seeing her grief. He should not be edging closer and closer to her.

A low, warning growl came from Atlas.

The doctor stopped his advance.

Lily's gaze crashed with Atlas's. "It's a sexual attraction to criminals."

He blinked at her.

"I've written a few papers on the intense attraction, the lust and the consuming need, that certain people can feel for individuals that they know to be violent and dangerous."

Well, well, well. "Do *you* have an attraction to those who are violent and dangerous, Lily?" He was fascinated by her. And that very fascination was *dangerous*. He'd told the woman to stay away, hadn't he? But she hadn't listened.

Her lips tightened. "Some women think they can somehow fix deviant men."

He completely ignored Phillip Owen. "Isn't that what you're trying to do?"

"I want to understand deviance. Understanding is the first step."

"The first step in what?" But Atlas thought he knew. Oh, poor Lily. She thought she could cure monsters, didn't she? Precious. Admirable. But...

Not happening. "What if they don't want to be cured?"

"This is about stopping violence. About preventing death."

Um, was it? He edged ever closer to her. He loved that warm vanilla scent. Just made him want to drink her in. Consume her. "You wanted to talk to me. You wanted me for your research." No, actually, he thought she'd wanted him...

Because a serial killer is at work in Dallas. And you thought I was him.

Until the bastard had taken Atlas. And that was something they had not discussed. He just hadn't been able to get Lily alone for long enough, not yet. They'd had to talk with the local cops, had EMTs hovering around them, gone to the hospital just to be met with doctors and nurses and...

No good privacy. At least, not privacy for longer than a few moments. So they hadn't been given the opportunity to talk about the serial killer who'd been picking prey from Dallas. *Disemboweling* his victims. A very distinct calling card. Since Lily had mentioned that particular process more than once, he knew she was already thinking about the serial. They'd get into a full discussion about the killer, once he had her away from the hospital. And alone with him.

For the moment, though...

You want to understand me, huh, sweets? Understand my deviance? Fine. Then I will let you into my darkness. "Consider your all-access pass granted."

Her brow furrowed. "You...are you saying that you will agree to meet with me? You'll talk with me? After *weeks* of avoiding me completely? Of literally having me thrown out of your building?"

"That's not very nice," Phillip mumbled.

"I'm not typically mistaken for being a *nice* man." The avoidance had been for Lily's own protection. But she had been persistent, and now, she'd made a fatal mistake. "You saved my life."

She didn't even blink. "Technically, I think I saved your life and the lives of those six men who work for you." A pause. "I did *not* save Benedict."

He didn't want her focusing on the detective. Her tears had stopped, and Atlas did not want them falling again. "I figure that I owe you." True enough, he did owe her. But, more, when it came to Lily...

I am just not letting you get away.

Footsteps thudded nearby. Atlas turned toward the sound just as Desmond appeared in the doorway again.

"The limo is being brought around to the front of the hospital," Desmond told him.

Excellent. "We'll need clothes," he said. Then Atlas shrugged. "Though I suppose we could just walk out in the hospital gowns. That's always an option." Atlas was curious as he focused on Desmond. "Has the press gotten wind of the story?"

"Absolutely. They are waiting outside."

"Um. Then shots of my naked ass in this hospital gown would be splashed everywhere." He didn't care about his ass. But Lily...he didn't want vulnerable shots of her taken. "So, yeah, guess we'll be needing those clothes." A brief pause. "Desmond?"

He'd already ducked out of the doorway.

But Desmond returned almost instantly. "Already got

it," Desmond retorted as he tossed a duffle bag toward him. "Things for you and for the lady."

And *that* was why Desmond was his right hand. The guy was a miracle worker. Atlas caught the bag in his left hand. "Perfect." He slanted a glance at Phillip. The doc was still staring at Lily with wide eyes and far too much admiration on his face. *Mooney eyes.* The doctor clearly had a crush or hero worship or some shit that would be stopping. "Your services are no longer needed, Dr. Owen, but thanks so much for all that you've done." Well, damn, maybe he *could* be nice. So what if the words held a hard, brittle edge? They'd still been mostly polite.

Dr. Owen snapped to attention. Face flushing, he whipped toward Atlas. "You are my patient. *She* is my patient. She has a concussion. Granted, her injuries were milder than yours, but I am the medical professional, Mr. Bennett. Not you. Therefore, I will say when my services are needed or not needed."

"Is Lily in danger?" He and Lily had both agreed that they could hear each other's medical info. One of the requirements for them to be able to stay together during so many of the exams.

"No...she...she should be fine. Her responses are all normal. Neither of your scans showed signs of brain bleeding or fractures."

Good. Lily was not in jeopardy. Time to drop all pretense. Time for Phillip to get the hell out of their way. "Desmond, escort the doc from the room, will you? Lily needs privacy to change."

Desmond advanced and wrapped one hand around the doc's right shoulder. "Let's go."

The doc jumped. At least two inches. "Wh-what? What are you doing?"

"The door is this way," Desmond informed him, voice courteous—far more courteous than Atlas's had been, but then his head of security added, "and, FYI, you getting an ass kicking if you stay in the room and watch the lady change is..." Desmond pointed toward Atlas, "...that way."

"*What?*" Shock. Horror. Fear.

The doc scrambled and wisely chose to get the hell out of that exam room. Such a good life choice. The door clicked shut behind him. For a moment, Atlas stared at the closed door.

"Is that how things usually work in your world? You treat people terribly, make demands, and get your hired muscle to ensure things go the way you want?" A considering pause from Lily. "By the way, the back of your gown is gaping open." She cleared her throat. "You have a great ass, even if your attitude leaves much to be desired."

He felt a smile tug at his lips. Weird to smile after all that had happened that night. He rolled back his shoulders and marched for the exam table. Atlas set the duffle bag on top of the table and pulled out the items inside. A black bra. Matching panties.

"Those can't be in your size," she murmured.

"Nope, but they are in yours." The panties and bra dangled from his fingers.

"And how did your head of security know my size?"

He turned toward her, still holding the underwear. "Because from the first moment that you reached out, requesting that initial one-on-one chat, I made it a point to learn every single thing that I could about you."

"Everything...like the size of my underwear?"

"Um. I believe in being thorough." Always.

She grabbed for the panties. And the bra. "So do I." Her fingers brushed against his.

He felt the spark at her touch, just as he'd felt it before. Even when they'd been in that damn basement.

She yanked her hand—and the underwear—back from him as if she'd been burned.

Surely, she wasn't afraid of him? Or his touch? Perhaps she should realize that trust was going to be necessary in their relationship. "Didn't you once spend a month interviewing that serial bomber from Chicago?" Atlas asked the question even though he knew the answer.

Her gaze didn't falter. "Yes."

"He wouldn't talk with anyone else, but he agreed to chat with you. For hours and hours. Told you how he created the bombs, where he planted them, and even how he timed the explosions."

Her head inclined. "Richard Hawthorne told me all of that."

He reached into the bag. Pulled out sweatpants. Far too small for him. Just as the sweatshirt he pulled out was too small. He handed both to her. "I suppose you became a bit of an expert on bombs after all that time with Richard."

"How about you just get right to the point?" She curled her hands around the clothing. "Are you asking me if I set the bomb at the cabin?"

Not exactly. "I'm asking...*could* you have set the bomb? If you wanted to do so, of course."

Her eyes glittered at him. "Yes. I could have set the bomb. Did I do it? No."

He smiled at her. *Trust.* He'd be the one who showed it first. "I'll change first, then I'll go outside so you can have your privacy."

She whipped around, giving him her back. "I won't look at you."

"Why the fuck not? I'm not shy." He hadn't told her not

to look. In fact, "Look all you want, sweets. Have at me." He ripped away the hospital gown, balled it up, and tossed it into the nearby garbage can.

Her shoulders stiffened, but she didn't look back. "I am trying to give you privacy. We are going to have a professional relationship—"

His laughter cut through her words. "I just asked you if you set a bomb that killed a cop, and you think I'm gonna be professional?"

"I did *not* kill Benedict!" Anger flashed in her words.

No, Atlas didn't think that she'd killed the cop, but she had cried for him. "Did you fuck him?"

Now she did whip around. Red fired in her cheeks.

"Sorry. I already put on my jogging pants." He had. "You missed the main show."

Her gaze immediately dropped at his words. Only to whip back up. "You're *playing* with me."

"Well, admittedly, I'm not some professional when it comes to mind games, not like you are, but I do know how to get by." That ability came from having a sadistic prick of a father who'd raised him. Molded him. Tried to make him into the worst beast on earth.

Her gaze burned at him. "I did not fuck the poor, dead detective. I met him a few weeks ago. When I first came to the city."

"When you came to meet *me*."

"When I came...to meet you."

Someone was not telling the full truth. Atlas sighed. "You came to the city because you understood a serial was at play. You thought I was that serial." He waited for her denial.

None came.

Interesting.

"Benedict was working those homicides," she said. "That is how our paths crossed."

Of course, Lily would have done her recon work. Talking to the homicide detective would have been step one for her. She'd probably talked to the ME. Maybe the friends and family members of the victims. He knew she was a very thorough individual.

Something they had in common. "Your path *crossed* with Benedict." The cop who'd wanted Atlas locked in a cage. He was curious—had Benedict told her anything about their previous encounters? He'd find out, later. For now, deliberately, Atlas said, "Your paths crossed, and you went out with him. On dates." Was that jealousy bubbling beneath the surface? Kinda felt like it. Then again, he'd never been jealous before, so he wasn't really certain. Maybe it was just rage. Some leftover adrenaline or...

I don't want her dating anyone else. I sure as hell don't want her fucking anyone else.

Okay, it was jealousy.

A blink from Lily. "How did you know that Benedict and I went out?"

"You dated him."

"We went on *business* dinners."

Screw that. Detective Benedict Swain had wanted to get in her pants. But Lily had said that she had not fucked the dead cop, so Benedict's goal had never been achieved. Good to know. "I told you, I do my due diligence."

She stepped closer. "You were watching me. All that time?"

Not *all* that time. He did have a business empire to run. Instead of directly answering, he queried, "Weren't you watching me? Isn't that how you knew I'd been taken? One good stalking does deserve another."

Lily sucked in a breath. "I am not a stalker."

He stared at her.

"Are you?" she threw back.

He smiled.

She backed up a step. That was not the usual response to his smile. In fact, he'd learned early on that his smile was one of his best weapons. It flashed his dimples. It made his eyes sparkle. It made him look more attractive. More inviting. Women usually came closer when he used his grin.

But Lily sensed the threat. She backed away.

And that is why I will enjoy her so much.

Then her lashes flickered. "Did you...did you deliberately allow yourself to get taken?"

"Why would I do that?"

"You tell me."

So I could kill the bastard. A man I knew was hunting in my city. A predator who needed to be removed from this earth.

Just as Atlas had removed other predators.

But, ah, no, deliberately getting *taken* had not been the plan. He'd truly been distracted. By her. Thinking too much about her. Wondering what she was doing. Who she was doing it with. Wondering if he could hide his true self from her for long.

I sure as hell never counted on you, Lily. Atlas's plan had been to eventually eliminate the serial working on *his* turf. He'd never counted on getting knocked out and waking up cuffed to his new fantasy.

Instead of saying all of that, Atlas extended one palm toward her. "You wanted to interview me. You wanted my secrets. Like I said, I think you've earned an all-access pass into my life, but that pass will come with a few conditions."

She didn't take his hand. "If it's all-access, how can it have conditions?"

She was going to be so much fun.

"You have nine scars on your chest," Lily noted without even batting one long eyelash. "Nine victims were linked to your father. Did he put those marks on you, or did you carve them into your skin yourself?"

"So you checked out my chest. Good to know. I've been checking out yours, too." But his smile slowly faded. Perhaps she would not be as fun as he'd anticipated. "My scars have nothing to do with my father's victims." Now he was disappointed because he'd hoped for more from her—

"Do they have to do with your victims?"

His heartbeat kicked up. Did she know what he'd been doing? His extracurricular activities? Or was that just a stab in the dark? "Call me crazy, but I am pretty sure you said I was hero material when we were in the basement. Do heroes typically have victims?"

Her lips parted. Lovely lips.

"Also thought you said you were wrong about me," he murmured. "Pretty sure I remember that, too, but, then again, I do have a concussion so..."

"In my experience, people are rarely just one thing in this world. Take my mother, for example. She was my room mom in school. The leader of the neighborhood watch group. She sat on the board for two area homeless shelters." A shrug. "She also killed men who pissed her off."

"Do you think I kill people who piss me off?" Dammit, this was not the place or the time for this talk. "Hold the thought." Because he didn't want anyone else barging in on them. For all he knew, the besotted Dr. Phillip Owen would be coming to get another look at Lily. "You need to get dressed. I'll wait outside while you do." He'd block the door so no one would get to her. "As far as the pass into my life is concerned, I'll tell you about my conditions once we are in my limo."

She stared straight at him, then nodded.

Unease had his gut tightening. He couldn't predict Lily's actions, and that worried him. The woman could be very dangerous to him, he knew that. She was smart and far too much of an expert when it came to killers.

What will she do when she sees my full darkness?

As he stared at her, her hands darted behind her back.

"Lily—"

She dropped the hospital gown. The paper gown fell, and Lily stood before him wearing only a white pair of panties and a white bra that cupped her breasts ever so wonderfully.

What in the sweet fuck is happening right now? Why was Lily stripping for him? Not that he was complaining. Oh, hell no, he was not. If she wanted to strip completely, that was totally the woman's prerogative. She could go right ahead.

"I kept my underwear on for my physical exam with Dr. Owen," she said. "No sense in ditching them." One eyebrow quirked at him. "And I thought one scar sharing deserved another."

A long, twisting scar cut across her stomach. It had taken him a moment to notice the scar. Sue him, he'd been distracted by her breasts.

"My mother didn't give me this, of course." Her fingers fluttered along the scar. "She never used knives. She preferred poison. A more delicate method of death. At least, that's what she always said. But when you've seen people vomiting blood and screaming in pain, and you watched their whole bodies lurch forward and heave as they fight for survival, well, I personally don't think there is anything delicate about that method of death. I think it is quite brutal."

His dick was saluting. Her breasts spilled forward against the bra she wore. The panties—bikini cut. Hugging her hips. Leaving far too little to the imagination. Desire poured through his veins. He wanted to grab her, lift her up, put her on that exam table, and fuck her until she screamed his name.

But...

Rage twisted in him. A dangerous, seething beast. And when Atlas stepped forward, lust wasn't controlling him. That rage was. His hand lifted and touched the twisting scar on her stomach. Not red and angry. White, faded. Old. "Who the hell did this to you? Who put a knife in your skin?"

A name was all he needed. Once he had the name, he had enough power to easily find the individual. Then death would come.

Because you did not take a fucking knife to Lily.

"It was my first interview with a serial. Well, with a serial who wasn't my own mother." Her hand reached down, and her fingers curled around his. "Take a breath, Atlas. It's okay, I promise. It doesn't hurt me any longer." Softer. "You don't have to be so careful with me."

But he thought that he did. "James Hadley." He knew the first serial she'd interviewed. *Madman Hadley.* She'd interviewed him back when she'd been a resident and on her journey to becoming a psychiatrist.

"You *have* been researching me. Consider me impressed."

Researching. Stalking. Learning every single detail. That was what he did with his enemies. But, she wasn't going to be an enemy. She would be something far more complex. "There was no record of him attacking you."

"That is because a public reporting of that incident would have been highly embarrassing for the warden at James Hadley's maximum security prison." Her lips pulled down. "James was kept in isolation. He should have been thoroughly searched by the guards before coming into the interview session with me, and, yet, somehow, he managed to conceal a shiv he'd carefully sharpened. The guards didn't put cuffs on him. I remembered thinking he should have cuffs. We were talking one moment, and in the next instant, he was across the table, and he was on me. The shiv slashed across my stomach."

"He's dead."

"Yes, I was present when the doctor administered the midazoluam that relaxed him, the pancuronium that paralyzed him, and the potassium chloride that stopped his heart." Flat. Utterly emotionless.

His fingers brushed over the scar. "What happened after he slashed you?"

"I broke his nose. I grabbed the shiv and attacked him with it. He thought he was going to get one more victim before he went to the grave. He was wrong."

She stood before him, clad in her underwear, seemingly defenseless, vulnerable, but he realized exactly what she was doing.

She was showing herself to be just as much of a predator as Atlas was.

How fantastic.

"The guards pulled me off him. And in return for me not blasting that particular tale to the media, the warden gave me full access to any prisoner I wanted to interview." She shivered. "Turns out, I like all-access passes."

But goosebumps had risen on her skin.

"I've learned a great deal about deviant behavior since that encounter. About predators." She wet her lips.

He wanted her mouth. "And now you're here. Wanting to get in my head. Wanting to know all about *me*."

"Are you deviant, Atlas? Do dark desires run in your veins?"

Plenty of dark desires were surging through his veins right then. Mostly, the urge to fuck her until she shattered into a million pieces. Until they both did. Was that so much to ask? He didn't think so. "Guess you'll find out," he finally said because...

That was the deal, right?

The all-access pass. Probably a horrible mistake.

He didn't care. His head lowered toward her. Her head tilted back, and he was also sure that her toes pressed into the floor so that she rose up toward him, just a bit.

He didn't take her mouth, though, not yet. Because if he did kiss her, he wouldn't stop, and their first time to fuck shouldn't be in a hospital exam room. When she started screaming, he didn't want orderlies or that prick Dr. Owen trying to rush inside.

"I am going to take you," he told her. Very clearly. There should be no confusion between them. "You leave this hospital with me, and I will fuck you eventually."

"I don't typically fuck my subjects. Not my modus operandi. But thanks so much for assuming the worst about me."

Had she assumed the worst about him? "Your subjects are usually psychopathic killers."

"And you're not?"

So she *had* assumed the worst, but he replied, "You tell me."

A little roll of her shoulders. "I guess I'll find out."

Yeah, they needed to get the hell out of there, now. "Get dressed, Lily."

She quirked a brow at him. "Why do you seem afraid of little old me? Here I am, making myself vulnerable. You're partially dressed. I'm partially dressed. You showed me your scars. I showed you mine. I am putting us on completely equal footing."

Bullshit. She was attempting to manipulate him. Soon enough, she would learn that he wasn't easy to manipulate. "This some sort of shrink tactic so that I'll reveal all to you?"

"All your deep, dark secrets?" she elaborated.

Yeah, those. He had so many of those that they often threatened to pull him down into the ground. Bury him.

Her hands rose. Her fingertips sank into the thickness of his hair. "I don't have to use any sneaky tactics. You'll reveal everything to me no matter what."

"And why would I do that?" It was interesting that she thought he'd just go straight to being an open book with her. Interesting. Naïve. Perhaps a shade past delusional.

But she just blinked those amazing eyes of hers. "Well, because, in your very soul, haven't you always wanted someone to see the real you? To *know* the real you?"

The real him would terrify most people.

"I'm that someone," she said.

She shouldn't be touching him. Shouldn't be tempting him. "Run away." A rasp. One he had not meant to make. But some part of him, a faint glimmer of what could have been goodness, wanted him to protect this woman.

Protect her from myself.

"Run away while you can," he added roughly. Because if he had her...

Atlas already knew he would not let her go.

Love at first sight didn't exist for monsters. Not a thing. Mostly because love wasn't a real thing. But obsession was, and he already knew she was going to be his greatest obsession.

She'd stripped to match him.

She'd shared her scars.

"Why would I run away from you?" Lily asked as her head tilted to the right. "I've been working to get you alone for the last month." But her fingers slid out of his hair. Dropped back to her side. "You are taking me home with you?"

"If you weren't sporting a bruise around your wrist, I'd be handcuffing you to my side." True story.

"Handcuffing me seems rather excessive."

"I'm an excessive kind of person."

"Obsessive?" she asked, sweetly. "Sorry, did you say *excessive* or *obsessive?*"

Lily knew exactly what he'd said. Atlas took a step back. "The bastard who took us wasn't caught."

She reached for the new sweatshirt. Yanked it over her head. It fell to mid-thigh luckily, covering up his temptation.

"Not a perfect fit," she noted, "but super soft. I'll be sure to thank Desmond."

He had the feeling she knew plenty about his head of security. *Excessive or obsessive?* Ah, but he was betting she could be quite obsessive, too. Although she might prefer the term *thorough.*

She tugged on the sweatpants. They fit her perfectly. Her feet shoved into the tennis shoes Desmond had also brought in the bag.

He yanked on his shirt, too. His body ached, and he was pretty sure the skin along his ribs was about a dozen different colors. The bastard who'd taken him had played damn hard.

"Be careful with that head of yours," she chided. "You were hit with a tire iron. You're lucky you didn't die right then and there." She bit her lower lip. "Maybe Dr. Owen had the right idea about you staying longer for observation."

She'd talked plenty with the cops who'd come rushing to the scene. Those cops had all known Benedict, and they'd been furious, worried, desperate.

The firefighters hadn't let anyone get close to the cabin. And even the bomb squad had come rushing to the scene— eventually.

Lily had given a statement to the cops even as the EMTs had examined her. She'd told them about seeing Atlas get attacked, about calling Benedict for help, leaving her phone turned on as she ran to help Atlas...

Then getting knocked out by the attacker, too.

They'd eventually been dragged into the cabin. Dragged, carried—he had no clue. According to her tale, Lily had woken up when they were near the basement door, just as the perp had cuffed them together.

Then Lily and Atlas had taken their joint tumble down the stairs.

"Atlas?" Lily prompted.

He swallowed. Realized he'd clenched his hands into fists. Lily could have broken her neck on the tumble down the stairs. He could have woken up to find himself cuffed to a dead woman in the basement.

What in the hell would he have done then?

"You're staying with me," he rumbled.

She blinked. "For the rest of the night?"

Not like there was much night left.

But Lily nodded. "Okay, that's good. I am a doctor, just saying."

"I am aware." Of so many things about her.

A quick sigh escaped her. "I meant that because I am a doctor, I could keep an eye on you. If you won't stay here at the hospital, then at least you'll have me to make certain nothing bad happens to you. I can monitor your condition."

Plenty of bad things had already happened. And would happen again. "He got away, Lily."

She inched toward him. "The cops are looking for him. He probably left evidence behind."

Seriously? His brows shot up. "You mean evidence, in the cabin that must have burned down to its very foundation?"

"Yes." A wince. "In there." Then a nibble along her lower lip. "*If* it burned to its foundation, we won't find anything."

Obviously. Thus the reason the bomb had been a very wise plan of attack. A good way of covering the perp's tracks. "He will know who you are."

"Not like we exchanged names during our short fight scene—"

"The press is already spreading the story about what happened tonight. Your name will be featured prominently. I'm big news. You're big news. Pair us together, sweets, and we're the lead story everywhere."

She swallowed. "I don't like being the lead."

"'If it bleeds, it leads,'" he quoted. "That's the way it's always supposed to work in the news. I'm bloody. A detective is dead. A killer is on the loose. There is no getting around the fact that everyone will be talking about us."

Her delicate nostrils flared.

"When we leave, photos will be taken of us." He

probably could have avoided the photos. He didn't want to do so. The sooner that the world knew Lily was under his protection, the better.

"So he knows who I am." She nodded. Her voice was very level. No fear from Lily. "He knows who you are, too. Not to tell you your business but...*you* were the target, not me. You need to get Desmond to step up your protection detail."

Oh, he'd be stepping up his detail. "You're staying with me."

"Again, yes, I'll stay tonight—"

"No, sweets." He cut through her words. Even smiled at her.

Her gaze dipped to his mouth. "Your smile is scary."

She was the first who'd noticed that.

"But I still like it," she added.

And I could like you.

"How long will I be staying with you?" Lily asked him, voice thoughtful, as her gaze lifted to pin his once again.

Forever. That was the reply that wanted to spring to his lips. But forever with him would be a very dangerous thing. So Atlas compromised and said, "Until our attacker is caught."

"Caught? By the police?" A pause. "By the Feds? Because I'm sure we'll be seeing them soon."

He stared at her. He really liked the gold in her eyes.

"Or by you?" she whispered.

He let his smile stretch. She *had* been doing her homework. Someone deserved a gold star. "You'll stay with me," he repeated. "Until he's caught...or until I put him in the ground."

Chapter Four

Julia Tutwiler Prison For Women
   Wetumpka, Alabama

Six months ago...

"Why, Lily?" Magnolia's voice was annoyed. Disgruntled. "Why on earth do you want to talk to them? They aren't going to be like you. You aren't going to have some magical connection. It's not going to be all—snap. " She snapped her fingers. Polish gleamed on her painted nails. A soft peach. A woman on death row with perfectly manicured hands. "You have a soulmate. Someone who understands your poor, traumatic past." A huff. "Everyone is a victim these days. Have you noticed? It's so tiresome."

Lily kept her spine perfectly straight. "My mother is a serial killer. She's on death row. Sorry to point this out, but that pretty much does qualify as me having a traumatic past."

"Oh, pooh."

Pooh. Because her mother didn't curse. After all, she was a lady. A murdering lady, but a lady, nonetheless. Lily almost rolled her eyes. She would have, if she hadn't known such a gesture would completely set off Magnolia. Lots of things set off Magnolia in this world.

"You have an *interesting* past," Magnolia corrected her. "You have a mother who is world-famous. A woman who has gotten movies and books written about her. I am a celebrity." A pleased grin. "Because of me, you are, too. You are famous because of *me*. Never forget that."

"I never wanted to be famous." In fact, she'd spent most of her life trying to hide in the shadows. She liked the shadows. The sun was far too bright. If you weren't careful, it would burn you.

"Well, *I* never wanted to be locked away in prison, but here I am...because of you." A despondent sigh. "The things we do for our children."

Lily maintained her expression. "Do you regret that? Being locked up, because of me?" *It wasn't my fault. Blame me all you want, but no one else made you kill. You chose everything you did.*

"I have no regrets in this life. There is no point in regret. I've told you this before. Regret does nothing but waste energy and give you a headache. I hate headaches."

Yes. Her mother did hate regrets. And bad language. And boring parties. And men who lied to her. Men who used her. She hated them most of all. "I'm not looking for a soulmate." There would never be a soulmate for her in this world.

"Of course, you are." Magnolia rolled *her* eyes. "You don't want to be alone. Humans are not solitary creatures.

We crave companionship. Not like we want to walk through the giant void of life all alone."

"That should be on a greeting card."

Magnolia snapped to attention. "Lily Oleander Gallo. Did you just make a joke? Is the sky falling? The world ending?"

"Thank you, Mother. Always nice to be appreciated."

"I do appreciate you." Softer. "You are the one thing in my life I appreciate above all else. You are my forever companion. The reason I will never walk through the void alone. Even at my worst, at my most damaged, you never turned on me. You never will."

Lily's chest ached.

"I appreciate you, my beautiful daughter, but you are far too serious. When you were younger, I used to worry that you didn't even know how to smile." Magnolia leaned forward. "You want to find the others out there because you want to think that you don't all have to turn out like your parents. Fair enough. Done. I'll go ahead and make a prediction right here and now. They won't *all* be wretchedly evil. *I'm* not wretchedly evil. I was simply getting rid of the disappointments in my life."

"No, you were murdering men, Mother."

"*Disappointments.*"

They stared at each other.

"They lie to you, Lily." Her mother wet her lips. "They use you. They twist up your goodness. Then they try to cast you aside when they are done."

Lily leaned forward, her pose matching her mother's. No, mirroring hers. "Got to say, walking through the void all alone sounds way better than leaving a pile of bodies in my wake."

Magnolia didn't blink. "The trick is to eliminate them before they eliminate you."

Yes, her mother had perfected that trick. Or, she'd *almost* perfected it. The *almost* part that had led to her being locked away.

"I tried to love," her mother admitted. "I tried to love them all. Maybe…" Softer. "Maybe part of the problem was on my end. I can love you. I just do. No effort. It's like breathing with you. But the others…" A shake of her head. "The connection isn't there. They disappoint me. Then they die." Her gaze sharpened. "Do you think it will be the same for you? Do you think you won't be able to love a mate?"

"I'm not looking for a mate." She would not make that mistake. "I'm looking for—"

"Someone to understand your darkness. Someone who won't fear you. Someone who can protect you, even from yourself." A nod. "That's what I wanted, too. But I never found that person."

Lily rose. The chair legs screeched as they slid over the floor. "Of course, you did, Mother. You have me."

"Yes, I do, don't I?" A slow smile bloomed on Magnolia's face. She'd never had trouble smiling. She used her smile as a trick—a weapon—all the time.

Lily turned for the door.

"Be careful." A rare warning from Magnolia.

Lily darted a glance at the watchful guard. Jesse Baker hadn't made a sound during her talk with Magnolia. She knew he'd paid careful attention to every word, though, and would probably report the conversation immediately to the warden.

"There's an old saying," Magnolia told her. "'The apple doesn't fall far from the tree.'"

Lily looked over her shoulder at her mother. "I am not you." *I will not be like you. I can change. I can stop.*

"Perhaps not, but the others could be just like their parents. And if you get attacked again, prison guards might not be there to pull a killer off you. You might not walk away with a jagged scar on your stomach. You might not walk away at all." Magnolia's lips pressed together. "If that happens, I will be very upset."

"Oh, no. I can't have you upset. Not like I want you to start poisoning guards."

The guard choked.

"I was joking," Lily told him.

But...

She hadn't been. Because as Magnolia had pointed out before, she wasn't really the type to joke. Lily spent her days and nights being far too serious. Far too aware of the darkness that was waiting to wrap around her like the greedy lover that it was.

For her whole life, she'd walked a tightrope with her mother. Always trying to keep Magnolia content. Always trying to keep her mother's emotions regulated. Because when Magnolia wasn't content, when she wasn't controlled...

She tended to murder someone.

"If my mother offers you any tea," she told the guard, "don't drink it."

A sharp gasp from Magnolia. "As if I would do that! Jesse is my friend!"

Lily raised an eyebrow.

"Besides, they don't just *give* me teapots here in maximum security, Lily." A huff from her mother. "Not like one can just snag poison from thin air."

The guard relaxed.

Then Magnolia...winked.

Chapter Five

Present day...

Atlas kept one arm wrapped around Lily as they left the hospital. As she'd expected, reporters waited like the hungry predators that they were.

But it wasn't just reporters outside. Hospital guards. Cops. Some of Atlas's own security personnel.

The sea of faces passed Lily in a blur. Her mind was spinning, her chest aching, but she made sure to keep her game face on. Long ago, she'd learned to wear that face. The wrong emotion, the wrong expression could lead to chaos.

She was too good to make amateur mistakes.

So why did you strip in front of Atlas? Why are you riding off into the darkness with him right now without a single protest?

Her chest felt hollow when she thought of Benedict Swain. The detective was dead. Not like he could have survived those flames. Soon enough, the wreckage of the little cabin in the woods would be searched. His remains unearthed. There would be more grieving. A funeral.

She'd always hated funerals. Ever since she discovered how much her mother enjoyed them. Black had been Magnolia's favorite color, and she looked extra fragile when she had tear tracks on her cheeks.

Desmond stood at attention near the rear of the limo. His gaze swept the crowd, and she knew he was searching for threats. Desmond Yoruba had been working with Atlas for years. Actually, they'd been friends long before Desmond had become Atlas's head of security. They'd met at college.

Desmond, a Nigerian immigrant. A man who'd been forced to be a child soldier and see traumas no one should face before his family had been able to rescue him, and they'd fled to the US. Desmond had grown up to be determined, deadly, and to be the right hand of one of the most powerful billionaires in the world.

A billionaire who just happened to be the son of a serial killer. And a billionaire who'd been kidnapped and nearly murdered that night.

Only for his head of security to sweep in with a brigade of armed personnel. She did wonder, if Desmond and those armed guards had found Atlas's attacker in that cabin, what would they have done?

Killed him on the spot.

"How do you know Lily Gallo?" A desperate shout from a nearby reporter. "Atlas, Atlas! Are you romantically involved with Lily Gallo?"

No, not yet. Though they had seen each other semi-nude so...

"Were you together when you were taken?"

No, I was just doing my due diligence and surveilling him. I saw the attack from a distance and ran to help.

"What do you have to say to the man who abducted you?"

The questions fired from the crowd.

She didn't think that Atlas was going to stop and respond. What would be the point of that? But...

Just as they reached the open door of the limo...

Atlas paused.

She saw Desmond shake his head in a short, negative gesture. A clear warning to Atlas. But Atlas chose to ignore the warning.

"I do have a message to deliver to that piece of shit," Atlas announced.

Oh, no.

"You had your shot at me," Atlas said, voice clear, unflinching. No, more than that, *threatening*. "Now it's my turn."

She glanced back at him.

A cold, dangerous smile curved his lips. His dimples flashed, but instead of reassuring her, those dimples sent a shiver down her spine. The truth was, when Lily saw those dimples, she thought of a shark. Weird but...

By the time you saw a shark's teeth coming at you, it was far too late to flee.

By the time you saw Atlas's dimples...

The danger is already right in front of you.

"Do you believe your attacker will come at you again? Is that what you're saying?" The words fired from a redhead in a black suit.

"What does Lily Gallo have to do with your attack?" A hard question from a man in jeans and a blue polo.

Atlas had his hand on the curve of Lily's back. The

spotlight was dead on them. She'd always hated the spotlight. And being trapped in a barrage of reporters was truly a scene straight from her nightmares.

There had been another moment in her life far too much like this one. When she'd left the hospital after her poisoning, after seven days of clinging to life, of fighting, only to finally walk out into the world again...

A frenzied swarm of reporters had been waiting for her. Their questions had blasted at her.

"Lily Gallo! Lily Gallo! What's it like to know your mother nearly killed you?"

"Lily! Is it true that your mother is a serial killer?"

"Can you ever forgive your mother?"

The voices from the past blurred with the shouted questions of the present. You weren't supposed to have to ever relive the same hell twice, but this certainly felt like the same nightmare to her in that instant.

Her heart raced, her breaths came too fast, and—*enough.* She didn't have to answer their questions. This wasn't her press party. Atlas had been the target. Atlas had also been the one to get his limo parked out front when he *could* have gotten the limo brought to the rear of the hospital. The man had donated a wing to the hospital, she knew he could have gotten the administrators to help him make a quiet exit. But, no, he'd wanted this scene. He liked the spotlight. She hated it.

He'd also deliberately sought the attention of the reporters because Atlas had wanted to issue a public challenge to his attacker. A very bold and dangerous move.

This was his show, not hers, so she shot forward and ducked into the car. Ducked, dove, whatever. She got inside, and, rather surprisingly to her, once she leapt in, Atlas followed.

"About damn time," Desmond groused. He slammed the door shut.

She'd thought Desmond might get in the rear of the limo with them, but, as if the driver had just been waiting for Atlas to get inside that vehicle...

The limo immediately pulled away.

"You turned to ice in front of the reporters. Did the scene bring back too many memories?"

She perched on the leather seat. A mini-bar waited in the back of the limo. Soft lighting trailed from the limo's floor and near the ceiling. At least a dozen people could easily have reclined in the rear of the limo.

But it wasn't a dozen people. It was just her. Just Atlas.

He lounged in the seat right beside her. Taking up way too much space. His leg brushed against hers, and the move should have annoyed her, but, oddly enough, it didn't. He felt strangely warm. His crisp, masculine scent teased her nose. And, as before, she felt drawn to him.

Why?

Was it because of the darkness she carried? Was she just responding to someone who might be...

Just like me?

Oh, great. Her mother would be laughing herself silly. Saying that Lily was truly after a soulmate that she would never find.

Atlas spoke slowly, thoughtfully, his deep voice rumbling and seeming to sink into her very skin, "After you were poisoned, you came out of the hospital, terrified, far too thin, with heavy shadows beneath your eyes and skin pale as a ghost. The reporters filmed every second of that hell for you." His arm stretched out on the top of the seat. "What were you then, nineteen? Twenty?"

Her breath shuddered out. She suspected he knew the

answer, but she still replied, "I was eighteen." Just old enough that the reporters had thought they didn't need to go as easily on her. Her story was too sensational for easy. "I'm surprised you are aware of what happened that day."

"I looked for the videos. I watched them. I watched you."

"*After* I tried to get interviews with you?" Again, he was being thorough.

"Sure." A casual answer. But...one that she feared held the hint of a lie. But, why would he have watched the videos about her before she'd ever approached him?

She looked back through the window on the right. The reporters were still filming them. Some just with their personal phones. Others with their camera crews because Atlas was big business. People like Atlas weren't supposed to be taken by killers.

Then again, people like Atlas weren't supposed to threaten killers in front of a hungry press, either. "Was that wise, do you think?" Lily tucked a lock of hair behind her left ear.

"Finding old videos of you? Watching them on loop? Probably not. However, those videos told me a lot about you. Like when you tuck hair behind your left ear, you feel threatened. You make that move when you're trying to buy yourself a beat of time."

Lily stilled. "I didn't realize you were a behavioral expert."

"I'm not. I am a Lily expert." He shifted position, moving his arm from the top of the seat. "Should we discuss our ground rules?"

The limo was driving down the street. It swept past the streetlights. Past the heavy buildings of downtown Dallas. A massive city. Sprawling. Over 1.3 million residents. The city teemed with life at every possible hour. So they weren't sweeping down deserted roads. Cars and people were everywhere. Vehicles buzzing past.

Yet that world seemed incredibly distant. She and Atlas were secluded away from everyone else. Maybe that was good. Maybe that was bad. Lily cleared her throat. "Before we get to rules, I need to stop by my rental house and pick up my personal belongings."

"Desmond is on the case. He'll have everything you need brought to my house."

Her brows climbed. "I haven't told Desmond where I was staying."

"You didn't need to tell him. I did it."

She nodded. "I get it. Fine. You're the all-knowing Oz. You dug into my life. Wanted to learn everything about me because..." But she stopped.

His expression was shadowed in the dim lighting that filled the exterior of the limo. "Please, do continue. Don't leave me in suspense."

"You were trying to decide what sort of threat I would be to you. So you tried to learn my weaknesses. Probably my strengths, too. Got to know those, don't you? The better to defend against them."

"Lily, Lily, Lily. You act as if we are enemies." A pause. "Is that what we are? Do you always get naked with your enemies?"

He was baiting her. As to why she'd gotten *almost* naked with him, yes, that had probably not been her best moment. Moments of weakness happened, though, when you were on a knife's edge of adrenaline, when grief shook your core and threatened to rip you apart, and guilt wanted to gut you like a fish.

Benedict is dead because of me. He came to help me. If only he'd gotten out of the cabin...

Atlas reached out. His fingers curled under her chin as he forced her to tilt her head up. She hadn't realized she'd looked down.

"Enemies, Lily? Or lovers?"

A weak laugh came from her. "Yes, I do get naked with lovers. That's sort of a necessity," she responded, going back to his earlier question. *Do you always get naked with your enemies?*

But Atlas shook his head. "What are we going to be? Enemies or lovers?"

"We don't have to be either." They did not. She really, really needed to put some space between them. She normally could be completely contained. Totally controlled. She didn't cross lines but...

I was kidnapped tonight. Shoved down a staircase. A cop died in a blaze right in front of me. And now...now...

She wet her lips. "We could be colleagues. I think I could learn a great deal from you. You could help my research considerably." As she'd explained in her emails and during her—very brief—phone calls with him.

His jaw hardened. "Research into the children of serial killers."

"Yes." Soft.

"Do I look like someone who likes to have his dark secrets dragged into the light?"

No, he did not, in fact, look like that type of person. "You're the one who offered me a pass into your life."

His thumb rose to brush over her lower lip. "Why me, Lily? There are others out there. Plenty of them. When I told you I wasn't interested, you could have just walked away."

Yes, she could have. Only..."You came from blood and death and pain."

"Thanks for the reminder." Mocking. "Actually, I came from nothing. From a father who was too damn good-looking. He used his looks to his advantage. Ted Bundy had nothing on my old man. He could charm any coed, any so-called happily married wife. He flashed his dimples, and his prey jumped into his car and didn't look back."

"Your mother was his high school sweetheart."

He raised his brows. "Is that what she was?"

"She became pregnant with you. Her parents wanted her to give you up for adoption. She didn't. She kept you."

"She kept me for seven years, until she learned what a monster I was."

"*He* was," she corrected, softly.

"That's fun. You think she didn't always know?"

This was news to Lily. His mother had always proclaimed ignorance for the crimes.

"Don't we all have to be as evil as they are? Isn't that what you and your *research* are going to show?" Hard, angry words, but his thumb brushed so gently over her lower lip. A sensual caress. "That we are just as fucked up as they are?"

"I don't see you out murdering college coeds." Her tongue touched the tip of his finger.

Atlas stilled.

"And I don't believe that I've murdered any of my previous lovers. They're all alive and well. No worries there. The point of my work isn't to show that we're as deviant as they are. The point is to see why we didn't turn out like them." Why on earth had she licked his finger? She hadn't meant to do that. Had she?

A low growl came from Atlas. "I was given up for

adoption at seven. I bounced around more foster homes than you could count because, shockingly, no one was interested in the kid of a serial killer."

Her chest seemed to ache.

"Everyone had always stared at me like they thought I was the devil. No, the devil's son." There was no emotion in his voice. No pain. No grief. He might as well have been talking about the weather as he said, "I ignored them all. Not like I wanted their affection—not like any would be given. My own mother had kicked me out. Why would they want me?"

I want you. Words that whispered through her mind.

"She tossed me away like I was trash. I bounced around foster homes. Never fit. Never stayed anywhere. I was taunted and hit and bullied by the other kids..."

The ache in her chest grew worse. "Atlas..."

"Until I fought back. Until I showed them how vicious I could be. Some people only understand strength. Some only understand pain."

"What did you do?"

His thumb moved from her lip, but his hand still curled around her jaw. "Never attacks that were too blatant. I picked my moments. Chose my punishments in the most effective ways possible."

His words should have chilled her. They didn't. Instead, she found herself angry that anyone had sought to hurt him. He'd just been a kid. Lost. Lonely. But she couldn't focus on the child he'd been. The dangerous man that he was—that man was before her. "Your IQ is off the charts," Lily noted.

"IQ is bullshit. People are smart in a million ways that tests don't measure."

He was still touching her, cradling her jaw. She was still

far too sensitive to his touch. "Based on the measured results you have, you're a certified genius. That genius helped you to build the largest research and development firm in the United States."

His hand lingered, as if he didn't want to stop touching her. "I made good investments."

"You got a full ride to college. You dropped out during your second year, though."

"I'd learned enough."

"You started your company one week after quitting."

"I don't like the term 'quitting'—I prefer to think of it as realigning. Quitting has such a negative connotation, don't you think?"

"You *realigned* very well. You went from not having a home of your own to owning twelve different homes in five countries. By any standard, you're a success story, but if you add in your father...well, you see why I am interested in the way you turned out." Interested. Fascinated. Far too consumed with knowing everything about him.

"Yeah, my old man made for quite the *interesting* college essay piece, I've got to say." Rough laughter. "What about you? Don't you see yourself as a success? The psychiatrist who writes best-selling books on the criminal mind. Heard you were even offered a few movie deals."

Goosebumps rose on her skin. "My mother is into the movie deals, not me."

"Is it true that you still visit her once a month? Even after she tried to kill you?"

She felt the dig in her heart. "My mother never tried to kill me."

"Okay, so, here's a ground rule. We'll call it our first one. I don't lie to you. You don't lie to me. You stripped naked—"

"You keep harping on that. Surely, I'm not the first woman who has stripped in front of you. And I wasn't completely naked. Neither were you."

Laughter slipped from him. A deep, dark, oddly sexy laughter. "Oh, sweetness, I never harp. Cute, though."

Finally, finally, his hand moved away. *He* moved away.

"We'll be at Preston Hollow soon enough," he murmured.

Ah, yes, his home in the ever-so-prestigious Preston Hollow. Billionaire row with lush, private properties. And top-of-the-line security.

"So let's get our agreement down, shall we? First, my terms. Then yours. Sound fair?"

"Yes." She pressed her hands against the top of her thighs. Her wrist ached. The bruising was getting worse.

"You don't lie to me. I won't lie to you."

She'd never bared her soul completely with anyone. Not even her mother. *Especially* not her mother. "Before we start, I must insist on personally going to my rental property. I have the keys, after all. My property, then your place."

"Desmond doesn't need keys for your rental."

She licked her lower lip. "That's called breaking and entering."

"That's called getting inside."

"Are you always this..." *Difficult.* "Challenging?"

"Yeah, I am. Think you can handle that?"

"In my sleep." A challenging billionaire was nothing compared to the murderers she'd faced. "This is a nonnegotiable point for me. I have to stop by my rental house. I have confidential material there that I must obtain."

Silence.

"Lily." A sigh of her name. "Is this the part where you

confess that you came to Dallas because you thought I was *already* a murdering psycho, just like my father?"

She squared her shoulders. "Atlas." Deliberately, she sighed his name, too. "Is this the part where you *confess* to being a murderer?"

Chapter Six

He couldn't help it. Booming laughter escaped from Atlas. As if he'd ever give up anything that easily.

"Right." A sniff from Lily. A cute, little annoyed sniff. She was just being so delightful. So serious and intense as she accused him of being a serial killer. "Didn't think you would fess up. Especially since I now believe you are his target, and not, in fact, the killer that Benedict and I had begun to hunt in the area."

Now *that* stopped his laughter. "You were hunting with Benedict?"

"A predator has disemboweled two individuals in the Dallas area. Sure, most officials will say a perpetrator must have three or more vics before earning the moniker of *serial killer,* but I say...if the signs are there, why wait when you know what's happening?" Very deliberate. "I told Benedict after the first kill that I was concerned a serial was at work."

Again, Atlas asked his question, "You were hunting with Benedict?" Because he needed to be clear on this point.

"I came to town after I learned of the first murder. The

method was very unusual. Deliberately painful. The killer clearly had the end goal of making his victim suffer as much as possible. I was...already looking into the Dallas area because of you, but the murder of William Lloyd did speed along my process."

William Lloyd. Billy Lloyd. Petty thief turned drug dealer. A guy tied to the fentanyl overdose of three Dallas teens.

"Victim number two turned up shortly after that," she added.

Yes, he was aware. Conry Harding had been the second kill. A suspected domestic abuser. An accused rapist. The son of a very wealthy real estate mogul. Conry had never actually spent any time behind prison bars.

But he'd sure gotten one gory ending to his life.

"After the second victim, there was no denying what was happening." Cool words. Except they frayed just a bit around the edges. "The killer only had three weeks in between the murders. That time frame alarmed me."

"Oh." A nod. "That alarmed you. *That* part. Not the fact that he'd pulled their insides to the outside. Sure. The time frame is the concerning part of the equation."

She exhaled. "With a first kill, predators can take years to build up to the actual attack. There should have been some sort of cooling off period after he murdered William Lloyd. Three weeks after the first murder—*if* it was even the first—that told me that our predator was especially dangerous. He *liked* it too much." She slid across the limo and pressed the button to lower the screen that separated them from the driver.

With barely a hiss of sound, the screen lowered.

"I'm going to need you to make a pitstop," Lily told the driver right before she rattled off her address.

Atlas was well aware of her address. He should be, after all, considering that he owned the property. A new acquisition. As in, new from a week ago.

"Boss?" From the driver. Carl Hansen had been his driver for the last three years. The man was also a bodyguard, former Delta Force. Quiet. Intense.

"Take us there," Atlas replied smoothly. Then he was sliding forward. Her finger still pressed to the control for the screen. His covered hers. Pushed down so that the privacy screen slid back into place. He was so close to Lily that he could drink up her vanilla scent. He could practically feel her warmth in the air.

But he could also see the faint shiver that slid over her skin. "Lily." Atlas liked saying her name. "Are you afraid of me?"

She pulled her hand away from his. Her head turned toward him. Their mouths were inches apart. "Should I be?"

He wanted her mouth. "I try not to hurt innocent things in this world."

"Don't make that mistake about me. I'm not innocent."

An immediate response. One that very much intrigued him all the more. "Oh?" Mild curiosity when he was really consumed by the desire to learn every detail about her. "How many people have you killed?"

She jerked. Hard.

Oh, Lily. Have you done something terrible? Do tell me all about it.

"I think we were talking about the killer currently hunting in Dallas," she reminded him.

Yes, but he would rather talk about Lily, and not that killer. Still, he'd let her direct the conversation. For now.

"You want us going to your rental because all of your files on the perp are there." Fine. He'd like to see those files.

"The files on *all* my research subjects are there. If I'm not staying at the rental—"

"You won't be." They needed to be clear on this. "For the foreseeable future, you will be with me." Done. He didn't intend to let her out of his grasp. His mind practically spun as he considered all the ways that he could bind Lily to him. For her protection, of course.

And because of his growing obsession.

"If I'm going to be at your place, then I need my research. It's too important to me. I can't lose it."

"Surely, you have computer backups. In the cloud, yes?" He couldn't wait to see that research.

"There are things at the rental I need. I will be collecting them."

So interesting. And a bit mysterious. As for another interesting point... "When I woke up in the basement, you said I was in danger of being disemboweled. You think the man who took me—who took *us*—is the predator that you and Benedict were hunting."

She didn't speak.

"Why, Lily?" He settled back into his seat. The one right next to her. His thigh brushed against her leg. "What made you think that sadistic prick had turned his attention to me?" His lips pressed together. He choked down his rage at the idea of that sonofabitch *touching* Lily. "I don't remember a bomb being part of his MO."

"Punishment is his MO." She shifted a bit on the seat. "Punishment can come in all sorts of forms."

She was not wrong about that. "How did you decide that this, uh, punishment killer had come after me? I'm not a drug dealer. I'm not a rapist. In fact, I have no criminal record." *Despite the efforts of one very enterprising cop.*

"Benedict warned me about you."

That would be the enterprising cop in question. Now they were getting to the good stuff. "Did he?"

"He was convinced that you were basically running the underworld here in Dallas."

Atlas laughed again. Okay, for such a seemingly serious woman, she was filling him with delight. "I have no interest in running the underworld. I am fully occupied running my billion-dollar company and employing thousands of people, but thanks so much."

"Appearances can be deceiving."

Just that. Those four casual words. Atlas fought his smile because he really should not enjoy her this much, not under the circumstances. They could have been killed that night. Benedict—prick that he had been—was dead. "Benedict hated me." True story. "He could never find a single shred of evidence to tie me to any crimes." *Because I don't leave evidence behind. What am I? An amateur?* "Benedict was convinced I was as twisted as my father, and he couldn't wait to lock me away."

A delicate throat clearing. "He was not a fan of yours, no."

His eyes narrowed. "Was that a joke?"

"It was a statement of fact. Benedict thought you were guilty of an assortment of crimes, and I believe this punishment killer also thought you were guilty. As to why I decided he was the one who'd taken us...I read the ME's reports on the two previous vics. Both suffered blows to the rear of the head that would have incapacitated them. Both were taken from dark parking lots, with no witnesses around, as if the perp had been watching them. Learning their routines. Waiting for the perfect moment to strike."

Yes. Atlas had even altered his routine just so he could have time in a dark parking lot to find the bastard. These details were not news, but Atlas said nothing.

"They were cuffed. The cuffs had bitten deeply into their skin as they struggled. The handcuffs left very distinct markings on them."

Now, he just could not help himself. He reached out and snagged her injured wrist. He hated that anything had been left on her skin but... "Marks like these?"

"Much deeper, but clearly consistent with handcuffs being locked around their wrists. The information about the blow to the head and the handcuffs was never released to the public. Only our killer would know that intel."

"So based on some head wounds and cuff marks, you decided the killer had come after me." Why not?

But his serious Lily just nodded. "I think the killer was working up to you the entire time. I think he believes he is eliminating evil. You are evil...to him, anyway."

He loved touching her soft skin. "But you originally thought *I* was the predator, didn't you? That I was the one punishing? Pretty sure I remember you apologizing for being wrong about me. Things were a little hazy when I first woke up in that pit of hell, but those words stood out."

"I, um, I don't know that I apologized."

"No? Well, then you clearly *should* apologize. Go ahead. Because if you think a man is a savage killer, you should apologize when you're wrong about that important point." They'd turned and were heading toward her rental. About five minutes away. He recognized the streets. Perhaps he'd driven by her place a time or two. "I think I do deserve an apology," he decided. "A lovely, heartfelt apology because you have wounded me so greatly."

"Fine." Bit out. "I'm sorry that I thought you were disemboweling people. There. Better?"

He winced and let her go. "Disembowelment never would be my chosen method. Why the hell would you want to get so gory with someone? Can you imagine the crime scene cleanup that would be involved? I mean, you might as well just put on a hazmat suit because the blood splatter from that kind of thing would be horrific."

Lily appeared all the more concerned by his response. Her tension just thickened. "Ahem." Another throat clearing from her. "I suspect our killer used this method because disemboweling has been a form of punishment for crimes going back to ancient times."

Of course, she would be an expert on the topic. Shocking. And now the guy was "our killer," was he? For the record, though, "It's not a form of punishment I'd ever use." His father had been into blood and gore. Mess. Horror.

I am not him.

"No, I think you're far more sophisticated than that. If you had talked with me sooner, I would have understood that about you. I don't believe you would go for the torture element at all. You'd simply kill your prey and move on."

He didn't tense. Didn't draw in a sudden breath. Didn't even blink. But he knew how to respond. When an enemy was getting too close, you simply had to throw them off target. Not that he wanted her to be his enemy... "Do you always get semi-naked when you think you're facing a killer?"

"Back to that, are you? I think we've covered that I was trying to put us on equal footing."

"I think you were trying to get naked with me. Full disclosure, you can do it anytime. There is nothing more that I would enjoy than fucking you until you scream with pleasure."

Silence. The thick, tense kind that could completely fill a car.

He began to smile. *Now I am back in control, and she—*

"Does that usually work?" Lily asked in her calm voice. "When people get too close, when people say things that make you uncomfortable, you strike out? Maybe you say something shocking to disconcert them so that you have the upper hand?"

Uh, yeah. Except she didn't seem particularly disconcerted. *Point for Lily.*

Before he could respond, she added, "I think *you* were trying to get naked with *me*. I believe you wanted me to see your scars, Atlas."

"Why would I want you to see them?"

"Because a part of you wanted to warn me about what I would be facing."

You have no idea, sweets.

She continued, "I also do think you want to fuck me. I don't believe that is a lie."

Fast, hard laughter escaped him. "Thank you for that. My dick is currently as hard as a rock, and I keep imagining you riding me in this limo. I definitely want to fuck you. Want to do it until you scream and come for me."

A swift inhale from Lily. Was she going to tell him to screw off? To shut his dirty mouth? He waited in anticipation.

"I'd be lying if I said I didn't feel the attraction between us, too."

Holy fuck. Holy. *Fuck.* His hands clenched into fists as

he tried to fight the urge to grab her. Everything she said and did just drew him to her all the more. Okay, was the woman a freaking witch? Because he sure as shit felt like he was falling under her spell.

Maybe it's the blow to the head. Maybe that prick doctor was right, and I should have stayed at the hospital.

"It's basic, isn't it?" Lily asked in her soft, husky, sensual voice. "Primal. And, honestly, a bit frightening."

This woman, *this woman*—

"Just so you understand, I have to trust you in order to fuck you."

Had she just said those words or was he so far gone that he'd imagined them? It *had* been a bastard of a day. Or, uh, night.

"I don't fuck monsters," Lily told him primly.

You will be fucking me. So she might have to make an exception to that monster rule. However, he could give her one truth. "I'm not the punishment killer currently running around Dallas." *Fuck me, Lily. Fuck me right here, right now.*

The limo turned again. Accelerated a bit, only to slow down moments later.

"No." Lily sighed. "But you were trying to catch him, weren't you? Not like you'd just randomly be in a parking lot without security. Not you. Your behavior changed about two weeks ago. Suddenly, there were more vulnerable moments for you. Moments when you wanted him to attack." She eased closer. "You were setting a trap for him. Even as he was hunting you. Did you get a warning that he was coming? Did he reach out to you in some way? Because I believe that he contacted his other victims. I think he liked to play with them before he attacked. Part of the thrill of the kill."

His heart beat steadily, but he was aware of every single thud. Far too aware. *Boom. Boom. Boom.* "And why do you believe that?"

"Another bit that Benedict made sure wasn't leaked to the media. He found a note at William Lloyd's house. Simple, to the point. *'You'll pay.'*"

Boom. Boom. Boom. Was his heart beating faster? He inhaled slowly. Exhaled the same way. "Did the second victim get a similar note?"

"Not that the cops found."

Um.

"Did *you* get a note?" Lily pressed.

"I get far too much correspondence. Am I really supposed to remember one letter?" He looked beyond the window. "We're here." Desmond had beaten them. He could see Desmond standing near her front door, but when Desmond caught sight of the limo, he immediately turned toward them. "Unfortunately, we did not get to go over those ground rules, did we?"

"I think we have a basic understanding. You don't lie to me. I don't lie to you."

"Ah, yes." The limo stopped. "Basic." He hadn't *technically* lied to her about the note from the killer. He did get far too much correspondence. The note had also been useless. No prints. No distinguishing marks. No help at all.

Atlas leaned forward. He'd be exiting first.

But she curled her fingers around his arm. "When does the part about you *not* lying to me start?"

Fucking her in the limo would have been a dream. But he'd settle for fucking her in the comfort of his king-size bed, when he had her safely locked in his home. That way, he could take his time with her. "I did not kill William Lloyd or Conry Harding." Absolute truth. "And if some fucker thinks he is going to play with me, going to hunt *me*, then I believe I am well within my rights to defend myself." Another truth. "Now, if that frightens you too much, we can stop this partnership right now." They would not, in fact, stop. And he didn't think *partnership* was the right word. But he was just pushing to see what she'd say, so he didn't think semantics truly mattered.

"You do not frighten me."

No? "Now who is lying?" Atlas couldn't help it. He brushed his lips over hers. She was simply too tempting. "You're so afraid that you're shivering. You talk a good game, Lily Gallo, but when it comes down to the cold, stark truth..." Atlas began to lift his head and move back.

Her fingers flew up and sank into his hair. She yanked him back to her. Kissed him. Hard. Desperately. Her lips parted, her tongue met his. She kissed with a frantic, hurried need that electrified him. She didn't kiss him as if she was afraid. Quite the opposite. She kissed him as if she'd been starving for him.

Where the hell have you been my whole life, Lily?

She ripped her mouth away, breath heaving. "I'm not shivering from fear." Just those stark words. Then she bolted from the limo.

Well, well, well... He smiled.

She dipped her head back inside. "For the record, I already knew you didn't kill Conry or William. If I thought you had, I wouldn't have been in the limo with you. Ground rule one—no lies, not from either of us. From this moment forward, no lies, understand?"

But he lied so well. And so often.

"Two...we trust each other."

He trusted Desmond. And maybe one or two other

people. Would Lily soon be part of that ever-so-elite group? Time would tell.

"Rule three..."

Someone was certainly spouting out ground rules quickly.

Her breath heaved. *"We don't hurt each other."*

He climbed from the vehicle. She backed up.

Not like he could have that. He didn't want her retreating from him. He wanted her running to him, always. His hands snaked out and curled over her shoulders. He could still taste her, and he wanted ever so much *more*. "Lily, trust isn't easy for me. It has to be earned." Usually, earned in blood. So he would make no promises on that score, not yet. "But I vow to you here and now, I will never, ever hurt you." He smiled at her, knowing the nearby streetlamp would catch his dimples. The smile that reassured others, but not his Lily. *My Lily*. Oh, what a dangerous but tempting thought. "How about you promise to trust me? And I promise to never hurt you? That fair?" Probably not, but it was what it was.

"Aren't you worried that I *will* hurt you?" A careful question.

He opened his mouth to respond.

"Atlas!" A bellow from Desmond. "We have a problem!"

Instantly, he'd thrust Lily behind him. He pushed her toward the still open limo door.

"Some bastard broke into her fucking house!" Desmond shouted.

He wasn't pushing Lily any longer. She'd whipped away from Atlas, maneuvered around him, and she ran straight for her front door.

Chapter Seven

Julia Tutwiler Prison For Women
  Wetumpka, Alabama

Three months ago...

"Do you still feel guilty?" Magnolia asked her.

Lily looked up from the files in front of her.

"Guilt is a useless emotion," Magnolia added. "Wastes time. Energy. I personally never bother with it."

"What, exactly, would I feel guilty about, Mother?" Lily was highly aware of the guard to the right. Blond, slightly rounded shoulders. Tall. Jesse Baker was typically the guard given watch duty when Lily was in visiting sessions with her mother.

"Oh, knowing you...anything." Her mother's hand waved vaguely. A light, coral polish on her nails today. "You blame yourself for all sorts of things that aren't your responsibility. Even as a child, you were far too serious.

94

Always thinking the weight of the world was on your shoulders."

Her mother wasn't talking about the weight of the—wait. "Atlas."

Magnolia blinked her glorious eyes. "Hmmm?"

She shut her files. "How do you know?"

"Know what, darling?"

That I am looking into Atlas Bennett. That I am fascinated by him. No, no, fascinated was the wrong word. She was merely conducting research. That was all. Research. Just like she and her friend Sloane researched their other subjects.

"Names are important, you know," her mother said. "Take me, for example. I was named for the Magnolia. A name that fits me perfectly. Beauty. Dignity. Southern charm."

Yes, nowhere in that description was *murderous predator.* So perhaps it wasn't the most perfect name ever.

"And you..." Magnolia turned her waving hand toward Lily. "My precious daughter. Named after the beautiful lily."

Lily's jaw locked. "Many lilies are extremely poisonous." One of her mother's little jokes. *You literally named me for poison.* "They cause vomiting, mouth pain, and weakness."

Magnolia smiled. "Isn't that fun?"

"Not to the people vomiting."

A delighted laugh escaped Magnolia. "You are telling more jokes lately! I find that wonderful. Maybe you are finally coming out of that shell of yours!"

She wasn't a turtle. "That wasn't a joke. I don't think the people vomiting would find it very fun." An inhale. "I was serious."

"Aren't you always?" Magnolia's lips pulled down. "How did I wind up with such a serious child?"

Maybe because you're a murderer, and I grew up knowing that dark truth. Lily also had never been particularly amused by her name. She didn't think her mother had given it to her because lilies were beautiful. But because they were poison.

Magnolia settled a bit more comfortably in her chair. "Beautiful things can be dangerous. They should not be underestimated in this world. Carry your name with pride."

Like it was easy to carry a name given by your serial killer mother. There was a reason Lily had always made sure she used her father's surname of Gallo and not her mother's maiden name of Calhoun.

Something has to separate us.

"Of course, your middle name *is* Oleander," her mother murmured. Those big, wide eyes blinked innocently. "Are you going to accuse me of some wicked intent with that one, too?" A blink. "Honestly, darling, you should be grateful I gave you such beautiful names."

Her palms were slick with sweat. Her mother was playing games. Oleanders were poisonous. In some cases, fatal. Severe cases of oleander poisoning could result in heart paralysis because the oleander contained cardiac glycosides.

"Do you still journal, my Lily?" Magnolia asked with a flutter of her lashes. "When you were a child, you were always scribbling away in your diary."

No, she had not been. As a child, she'd never kept a diary. She'd also never had any close friends. Magnolia hadn't liked for the other children to visit their house.

"The therapist here tells me that it would be very beneficial for me to keep a recording of my thoughts. My emotions." Her mother pressed her lips together. Slowly released them. "I suppose I could give it a try. I do want to cooperate as much as possible."

Her mother had *always* written down her thoughts and emotions. She was the one who'd kept journals.

And Lily had been the one to dispose of them so they could not be used against Magnolia. Well, most of them. She'd kept one.

Did her mother know that? Lily suspected that she did.

"Keep a journal," her mother urged her. "Maybe it will help you, too."

You want me to read your journal again, don't you? I've read it a thousand times. There is nothing inside that will help me. Time to change the subject. "Are you still in contact with the doctor from Louisiana?"

"Who?" A faint pucker between Magnolia's brows.

"The man who offered marriage," she reminded her.

"Oh, right. We'll see what happens. You just have to be very, very careful with men. You never know what burdens they carry. We *all* carry burdens in this world."

Again, Lily knew the phrasing was deliberate. All the talk about names...about carrying burdens...the world...

You know, don't you, Mother? But *how* did she know?

"You've centered in on your first test subject," Magnolia murmured.

Yes, she had.

Atlas Bennett.

Atlas. Named for the Titan of Greek myth. The one who bore the weight of the world on his shoulders.

"Do you think he'll carry your burdens? Take some of your darkness away?" Magnolia shook her head. "I doubt it, darling. I think he'll just pull you under with him. The weight might just crush you both." A shrug. "I always worried you'd be attracted to the wrong kind of man. I mean, just look at the failure of your last relationship."

She wasn't talking about that relationship with Magnolia.

"He was a user," Magnolia said. "Tried to warn you about that. You didn't listen." Her lips pursed. "Will you listen this time?"

"I'm not attracted to research subjects."

"That's not what he will be."

Their gazes held. Fought.

"Live up to *your* name," her mother urged her.

That was the problem. She already had. *And now I have to find a way to stop. Someone has to help me stop.* Because she wasn't sure if she was strong enough to do it herself.

Chapter Eight

Present day...

Lily ran toward the open front door of her rental house. She could see the shattered doorbell camera, broken and smashed into pieces on the narrow porch. The lock on the door had been broken, too, apparently banged to hell and back, and a discarded hammer—the hammer from the small shed in the back of the property, a hammer Lily had used just days before—had been dropped near the door. Her hands flew out to push the door open.

"Nope." Atlas's arms curled around her stomach, and he hauled her back. "Did we learn *anything* from the explosion tonight? Let's not run straight into traps. Don't particularly want to watch you burn in front of my eyes."

She struggled in his grip. "I have to get inside!"

Again... "Nope." He lifted her off her feet, completely ignored her struggles, and carried her back toward the limo. Where he basically hurled her inside as if she weighed nothing and tossing her was the easiest thing in the world.

99

She landed on the seat and immediately surged forward.

But Atlas blocked her exit. "Do I honestly look like I will allow you to die tonight?"

"It's *my* house!"

"No, technically, it's mine. I own it. You are the tenant who broke the terms of her lease when she started painting and doing repair projects without authorization."

"*What?*" Since when did he own it? When?

"That's probably like check or checkmate. Me, owning your place. Didn't see that coming, did you? So much for being the all-knowing Lily."

"*Atlas.*" She'd never claimed to be all-knowing. And when had he bought her house?

All traces of humor fled. "You're not going near the house right now. So get over it. Desmond is calling the cops. After tonight's very, shall we say...*hot* events, I want a bomb squad checking the property before you get anywhere near it." Flat. Hard.

And...

Smart, dammit. Smart. She should never have just run inside. The perp had made it clear her house had been invaded. Thus, the broken lock and smashed doorbell camera. Correction—Atlas's house. Only it had not belonged to him when she moved in. Lily was certain of that fact.

"Thinking more clearly now? Excellent. We won't have long before the cops arrive." He climbed into the limo. Slammed the door after him. "Tell me, Lily, what is inside that the cops should not discover?"

"I have no idea what you mean." It was good that he was inside the limo. If a shooter was out there, he would have made too big of a target.

A shooter? So now you're worried about gunfire? Her hands twisted in her lap. The punishment killer hadn't shot victims before, but, as she'd told Atlas, there were plenty of ways to punish someone. And killers evolved. The most dangerous ones *always* evolved.

Everything was getting all twisted and confused. She needed to think through all of the events from the night.

She also needed her files. Her laptop. Her...

I need my mother's diary.

"I will ask you one more time, sweets, but please don't play games with me. We don't have time for them right now." A beat of silence. "What is inside that the cops can't find? I can't help you—I can't protect you—if I don't know what I am supposed to hide."

Her breath sawed in and out. "My research is in there. My laptop. Files on the adult children of serial killers. Most of that is public information. But I just... some of that material I discovered on my own. Some of the individuals don't even know who their parents were— *are.*"

"Well, that's fun. Who doesn't love to get the shocking news that mommy dearest or daddy dearest is a sadistic killer?"

"I didn't tell them. I haven't confronted anyone. *You* are the first for me." Though her friend Sloane was tracking others.

"Sorry, but the question has to be asked, how can you be so certain *you* are right? What if you tell someone the wrong news about a serial killing parent?"

"I am thorough."

"Oh, well, that clears it up. I mean, if you're *thorough* about it." He looked back over his shoulder at the house. "Tick tock. What can't the cops find? We both know you have something you want hidden. You were far too desperate to get in that house."

Yes, she had been desperate. Panicked. "A diary," she whispered.

His head swiveled toward her. "Yours?"

"Yes." No. She wasn't supposed to lie to him. The lie had just slipped out. "It's...personal information." That was true. "Information that I don't want others to see."

"Where is the diary?"

"Underneath the loose board in the bedroom. The board two over from the nightstand. To the right." Her breath came faster. "The cops will not search there. They won't think to yank up a board, but..." *But I'm worried.* They wouldn't look under the board unless there was a reason to search there. A reason as in, someone else had ripped up the board already. Someone—the intruder.

But in order for that to happen...

The intruder would have needed to be watching me very closely.

She swallowed. "That diary can't reach the cops." It would be disastrous.

"So you've been that naughty, hmm, Lily?"

Yes. "Atlas..."

"Your research and your diary. Those are the important items inside. Got it. Anything else? Anything else my nimble fingers should grab when I have the opportunity?"

Nothing that could jeopardize her.

But that diary...

If it fell into the wrong hands...

Her house of cards could come crashing down. "Just the diary. It's what I need."

"You saved my life. The least I can do is retrieve a book for you."

She grabbed his hand and held on tightly. "But not until it's safe. Not until we are sure it's not a trap."

"Ah, sweets, you're saying I'm more valuable than a book? I am touched."

"Atlas..."

His lips brushed over hers. "I'll get it when the moment is right. Trust me."

Trust...

Trust would be necessary in their relationship.

I have to trust you in order to fuck you.

* * *

SHE STARED AT THE FLASHING, blue lights. Nearly eight a.m. Exhaustion pulled at her even as the sun rose higher in the sky. She was long past the point of running on adrenaline. Now, Lily knew she was running on fumes. Wasn't that the old saying?

Because it was Atlas and because of what had happened before, a full force of cops had rushed to the little house on the cul-de-sac. The bomb sniffing dogs were brought out. The home thoroughly searched.

No bomb was found.

But apparently, something bad *had* been discovered. Because the cops had been extra intent as they systematically examined every inch of the property.

She hadn't been allowed inside yet, but Atlas had. Atlas and his magic reach and his new ownership of *her* rental. He'd been escorted in by two uniforms while she waited outside.

Her hands twisted nervously together.

Desmond was at her side. Silent. Steady. Intense.

Carl waited near the limo. Just as steady and intense.

Desmond had introduced her to Carl while she'd been waiting for the madness at her house to settle down.

As for Atlas...he appeared in her doorway, his hands loose at his sides. His expression was extra grim as he began to march toward her.

Oh, no. There was no sign of the diary. She felt heat stinging her cheeks. She should have destroyed that diary so long ago. Why the hell hadn't she? *Why?*

Because it was the only proof I had that she actually loved me.

Too bad it held all sorts of other proof, too.

Atlas came right up to her. Desmond immediately stepped away to give them privacy.

"It's bad," Atlas said.

Bad?

He pulled her into his arms. "Mission accomplished," he breathed into her ear.

She shuddered, and relief made her lightheaded.

"It's okay. I got it. It's tucked inside my sweatshirt. No one ever saw me take it, I promise. Now let's get the hell out of here. I'll describe the fucking mess when I get you safely in the limo."

She eased back. One step. Their bodies no longer touched. Her eyes flew to his face. Though she very much didn't like the *fucking mess* part, she had to say, "I could kiss you right now," she told him.

"Hold the thought." He glanced over his shoulder. "Dammit."

Uniformed cops were coming toward them. That tracked because there had to be more questions, and there was—

Wait. She'd just caught sight of someone else. An FBI agent that she recognized. One that had her stiffening because FBI Special Agent Gage Emerick was not a fan of hers. In fact, quite the opposite.

I know what you did. I just can't prove it.

He'd certainly gotten to Dallas far faster than she'd anticipated.

"What's wrong?" Atlas asked as he felt her tension. Then, upon spotting the man heading toward them with a determined stride, "Who the fuck is that joker?"

An FBI agent. A man who thinks I'm a killer. And...

Her ex.

No time to explain all of that, though, because Gage had closed in too quickly.

"Lily." Gage stopped about two feet away from her. Wrinkled suit. Finger-combed hair. She recognized the signs of someone who had been traveling all night. "I hear you've had quite the exciting twelve hours." His gaze raked her.

She inclined her head toward him. "Being abducted doesn't count as exciting. It counts as terrifying."

"*Were* you terrified?" He flashed his ID and waved away the local authorities. "FBI. I'll be talking to the vic. Give us some time."

She was aware of Atlas shifting his body closer to her. Atlas lifted his hand, and Desmond immediately began walking back their way.

The limo driver remained near the vehicle.

"Weird to think of you as terrified." A slight, considering pause. "Because I wasn't sure anything could scare you." Gage smiled at her. That perfect, pearly white grin. Then he reached out and put his arms around her. He hugged her, the embrace hard, and Lily stood statue-still in his arms.

"Excuse me." Atlas's arctic voice. "I'm not exactly an

expert in these situations, but is embracing a vic the way to go? Especially when she damn well does not *want* the embrace?"

Gage let her go.

Lily immediately backed up. No, not backed up. She edged toward Atlas. *Why did I do that?*

"Lily." Atlas wrapped an arm around her shoulders, and he pulled her against his body. "Are you going to introduce me?"

She hadn't stiffened when he wrapped his arm around her shoulders. Because honestly, his touch reassured her. Odd because no one's touch had ever reassured her in this world. Truth be told, she didn't really like physical touch. She certainly had not liked the hug that Gage had just given to her. They were *not* at a hugging stage.

Physical touch was not exactly her love language. She was more an acts-of-service woman.

He found the diary and smuggled it out before the cops could see it, no questions asked.

If that didn't count as an act of service, she wasn't sure what did.

"This is FBI Special Agent Gage Emerick." She settled a bit more comfortably against Atlas, her body softening as growing exhaustion pulled at her. "I'm sure he knows who you are..." That had to be the whole reason Gage had made an appearance. He came out for the big guns. "But, just so I do this bit right, Gage, meet Atlas Bennett."

Gage extended his hand toward Atlas.

A brief hesitation, then Atlas reached out to take the offered hand. "How do you know Lily?" Atlas asked the Fed.

"We dated—*damn, that is quite the grip you've got there.*"

Atlas released him. "Lily is with me."

Gage stretched out his fingers. "With you? What the hell does that mean?"

"It means she's moving in with me. The events tonight have sped up our process a bit, but, from here on out, Lily... Is. With. Me."

He'd just gotten way territorial. And she had no idea why. So what if she'd dated the Fed? Why did that matter?

Gage's brows shot up as he assessed her again. "So you're dating billionaires now, Lily? That's new."

She wasn't exactly dating Atlas. She could feel the edge of the diary pressing against her. He *had* gotten it for her. Truly, she wanted to kiss the man.

"Did I just see you exiting the house, Atlas?" Gage asked. "Thought it was a crime scene."

"It's *my* house." Arrogant. Commanding. What she was starting to think of as typical Atlas. "So I went in to survey the damage. As you can see, I didn't bring anything out with me. Not like I was tampering with evidence."

Gage's watchful stare drifted from Atlas back to her. "You been inside, Lily? You see if anything was taken?"

"I haven't been inside yet."

"Her laptop is missing," Atlas revealed.

It was? Oh, *damn*. Not good. As if the break-in had ever been a *good* sign.

"Lily told me where it should have been. It wasn't there. It appears...other things were taken, but the damage is so severe that it's hard to tell right now."

"Severe damage?" she breathed.

A curt nod.

Oh, no. "Were my files there, Atlas?"

Appearing apologetic, he told her, "I believe they were taken."

Disaster. She would have to call Sloane right away and alert her friend except—no phone. Her phone had been smashed back at the cabin. *Then* the flames had probably destroyed it. A new phone would be a necessity. She would have to reach out to her friend, ASAP. She *should* have called Sloane already, not like she wanted Sloane finding out about the attack and the cabin fire on the news.

I messed up. Wasn't thinking clearly. Sloane is going to panic.

"Lily?" Gage's voice drew her attention back to him. "They let him in, but not you? You *were* living here, correct? That's the information I was given on my way over."

"Why the hell *are* you here?" Atlas asked.

"I'm a Fed. I work BAU. That's Behavioral Analysis—"

"I know what it is," Atlas growled.

"I was brought in just for you, Atlas." A flashy smile. "The people in charge at the Bureau view you as very important. Rest assured, I will not rest until the perp responsible for your abduction and for the murder of Detective Benedict Swain is apprehended." He scraped a hand over his jaw. "I learned Lily was taken, too." Rougher. "When word reached me about this break-in at her address, I immediately came to the scene." His hand fell. His eyes raked her. "You're the one who needs to see what happened in there, Lily. Come on. I'll take you in." He reached out to grasp her hand.

Atlas pulled her back. "Why did the two of you stop dating?"

Cops buzzed around them. A dull throb began behind her left eye. "Really not the place for this." The last thing she wanted was to rehash her relationship with Gage. Especially considering that some perp had broken into her house. Stolen from her. *My work. Gone.*

"I'm curious." Atlas brushed a kiss across her temple, right near the throbbing. And the pain seemed to ease.

What in the world?

"Why would anyone ever let you go?" Atlas murmured. "What kind of idiot would let you slip through his fingers?"

Her head turned toward Atlas. Now wasn't the time to mock the Fed. "It wasn't serious." They'd had sex. Twice. This did not seem to be the appropriate place to announce that news. Some things were private. "Then I learned Gage had ulterior motives for wanting to be close to me."

"*That hurts, Lily.*" A dramatic pronouncement from Gage. "I've always cared for you."

She glanced back to see him place his hand over his heart. Seriously, that move was too much, even for him.

"We were friends all through med school," he added. "Even when I dropped out to join the Bureau, we kept in touch. It was natural for me to be curious about you. And... some pieces of the puzzle just didn't add up for me. Questions had to be asked." His hand slid back to his side. The movement had his fingers sliding near the holster on his hip. "But just because I had a job to do, it didn't mean that I did not care. Again, I'll repeat, I've always cared." His eyes glittered.

"Yeah, that bullshit needs to stop." Now Atlas moved in front of her. "*I'll* repeat, Lily is with me. Any relationship you had with her is dead and buried." Snapped.

Desmond watched from close by, saying nothing.

"Huh." Gage rocked back on his heels. "I'm a bit curious. Are you *good* at burying things, Atlas? Because there have been some rumors about you..."

Atlas just laughed. "Fuck around," he advised the Fed, "and, as the saying goes, you will find out."

Chapter Nine

She knew her mouth dropped open.

No, no, no. Did Atlas just threaten to bury a Fed? Right in front of me?

"Are you threatening me?" Gage asked bluntly.

"Of course, he isn't!" She elbowed her way to Atlas's side.

But Atlas and Gage stared straight at each other. The tension between them was thick enough to suffocate a person. She certainly felt suffocated. "I do not need testosterone crap," she snapped. "Someone broke into my house and apparently stole some of my possessions, and all this happened *after* I was abducted! Believe me, things are bad enough for me already. I don't need the two of you arguing right now!"

Immediately, Gage's head swung toward her. "You're so sure this happened *after* you and Atlas were taken? You think it was the same perp?"

Ah...

"Is that what you're saying Lily?" Gage pressed.

She glanced toward her open front door. A female cop

in uniform had just exited the home. "I think it is certainly a possibility that we can't overlook."

"Why would he come here? Why would he break into your place?"

She wet her lips. "Because maybe he wanted to know more about me. The whole know-your-enemies bit." The throbbing in her head was getting so much worse. Her gaze cut back to Gage. "Or maybe the perp just wanted to see what all I knew about him."

"Fuck." Gage shook his head. "How many times do I have to tell you? You aren't a Fed, Lily. Don't hunt the predators. Don't screw around with them."

Her shoulders stiffened.

But Atlas reached over and took her hand. Casually, he brought it to his lips and kissed the back of her knuckles. He acted as if it was a move he made all the time. It was not. It was the first time he'd ever kissed her knuckles, and such a small caress should not have sent a tremor of electricity surging through her veins.

But it did.

She sucked in a breath. Just like that, her gaze was on Atlas, not Gage. She found Atlas's eyes right on her, too.

"Screw around all you like," he invited her. "It's because of you that I'm standing here right now."

Holding her gaze, he bent his head and kissed her knuckles once more.

Gage cleared his throat. "If you want to check out the interior of the house, Lily, then you need to come with me."

Atlas had retrieved her diary. That had been priority one. But, sure, looking inside was a fine plan. She wanted to see what the intruder had done. *What he took from me.* She pulled away from Atlas.

"Don't touch anything," Gage warned her.

She sighed. "Not my first crime scene." And her prints were already going to be on everything. But she followed him down the narrow sidewalk and up the steps. Lily was highly conscious of the fact that Atlas trailed right on her heels. She was also conscious of the fact that, for some reason, his presence made her feel better.

No one had ever made her feel *better* in this world.

She was probably just too tired. How many hours was she running on with no sleep? She would be crashing soon.

One of the uniformed cops tried to block them from entering.

But Gage flashed his badge, and they got in. The first thing she noticed—

Not a single thing is touched in the den. The sofa still had a cozy blanket tossed over the side. Her book was still half-open on the sofa cushion. The bookshelf still had all her titles in perfect position. The TV was off, with the remote on the coffee table. A glance to the right showed her kitchen in similar shape. Clean kitchen table. Dishes stacked neatly behind the glass doors of her cabinets. Dish soap and brush still near the sink.

From this position, it looked like no break-in had occurred at all.

But then they went into her bedroom.

Absolute chaos. The mattress had been cut open. Stuffing was everywhere, like a snowstorm had hit the bedroom. The books on the shelves in that room had all been pulled out, ripped open. Pages littered the floor. Every drawer of her chest had been pulled open. Her clothes ransacked. A glance inside the closet showed her that the items in there had been pulled from the hangers. Some looked slashed.

There was a whole lot of rage in her bedroom. As if the intruder had become—

"What do you see?" Gage asked her.

"Destruction."

"Ah, come on. You can do better than that."

She blinked quickly. Yes, she could. "He knew what he was looking for."

"Your laptop?"

"Yes." It was missing. But it was more than that. She edged toward the desk. Two uniformed cops were buzzing in the bedroom. The desk drawers hung open. An empty manila file had fallen near the desk chair, a desk chair that had been tossed to the floor. "My files appear to be gone." She'd had two dozen case files for her research on the adult children of serial killers. "But there is so much chaos here, it's hard to tell for certain. I'll need to clean up in order to properly assess everything."

"Yeah." Gage jerked his thumb toward the cops. "They're not gonna let you clean anything, not anytime soon." A low whistle escaped him. "So, where was your murder wall and did he find it?"

Her gaze darted to Atlas. His stare was already on her.

"Come on, Lily," Gage chided, pulling her focus back to him. "Where was it? Where was the info you had on the case you were working with Detective Benedict Swain? You think you've got a punishment killer at play in Dallas, don't you?"

She didn't respond.

"Oh, come on. All the signs are there. He's making them suffer. He wants them to hurt for their crimes. The guy has punishment written all over him. Don't deny it. You and I both know that's the type of perp you have hunting in

Dallas, and I'm sure you told Detective Swain that very thing."

He'd definitely been doing his homework on the way to Dallas. "I didn't have a murder wall here."

"Lily." A sigh. "It's me. No need for BS. We both know you live for things like this case. The killer must have fascinated you from the moment you learned about him. You would have plotted out every detail. The vics. Their connections. The would-be suspects." His attention shifted to Atlas.

Her breathing remained steady even as her heartbeat raced. "Benedict—Detective Swain—had a file with *his* findings and suspicions. I'd suggest you go look at the police station for that data."

A half-smile curved Gage's lips. But it was a smile that held no humor. No dimples flashed when he smiled. Just those perfectly white teeth. "Want to hear a weird thing about that?"

Not particularly.

"Benedict *did* have files at the station, on his computer, but, looks like they were wiped. Techs are working on things now. But it's not looking good. Benedict's computer was completely scrubbed."

That made zero sense. "There will be a backup," she said. "The cloud."

"There is no backup." Flat. "Located a few physical files, Most of those, actually, contained info about Atlas. But pretty much everything else is missing, and don't you find that suspicious?" He lifted his right hand and indicated the trashed bedroom. "Especially in light of this?"

One hundred percent, yes, it was suspicious. "When did you discover the detective's files were wiped?" Just how long had Gage been in town? She'd originally believed that he'd driven all night or even flown in, but maybe...maybe he'd been in Dallas far longer than she suspected. Maybe his clothing appeared wrinkled because he'd been *working the case* all night long.

"His captain figured it out, not me. The captain made the discovery about one hour after Benedict died. So someone worked very, very quickly. Someone who knew his way around tech. Someone who had no trouble bypassing the security in place at the PD." Once again, Gage's attention shifted to Atlas. "Got to ask, do you happen to know anyone like that?"

"Sure." An easy response from Atlas. "I could do it. In my sleep."

Oh, no. "He *didn't* do it," she rushed to say. And, yes, she physically even jumped in front of Atlas. Why did she do that? No clue. Just some weird, instinctive thing. Like she had to personally protect him. "Atlas was with me all night. I can assure you that he never stopped to hack police files. Never pulled away long enough to give anyone orders to hack them."

"He was with you *all* night?" Gage emphasized the *all* even as he raised his brows. "Lying so quickly for him? Look, just take a breath, Lily."

She was about to take a swing at him. "I'm not *lying*." On this point, she was not. "We were questioned by the cops together at the cabin. We left that scene in an ambulance together. We went to the hospital—"

"And you were fucking holding hands the whole time?" Gage sliced through her words, voice tight. "Bullshit, Lily. *Bullshit.* Don't cover for him when—"

"Lily? Are you ready to leave?" Atlas's very polite voice.

Too polite.

Goosebumps rose onto her skin as her head swung toward him.

He was watching her with a faint smile on his lips. The dimples just starting to flash. *Uh, oh.* "Leaving sounds great." It sounded like heaven. She forced herself to bob her head toward Gage. "I can't tell yet what all is missing. There is too much chaos. Once the crime scene team is done, and I have the all clear to come back, I'll do a complete review."

Gage's jaw hardened. "That's it?"

"It's been a really long night. So, yes, that's it."

"Lily." Her name came from between Gage's clenched teeth. "*Give me something to work with.*"

Why? So you can try to lock up Atlas? Or me?

"I don't appreciate the tone that you're using with Lily, and I'd wager she doesn't like it, either." Again, Atlas's voice was brutally...polite.

Which seemed oddly intimidating. She grimaced. "I am not a fan," she agreed. Then she was the one reaching out for Atlas, mostly because she was worried about just what he might do next. He seemed far too controlled, and those peeking dimples and that cold grin were a stark warning. One that Gage didn't seem to understand. "Let's go."

Atlas's hand flew up and caught hers. But then he turned her wrist. Shoved up the sleeve on the sweatshirt. "For your edification, Agent Emerick, we weren't holding hands the whole time. She was cuffed to me. Every damn moment in the basement. *Every moment.* She fought to save me. Then when we went to the hospital, where plenty of people saw us both. Yes, we were separated during some imaging scans, but that separation was very, very brief. Check with the nurses. Check with Dr. Phillip Owen. Lily and I stayed together nearly every single moment. She's not *lying* to you, and don't ever fucking accuse her of lying—or of any other crime—again. If you do that shit in front of me, it will be a fatal mistake."

But Gage surged toward him. "That's the second time you've threatened—"

"You think I don't have pull at the FBI, dumbass?" Still a polite tone, but savage words. "I had dinner with the deputy director last week. You do not want to screw around with me. Get on my bad side, and it will be the worst mistake you'll ever make." His fingers slid lightly over her bruised wrist. "Come on, sweets, let's get you to bed."

Gage was gaping at him. Atlas hadn't threatened the Fed's life. He'd threatened to take away his job, his power. A far more effective threat to someone like Gage.

She didn't want to stay in that bedroom another moment. What she hadn't told Gage...she could see rage there. Feel it. The person searching her room had grown increasingly angry—and all of that rage had been directed at her. There had been no need to smash the small, ceramic pieces on her bookshelves. The little dragons had just been fun pieces that she'd picked up because she liked the whimsy of them. She'd had some of those little book dragons for years.

But...

The intruder had smashed them. Just as he'd slashed the artwork on her walls. He'd gone right to the heart of the house—her most intimate spot—and he'd destroyed everything he saw.

What a sonofabitch.

Not a clinical term but...

"How long have the two of you been involved?" Gage asked. He'd followed them through the house and onto the porch.

Her gaze swept the exterior scene. A local news van had just parked. Desmond paced impatiently near the limo. She didn't see Carl. Wait, was he behind the limo's steering wheel? Yes, yes, he was.

Carl and Desmond were ready for a getaway. Good, so was she.

"How long?" Gage pressed.

Since they weren't involved and Atlas had just done that whole spiel about Gage not accusing her of being a liar, Lily figured she'd just keep quiet and, uh, not lie.

"Lily began emailing me quite some time ago." Atlas's calm and cool voice. "I'm sure I can dig up the first note if you want a specific date, but, frankly, you're just annoying me so I don't feel like going to the effort." Atlas threaded his fingers with hers as they walked down the sidewalk and toward the limo, but he paused and turned back toward the Fed. "We were victims tonight. In light of this break-in, my Lily was a victim *twice*. I would think that someone who cares about her would be showing a bit more kindness under the circumstances. Perhaps some sympathy. And not just acting like a jealous prick because she found someone better to fuck."

What?

"Your loss," Atlas continued seeming to be utterly unconcerned with Gage. "But I'm not a dumbass like you so I won't make your mistakes. Have to admit, it was not exactly a pleasure meeting you, and, unfortunately, I'm sure our paths will cross again."

Yes, okay, *done*. She dragged him toward the limo. Double timed it because she was a bit worried about what he might say next.

"Is he being a pain in the ass?" Desmond asked softly when she passed him.

"Major," she responded.

"Want me to eliminate him?"

Wait, what? It took her a beat to realize he was talking about Gage, not Atlas. He was offering to eliminate *Gage*. "He's a Fed. And no one is eliminating *anyone*."

Desmond shrugged. "Tell me if you change your mind."

"I am not changing my mind." She pushed Atlas's broad back to get him in the limo. The blonde newscaster from Channel Five had just hopped out of her van and was torpedoing toward them.

Lily hurried in the limo after Atlas. Desmond slammed the door behind them, then assumed a protective position outside the vehicle. And, Carl, bless him, took off.

Her breath heaved in and out. In and out. And her hand extended toward Atlas. "I believe you have something that belongs to me?" She needed that diary back.

But, instead of handing it to her, he settled a bit more comfortably against the leather seat. Then he smiled. Those dimples were a flashing red light. *Danger. Danger.*

Her heart thudded hard in her chest.

And he asked, "What is it worth to you?"

* * *

Desmond Yoruba watched the limo drive away. Lily Gallo made him want to smile. She'd looked so horrified by his offer. Not exactly what he and Atlas had expected when they'd begun digging into the woman's life.

Desmond had thought she'd be colder. More controlled. *Lethal.* And, she probably was lethal, but the woman clearly did not have a full killer instinct. At least, not yet. Maybe that would change after she spent more time with Atlas. Atlas had a way of pulling out a person's dark side.

119

"You gonna lie for your boss?"

Ah, that would be the prick Fed. Desmond turned toward him, quirking a brow.

"FBI Special Agent Gage Emerick," he said, introducing himself and offering his hand.

Desmond knew the name. He was sure that Atlas had recognized it, too. After all, they'd come across the man when they did Lily's initial background report, though he was sure that Atlas had played it cool and probably acted as if he knew nothing about the guy. That was Atlas's way, always keeping his secrets close.

Gage Emerick had been Lily's last lover. Over a year ago. Then, almost overnight, Lily had seemingly severed all contact with the man.

What did you do to piss off Lily Gallo?

"You're Desmond Yoruba, aren't you?" Gage asked as he wiggled his fingers.

Ah. So Gage had been doing his research, too. Not exactly surprising. Desmond took the offered hand, found the grip a little too weak, and let the man go. "Guilty."

Gage frowned at him. "At least you didn't try to break my hand the way Atlas did. The dude clearly has something to prove."

No, Atlas had probably just been pissed. Maybe jealous, too. Jealousy would be new for Atlas. His friend might not know how to handle the emotion. "He doesn't like people touching things that belong to him."

Gage backed up a step. "So...wait, are you talking about Lily? Me and Lily? I haven't *touched* her in—"

"You touched her here today. I saw you. So did he. We both also saw how you looked at her. You should be careful. You really don't want Atlas as an enemy."

"More threats. Noted." A muscle flexed along Gage's

jaw. "Atlas Bennett was abducted. Maybe I'm trying to *help* him and Lily? How about we all consider that option? I'm with the Behavior Analysis Unit, and I am good at my job. I know killers."

Give yourself a cookie. I know them, too. Because I was turned into one when I was just a kid. Information he did not share with most people. "Are you as good as Lily?" Desmond asked instead. The question was a deliberate taunt. "Do you know them as well as she does? Because I'm pretty sure she's an expert." Then, because he could sense some blood in the water, he added, "Is that why you and Lily were so close, for so long? Because she was helping you to *know* killers?"

"I'm not the bad guy here." Faint lines bracketed Gage's mouth. "I care about Lily. I want to keep her safe." He pointed back toward the house. "Someone out there clearly wants to hurt her."

It did appear that Lily had attracted too much of the perp's attention.

"Your boss was abducted when *you* were supposed to be keeping him safe. So you can see where I'm concerned. I'm worried that maybe you and Atlas Bennett aren't up to the task of protecting Lily."

Desmond narrowed his eyes. "I can do my job."

"Really? Then where were you when Atlas was taken?"

Oh, such a prick.

"If you were doing your job, just how did Atlas get taken?"

Desmond just stared at him.

"Did he ditch his protective detail?" Gage pressed. "Give you orders to stand down? If so, why would he do something like that?" Gage's hand returned to his side. Rested near his holster. "Because you're supposed to be the best out there when it comes to security. At least, that's the word I picked up."

Who'd given him that word? And when?

"In order for your boss to get taken, you *must* have been told to stand down. Ordered to give him space. Otherwise, hell, it just looks like you're guilty. Like you left your boss vulnerable so that he could be killed."

Desmond raised his eyebrows. "You're accusing me of being involved?"

"*Are* you involved?"

Desmond laughed. "You are not very good at mind games. No wonder Lily grew tired of you." Shaking his head, he turned away.

But the Fed curled a hand around his shoulder.

"Lily *is* good at mind games. Never forget that. And you didn't answer my question. Not *any* of them, actually."

He glanced back at Gage Emerick. Staring the Fed dead in the eyes, Desmond replied, "I was not involved in the abduction. I was told that Atlas did not need security yesterday evening. He had other plans."

"Plans...that involved Lily?"

He had no comment for that one.

Gage leaned closer. "Does Atlas typically have security with him, everywhere he goes?"

"You have the wrong impression of him. Atlas goes where he wants, and he does what he wants."

"Jeez. Sounds like the man is a security nightmare."

You have no idea. And you don't want to know about my nightmares. "He pays well."

"Well enough to cover up something like say...a murder?"

Desmond laughed. In the guy's face. Again, the Fed was just not good enough at mind games. "Don't know the meaning of being subtle, do you, Agent Emerick? FYI, I signed a nondisclosure agreement the day I accepted my job with Atlas. He requires an NDA from everyone in his inner circle."

"Has Lily signed one of those already?"

Not yet, but he had a feeling she would be signing one very soon.

One of the uniformed cops called for Gage. He hesitated. "I will be in charge of this investigation."

"I'm sure the locals will love to know that. A break-in doesn't seem to be high enough priority for a Fed, but you do you."

"I'm not just talking about the break-in. I'm talking about the serial killer hunting in Dallas. I will apprehend him. See you again soon." With that, he turned on his heel and marched toward the waiting cops.

Desmond watched him go. Oh, yes, that man would be a problem.

It was good that Atlas excelled when it came to eliminating problems.

Chapter Ten

THE FED WOULD BE A PAIN IN THE ASS, BUT ATLAS would handle him, no problem. He did know the deputy director of the FBI. Hell, he knew all of the deputy director's secret sins, so if some leverage was needed in order to get Gage Emerick pulled back, then Atlas could take care of that situation in a blink.

Gage wasn't a major concern for him. Except... "Why in the hell did you fuck him?" Ah, yes, that was indeed jealousy stirring in him. Not something he usually experienced, but the instant that prick had come close to Lily, the moment he'd touched her...Embraced her...

I wanted to break his hands.

Clearly, he was still suffering aftereffects of adrenaline and fury from the night he'd had. After some deep sleep, he'd be back to normal. Or as normal as he could get.

Normal wasn't exactly in his wheelhouse.

Lily's hand remained extended toward him. "Give me the diary."

He lifted up his shirt and pulled out the faded leather

book. "I took evidence from a crime scene for you." Just so they were clear about what he'd done. Not the easiest trick ever, pulling a sleight of hand and getting the book so all the nearby cops hadn't seen him.

Good thing he'd been a magic buff once upon a time. He was good at making things vanish.

Certain people, too. They could vanish and never be found.

"You retrieved my property," Lily clarified. "No big deal."

A leather tie bound the book. "I am so curious about you," he murmured. "If I open this book, will I find all of your secrets?"

"*Don't play games with me.*"

Uh, oh, She hadn't sounded cool and in control. Her words had frayed around the edges. His gaze lifted to pin her. "Why not? You're playing them with me."

She sucked in a breath. "I am not."

"You fucked a Fed who thinks I'm a murderer." Really, he didn't care that Gage Emerick believed he was a killer. He did care that Lily had fucked him. "Why?"

"Uh, why did I have sex with him? Or why does he think you're a murderer? Because if it's the latter, you'd have to ask Gage where he came up with that idea."

"It's the former." Gritted. "Why did you fuck him?"

Her delicate nostrils flared. "Because we were involved. We'd known each other for years. We dated. I...thought he understood me." A quick clearing of her throat. "I was wrong." She kept her hand extended and then...

In a fast swipe, she snatched the diary from him.

He smiled at her.

She brought the diary to her chest. Held it tightly.

"Maybe you should burn that," he advised her. "Don't want it falling into the wrong hands. By the way, you never answered my *other* question."

"You'll have to be more specific." She clutched the diary in a too-tight grip. "You've asked me a lot of questions."

"What is the diary worth to you? Considering I just stole it for you—"

"You didn't steal it because it's my property. You simply retrieved it for me."

Ah, yes, an important clarification. One he was sure the authorities would appreciate. "You didn't want the cops reading what was inside the diary. I *retrieved* it before they could find it in order to protect you. Understand that I will *always* protect you, and I don't really give a shit if that means I have to break the law. I'd bend it, I'd break it. I'd do it for you in a heartbeat."

Surprise came and went on her lovely face. "Thank you." Whispered. "For, um, getting the diary back for me." She lowered the diary and put it on the seat beside her body. On the side *away* from him. Her fingers remained on the book's cover.

Atlas tilted his head. "Do you have confessions in there? A list of dark deeds? I am intrigued. Just what sins have you committed? Come on, Lily. Tell me yours, and perhaps I'll tell you mine."

Her breath caught.

"Isn't that what you want from your all-access pass into my life?" Atlas prompted. "My sins?"

"I want you..." Her fingers slid along the surface of the closed diary. "I need you to be better than the past. I have to be better, too. We can't be like them."

His jaw hardened. "I'm nothing like my father."

"A twisted, sadistic killer with no conscience?"

Well, she'd certainly gone right to the heart of the matter.

"No," Lily continued. "I don't think you are like him."

On this, they could agree. But... "Do you wonder...do you fear that I might be worse?" Atlas asked.

Chapter Eleven

"My father had no control. He was like a wild animal when he attacked. He enjoyed causing others to suffer." As a rule, Atlas didn't discuss his father. Plenty of people had wanted to talk to him about his father over the years—reporters, private investigators, women who just loved the thrill of fucking a villain and they thought Atlas was that villain...

The devil's son.

Typically, Atlas just had one response for them all. *He's burning in hell. He's exactly where he needs to be.* But, Lily wasn't like the others. And he actually found himself wanting to talk more with her. Because maybe...

Does she understand? Could she understand?

Instead of appearing alarmed, Lily nodded as she stared out of the window. "I never wanted to be like my mother."

Ah, sweet Lily. "I just met your ex-lover. He's still alive and breathing. I'd say that means you *aren't* like her."

Her long lashes flickered as her head tilted, and her stare shifted to the diary near her. "As far as what the book is worth—it's worth a great deal to me. The diary, that is." A long inhale. Her shoulders straightened. Her spine stiffened. "You helped me a great deal by retrieving it. Retrieving, not stealing. So tell me what you want. Tell me how I can repay you." Her gaze came back to him. "Make your demands."

I want you to fuck me. The words would be so easy to say. When Lily was near—even if they were handcuffed in hell—he wanted her. His physical reaction to her was so far over the top that it should probably scare him. Then again, plenty of things in this world should have scared him.

They never had. Truth be told, Atlas could not remember the last time he'd ever been afraid of anything or anyone.

Maybe I never have been. Because maybe his emotions didn't work properly.

But...as he stared at Lily...

He didn't want her fucking him because she *owed* him. He also didn't want to say those words to her because—Lily wasn't some whore. She wouldn't trade her body for a damn book, no matter how important it was to her, and he would never, ever cheapen Lily in any way. He could want her, he could lust after her, but...

I will not hurt her. Not Lily. She'd be the one thing in this world that he never damaged. The one thing he protected. He could have one thing, couldn't he? "You saved my life. Giving you a book is the least I could do. Consider the matter settled." He closed his eyes. Maybe it would be easier to keep his control—because it was far too frayed—if he didn't look straight at Lily. "You still shouldn't have fucked the Fed," he muttered. "He wasn't worthy of you." Maybe he should go back and break the guy's fingers so he'd know not to touch her.

Wait. Was that over the top? Maybe. Probably. He

really did need some sleep. He'd think more clearly after sleeping. And his damn head had been aching dully all night.

He heard the rustle of her clothing. He figured she was scooting away.

Instead, her leg brushed against him. "Let me guess...I shouldn't have fucked Gage, but I should fuck you? Because you're...uh, *worthy* of me? Does that pickup line always work for you?"

"I don't usually have to bother with pickup lines. Honestly, a lot of talking isn't needed. Women fuck me because I'm stupid rich."

"Well, I don't fuck men because they're stupid rich."

"No, I didn't think you did that. I think you are very, very choosy when it comes to your lovers." He actually knew every lover she'd had. Their names were in his Lily file. In case he had to kill them.

A joke, of course...

Or maybe not. He kept his eyes closed but not seeing her wasn't helping with the temptation he felt. If anything, his senses seemed heightened. Her vanilla scent enveloped him, the softness of her leg against his maddened him. He wanted to reach out, lock his hands around her waist, lift her up, and fuck her right there. In the back of the moving limo. "I am not worthy of you, don't make that mistake."

"Uh, you're kinda running hot and cold on me."

His eyes opened. His head turned toward her. "I will not be an easy lover. You need to know exactly what you'll get with me. I am demanding. With you, I will be possessive." Probably to an extreme degree.

"And you *aren't* with others?"

"You will be different." *And I may not be able to let go.*

"I've always been different. That's the problem."

No, that was the perk. "You don't need to worry about me today. Or tomorrow."

A little line appeared between her brows.

"I won't fuck you when you're falling off an adrenaline high. I won't take you when fear still beats in your heart or when you're dead on your feet from exhaustion. There won't be any excuses later, no reasons for regret. You'll come to me, you'll choose me...and I will possess you."

She wet her lips. "So, you've basically told me that you're a walking red flag. Yet you still expect me to choose you. To fuck you."

"Ah, sweets, you really going to tell me that you don't enjoy a red flag?"

"Red flags are dangerous."

"I will *never* be dangerous to you. You have my word. I'd cut off both my hands before I hurt you."

"No need to get bloody. I like your hands." Her gaze did not waver. "I like the way I feel when you touch me."

Every muscle in his body tightened. *Oh, Lily, you do not know how dangerous the beast I carry truly is, and he wants you. You're making so many mistakes with me.*

"You seem incredibly certain of yourself." The gold gleamed in the darkness of her eyes.

"I'm not. Not when it comes to you. Forty-eight hours." That was the clock he was running. "I figure in forty-eight hours, you'll either tell me to fuck off...or you'll say, '*Fuck me.*'"

"I've *never* jumped into bed with someone forty-eight hours after meeting them."

No, not his careful Lily. "Good thing you've known me much longer than forty-eight hours."

"Atlas—"

"That's how long you get to decide. Will we be real

lovers? Or just pretend? Because if I'm a line you don't want to cross, a monster you just can't handle, I will keep my hands off you. The world can think you belong to me, that cover will protect you, my guards will protect you, *I* will protect you, but if you don't want to be in my bed...I will stay away." The choice would be hers.

Forty-eight hours.

The clock was ticking.

"You are very blunt," Lily noted.

"With you, yeah, I am." Why? "I feel like I don't have to pretend as much with you. I know how to play the game. I *could* be a charming asshole, but I don't want to do that." A pause. "I don't want to hide who I am with you. So I'm saying what I feel. I. Want. You."

"It's probably adrenaline. It's confusing you. Making your emotions and your, ah, lust, seem heightened." She swallowed. "We've had one hell of a first date."

A first date? His eyes narrowed. "Are you joking with me?"

"I have a terrible sense of humor. Ask anyone."

"I don't care what anyone else says. I care..." *About you. Whoa. Bad. So bad.* "I want to know what you say. What you think."

"I say it's probably the adrenaline impacting us both. I mean, you're handsome. Obviously. And I do feel some attraction to you—"

"Some? Ah, Lily, just stab me in the heart, why don't you?"

"No." Sharp. "I won't."

He already knew that. But he took her hand, lifting it off the diary, and he placed it over his heart. "*Some* attraction? Some? I feel more than *some* for you. I knew you were going to be a problem from that very first email." He kept his hand curled around hers. "Kiss me, and tell me that you don't feel the connection, too. I'm not talking about *some* mild attraction. I'm talking a consuming lust that makes you want to forget every single rule you've ever followed." He suspected she followed lots of rules. "And just take what you want."

"I..." A ragged breath. "Too much has happened. I'm too tired. Too on edge. I am not in control right now."

"I am." Barely. "I'll keep you safe."

She wasn't going to do it. She wasn't going to kiss him. Too bad. He'd really wanted her mouth.

She leapt toward him. Straddled him. His unpredictable Lily. She pressed her mouth to his, and she kissed him as if she had forgotten every rule. Her mouth was hungry and eager and so incredibly sweet, and she had to feel the giant dick shoving against her.

His hands dropped to her waist. Hers pressed to his jaw. His tongue thrust into her mouth, and he took and took, and when she moaned, he greedily swallowed the sound.

She was warm and soft and sexy. Every single thing he wanted—the *only* thing he wanted. Her hips rocked against him as she rode his dick through their clothes. Over and over, and she kept kissing him. Open-mouthed, sweet tongue, hungry need. Driving him wild. Closer and closer to the edge, but he held on to his control with both hands because he'd made a promise to Lily.

He would not break his word. Not to her.

But he took her mouth. He kissed her, he savored her, he kept his hands on her waist, the grip probably too tight, but by holding them there, he didn't touch her in other places. Places that tempted and beckoned. Places like the soft heat between her thighs. He didn't slide his hands down to her core. Didn't stroke her through the soft sweats.

Didn't shove the sweat pants aside, shove aside the panties she wore, and touch her bare skin. Didn't stroke her clit the way he wanted. Didn't thrust one finger into her, then another, to see how tight she'd feel. But he could imagine... imagine all of that so easily. Could almost feel her clinging tightly to him as he stroked and stroked and...

A low hiss of sound.

The privacy screen in the limo, lowering a bit. "Boss." Carl's voice. "We're approaching the estate." Another hiss as the screen raised back into place.

I want her in my home. Locked behind my gates. Safe. Protected.

Odd. When he'd never been much for protecting anyone in this world. He'd grown up to be a destroyer.

Her mouth pulled from his. Her head lifted. She straddled him as they remained in the back of that limo, one leg on either side of his, her knees pushing into the seat, her fingers on his cheeks and jaw even as his hands remained curled around her waist. The tension was thick between them. Her breath came in ragged pants. Hell, so did his. All he wanted was to strip her and take her.

Control. Because...not yet. He could not screw this up yet. He'd given her forty-eight hours. He could be a man of his word. After all, she'd just been a woman of hers. "You were right," he said, aware that his voice came out extra rough and rumbly.

"Right?" Her voice was husky. Tempting. "About what?"

"You did give me the best kiss of my life." He could admit it. As if there were any comparison. He'd pretty much been on the verge of coming just from kissing her and dry humping her in the back of the limo.

She blinked at him.

"Aw, sweets, don't you remember?" He smiled at her. "You promised me the best kiss of my life if I got you out of that basement. I delivered. And so did you."

Her lips pressed together. Then, "I think it was the best kiss of my life, too."

His smile stretched. "Just so you know, when I do get you naked, I will be the best fuck of your life, too."

She nodded. "I believe you." Very serious.

He had to kiss her again even as the limo slowed. They'd reached his house and gone through the gates at the end of the drive. Gently, carefully, he lifted her off him and slid her back to her seat. When the vehicle parked, he didn't wait for Carl to come around for them. Atlas opened the door and reached back with his right hand for her.

She'd grabbed for her diary. She held it fiercely with her right hand, but her left reached for him. He pulled her out of the limo, and her gaze darted over the massive exterior of his house, perfectly revealed now by the bright sunlight.

A low whistle came from her. "Wow. All of this space..."

Fourteen thousand square feet.

"All for you?" Lily turned her head toward him.

"No." Not just him. "You're here, too." Had he blown thirty-four million on the house? He fucking had. Had he once spent months sleeping on the floor of one of his foster homes? Had he once been locked in a closet for damn days and now he had fucking claustrophobia that would try to slip up on him so he liked open spaces and open rooms and—

"Yes, I am here, too." Her fingers squeezed his. "I also imagine there are security personnel who are here?"

Damn straight, there were. "They will be patrolling the grounds. And cameras are everywhere." He led her inside the Spanish Revival style house. Walls of windows provided views in every direction, and sunlight spilled through the rooms. Venetian, hand-blown glass chandeliers hung overhead, and as he took her through the house, they passed several stained-glass windows. What the hell could he say? He'd liked the stained-glass when he'd first seen it in Italy. They walked up the curving staircase, and he was aware of Lily taking everything in, but not saying a word.

Through her eyes he could realize that, yeah, the place was over the top. Too big. Too expensive, too...

Screw it. "I had nothing." Flat. They were at the top of the stairs. He turned to the right. Opened the door to the bedroom next to his. "When I was growing up, I never had a home that was *mine*. I was shuffled around, forgotten. Excluded. I would carry my belongings in a trash bag from one place to the other." Such a sad pile of belongings. Donated clothing in a trash bag. Tennis shoes with worn soles and holes in the toes.

Her gaze darted around the house. "This is no trash bag."

No, it wasn't. He opened the bedroom door. "Guest room." Curt. Because he'd noticed the darkening shadows beneath her eyes and the slight sway of her body. "You won't be disturbed. Sleep as long as you want. A bathroom is connected."

"I...didn't get clothes. From my place, I mean."

He let go of her hand, but only so his fingers could rise and cup her chin. "You didn't get the clothes because they were slashed to pieces."

She winced.

"Don't worry. By the time you wake up, I'll have a whole new wardrobe for you." He'd snap his fingers, and it would be done. There were benefits to being rich as fuck.

When he'd been a kid, he had to steal to get what he wanted.

Not any longer.

But she shook her head. "Unnecessary. I can pay for them myself."

"Sure, you could. You could also have let me die yet you jumped in to save me, so...I'm buying you the damn clothes."

She lingered near the door, clearly about to argue with him. Argue, when she should have been sleeping. She'd gotten hit by their attacker, too. He frowned at her. "How's your head?" At the hospital, the doctors and nurses hadn't seemed as concerned with Lily's injuries. Something that had pissed Atlas off. Sure, he had more physical bruising on his body, but she'd been hurt, too. He'd even insisted that she be examined first.

"I'm fine." A note of worry as her gaze scanned him. "What about you?"

"Never better." Every part of him hurt.

"I thought we weren't lying to each other." She swayed a little on her feet.

Obviously, he was going to have to take care of her. He hadn't taken care of anyone before. Without hesitation, he swept her into his arms.

"Atlas! Stop! You took a blow to the head from the creep —you should not be carrying me around!"

You took one, too. He ignored her words and carried her into the bedroom. "I wasn't the only one who got knocked out. Hate to remind you, but you took a blow, too."

"I'm not carrying you!"

No, she was not. "Probably want to kick off your shoes."

Her right arm had flown behind his neck as she held on.

"What are you doing?" Her left hand now held her precious diary.

Oh, but I need to peek inside those pages. Later. For now, though... "I'm getting you in bed." Because they didn't need to fight about clothing when she was about to collapse.

He heard her shoes hit the floor.

"Good girl," Atlas praised.

She growled at him.

"Oh, sorry." A laugh slid from him. "Bad girl. Very, very bad."

"I'm a woman."

Oh, yes, you sure as hell are. "And are you bad?" He lowered her onto the bed.

"I guess you'll find out."

He wanted to keep touching her. "Need me to help you strip?" He'd be happy to oblige.

"I have it, thanks."

He stepped back, but didn't leave, not yet. "I know you enjoy stripping in front of me, so, by all means, go ahead." Atlas tried to sound magnanimous. "Don't let me stop you."

"Again, I've got it, thanks." And she hauled part of the comforter over her still-dressed body. The fluffy comforter covered her—and her diary. "Where will you be?"

"Right next door, of course." As if he'd go a greater distance than that. "Unless you want me to sleep with you, and, in that case, I can climb into bed with you right now." He rather liked that idea.

"I'll be fine here." That slightly pointed chin of hers angled up. "Alone."

"Sure about that? You could have nightmares. If you have them, all you have to do is call for me." He'd come running. True story.

"I always have nightmares. They won't be anything new, and they won't be anything that I can't handle."

Her words gave him pause. "Maybe you'll tell me about your nightmares one day soon."

She stared at him.

Right. Today was not the day to hear her nightmares. He turned away. "Scream if you need me. I truly will come running." His hand reached for the door.

"Thank you, Atlas."

His hand hung in the air.

"If I'd gone back to my home by myself and found that destruction..." Her words trailed away.

What if you'd gone there without me and found that prick waiting for you? "He knows who you are, Lily." Growled. "He knows where you live."

"It's more than that. He knows about my research. He has my files."

Now Atlas glanced back at her. "Files on me."

"On you, on at least a dozen adult children of serial killers and..." An exhale. "The locations of those individuals are listed in files. The crimes of their parents and, um...." She bit her lower lip.

He waited even as exhaustion pulled at him. His body ached in a million places. Pain he hadn't noticed when he was touching her. Kissing her.

"For some of them, I suspected that they might be tied to current...incidents. I just didn't have enough evidence to completely prove those suspicions yet."

Yeah, he'd rather thought that might be the case. Lily believed some of her would-be subjects had followed in the footsteps of their parents and become killers. "Like me, huh? Like when you suspected I might be the one killing in Dallas?"

A nod.

"We'll deal with it," he said, because they would. "After we've slept, we've eaten, and I don't feel like a human punching bag any longer."

Another nod. "Thank you." Soft.

Ah, she should not thank him. Being with him would probably turn out to be a disaster for her. He looked away and reached for the doorknob.

"In my nightmares..." Lily's voice drifted to him. "I'm dying. I can feel the darkness reaching out to swallow me whole."

He exhaled. "In my nightmares..." His spine straightened. "I am the darkness." And death was all around him.

But that wasn't just the case in his nightmares. It was like that in his real life, too.

I am the darkness. He'd been carrying the weight of evil on his shoulders his entire life.

Chapter Twelve

LILY CREPT TOWARD ATLAS'S BEDROOM. SHE'D SLEPT for an hour. It had been a fitful sleep. Unease kept pulling at her. She'd told Dr. Owen that she would keep an eye on Atlas. She had to check on him.

His door was unlocked. She turned the knob and slipped inside.

Darkness.

His curtains were drawn over the windows. Had to be those heavy, blackout curtains because no light at all drifted into the bedroom. The guest room had been the same way, and that darkness had enveloped her.

But worry had stopped her from sleeping too deeply.

She tiptoed toward the bed. Her eyes had adjusted to the dark, and she could see his heavy form in the middle of the bed, and she—

"Decided not to wait the full forty-eight hours, huh?"

Lily froze. "I was...checking on you."

"Bad idea, Lily."

She thought the opposite. A good, responsible idea. "You have a concussion, Atlas."

141

"So do you, Lily. That happens when we both get knocked out."

Hers had not been as bad as his. She knew how to assess her own condition. Besides, imaging had been performed on them both at the hospital. "I am fine. There is no need to be concerned about my welfare."

"Yeah, whatever. A concussion is a concussion, so don't bullshit me."

"There are levels of trauma. All blows to the head are certainly not the same." Her lips tightened. He was cranky and clearly aware. No confusion from Atlas. "So...you're okay?"

"No, I am not okay. I'm horny as hell, and I'm about to pounce on you. *Go back to your room.*"

A sniff. "You don't have to be rude about it. I was simply trying to look after you."

"*And I'm trying not to fuck you. Go back to your room.*"

She turned on her heel. "Remember how you said to scream if I needed you?"

"Lily..."

"Scream if you need me." She took another step toward the open bedroom door.

"If you're really worried, you could always just climb into bed with me."

A shiver skated down her body. "Not sure that's the best idea."

"Ah..." The covers shifted. A faint rustle of sound. "Don't trust yourself with me, hmm?"

Actually, she wasn't quite sure that she did. "Any blurry vision? Dizziness? Confusion?" A checklist she should have gone over before. But she'd been distracted by the break-in at her place. Her own exhaustion had swept over her and... hell, she'd just been a crappy caregiver for him. Case closed.

"I only see one of you. Granted, you're cloaked in shadows, but that's because it's dark in here. I'm not the least bit dizzy, though I am damn sleepy. As to the confusion, I am perfectly aware. I know what I want. I know what I will have."

His words seemed to wrap around her. "Sorry I woke you. Just, um, doing my due diligence." She began to dart through the open doorway.

"I was dreaming about you."

And just like that, her feet rooted to the spot. "Dreams or nightmares?"

"A dream. The sweetest one. Want to know what you were doing in the dream?"

"I think I can guess." *Fucking you. Coming for you. Making you come.* He was such a dangerous man. More dangerous to her than Lily had ever anticipated. She squared her shoulders. "Sorry to disturb you. I'll see you again in a few hours—"

"You were marrying me."

Nothing could have shocked her more.

"I hope you have sweet dreams, too, Lily."

She fled his room. She did leave the door open, though, the better to hear him if he should call out for her. Lily raced back to her guest room and practically jumped into the bed. She still wore her sweatshirt and the sweat pants, her underwear and bra, even her socks. She...

He dreamed about marrying me?

She did not know what in the world to think in response to his dream. Her eyes closed. Her fingers clenched around the covers. Tension held her in a tight, desperate grip even as the darkness of the room settled around her like a lover.

Lover. Atlas would be her lover. She understood that, deep inside. The awareness between them was too absolute.

Too consuming. If she didn't discover what it was like to be with him—fully with him, at least once—well, then she'd be regretting that choice for the rest of her life.

She already had enough regrets. No sense adding another one to the pile.

I won't ever marry Atlas. But I will fuck him before we are done.

* * *

It was the chirping of birds that woke her. Her eyes opened, slowly, awareness trickling back to her. Her gaze darted around, eventually falling on the bedside clock. But when she saw those glowing digits, shock rocked through her. *Nearly four p.m.* Wow. Her brain still felt foggy, her body heavy, and it took her a moment—a few moments—to process where she was. And what was happening.

I'm in the guest room. Atlas's guest room. I hid the diary under the mattress. I'm safe here.

She sat up, frowning. She knew the time because the digits glowed, but the blackout curtains prevented light from filling the room. Her hand flew out to hit the lamp on the nightstand. The lamp's illumination spilled on at her touch, and she spotted the high-end bags waiting at the foot of the bed. A pang of unease slid through her. She'd slept so deeply that she hadn't heard anyone enter the room to drop off those bags?

She brushed aside the unease. Got out of bed. She showered in the huge guest bath, enjoying the blasts from the double shower heads. A toiletry supply had been included with her new purchases. Toothpaste. Shampoo. Conditioner. Body lotion. Makeup. Even her favorite brand and shade of lipstick.

Atlas's way of saying he knew everything about her. Or, at least, a sign showing he knew far too much.

She dressed in new underwear—a black bra and matching, silky panties. Black pants, flats, and a pale blue top. The top had long sleeves, and those sleeves hid the bruising on her wrist. Bruising that was now dark and vivid. Because she still seemed a little too pale and the circles under her eyes hadn't vanished, she used the makeup quickly like the shield it was, even sliding on a quick swipe of the soft red lipstick. Her mother had always told her that a bit of red lipstick could be a woman's best friend.

Then again, poison had actually been her mother's best friend for years so...

Lily left the guest room. She approached the room next door, lifted her hand, and rapped quickly on the closed door. "Atlas?" His door had been open before.

"Down here, sweets."

She jerked at the call, then made her way to the balcony that overlooked the lower floor. Because Atlas's voice had come from below her.

He quirked a brow as he stared up at her. "Sleeping Beauty finally decided to wake up, huh? Good for you." He peered at his watch. "The Feds will be here soon so you woke up just in time. I'm sure they will be bringing local cops with them. My lawyer is gonna join the party, kind of a nonnegotiable. Theodora would be pissed if I talked to the Feds without her present."

Well, she certainly didn't want Theodora pissed.

"Just so you know, the authorities want to interview us both, but we are *not* going to be separated for that interview."

Her hands curled around the balcony's railing. "Another nonnegotiable point for you?"

"Absolutely." His head tilted as he focused on her once again. "If they push on that point, I'll just explain that I can't be parted from the love of my life. I'm too distraught over how close we both came to dying."

The wood was smooth and hard beneath her grip. "The love of your life?" She'd never been called that before. Probably never would be again.

"I'll inform them that we'd been dating. Casually, of course, before last night."

"Casually." A nod. She should not have this conversation while she was upstairs and he was downstairs, so Lily let go of the balcony railing and began to head down to him. "When you casually date someone," she inquired, "do you always have security toss them out of your building?" Was that part of his courting ritual?

"Occasionally." He moved to position his body at the foot of the stairs. He wore black pants. A crisp, white shirt that he'd rolled up to the elbows. He'd left the top two—maybe three—buttons undone on the shirt. No shadows under his eyes. His blue eyes appeared extra electric. His skin tan, golden, not pale. His hair was combed back, thick and lustrous, and his chiseled jaw had been cleanly shaven. There was no sign of tiredness or pain or—well, any issues at all. No one would ever have looked at him and thought the man had been kidnapped and nearly murdered the night before.

Her steps faltered as she gazed into his eyes. His stare had heated even more as she approached him, and there was no denying the lust she could see staring back at her.

"Pleasant dreams?" he asked politely.

"I don't remember them." Total lie. She remembered them perfectly. She'd woken from one nightmare with her heart racing and sweat covering her body. Lily had leapt from the bed and rushed to his still open doorway. *My second visit to his room.* She'd peeked inside, terrified that he'd be just as he had been in her nightmare.

Dead. Covered in so much blood. And his stomach slashed open—

But he'd been sleeping. His breathing slow and steady, so she'd slipped out of his room without a word and gone back to sleep.

That was the second time I checked on him. I didn't want to wake him that time. I ran away. I—

"Really?" One dark eyebrow quirked. "Not even the nightmare that sent you running to me?"

Her breath caught. "You were awake?"

An incline of his head. "The floorboard right outside my door creaks. I heard you when you stepped on it."

He must have very good hearing.

"Figured I shouldn't say anything, though, because if I did and if you'd come closer, I would have just grabbed you and hauled you into bed with me. My control was at its weakest then." He rolled back his shoulders. "I'm better now. Got all the sleep I needed."

She could use about twelve hours more.

His head cocked to the side. "Gonna stay on those stairs a bit longer or can I get you something to eat?"

Her stomach decided to growl hungrily because she truly could not remember the last thing she'd eaten. Had it been a bagel yesterday? "Food, please." She continued her climb down the stairs. Slow, deliberate steps.

"Such polite manners." He watched her with a faint grin on his lips, his dimples barely held in check. "Your mother must have taught you well—" Atlas stopped. His eyes closed briefly before reopening. "Fuck."

She kept walking. Only stopped when she was on eye level with him.

"That was just a damn poor choice of words. A stupid joke." He shook his head. "I didn't mean to suggest you were like her."

No? Plenty of people had certainly made that suggestion over the years. "My mother taught me many things. Never doubt that. Never forget that." It would be a dire mistake to do so. "What did your father teach you?"

His hand lifted, and he tucked a lock of hair behind her ear. His fingers lingered against her cheek. "He taught me how to break delicate things." A pause. "But I won't break you."

"Atlas..." She ached for him. *I'm not delicate.*

But he stepped back. His hand fell. "I've got my personal chef waiting in the kitchen. Tell me whatever you want and it's yours. Roland is exceptional."

You. I want you. "Your own personal chef, huh?"

He shrugged. "Are you gonna tell me it's too much to have a personal chef? Too over the top? Save yourself the effort. I can't cook for shit. Roland is worth his weight in gold."

"I was not going to say any of that."

"No?"

"No. I was going to say...how about some eggs? Scrambled? I can make them myself, though. It's not a big deal. No need to bother Roland."

"You realize it's close to five p.m."

Yeah, she did. It was actually 4:30. She'd dressed quickly, but it had taken a bit to blow dry her hair. "I like breakfast for dinner. Um, maybe some toast, too, if that's okay?" Then she shook her head. "It's your house. I don't want to be any trouble. Just—I'll eat whatever you're eating."

"I had a steak an hour ago while you slept. That would have been right before I brought in the clothes for you. You looked peaceful, and you weren't crying out again, so I didn't wake you."

Crying out...again? "Did I cry out before?" A careful question. She'd never let a lover stay with her during the night. Mostly because she was afraid that she might say the wrong thing in the middle of a nightmare.

His electric gaze pinned her. "I'm not dead, Lily. But it's kind of you to worry about me. To have nightmares where you plead for me."

Crap. She had zero memory of him being in her room. But she did remember begging in one of her nightmares. Begging for him to be alive. To stay with her.

He turned away. Paced back from the staircase. "The authorities will be here soon."

Yes, right. He'd mentioned them. Lily climbed down the few remaining stairs and paused on the landing.

"They have more questions, and I'm sure that annoying prick ex of yours will be in charge of the interviews with us. But you won't be talking to any cops or Feds until you've eaten. They can wait. Not like I want you fainting from hunger on me."

Not like she wanted to faint from hunger on him, either.

Before she could say anything else, he headed down a hallway to the right and vanished. Uncertain, she remained near the bottom of the stairs. Was she supposed to follow him? Was he coming right back? He'd probably gone to talk to his chef. She seriously didn't need a chef for scrambled eggs. She could take care of the eggs and toast in five minutes. Her arms wrapped around her body as she began to stroll through his house. The den waited nearby, so she entered the sprawling room. The stained-glass windows in the den were gorgeous. And marble was everywhere. She paused in front of a gigantic, white marble fireplace. No soft touches, no photos. Stark artwork. All abstract. One piece of art was a white canvas with hard, angry streaks of black and red savaged across its surface.

"What do you see in that one?" Atlas asked.

She'd almost jumped at his voice. He hadn't made a sound as he returned to her. She breathed slowly, in and out, before querying, "Is this supposed to be an ink blot test? Rorschach?" Where it was really all about the individual and what was inside the person, not what was in the image?

"No test at all. Just me, being curious about you. What do you see, Lily?"

That was easy. "I see blood and death." The red splattered across the canvas just like blood.

"Yeah, me, too."

She turned toward him. "Maybe we are more alike than we realize."

But he shook his head. *No.* And her heart seemed to sink.

"Lily Gallo," Atlas said her name as if tasting it. Savoring it. "I will give you my secrets," he promised. "I'll let you slice open my skin and dig into my heart. I will let you leave me as bloody as that painting."

"That's...not exactly what I'm intending to do." She wasn't a killer intent on slicing him open.

"I'll let you in, but you have to let me do the same with you. To you. You have to show me all of the secrets you've hidden so deeply. That's what the strip show at the hospital was about, right? Us being equal? On even footing. One scar for another."

Yes, it had been about pain for pain. Secret for secret. Scar for scar.

"I like that idea," Atlas rumbled. "I want us to continue that way."

She dipped her head. "Fine."

"There will be a nondisclosure agreement you have to sign." Casual. "It's standard for people who are close to me."

A nondisclosure agreement? "Uh, that goes against the whole purpose of my work." She was trying to learn from the children of serial killers. To develop case files that could potentially help others out there.

"Yeah, well, too bad."

Too bad? Her temper began to stir. "You could be ash right now if I hadn't gotten us out of that cabin!"

"The way Benedict is ash?"

Savage attack. She sucked in a hard breath. She'd had nightmares about Benedict, too. In one of those hellish visions, she'd been crying over Atlas, begging him to live. Only he'd transformed into Benedict in a flash. A Benedict who burned right in front of her. She blinked quickly, aware that sudden tears had filled her eyes.

Atlas's jaw tightened. "Stop feeling guilty," he ordered her as his watchful stare did not leave her face. That stare hardened as he seemed to note the moisture gathering in her eyes. "You told him to get out of that cabin. Several times. You told us all to leave. I listened to you. I will always listen to you. So you should listen to me, too. Benedict Swain chose that fate. He should have gotten his damn ass out of there. For some reason, you have yourself convinced he was a good guy. In truth, he was a pain in my ass. He made it clear on numerous occasions that he thought I was as fucked up as my father. He kept pushing into my business because he wanted to take *me* down." Atlas raked a hand through his hair. "You should look a bit harder at some of his previous cases. All the facts might not align the way you expect. He might not be what you expect."

"What are you saying? That he was dirty? That he broke the law?"

"I'm saying take a look for yourself. Don't feel guilty because he didn't listen to you and get the hell out of there when he had the chance."

"Too bad," she snapped right back at him. She blinked again, aware that one of the tears had slid down her cheek. She swiped it away. "I do feel guilty. I can't turn that emotion on and off. It just is."

"You can't turn any of your emotions on and off, can you? You just feel them all the time. Do they ever threaten to rip you apart?"

His words had just pierced through her. "Can you turn off your emotions?" Something that made her very, very curious.

"What emotions?" A shrug of his broad shoulders. "I typically don't feel much at all. Isn't that the hallmark of a psychopath?"

She inhaled.

He raised his hand, and his fingers brushed away another teardrop. "He's not worth your tears." His hand pulled back. "Here are some fun facts about me that you can add to your Atlas file. Or book. Or whatever the hell you want to call it. Fact one, I lack empathy. As a general rule, I tend to be exceptionally cold-hearted. Ask anyone who has done business with me. I'm a straight-up bastard. I have no regrets in life. I don't feel remorse. Guilt isn't a companion I carry."

"Four percent of the population counts as being, um, under the psychopathic umbrella." Something she felt compelled to note. "Not all psychopaths are killers. Most actually make for great CEOs. Doctors. Lawyers."

A soft chuckle. "Oh, it's an umbrella, is it? Didn't realize it was raining psychopaths. Good to know."

"Don't mock me, Atlas."

He leaned toward her. His crisp scent teased her nose. "Then don't bullshit me. You think I'm a psychopath? Call me on it. You think I'm a bastard? *Call me on it.* You want to know me, the real me, then you say what you think. You hold nothing back. I'm giving you my terms. We didn't get to discuss them fully before, so we are doing it right now. Agree or we're done."

Well, well. "Awful moody for someone who claims not to feel very much. Did someone wake up on the wrong side of the bed?"

His lips parted. His blue stare *blazed*. "I woke up fucking horny, and you weren't there. I slipped into your room to drop off those packages, and you were curled up in the bed, sexy as hell, and all I wanted was to take you."

Um...

"I didn't. I walked away like a *gentleman*. When that is not who I am. I'm warning you. Agree or—"

"We're done?" She rolled one shoulder. She would not be intimidated. She'd faced off with far worse men, and she was calling his bluff. "I don't think we're done, no matter what I say. If I agree or don't, it won't change. You brought me into your home because you wanted me here. And we both know a killer is still hunting in this town."

He growled.

Why on earth was the animalistic sound so sexy?

"You are definitely in a mood today. Maybe you're just so used to masking your emotions that you don't know what do when they batter at you so hard." She raised one hand

and placed it against his chest. Over his heart. "Is it racing too fast? Do you feel like you're about to jump out of your skin?" Because that was certainly how she felt. She tended to feel that way when he was near.

"When you touch me, I want to fuck you."

Ah, brutal honesty, huh?

But his head tilted as he studied her. "You want to fuck me, too."

She did. "Our forty-eight hours aren't up yet."

"Are you counting down? Because I am."

She was. And wondering if she'd make it through the full forty-eight. Did she even want to make it that long?

He took a step back.

Her hand fell.

Atlas rolled his shoulders. "Everything I say with you will be off the record. I'm not gonna wind up in one of your books or in one of your journal articles. You can learn about me. About my secrets. But that info is for you alone."

Hardly a scientific benefit but...

Maybe this wasn't just about science.

Maybe it had never been.

Cut to the chase. "Do you feel it?" she asked him, suddenly just needing to know and to hell with the consequences.

"Feel what?"

She was just going to tell him and put her soul bare before him. "It surges inside, pushing, pulsing. It grows in your weak moments. When you think about how very easy it would be to stop being good. To let go. To forget the rules that are in place."

"Lily?"

"Do you feel it?" she asked him again. "Do you fight it

every single day? Because I think you do. I think..." A ragged exhale. "I think you might be just like me—"

His mouth took hers. With a ravenous, consuming need.

She kissed him back with desperation. Because maybe... maybe she was tired of being alone in the dark. Maybe she was tired of fighting the dark.

Maybe it was time to let the darkness consume her. And if it did consume her, then maybe that was just the way it was meant to be—

"Mr. Bennett?" A man cleared his throat. "Her eggs and toast are ready."

Dammit.

Atlas pulled back. "Hold the thought, my Lily." Lust burned in his gaze. "Hold it. We shall revisit. Very, very soon."

The words were a promise and perhaps a threat, too.

Chapter Thirteen

HIS LAWYER ARRIVED FIRST. PERFECTLY ON TIME, AS Theodora Shore always was. Her high heels clicked across his marble floor, and her right hand tightly gripped her briefcase. Her first words upon entering his house were a disgruntled, "Desmond warned me this was going to be a clusterfuck."

He'd expected Desmond to warn her. After all, the two had been fucking for the last six months.

She stopped in the middle of the foyer. "So? Where is she?" Her brows shot up. Her hair was cut in a short bob to frame her face. When she looked to the left, then to the right, her hoop earrings swung slightly. "I assume I'll be repping the shrink, too?"

"She's talking to Roland." After eating, Lily had insisted on going into the kitchen to thank the chef for her eggs and toast. Atlas did wonder, though, if she'd also run in there just to escape him. Things had certainly accelerated quickly in the den during their little discussion. *Oh, Lily, what have you been hiding from the world?* He could not wait to discover everything about her. "And, yes, you will be representing her."

A grunt from Theodora as she hurried toward his dining room and plopped down the briefcase. The dishes from Lily's breakfast/dinner had already been cleared away. "The Feds were on my tail while I drove here. They literally pulled in right behind me." A huff. "Typical black SUVs. Why can't they ever show any creativity? Makes me crazy. Just once, I'd love to see a Fed pull up in a flashy, little convertible. Wouldn't that be fun? But those guys don't understand fun." Her earrings bobbed again. "So, okay, it's good that they are meeting *here*. My request, by the way, because I'm selling this as you being the traumatized victim and you also being a celebrity so we're trying to not have a shitshow at the local PD or FBI office or..." An inhale as her dark gaze swept up and down his body. Then up again. "Could you *try* to look more traumatized and less GQ? Jeez." Another exhale. "And tell me that you were the victim. Say it to my face, will you? I need to hear the actual words coming from you."

"I was the victim." He shrugged.

"OhmyGod. That doesn't sound believable. At all. The insufferable shrug helped nothing, by the way. So don't do it again."

One of the things that he liked about Theodora. She never bullshitted him.

"We want the cops to move the hell on from you. We don't want a shitshow, but with that detective being dead..." Theodora grimaced. "Did you hear they will probably have to use dental records to identify him? What a horrible way to go." A shudder slid over her body.

"Yes." Lily's voice was very clear. Very controlled as she strolled into the dining room. "It was a horrible way for someone to die. But I hope it happened quickly. I hope the flames were so intense that there was no time for suffering and that Benedict died instantly."

Theodora swiveled to face her. "You..." Her gaze assessed Lily. "You are not a ray of sunshine. Oh, no." Real worry. "Are you going to be as bad as Atlas?"

She could be worse. He was still working that out.

The doorbell pealed, echoing through the house.

"*Victims*," Theodora stressed. "Please remember, you are both victims."

"It's easy to remember the truth," Lily returned as a little furrow appeared between her eyes. "Why would we say that we were anything else?"

"Could you just say for me—really quickly because I need to hear it—*I am the victim*."

Lily's chin tilted up. Her shoulders squared. Her eyes didn't blink. "I am the victim."

"You might as well have just said *I'm a freaking vampire* because that did not work at all. People, we are about to be seriously screwed."

No, they weren't. Because Atlas had a plan. It had come to him...in a wonderful dream. "Trust me, I've got this."

"Screwed," Theodora repeated. "In the worst way."

* * *

"I WOULD HAVE PREFERRED to have this conversation downtown," Gage Emerick announced.

Their little party was all gathered around the dining room table. Gage, a female agent named Sharon Hinkle, a police detective—Kurt Wry, a man Atlas knew had worked with Benedict more than a few times. Those three sat opposite of Theodora, Atlas, and Lily.

"We certainly appreciate you coming here," Theodora replied in her cool and professional tone. Her courtroom voice. "Especially since my client is still recovering from his ordeal. Oh, sorry, my *clients* are recovering. Because I am representing them both."

Gage kept looking at Lily. There was far too much focus in the Fed's stare. The man could look away from her anytime.

Atlas's fingers tapped on the top of the dining room table.

"I would like to speak with your *clients* individually." Gage thrust back his shoulders. "The interview process works better that way."

Deliberately, Atlas reached over and took Lily's hand. His fingers twined with hers. "I'm afraid that my fiancée and I are a package deal."

Her hand jerked in his. To cover the move, he brought her hand to his mouth. Atlas pressed a kiss to her knuckles. "Thank you for saying yes, my love."

"*Since when the fuck did you two get engaged?*" Gage thundered.

"Since about seven hours ago, when Lily was in my bedroom and I realized how close I came to losing her." He stared into Lily's eyes. Should he have gone with this story? Ah, screw it. *Another tie to bind her to me.* After her reveal in front of his favorite painting, he was all in with her. "You just can't let some people escape."

Lily had frozen.

"Really?" Gage's doubt was evident. "That's a weird thing to say."

"I don't find it weird at all."

"Huh. Well, see, I questioned a guard at your main office earlier today, and he told me that you'd had Lily tossed out of your building. That you'd given orders for her not to be allowed onto the premises again." A twist of his lips. "Weird that you want her to marry you after kicking her out so recently. Talk about mixed messages."

That guard would be handled. ASAP.

"Want to explain that to me?" Gage pressed. "You, barring the woman you love from your own building? Having her tossed out?"

"I am deeply ashamed of my actions." Did he sound suitably ashamed? Theodora had just winced, so probably not. He tried again, "I was trying to fight my feelings for Lily. I was an idiot." His gaze caressed the delicate lines of Lily's face. "I thought she'd destroy me." Truth poured in those words. Maybe he'd just stick to the truth as much as possible. "Self-preservation mode at its worst. I didn't realize that she would make me better. Stronger. Now I see that I can't live without her."

"Uh, huh." More doubt from Gage.

"She risked her life to save me. She could have died when she jumped on the attacker's back. She could have died in that basement." He and Lily would have to talk about that scene, very soon. She would never take those risks again. "I will not let someone so brave and caring slip away from me. We're getting married." Done. *Almost exactly like my dream.*

No, in his dream, she'd been wearing a white dress. Standing in front of a priest. Atlas had been vowing to love her forever.

Love. *I've never loved. Like I told Lily, I'm a damn psychopath.* The label had been tossed onto him when he was thirteen years old. One of the counselors at his group home had called Atlas a psychopath when he'd thought Atlas wasn't close enough to overhear him.

"*This isn't oppositional defiance. Have you looked into that kid's eyes? Seen how he acts? He's ice cold. Frozen inside. Nothing touches him. He's a freaking psychopath just like his father, and he scares the shit out of me. I don't want to be alone with him. Do you hear me? Don't leave me alone with Atlas. Not ever.*"

A forty-year-old man had been terrified of a thirteen-year-old kid.

"Lily?" Gage prompted. His voice drew Atlas back to the present. "Got something you want to add? By the way, I don't see a ring on your finger."

Lily didn't have on any rings. No jewelry at all. He'd handle that problem. Atlas made a mental note to get her an engagement ring. One that included a tracking device. The better to make certain that Lily never vanished on him. The watch he was currently wearing had a similar tracker. When he'd been taken from the parking lot, Desmond and the security team had found Atlas at the cabin by following another tracker that he'd had on him at the time. Atlas had made it a point to always have a tracker on him. Especially with the dangerous games he tended to play.

"No ring yet." She exhaled. "But you heard what Atlas said. He can't let me slip away."

"You two are *seriously* getting married?" Now it wasn't just doubt. Anger hummed in Gage's voice. And damn if the man didn't jump to his feet.

Atlas turned his head so that his gaze locked with the angry Fed's. "Some people don't value what they have. That will not be my mistake. I will value Lily for the rest of my life." *Unlike you, you dumbass tool.*

Gage glared at him as he loomed at the table.

"Uh, excuse me?" Theodora cleared her throat. "Are

you going to harp on my clients' romantic relationship or do you have questions about the actual killer who took them?"

Gage's Adam's apple bobbed. "Did either of you ever see the killer's face?" He kept standing.

The cop, Kurt Wry, tugged on the collar of his shirt. He looked like he wished he was anywhere but at that dining room table.

As for the female FBI agent, Sharon Hinkle, she was scribbling notes frantically on a small pad in front of her. Why all the scribbling? They hadn't even gotten to the real interview yet.

And, speaking of the interview...Gage's question about the killer...

"No." From Atlas. "I never saw him. He attacked while my back was turned." *While I was thinking about Lily and lowered my guard for just a moment because I was sure he wouldn't come for me quite so soon. He'd waited three weeks on taking his second victim. I thought I had more time. That I was still setting up my trap.*

Atlas had been wrong. He didn't like being wrong. Especially when his errors could prove fatal.

"No." From Lily. Softer. "I didn't see his face."

"Can you describe him at all?" Gage pushed.

Atlas could not.

"About six-foot-two, two hundred pounds. Wore all black. Moved fast. Showed no hesitation when he attacked Atlas." Lily's words were crisp. "I went up to him from behind. I jumped on his back, and I tried to pull him away from Atlas. We fought, and I...he threw me to the ground. That's when I hit my head. I..." She paused. Frowned. "No." Stronger. "He loomed over me once I hit the ground. I-I remember that. I was trying to get up, but he grabbed me by the shirt front. Then slammed me back onto the pavement. *That's* when things got blurry. I...passed out a bit."

She had never mentioned the prick slamming her into the pavement that way. His hold on her fingers tightened.

Sharon scribbled faster.

Kurt stopped tugging on his collar. He frowned at Lily.

"When we got out of the cabin, I remember seeing your car," she told Atlas. "Guessing maybe he dumped us in the trunk. Then drove us to the cabin?" A bit of uncertainty. "I woke up again when we were at the basement door. Right before he decided it would be lots of fun to shove us down that narrow staircase."

"Mr. Bennett's vehicle *was* recovered at the scene," FBI Agent Sharon Hinkle noted as her pen paused above the pad. When Atlas glanced her way, sympathy filled her eyes as she stared at Lily.

But a quick glance showed there was no sympathy on Gage's face. If anything, the prick looked furious. "Why were you targeted?" Gage demanded.

"Oh, my." Theodora leaned forward. "I think we should tone down the tension here. My clients are cooperating. Recounting as much as they remember. I'm sure if you reach out to the hospital, the staff who examined them can back up all of their injuries. The concussions, the bruising— it's all going to match up with the descriptions they are giving you."

Lily pulled her hand from Atlas's grasp. She tugged down her sleeve, pulling it over the dark band of bruising on her wrist.

"We've talked to the doctor in charge of the ER. Dr. Phillip Owen." Gage's jaw had clenched when he saw Lily's wrist. His eyes glittered now as he glared at Atlas. "Why were you targeted, Atlas?"

"I'm afraid you'd have to ask the perp that question." He curled his hand along the armrest on his chair. "Who knows what drives killers?"

Gage pointed at Lily. "She knows. She's made it her life's work to know." A nod. "So, Lily, how about you tell me why this killer targeted your new fiancé?"

Lily blinked. "Different killers have different motivations."

"Uh, huh. Sure they do. Got it. Understood."

Sharon was back to taking her industrious notes.

Detective Wry watched the interview but didn't say a word. Atlas wondered if that had been the deal. Gage told the detective he could attend the interview session provided that the local guy knew he wasn't to interfere.

"But you and Detective Benedict Swain had plenty of theories about this particular killer, didn't you? And let's cut through the BS," Gage directed with a huff. "I don't like wasting time, and you know it. The attack from behind, the handcuffs...you and Benedict had already been looking at a serial in this area who hunted and used that exact MO—"

"Serials require three kills," Sharon cut in to say as she glanced up from her pad. "There have only been two so far."

"Not if you count Benedict Swain as the third victim," Gage returned to his partner, his teeth clenched and the words tight. "The poor bastard wasn't gutted, and he didn't have his insides yanked out—"

"Oh, Jesus." Theodora flinched and put her hand to her mouth. "Tact, *tact*. I cannot handle gore, and now that image is in my head and it will never come out."

"Too bad. The vics didn't want to handle it, either, but they had no choice." Gage's nostrils flared. "The way I see it, Benedict was the third victim, at least if we believe that a serial killer is truly hunting in the city. I do happen to believe that. I happen to believe that a punishment-motivated killer is at work." His hands flattened on the dining room table. "But I want to know, why did this particular killer target you, Atlas? Just what crimes have you committed that made him think you should be next on his hit list? You were the intended victim, and poor Benedict died in your place."

Theodora jumped to her feet. "How dare you? *How dare you?* We are cooperating—my clients are cooperating after their harrowing experience—and you *dare* to accuse them of *committing crimes?*"

"I'm not accusing Lily of anything," Gage said. "Not this time."

Lily stiffened.

Not this time. Atlas caught that deliberate phrasing, and it certainly made him curious. Just what had the prick Fed accused her of before? And had that accusation been what ended their relationship?

"My clients are not going to answer anymore of your ridiculous questions." Theodora appeared to be in a fine fury now. "Atlas Bennett is a pillar of the community."

"Pillar," he repeated.

"He donates massively to local charities. Do you know he even recently built a cancer wing for children at the very hospital where he was treated last night?"

"I like helping others," Atlas murmured. "It's a calling."

"He is on the board of a dozen community organizations." Theodora was definitely fired up now. "He was given the key to the city."

"Twice," Atlas admitted. Not to brag. But, yeah, twice. He'd even led a parade in the city. Again, twice.

"How dare you suggest that Atlas has committed crimes

for which some madman thinks he should be punished? That is your implication, yes? The killer is targeting those he believes are guilty, at least in his mind. And you suspect Atlas is guilty of something." Theodora's slender shoulders heaved. "Such a horrible insult to an upstanding citizen like Atlas."

Gage didn't appear particularly impressed or intimidated in the face of her outrage. Instead, he said, "Bryan Mathers."

Well, well.

"Name ring a bell?" Gage prompted. "If not, let me help. He was your college roommate, Atlas. Sophomore year."

Yes, he had been. Bryan had also been a spoiled prick who drank too much and partied far too hard. "Random roommate assignment." Bryan had also been accused of rape by several girls on campus. But the charges had always been swept away. Mostly because Bryan's own mother had been an associate dean at the university.

"Bryan OD'd in your dorm room." Gage delivered that bit like it was a major news story.

"Yes, I am aware." Atlas nodded. "I warned him to give up the drug use. He didn't listen. Such a tragedy."

Gage gaped at him. "The needle was shoved directly in his throat. I don't know why the hell more of an investigation wasn't conducted at the time, but people don't usually inject full needles into their *necks* like that—"

"Bryan thought he was invincible. He would try anything. Always told me that nothing could hurt him." Nothing and no one. Bryan had been wrong. "If only I had been there that night, but, sadly, I'd already left the school. Two weeks before that, actually. I'd learned enough."

Gage's nostrils flared. "Landon Russell."

Ah, another blast from the past. Gage had certainly been a busy Fed.

"He was a chemist who worked in your research division."

Atlas laughed. He could feel Lily watching him, but he didn't glance her way, not yet. He let the smile linger on his lips. "I have quite a few chemists who work for me. Quite a few research divisions, too. Gonna need you to be far more specific."

"Landon cut corners. There was an accident in his lab. One man suffered third degree burns on half his body. That specific enough for you?"

Atlas tapped his chin. "I do recall Landon. If memory serves, he was fired immediately after that incident." He glanced at Theodora. "I'm sure you could check with HR on that. I believe he may have experienced a drinking problem. We have a zero tolerance policy for drinking on the job. I believe we even referred him to a substance abuse program for treatment."

"I remember him." Theodora's subdued response. "He refused treatment."

"He was in an auto accident after his dismissal from the company," Gage informed their group. "A mother and her son were killed in the car crash. He fled the scene on foot."

Atlas unclenched his back teeth. "Terrible."

"He was found dead, two months later."

"Two months?" Atlas repeated, but he knew this information. "It certainly took the cops a while to find him."

"He'd been dead the whole time. His remains—the bits left of him—were found about two miles from a popular hiking trail."

"*What does this have to do with my clients?*" Theodora snapped.

"Two victims," Gage fired back. "Those are two victims tied to Atlas Bennett."

Atlas grimaced. "I am not an FBI agent. I have not gone to Quantico for training. I am not some behavioral expert, but...they are not *my* victims. Unless you are implying that I killed them?" Atlas waited. No response from Gage. So he asked, voice cool, "Is that what you're saying? Are you accusing me of being a serial killer?"

Sharon put down her pen. "That's only two victims. We really need three for the serial designation."

"*Thank you, Sharon,*" Gage bit out. His glare remained on Atlas. "Benedict Swain thought there were more victims. Remember when I said he had a few physical files on you, Atlas?"

He tapped his chin. "I do remember you saying something about that. His computer was wiped, but some physical files were left in his desk. How incredibly convenient." *Files that point to me as being a killer. Lovely.*

"I read through those files," Gage told him.

"I would have been shocked and disappointed in your skills as an FBI agent if you had not." What in the hell had Lily ever seen in this jerk?

"There were lots of notes in those files. Names. Plenty of deaths. But—"

"But no concrete evidence." Now he was bored. "Benedict liked to make my life hell. He was convinced I was the boogeyman. Want to know why?" They could all just cut to the chase because he had zero patience left. "Because a million years ago, we happened to live in the same group home. To say we did not get along is an understatement. I thought that our paths would never cross again after I got out of that place, but then when I decided to return to Dallas, to set up my roots in the city that once, well...a city that once abandoned me." *Turned its freaking back on me but now I practically own the place.* "I came back here, looking for a fresh start, and then I see Benedict skulking around me. Only now he has a badge. A shiny badge, but the same old hate fuels him. He was determined to prove that I'm unworthy. That I'm evil. But he never had actual proof. That was the problem. And you don't have that proof, either."

"*We are done with this interview.*" Theodora was adamant. "Done. You will *not* accuse my client of—of murder! Of being some sort of *serial killer*—"

"Aren't you going to say something?" Gage snarled.

The snarled question was directed at Lily.

Now Atlas rose to his feet. "Watch it," he warned the Fed. "Because I have been cordial with you thus far." Time for that bit of cordialness to end. "Don't make me your enemy." Actually, it was too late for that. This lucky jerk had fucked Lily.

We are enemies. Because she is mine.

But did Gage heed his warning? Oh, no. Eyes on Lily, he said, "Benedict shared his suspicions with you. He must have done it. He must have told you, showed you the files. You were watching Atlas, too, weren't you? Following him because you thought he might just be the one who'd sliced up those people in Dallas—William Lloyd and Conry Harding. You thought that Atlas was the one doing the punishment kills, only then he was taken, wasn't he? Right in front of you?"

"What part of *enough* do you not understand?" Theodora heaved a sigh. "Hey, Detective Wry, I know you. You know me. Can you drag this jerk out of here? Or I guess I can call one of Atlas's many security guards and have them do the job."

Detective Wry rose. But he didn't actually move to do anything. He just stood there appearing all uncertain.

Sharon also rose. "We should go," she murmured. Sharon closed her pad. Tucked her pen into her small purse.

"Excellent! The voice of reason." Theodora beamed at her.

But Gage and Lily just stared at one another. "You know he's a killer," Gage told her.

Yeah, Atlas hated the dick. He figured he was entitled to that hate, though. A man comes into your house, he tells you that you're a killer, plus...*he fucked my lady*. Frankly, Atlas thought he was exhibiting amazing control. He hadn't beaten the ever loving hell out of the Fed...yet.

"And you're gonna stay in his house?" Gage asked her. "Let him lie to the world and say you're getting married? Bullshit. *Bullshit.* Come on, Lily, is your research really that important? So important that you'd lie like this in order to protect a monster?"

Oh, but it would be fun to drive his fist right into the agent's jaw. "Is it made of glass?" Atlas wondered. He bet that it was.

"What?" Gage whipped his head toward Atlas.

"Your jaw. When I punch you, will you go down instantly, will it break right away, or will I need to hit you a second time?" Because he could certainly oblige with a second hit. Or a third. Maybe a fourth, simply for fun.

Gage rounded the table and surged toward him. "You just threatened a federal officer."

Bring it, asshole. Atlas smiled at him. His hands fisted.

"No!" Theodora's high cry. "My client asked a question. A question is not a threat. You don't arrest people for *questions*. I'm calling security. We are done here. Done,

done, done. You try to cooperate, and then *this* happens." She grabbed her phone. "Desmond," she said immediately after putting the phone to her ear. "Code Atlas."

Code Atlas...Get guards in here because he's out of control.

Only Atlas wasn't out of control, not yet. And he would be perfectly controlled as he drove his fist into Gage's smug face.

"No." Lily stepped in front of Atlas. "Gage can actually take a punch really well. I've seen him do it. Gage's jaw is not made of glass."

He didn't want her between them. Atlas's hands settled on her shoulders.

"Yes." She nodded toward the Fed. Apparently, this retort was for him. "Benedict did share his suspicions about Atlas with me. But he had no direct proof of Atlas's involvement in any crime. Not one single real tie. What he did have was an obsession that I found troubling."

Gage's eyes narrowed to furious slits. "Lily..."

"Atlas was targeted. The killer wanted to hurt him, and he wanted to hurt anyone who came to help Atlas. That tells me the notion that this guy is just going after people who have done something wrong, that he is a dark avenging angel of some sort—that idea is wrong. He was ready to take down innocent people. *Innocent.* He set a trap. He let the fire burn." She swallowed. "The man who did that—I suspect he broke in my house. He came after me when Atlas and I escaped."

Atlas's grip tightened on her. "He's not getting you." *Never gonna happen.*

"I was in his way. I stopped him from achieving his goal. He won't like that. If I hadn't been there, maybe he would have gotten his high body count. But instead, everyone but Benedict got out. He failed in his main goal. I figure that failure had to unleash his rage. Perhaps in his mind, I'm now the one who has committed the biggest sin."

Gage took a step back. "I...I can protect you. If he's coming after you, I can keep you safe."

"I'm on it," Atlas assured him. "I have her." *And no one will ever take Lily from me.*

"Is that why she's in your house?" Gage wanted to know. "Why you're about to put a ring on her finger? Because you think that will protect her?"

"That and the army of guards who are about to burst inside." Because Desmond would respond instantly to Theodora. He always did.

As if on cue, the front door burst open. Four guards rushed inside and thundered toward the dining room, with Desmond in the lead.

"I believe we are done," Atlas said even as he motioned for the guards to hold their position. "As my lawyer indicated, multiple times, in fact."

Red tinted Gage's cheeks. "Not yet, we're not." His head angled down toward Lily. "I had an interesting talk with Magnolia recently."

Because Atlas still had his hands around Lily's shoulders, he felt the tension slide through her.

"She's worried about you," Gage added.

Lily laughed.

Atlas realized it was the first time he'd ever heard her laugh. But...he didn't think that was a real laugh. It was brittle. Mocking.

"I find that highly doubtful," Lily returned in a cool voice. "Though I suspect she is very annoyed with me, and therefore, she'd try to mislead you."

The red deepened in his cheeks. "She told me that you were hunting a serial killer."

"I don't do that. I'm not in the BAU. That's your department."

"Magnolia says...Lily, you believe you are going to find some kind of soulmate." Gage's stare shifted from Lily—to Atlas. He glared at Atlas over Lily's head. "Someone who understands you."

Well, well, well...

"He won't," Gage bit off. "He can't."

Oh, but Gage was very wrong. Shocking. "Don't be so sure of that. I understand Lily perfectly."

"Do you?" Gage challenged. Then he smiled. A smug bastard kind of smile. "David Warren."

Lily didn't tense. She trembled. He didn't like for Lily to tremble. Not unless her trembles were from the pleasure that he intended to give her. Instead of pleasure, though, his instincts said that Lily was afraid and that was why she trembled before him.

"Leave," Atlas ordered. "*Now.*"

The guards stepped forward. Agent Sharon Hinkle and Detective Kurt Wry immediately began to depart.

"Thank you for your time," Sharon murmured. Her gaze darted up to the chandelier. "Insane place you have here, by the way." She hurried for the front door, with Detective Wry right on her heels.

Only Gage lingered.

"David Warren is dead and buried," Lily said. "I don't really see how he is relevant to anything."

"Isn't he relevant?" Low. Gage's voice seemed to carry only to Lily and to Atlas. "Why the hell doesn't your fiancé know about him? Or are you scared of what he'll do if he does find out? Worried you'll get punished, Lily?"

Why in the hell would Lily ever get punished?

But, screw that. Using his grip on her, he pulled Lily back. Then he positioned himself in front of her. A deliberate choice. Because he needed the Fed to understand one basic fact. "Anyone who wants to hurt Lily will have to go through me." He wanted this prick far away from her.

"You don't know her." Gage shook his head. "I do. I know what makes her tick on the inside. I know the demons she fights. You won't help her. You'll destroy her."

The hell he would. "Should the guards drag your ass out? Or do you want to be a big boy and walk out on your own?"

Gage's lips flattened. He stomped away. Atlas watched him go, his body full of its own fury and his hands clenched because he really wanted to take a swing at the bastard.

Gage swung back around, pausing near the columns that marked the edge of the dining room. "I know what you are," he snarled at Atlas.

Oh, right. He'd practiced this part with Theodora. Atlas knew exactly what to say. *"I'm a victim."* A low, dangerous rumble of sound.

Theodora had just stepped to his side. Her jaw dropped at those words.

"Now get the fuck out," Atlas ordered Gage. "And stay the hell away from my fiancée."

Gage stormed out. The guards followed because they would know to make sure the Fed and his associates were fully escorted from the property. Not like anyone got to take a free search of the place without a warrant.

The silence in the dining room stretched. And stretched.

Finally, Theodora's heels clicked as she moved forward.

"I don't think you should use those particular words again." Hands on her hips, she angled to face him.

He quirked a brow at her. "You told me to say them."

"Yes, but somehow, when you say...*I'm a victim*...it comes out as a threat. I have no idea how, but it just does. You might as well have said *I am a killer*."

He shrugged. "Didn't say that." He'd never make that confession to a Fed.

"Right. Because you aren't one." She blew out a hard breath. "Are we going to sign the NDA before I leave?"

The NDA, right. He'd almost forgotten.

Atlas glanced back at Lily. "Ready to sign your life away to me?"

Fear filled her expression.

Shit, bad word choice. "Ah, Lily—"

"Give me the NDA." Flat.

Theodora opened her briefcase. She'd had it on the floor near the right wall. She pulled out the paperwork. "I, um, also have a standard contract for you, too, Lily, one that will prove I'm your lawyer going forward."

"I'll sign it, too. Just show me where."

But Theodora hesitated. "You should really read these. Thoroughly. How about I leave them and you can read them and then sign tomorrow?"

Too late. Lily flipped through the papers and slashed her signature next to the Xs. Then she slapped the pen down on the table. "Great. I gave you my life, Atlas." Her hands folded across her chest as she faced off with him. "What do I get in return?"

Tension burned between them. *Me. You get me, Lily.*

"Uh, do you want him to sign an NDA, too?" Theodora asked with a faint cough. "Because I'm your lawyer now, and I can draw up one for him. If there are things that you don't want him to discuss about you and your relationship—"

"Make it," Atlas pounced on that offer. Anything to put them on equal footing. Anything to get Lily to open up to him. To share with him. To banish the pain that he saw in her eyes because he wanted to take it away. He needed to take away all her hurt and fear and make her feel safe.

Lily's safety mattered to him more than anything.

She mattered. Dangerous. So very dangerous.

Theodora left them alone. The clicking of her heels faded away. Lily didn't move. Atlas felt nailed to the spot.

"I signed," Lily told him. "So now are you gonna tell me where you buried the bodies?"

So cute. He hadn't buried them. If he had, then Landon Russell's body never would have been found near that hiking trail. "No, this is the part where I put a fucking ring on your finger." His breath heaved out. "Lily Gallo, you're mine now."

Chapter Fourteen

Julia Tutwiler Prison For Women
   Wetumpka, Alabama

THREE WEEKS AGO...

"I'M WORRIED ABOUT LILY," FBI Agent Gage Emerick said as he sat in the small, private room at the maximum-security prison. His chair wobbled beneath him. Damn uneven legs.

"You broke my daughter's heart. You used her. You took her for granted. Yet *now* you claim to be worried? Don't insult my intelligence." Magnolia shook her head. "I really shouldn't have even agreed to see you today."

Yeah, well... "Why did you?"

"Boredom." A sigh. "And I typically enjoy visits from handsome men." Her full lips curved, just a bit. But the faint smile quickly faded. "Unless those men have hurt my

177

daughter. I don't like it at all when someone hurts my precious Lily."

Ah, yes. The moment he'd been waiting for. "Did David Warren hurt Lily?"

Magnolia's expression didn't change. Not even by a flicker of one long eyelash.

The woman was really quite lovely. Time had always been kind to Magnolia. Even in the garish orange prison garb, she somehow seemed...fashionable. Maybe it was the twist of her hair. The faint pink sheen on her lips.

The red polish on her nails.

If he didn't know better, he would have even thought she'd had the prison uniform tailored a bit. It didn't sag on her body. The collar fluffed—fuck, if that was even the term. The sleeves were well fitted and—

"Who is David Warren?"

He laughed. "Come on, this is widespread knowledge. The man did a media tour after your conviction." Why was she even trying to pretend with him? "You were dating him...years ago. Back before you were convicted of multiple homicides."

A roll of one shoulder. "I dated lots of men. I don't remember all of their names."

"But you remember the names of the men you killed, don't you?" He would bet those names—and the faces—were burned in her memory.

"I know the names of the men I was convicted of killing." A careful and deliberate distinction. "I'm innocent, of course. That would be why my conviction is on appeal." A shudder. "Death row. For me. Can you imagine? What a horrible miscarriage of justice. Honestly, *I* am the victim here."

The hell she was. "You were dating David Warren right around the time that Lily was poisoned."

Her gaze flickered to the watchful guard. "Jesse, do you know what's for dinner tonight? Wait, wait. Let me guess. Would it be...a meat patty? Beans? Perhaps even a piece of fruit for dessert? Oh, how incredibly exciting. Talk about a dining extravaganza. A real feast for the senses."

Magnolia was interesting. Intriguing. Borderline personality disorder, narcissistic, histrionic...

Charming beyond measure when she wanted to be. Brutal beyond thought when the urge struck her.

And she was Lily's mother. His Lily. He really fucking needed Lily back.

"Magnolia," he said her name deliberately.

Her attention returned to him. "I have no clue what Lily saw in you. You're far too stiff and boring to entertain my daughter for long."

"Lily...talked about our relationship with you?" It sure seemed that way, but it was hard for him to imagine Lily just opening up with her mother. Or, with anyone, really.

"Doesn't a daughter tell her mother everything?"

That wasn't an answer. Magnolia was sly that way. "You have a lot of...fans, Magnolia."

"I do." A delighted smile. "They adore me. They understand that I shouldn't be locked away. That I need help. That I must have my freedom."

Uh, no. The world would be a safer place with her locked away forever. "The warden told me that you receive more mail than anyone else at the prison." He knew to deliberately appeal to her pride. Her pride was a weakness for her.

"Some people are popular. Some aren't." Once again, she looked at the guard. "I'm popular, right, Jesse?"

"Yes, Ms. Magnolia. The most popular inmate here."

She beamed at him. Even blew him a kiss. But that beaming smile vanished as she sized up Gage once again.

Oh, yeah, this woman would poison me in a heartbeat. She'd offer me her tea and smile while I vomited blood on her floor. "The warden also told me that you get marriage offers. People willing to do just about anything for you."

"When you love someone, you have to prove that love."

Excitement had his heart pounding. "Is someone proving their love to you right now? Maybe a doctor in Louisiana?" The warden had told him the doctor had come to visit her several times. Gage had called in some favors from the Baton Rouge FBI office. Fun fact, Dr. Francis Locke had lost his medical license five years ago when one of his patients had died under extremely suspicious circumstances. Francis hadn't been charged with murder, just dismissed from the hospital while the insurance company had to foot a major wrongful death bill. But after reading the reports on the vic...

Did you murder her, you bastard? Because Gage thought that Dr. Francis Locke might just be guilty as sin.

"Lily and I talked about the doctor." A casual admission from Magnolia. "The doctor and I talked about Lily."

Oh, fuck. Gage straightened in his seat. "He's not a good man, Magnolia."

"Excuse me?"

"Your doctor friend? I think he might be a murderer. Tell me he doesn't know where Lily is. Tell me he doesn't know—"

"*You* don't know where Lily is." Her head tilted to the side. "Is she refusing to talk to you again?" She rocked forward. "Makes sense, seeing as how she's seeking her soulmate now."

"What?" Since when in the hell had Lily started to see someone else?

"I warned her, though, he's going to be too dangerous for her to handle. But Lily thinks she can face any threat."

Tension curled around his spine. "Who is her soulmate?"

"It's certainly not you." Disdain dropped from every word.

"Because I have a badge?"

"Because you won't kill for her. That's what she needs. A man to kill for her. Hmm." Now she frowned. Appeared a bit thoughtful. "He will."

"The doctor? Your doctor friend is going to kill—"

"We are done. The doctor and I. No more visits. No more letters. No more packages. He lied to me. Lily already told me about his poor, dead patient. I'm not concerned with him any longer."

Oh, shit. That probably meant the doc was dead somewhere.

"I was talking about Lily's new friend. Her soulmate. *He'll* kill for her."

She seemed way too certain of that. "Who is her friend?" *I need to find Lily. She moved out of her old place. Left no forwarding address. I have to find her.* Even his connections at the Bureau hadn't turned up anything on her yet.

Lily...shit, she'd been his ace in the hole. She'd helped him solve five high-profile cases and then...

"She thinks it has to be someone like her." A disgruntled sigh eased from Magnolia. "I keep telling her, there won't ever be anyone just like she is. But you know Lily. She's all about research, research, research. All research and no play makes Lily—" Magnolia stopped.

He waited.

But she said no more.

"What does it make her?" Gage prompted.

Nothing.

"Desperate?" Gage asked. "Vulnerable?"

"Lonely," Magnolia said. "And isn't that the greatest tragedy of all? To know that you will be forever alone in this world? That's why she thinks that she has to find the others like her. That they will somehow fill the void inside."

Hell. "She's…going after the children of serial killers, isn't she?" Because he'd stumbled on her research once, seen it on her laptop. She'd slammed the lid down closed when she caught him looking. Lily hadn't been working alone on that project, though. She had a friend, Sloane, who'd been just as caught up in the dark as she was.

Sloane's parents hadn't been serial killers. They'd been *killed* by a serial. "Is she with Sloane?"

"Who?"

"Sloane. Sloane Armstrong," he enunciated slowly. "Her friend."

"Sloane isn't her friend. Lily thinks she is but…deep down, we know the truth."

We?

"Sloane has always been a bit afraid of Lily. Just as you have been."

"I'm not scared of Lily."

"Aren't you?" A taunt. "Would you drink tea if she offered it to you?"

Hell, no. Dammit. He grabbed the edge of the table. "I need to find Lily. I know she comes to see you. Clearly, you know about her research. Look, I'm worried about her."

Her expression shifted, just a little bit.

"David Warren," he said softly. David was the reason

he'd never drink Lily's tea. "Others will look into him, too. I need to find Lily."

Again, her expression changed. It grew harder. Anger flashed in her eyes. "Let them look. He's ashes in the wind."

Wait, wait, wait. "He was cremated?" That hadn't been in the files—

Magnolia began to laugh. Delighted peals of laughter that sounded like a bell ringing. "You were never a match for her." More laughter. "But maybe he will be...maybe... maybe I was wrong."

"Who?"

More laughter. More fucking laughter, and she didn't answer him. When she left with the guard a few moments later, Magnolia was still laughing.

* * *

GAGE STRODE toward the prison's exit. The trip had been an utter waste. Magnolia had given him zero insights, and he needed to find—

"What's it worth to you?"

The low voice stopped him. He turned to find a guard trailing behind him. Tall, rounded shoulders. Blond hair. The guard who'd been in the room with him and Magnolia.

"I know where Lily Gallo went." The guard shuffled forward. A taser was clipped to his belt. A baton dangled next to it. "What's it worth?"

The guard was trying to get him to *pay* for the intel? Fuck. "I have five hundred dollars in my wallet."

"Done."

Hell. He should have offered the guy one hundred. They had to wait for Gage to get his wallet and ID back from the check-in desk and then...

He palmed the money to the guard, making sure that no one else saw the movement.

"Atlas Bennett. That's the one she went to see. Heard her say his name."

"You heard Lily say that to Magnolia?" The name Atlas Bennett hadn't just rung a bell. It had reverberated through him. Everyone knew Atlas. His father had been as twisted as they came.

Lily, stop playing with monsters. Didn't she get that they were just dragging her deeper into the dark?

"Nah. Didn't hear her tell Magnolia. Heard it when she was on the phone to someone, on her way out. Said she was going to Dallas to see him."

Hell, yes.

But he had an idea growing within him now. Because he had a source. "You ever hear any other useful bits while you're in there with Lily and Magnolia?"

The guard smiled at him. "You're gonna need more money."

"I can get it."

* * *

GAGE CLIMBED INTO HIS CAR, excitement filling him. He'd go to Lily, he'd convince her to take him back, they'd work together and—

His phone began ringing. He grabbed the phone, recognized the agent from Baton Rouge that he'd talked to before, and Gage put the phone to his ear. "Yo, listen, about Dr. Francis—"

"He's dead," the agent cut in to tell him. "Body is decomposing. Been dead in his greenhouse for days. No one

184

thought to look out back for him. It's...fuck, he smells. Hot as hell in there."

Tension swept through Gage. "How did he die?"

"The medical examiner suspects it was a heart attack. No sign of foul play. Guy seems to have been pruning his flowers, and then he just dropped dead. Shit happens, you know?"

Uh, yeah. Shit did happen.

And so did murder.

Chapter Fifteen

PRESENT DAY...

"SLOANE, Sloane, I am all right, I promise." Lily gripped the phone tightly in her hand. Since her phone was long gone, Atlas had brought her a replacement. "I'm in a safe place."

"Define *safe place* for me," Sloane Armstrong demanded, voice tight. "Because I saw the story on the news. The reporter said a cop is dead, and you were *kidnapped*. Nothing about that is *all right*."

"I'm with Atlas Bennett."

Silence.

Lily paced quickly across the guest room. She peeked out the curtains. Darkness had fallen again. The darkness had fallen long ago because it was edging close to midnight. She should have been asleep but, when you woke up at 4 p.m. you weren't exactly tired when midnight came rolling around.

"Atlas...Bennett." Sloane inhaled. "He's cooperating with you?"

Yes, this would be where things got tricky. "You will probably see stories soon that say he's my fiancé." After Gage had finally left, Atlas had begun pulling strings like crazy. He'd talked to certain powerful reporters, an effort to get *his* story out there. Probably because he realized Gage wanted to take him down.

But in getting *his* story out, Atlas had been very clear that she was linked to him. *His fiancée.*

"We don't talk for a few days, and suddenly you are engaged?" Sloane's voice rose. "That's fantastic! Congratulations!" Her enthusiasm poured over the line.

That was Sloane. Brighter, happier than Lily. They'd met in college. Sloane had been interested in pursuing a PhD in psychology while Lily had been determined to get her MD and work in the field of psychiatry. Sloane had been bright, bubbly, a flame that drew everyone to her. Lily...

I'll never be described as the flame that draws people close. Lily knew she was quiet, withdrawn.

But she and Sloane had sat next to each other in an abnormal psych class, and Sloane...Sloane had kept talking to her. Walking with her after class. Inviting her to lunch. Sloane had been the president of her sorority. She'd always had an eager circle of people around her. Lily had never understood why Sloane wanted to be her friend so badly.

Then she'd learned the truth.

Sloane glowed so brightly because her darkness was buried deep inside.

"Lily." The enthusiasm had faded from Sloane's voice. "You've said nothing here. This is making me nervous. Do you love him? Are you happy?"

"It's...not like that." She let the curtain fall back into place.

"Uh, yeah, yeah, it's exactly like that. You marry someone because you love them, no other reason."

"It's to keep me safe."

"*What?*"

"So, I don't want you to worry—"

"Too late! I'm worrying like mad! I'm about to jump on a plane and hunt you down because I am so worried about you!"

She fully believed that Sloane was about to take those very actions. "I believe the individual who took me—who took Atlas and I both—I think he broke into my rental house. He stole my laptop, Sloane."

"It's password protected," Sloane's instant response.

"You know he'll eventually get past any password protection. He also took my physical files." There was no getting around this. "He has the data on our potential subjects."

"Shit."

Yes.

"But so what?" Sloane demanded in the next breath. "Most of that intel is public information. And the stuff that isn't, what is he going to do with it?"

"I don't know." She turned from the window and stared back at the bed. "That's what worries me."

"Let me tell you what worries *me*. The guy took you. Then he—what? Broke into your house? That's not good on a thousand levels. Lily, he's got you in his sights. He's coming for you. You need an army around you, you need—oh, the engagement." Her breath heaved out. "Got it. I'm following along now. Atlas Bennett is giving you an army, isn't he?"

Yes, he was. "I'm pretty sure half a dozen guards are patrolling the grounds as we speak."

"He's telling the world you're under his protection. That's what the engagement is about."

Right. "Not like it was going to be about him taking one look at me and falling helplessly in love."

"Lily Gallo, you stop that right now! If the man has any sense, he absolutely would look at you and instantly fall in love! You're an amazing person, and, uh, hello—you *saved* his ass! He needs to be grateful to you. He needs to be thanking you. Preferably on his hands and knees in full grovel form. He needs to be—"

A soft knock on her closed door.

"Worshipping the very ground upon which you walk," Sloane finished tightly.

"Don't really think he's going to be doing that anytime soon," Lily told her.

The door opened. A few inches at first. Enough for Atlas to peek inside. "Thought I heard your voice." One dark eyebrow rose. "You're on the phone. Got it."

Not like I was in here talking to myself. She wasn't that far gone. Yet.

He started to back away.

"Atlas!" Lily called.

"*Is he with you right now?*" Sloane demanded.

He opened the door fully. He was dressed all in black, even black boots. And she could feel a tension clinging to his body.

Atlas was planning something.

"Yes," Lily said into the phone.

"Is that good...or bad?" Sloane wanted to know.

"Yes," Lily said again.

"Ohmygosh. I'm coming to you. I am getting on a plane, and I am coming to you."

"You don't need to do that!"

"You are my best friend. My family. I definitely need to do it. So expect me. It's a done deal. I figure I'll find you at his big-ass mansion."

Atlas filled the doorway. He didn't approach. Just stood there wearing all black, looking dangerous and sexy. His eyes were on her, seeming to brand her. He looked even bigger than normal. His shoulders so wide they almost touched the wood of the doorframe on either side of him. His right hand gripped a manila file.

"That's where I am," Lily agreed quietly. *In his big-ass mansion.* Though she wouldn't have described it quite that way.

"I am on my way. Seriously, moving now, as fast as I can get there. And don't you *dare* get kidnapped by some psycho killer again before I get to you, do you hear me? I will be so pissed at you if that shit happens."

"We're not supposed to call them that, Sloane."

"Fuck it. Like I care. A man kidnaps my best friend, he blows up a house and kills a cop, then he counts as a *psycho killer.* Sorry if he doesn't like the label, but that's too bad for him. You stay safe. Wait. Know what? Better plan. Stay close to Atlas Bennett. Stick to him like glue. No way his guards are gonna let anything bad happen to him again."

The guards were certainly working in overdrive.

"You do not get separated from Atlas. Twenty-four, seven, you stay with him, got me? Lily? Lily? You're not responding. I am giving you an order from your best friend."

Sloane was her only friend.

"Tell me that you will follow my order." A plea had

entered Sloane's voice. "I need to know you're safe. Tell me that you will stay with Atlas."

"I will stay with Atlas," she dutifully confirmed as she held his stare. "Twenty-four, seven."

His eyes gleamed.

"Goodbye, Sloane," she said.

"Stay alive, Lily," Sloane returned. "If you don't, I will never, ever forgive you. Friends don't die on friends, understand?"

"I understand."

Sloane hung up. Lily slowly lowered the phone. She put it on the nightstand, then stood by the bed, her hands rising to twist a bit awkwardly in front of her. "That was my friend Sloane."

He took a step into her bedroom.

"She's my partner in my research, too," Lily added. She forced her hands to release and fall to her sides.

He advanced another step.

"I wanted her to know what had happened—with our files, that is. She's insisting on flying here to see me. Told her that I was safe."

Another step. His eyes were locked right on her. Blazing so blue that it almost hurt to look into them. That gaze of his was really quite unsettling.

"I explained to her about the fake engagement bit. Said it was for my protection. Not real. Not because you looked at me and fell hopelessly in love." Immediately, she wanted to yank those words back. Why, oh, why had she just uttered them? So unnecessary. Why was she rambling? She didn't ramble. She didn't talk unnecessarily. Often, she'd been accused of not speaking enough. She was the shy one. The quiet one. The reserved one. Not the oversharing one.

That would be Sloane.

Atlas stopped right in front of her. He lifted the file. "The NDA. The one I signed for you. So you'll know that I'll go to my grave before I ever reveal secrets you tell me."

Not that she was a legal scholar, but Lily didn't think that was quite how NDAs worked. "You didn't have to sign that."

"Neither did you." A twist of his lips. "We both know I wasn't walking away from you, no matter what." He put the file on her nightstand. Hesitated just a moment.

"Atlas?"

His hand shoved into the pocket of his pants.

What was he doing?

He pulled something out of that pocket. And he...he reached for her left hand. She glanced down and realized—"Is that an *engagement* ring?"

Because now Atlas held a gleaming, glittering ring. What appeared to be an incredibly expensive ring. No way the man just casually had that thing lying around his house. "When did you get it? Where?"

"Lily..." A smile seemed to be in his voice. "It's me. I make phone calls, and things happen." Gently, he slid the ring onto her finger.

Lily shook her head. "It's...too much." And it was. She was certainly no expert when it came to jewelry—she typically didn't wear any jewelry at all. When you were going in prisons to interview killers far too often, you tended not to bother with jewelry. After all, you'd just be constantly taking the pieces on and off at check-in. Better to just not wear anything fancy. And this ring... She swallowed.

Fancy. Expensive. Too much for me.

"It's not enough," he said. "But it will do, for now."

What did that even mean? "It's full of diamonds." And

one very big sapphire gleamed in the middle of the diamonds.

"Loyalty. Trust."

She glanced up at him.

"That's what a sapphire is supposed to symbolize. Given our unique relationship, I thought the sapphire fit us. I will be loyal to you, Lily. Always. And I want you to trust me."

"I'll be loyal to you." She would be. "But will *you* trust me?"

"Yes."

The ring was slightly cool against her skin, and the fingers that still held hers—his slightly callused fingertips—were warm.

"There's a tracking device in the ring," he told her.

She'd rather thought there might be.

"If you ever get taken, I will find you." His head lowered toward hers. "Then I will kill the sonofabitch who took you."

"You say the sweetest things."

His eyes widened. His gaze searched hers, harder. "Lily, you just joked with me."

"I can do that, occasionally." Very, very occasionally.

His smile teased at his lips. But his dimples didn't bloom.

"You have a tracker on you, too, don't you?" she asked him.

"Um. I have quite a few trackers. One in my watch. One in my cuff links. One in a tie pin. Sort of depends on the day, but I will always have one close." His lips twisted. "I should have said one *was* in my cuff links. But I lost my favorite cuff links somewhere at the cabin when the killer took us."

So the cuff links had been how Desmond tracked him. "You wanted the killer to take you."

His head cocked to the right. "I give you an engagement ring, and you immediately start talking about killers. I'd hoped for a different response."

Had he really? Or was he just trying to distract her? "What sort of response did you want?"

"You vowing to love me forever would have been great."

She blinked.

His full dimples flashed at her. "That was a joke, Lily. I make them, too. Actually, I make them a lot more often than you do."

"I..." She swallowed because her mouth had gone way too dry. *You vowing to love me forever.* "I don't...I am never going to be the one laughing in the middle of a room." That sounded awkward. Fair enough, she felt awkward. Awkward, and Lily was too aware of the ring. "I will never joke easily. An occasional joke is all that you'll get from me. And, yes, my whole life, I have always been told that I am far too serious."

His dimples slowly faded.

"But that is who I am. You grow up with a mother who is a killer...you grow up always sensing something beneath the surface, always feeling like *you* have to be perfect or that something very bad can happen...and you don't joke a lot. You don't smile easily. Instead, you overthink. You worry. You try to plan for every scenario so that you can be safe. So that the people around you will be safe. And then one day, you realize that you don't even really know how to laugh anymore. Not like other people. Because you will never be carefree like them." *You wonder if you can ever be happy.* She didn't say that last part, though. She'd finally managed to clamp her lips shut.

Too much oversharing. Sloane would have been shocked. Lily *was* shocked.

He let go of her hand. Took a step back.

She'd revealed far too much. Why on earth had she done that?

Sloane is the one who laughs easily. Sloane is the one who smiles. Sloane is—

She wears a mask. Sloane learned to mask when she was a teen, and she does it like a pro.

Lily didn't like to bother with masks.

As he stared at her, Atlas's expression hardened. Then, seemingly through gritted teeth, he questioned, "Do you think I want you to fake smiles with me? To fake *any damn thing* with me?"

She backed up. Hit the side of the bed. "I—" Lily stopped. "No, no, of course not." Why had she said anything to him about—

"I fucking *don't*. If you smile, I want it to be real. I want you to mean it. I want you to mean everything that you do or say with me."

Okay.

"But, hell, yes, I would like for you to smile. I would *like* for you to be happy, and I have no idea why. My whole life, I've never cared if most people are happy or sad. Bored or thrilled. But for some reason, *you* matter."

Her heart began to beat faster.

"So, yes, fuck it all, I do want to see you smile. I want to hear you laugh. But I want it to be real. I want all of you to be *real* with me. No pretending. No holding back because you think I won't be able to handle the monster that lurks inside of you. The one that you can feel inside, pushing and growing in those weak moments that you told me about before."

He was going back to that, now?

"The one that wants you to stop being good. To just let go." His hand rose again. This time, though, his fingers slid under her jaw as he tipped back her head. "You keep your control every single moment, don't you?"

No, she didn't, not with him. And when she'd let her control break in the past...

David Warren.

She'd done something bad. Something that she would never be able to forget.

"You guard yourself too well, Lily. You don't let go, so you don't *feel*, do you?"

Anger stirred. "You're going to talk to me about not feeling? If memory serves, you were the one who said you didn't feel emotions." She'd never claimed not to feel them. Quite the opposite. Sometimes, she feared they would rip her apart. *You can turn them on and off? Tell me how. Please, tell me how. Tell me how to make the pain stop.*

"I told you that I *typically* didn't feel them. With you, I find myself feeling far too much."

That was good, wasn't it? Or could it be very bad? Maybe a bit of both?

"You have to let go of your control," Atlas warned her.

That was something that terrified Lily. She shook her head.

"Do you ever do it?" he asked. "Just let go?"

Not if she could help it. "Bad things happen," she whispered.

"Not with me. Because I'll keep you safe." His fingers skimmed over her skin. His thumb brushed across her lips. "Do you let go with your lovers, sweet Lily?"

No. She didn't. She wanted to let go. She wanted to

stop caring and overthinking and worrying and just get lost to pleasure with a lover, but she never had. Her head shook.

His thumb slid over her bottom lip with the slight movement. "Not even with that jackass Gage?"

No. Though she'd come close with him—

"Know what? Let's not fucking ever talk about him with you again, shall we? It's the best plan if we want him to keep living. Though, I am happy to eliminate him at any time."

Her tongue licked his thumb.

He sucked in a quick breath.

"Don't say things you don't mean," she chided him. Atlas was just trying to be outrageous. To frighten her away from him. Didn't he realize she could see the truth? He thought he was too dangerous, and he was trying to warn her away. That wasn't a villain thing to do. The villain didn't tell you to run so you could stay safe. A villain grabbed you and didn't let go no matter what you did.

"I would kill for you in an instant." He stared straight at her. "Never doubt that."

Staring into his eyes, she did not doubt his words. Not even for a minute. He would kill.

"Tell me about your orgasms, sweets."

What?

She jerked her chin away from his hold. Lily would have backed away, again, but the bed was right there, blocking her retreat.

"They're not something to brag about, huh? Because you've been with dumbasses? Because you couldn't let go with them?" His arms were at his sides now.

"They are fine," she said. "My orgasms are fine." How were they having this conversation?

He whistled. "Oh, fuck, that's terrible. If I ever give you

a *fine* orgasm, punch me in the face. Seriously, right in the face, and then I will do a thousand times better than *fine*."

No, he didn't understand. "It's...me. I can't—" A huff of air as she exhaled in frustration. "I can't be in the moment. I can't shut off my thoughts."

"Then use those thoughts. If you can't shut them off, then focus on me. When I'm fucking you, think about me and what I'm doing. Think about how it feels. Think about what you want. Think about my tongue sliding over your clit. Again and again." His voice deepened. Went guttural. "Think about my tongue sliding into you. My fingers and my tongue and—know what? Screw it. I'll prove to you that your orgasms should be far, far better than *fine*."

His hands flew up and locked around her waist. He lifted her up, holding her easily before he dropped her right into the middle of the bed. Then he was on top of her, hands moving to either side of her body, his powerful legs between her spread thighs as he crouched over her.

What is happening? What is happening? Things had gotten out of control in an instant. All because she'd said her orgasms were *fine*. And now he was between her legs. Looking all sexy and tough and like he truly wanted to eat her alive.

Her sex quivered. *Oh.* "F-forty-eight hours haven't passed yet." The only thing she could think to say. Her heart raced. And a heavy ache grew deep inside of her.

"I'm not fucking you, not with my dick, anyway. I'm putting my mouth on you."

She stopped breathing.

"My tongue is going *in* you."

You have to breathe, Lily. In and out. Breathe.

"Fingers and tongue, and I am going to do nothing but give you pleasure. Don't you want that, Lily? Pleasure just for you? Don't you want to let go and explode into a million pieces as you forget everything else and just let the orgasm take you?"

She would love that. For a time, to just know pleasure? Yes. Yes. *Yes, yes, yes.*

But it had never happened that way for her. Already, her hands were flying up and curling around his powerful arms. Unease, uncertainty, filled her. "That won't happen." Not for her. And maybe *fine* had been a stretch. Because she didn't always come with her lovers.

She'd had sex two times with Gage. But...both times...

I was too tense. He was frantic and hungry, and I wasn't there. I couldn't be there.

"You've been fucking the wrong men." A flat and brutal assertion. "The problem is now corrected. You're with the right man. A man who knows exactly how you need to be fucked. *Trust me.*"

Her gaze collided with his.

Pleasure...oh, the tempting promise of pleasure. His mouth on her. That wicked tongue of his, stroking her. Slowly, she nodded.

His dimples flashed. "Focus only on me."

She was too aware of her racing heart. Of the mad chorus of thoughts rolling in her head. *I won't be able to come for him. He'll get frustrated. He'll get impatient. He won't enjoy me.*

"Where do you want my hands, sweets?"

They weren't on her. They were beside her, pushing into the mattress.

"Where do you want them? Say it. Tell me."

"I want..." Why was this so hard? "Take off my pants." She'd already kicked off her shoes on her own.

He nodded. "Done." He eased back. His hand went to

her waist, and he unbuttoned the pants. Unzipped them. Slowly pulled them down over her hips and her legs and then he tossed them on the floor.

She wet her lips.

He was staring at the black panties she wore. He crouched between her legs—legs she'd spread wide. Maybe she'd even just spread them a bit wider. She waited for him to touch her.

He didn't.

"Talk to me," he ordered. "Where do you want my fingers?"

She closed her eyes. Maybe it would be easier if she didn't stare at him directly. "In me." Husky.

"Your wish is my command." His fingers slid over the crotch of her panties, and Lily hissed out a sharp breath.

Then those nimble fingers of his were darting under the edge of her panties. Rubbing over her clit, and she arched toward him, helpless. The spike of pleasure she felt shocked her. She bit her lower lip to hold back a moan when one long finger pressed into her. One, then another.

"Aw, Lily. You're so tight. But it's been a while, hasn't it? Because you were waiting for me."

No, no, she hadn't been waiting for him. She'd just been —*no one else understood.* She'd been tired of lovers who—

"Talk to me."

Her eyes opened.

His thumb pressed against her clit. Rubbed. "Tell me that you want me to lick you."

"I want..." *Say it.* "I want you to lick me."

His hand pulled back immediately. She arched, missing his touch, hating that he'd pulled back when she was enjoying the feel of his fingers against her.

Fabric tore. Ripped. Her panties? She craned to look down, now wanting to see him. Needing to see him.

"Not sorry at all about that." He tossed the scrap that had been her panties to the floor. His warm hands pressed to the inside of her thighs, and he slowly pushed them apart even more. "Watch me lick you." His head lowered.

His mouth got closer and closer and her breath heaved out because this was...he was...

His mouth touched her. A soft kiss.

She grabbed for the covers.

Because...

He stopped being so careful.

He began to lick her. To taste her. Demanding. Taking her over and over with his tongue. Tongue, lips. Tasting and licking and taking, and one hand left her thigh so that he could push his fingers into her as he took and took and licked her clit like he was maddened. Desperate and greedy and the emotions and needs surging through her were so strong that they scared her.

Can't let go. Can't.

"You can." His breath blew against her clit. "You can come for me, can't you, sweets? You can come against my mouth. You can come against my tongue." He licked her again. Again. He growled, and she *felt* the savage sound in her core. "You can come with my tongue in you." And his tongue was inside, replacing his fingers. Licking her. Lapping her up greedily before swiping back and sliding over her clit.

Her hips surged up toward him. Yet even as her hips slammed her toward his face and that wicked, wicked mouth, her hands flew down to push against his shoulders. To push him back.

She never wanted him to stop.

She wanted to stop herself.

She needed, and she feared, and if she let go, she'd be too vulnerable. Too exposed.

"Oh, my sweets, are you focusing on the way it feels when my tongue licks you?" He licked her again. That deep, dark voice pulled her. Compelled her. "On the way it feels when my fingers fuck you?" They were fucking her. In and out. In and out. Even as he licked and took and controlled her.

Control.

She didn't have control. It was gone. He had it all. He was working her body and controlling her and there was—

"You're going to come for me," he told her. "You're going to come hard against my mouth. Grind that sweet pussy against me."

She was grinding against him. Helplessly. Eagerly. She couldn't stop.

She didn't push at his shoulders. She clutched them. Drew him closer. Her nails bit into his skin. Her head tipped back against the pillow.

He was sucking her clit now. Sucking her even as those skillful fingers drove into her.

"I'm going to taste you when you come." A fierce promise from Atlas. "I'll taste everything. Every single drop—"

She shattered. No other word for it. Lily was shattering as she looked down at him between her thighs. Taking and tasting, and she shuddered because he was so powerful and strong and so focused on *her*. Licking. Stroking. Claiming.

She could not hold back the orgasm. It just exploded through her. Surging through every cell of her body. Detonating through her. So much pleasure that she could barely breathe. The bedroom seemed to dim. To spin. She arched and cried out, the sound of her own release shocking to her ears.

He licked her again. Kept using his mouth as she rode out the wave of release. Endless. That was how it felt. Not some brief flash of pleasure. Not a little pop that was gone before she even realized it happened. This was so much more.

This was...

Soul deep. Body wrenching. The kind of pleasure she'd dreamed of having.

The perfect release.

Her breathing slowed. Trembles still shook her body. His head lifted. Atlas licked his lips, as if he had to have one more taste of her, and he was determined to savor every drop.

She held his stare as reality came back. A reality where she'd just come harder than she ever had thought possible, and he was still fully dressed. Between her thighs. Her blouse was still on. Her bra.

Her panties were ripped and tossed somewhere.

And she didn't even care about them.

He began to rise. He eased back, but his gaze darted between her legs. "So fucking pretty."

Was she supposed to say thank you? Thank you for the best orgasm ever?

He climbed off the bed. She turned toward him, aware that she could feel aftershocks inside, little quivers that sent pulses of pleasure careening through her. She expected him to strip. To toss off his shirt. Ditch his boots and the black pants and to come and fuck her.

Forget their forty-eight hours. She wanted *more.*

But he...

Took a step away from the bed. "That's a taste, Lily. *My* taste."

"Atlas..."

"Forty-eight hours. You need to make up your mind fully in that time."

She'd just come against his mouth. If that didn't say she'd made up her mind and was ready to fuck, what did?

"Because when my dick gets in you, I am not going to give you up. I will be possessive. I will be jealous. I will be a total bastard when it comes to you because you will be *mine*." He reached out. Caught her hand. The engagement ring flashed. "I think you already are mine. I feel it in my bones." But he let her go.

She sat up. Pulled the blouse down to cover the V between her legs. "You didn't come."

"No, I didn't, though it was a damn near thing. Not like I want to come in my pants at this age." Those incredible eyes of his shot blue fire at her. "I'll come in you. The clock is ticking down on that."

She reached out the hand that he'd just released. Her fingers pressed right over the top of his belt. "I could taste you." He was clearly skilled at oral sex, and she'd never tried it. She should probably be up front about that lack of experience. "I've never gone down on a man, so you'll have to show me what you like."

A deep, hard *snarl*.

Her eyes widened.

"Lily, I am trying not to fuck you into oblivion. But you seem determined to push...My control will only last so long." An inhale. "Why no one else? You let them fuck your pussy but not your mouth?"

She flinched. Her hand dropped.

His hands curled around her shoulders. "I am a jealous

bastard. Be warned on that. *Why didn't you put your mouth—*"

"Because the fucks were fast and in the dark. Because I didn't show them my scars."

He frowned. Glanced down at her. "You...kept your shirt on. When I was tasting you...you kept your shirt on."

She had. She pulled the blouse lower.

"You stripped for me before."

Yes, she was aware of what she'd done. "You think I don't know that I've got issues?"

The faint lines near his eyes deepened. "*You have me.* Know that. Fuck the issues." His hand flew out to curl around hers as she held the shirt as a cover. "You don't want to be vulnerable. You don't want to be weak. You don't want to—"

"I don't want to explain to a lover that a murderer tried to cut me open, and in return, I nearly killed him. I was slitting his throat, in the process of cutting him from ear to ear with that stupid shiv, when the *three* guards finally hauled me off him." There. Dark. Bitter. Twisted truth.

And Atlas smiled at her. Those perfect dimples. He took her hand, and he brought it back to him. He raised his shirt, and he put her fingers against the scars that marked him.

"Landon Russell was far more dangerous than most people believed. I found him in the fucking woods shortly after the car wreck where he killed that mom and her kid, but that sonofabitch was ready for me. Furious that I'd let him go from his job, said it was my fault that everything was falling apart in his life. He drove a needle into me when I told him that he should turn himself over to the police. Fucking drugged me with some damn BS sedative and then he was driving a knife into me. Again and again."

Horror rolled through her.

"He should have given me a stronger drug." Casual. "Because it wore off as he was hacking at me. I took the knife. I slit his throat. I stabbed him in the heart. Then I left him for the animals. Figured they would take care of the sonofabitch's dead body. And they did. By the time the bastard was found, he was little more than bones."

"Atlas..."

"I really don't like needles. See, I had a run-in with another prick long ago who liked needles. Really turned me off them. Call me crazy, but I don't like it when sonsofbitches drive needles into my skin and try to pump me full of drugs."

She felt frozen. "Who—who was the other attacker?"

"Don't you know?"

She had a suspicion, yes. Because there was someone in his past who'd *died* of a drug overdose. "Bryan Mathers."

"Ding, ding. Right answer. My stupid prick of a college roommate." Anger hardened his face. "He was a total asshole, just so you know. Rumors had circulated about him, about him getting rough with girls, hurting them. He always denied the stories. Somehow, the accusations vanished. Power has a way of doing that, making trouble vanish."

"You have a great deal of power now." Something that was obvious.

"Yeah, I do. Once I was nothing. I'll never go back to that."

Not he'd *had* nothing, but *I was nothing.* "Not true."

His stare glittered.

"You've never been nothing, Atlas."

"Ah, sweets, you didn't see the way I was thrown away as a child."

Tears burned in her eyes. "You were never *nothing.*"

The blue of his gaze just electrified all the more. "I came back that last night, back to my college dorm, just to pick up some books I'd forgotten, and the bastard roommate I'd always hated was on top of a terrified redhead. He had his hand clamped over her mouth so she couldn't scream. Tears were pouring down her face." His right hand fisted, then released. "I yanked him off her. Told her to run the hell out of there. He was furious with me. Saying he was going to end me. The prick grabbed his fucking needle, and he came at me with it. I just took it from him. Snatched it right out of his damn hand, and, without even thinking about it, I shoved it into his neck."

"Atlas..."

"I had no idea what was in the needle. Didn't know how strong it was. I also didn't go get any help for him. I watched him fall. Then I got my books, and I walked out. By the time anyone found him, I was long gone from the campus. Always knew the girl wasn't going to tell anyone she saw me. She was far too glad that Bryan was dead."

He'd just confessed to two murders. After giving her the best orgasm of her life, he'd casually confessed to two *murders*. No, no. She shook her head. Not murder. Self-defense. He'd been attacked first in each instance.

He'd struck back.

"Doesn't make it better, though, does it?" He leaned down, putting his forehead against hers. "Oh, my Lily, I can practically see the wheels spinning in that beautiful mind of yours. Are you trying to excuse what I did? Justify it? I do that, you see. Justify it to myself so I can say I'm not like him. If they strike first, then I am fighting back. Maybe that way, if I am ever caught, Theodora can have a defense ready for me. Justifiable homicide." His head rose. His lips feathered over her brow. "I always let them have the first strike."

Is that why you were taken in the parking lot? You were letting that perp strike first?

"And then I end them," Atlas told her.

A shudder worked over her body.

His mouth moved—he pressed his lips to hers. "Is that revulsion?" Atlas asked her.

No, it wasn't. Should it have been? Because no part of her felt revulsion for Atlas. *You were never nothing.*

Another soft kiss. "This is why you have forty-eight hours. So you will know me completely. So you choose, understanding what you will get from me. What I am." Then he let her go. Paced away from her. He turned and positioned himself at the foot of the bed. "This is the part where you can grab the phone on that nightstand and call your annoying ex. You can tell Gage Emerick that I confessed all to you. You can take me down."

She did not reach for the phone.

"Or you can climb back in bed. You can pull the covers up over your head. You can pretend I gave you a great orgasm and that I said nothing after that amazing event. You can sleep, and this can be a dream."

She kept her stare on him. *Amazing, huh?* Yes, though, it had been. She still quivered.

"Or..." Atlas's deep voice rumbled, "you can accept me and all the dark parts that I have. Parts that I *swear* will never hurt you. Because I will not be like him, Lily. I will never be like my father. I have the urges inside me, the ones that you talked about before, the ones that rise and want to consume you, but I don't hurt the helpless. Not ever. I go after those who are coming for me. Those bastards? They'd hurt others. They'd given pain to women. Kids. They have killed. They are the ones who deserve the hell I bring." A slow exhale. "Does that make it all right? Probably not. But I don't really give a shit. It's who I am. What I do." He brought his hand to his lips. "Just so you know, you tasted delicious."

Her heart was drumming too hard, the sound echoing too loudly in her ears.

"Good night, Lily." He turned away. Walked for the door. Just dropped his bombshell and gave her a body-shaking orgasm and let the door shut softly behind him.

She stayed in place for all of five seconds. Then she was grabbing her discarded pants. Yanking them on. Toeing into her flats and tearing off after him. When she opened her door, he was already halfway down the stairs. "Atlas!" She raced to the top of the stairs.

He turned to look back at her. *Up* at her.

"Where are you going?" Lily asked him. Why hadn't he just gone into the bedroom right beside hers? *He was fully dressed. He always intended to leave the house.*

"You don't want to know."

"I do." He'd given her three choices. Turn him over to the Feds. Pull the cover over her head and pretend she hadn't heard his confession. Or accept him.

"Fine. Since I've decided to refuse you nothing..."

"*When* did you decide that?"

"Ah, Lily, it's what an all-access pass means."

No, that was not what it meant.

"I'm going to break into Detective Benedict Swain's house."

Her jaw dropped.

"I want to make sure there is nothing there that can bite me in the ass."

Okay. She forced her mouth to close. No sense continuing to gape at him.

"You don't want to commit a B&E with me." A half-smile. One dimple. "Go back to bed. Have sweet dreams."

Not happening. "I told you before, I tend to have nightmares." She crept down two steps. "Are you sure a B&E is wise?" It did not feel wise.

"Absolutely not. It's probably very unwise. But don't worry, I won't get caught. Not like it's my first time."

No, she doubted that it was. "Then I'll bow to your expertise." She eased down a few more steps.

He climbed up to meet her. "Lily..."

Her chin notched up. "Did I ever tell you about the time *I* killed a man?"

Atlas stiffened.

"No? Oh, that's right. I haven't told anyone. Not a single soul. Though I am going to tell you." She was. She was finally going to confess. To Atlas. But... "*After* we commit a felony together. Crimes are the ties that bind, aren't they? So let's go break into Benedict's house."

Chapter Sixteen

OUTSIDE THE LAST DROP BAR
  Shreveport, Louisiana

MEN WERE IDIOTS. Tonya Johnson had learned that fact long ago. Flash plenty of leg at them, let them see the curve of a boob, and they'd be helpless. So it was an easy enough matter to convince the fancy businessman to step into the dark alley behind the bar with her. All she had to do was flirt a bit. Bat her eyes. Rub one finger down between her breasts and the V of her shirt...let him see just a little bit of side boob.

He was practically drooling.

So he eagerly rushed outside with her when she made the suggestion for them to go enjoy a quieter scene. He kissed her up against the dirty, exterior wall of the bar. His hands ran all over her. And her hands ran all over him, too. Into his coat pocket. To nimbly open his wallet so that she could slide out the cash he'd been flashing around while buying drinks.

While he was panting in her ear and telling her how beautiful she was, she slipped off his watch. Tucked it in her bag. Oh, and those shiny cufflinks? The ones that looked like real gold? She took them, too.

"You are gorgeous," he was telling her, breath hot.

She rolled her eyes. What else could she snag from the guy? Tonya thought she'd gotten everything she needed. Time was ticking, and her partner needed to show his ass up. Not like she was going to actually screw this idiot even as his dick shoved against her.

"I have a hotel room," he said.

Yeah, because she knew he was only in town for a few days. *Important business.* That was what he'd bragged to her about.

Like she gave a damn about his business.

"I'd really prefer to kill you there instead of here."

Wait...

Tonya brought her hands between them. She started to shove the asshole away from her, then realized she must have misunderstood him. He'd probably said, *"I'd really prefer to kiss you there instead of here."* Kiss. Not kill. But he was all panty and raspy, so she'd misunderstood. "Oh, sugar, you can do far more than kiss me."

His head lifted. He stared down at her, his features mostly in shadow. There was barely any light in that alley. But she'd gotten a good look at him inside The Last Drop. A handsome man. She'd thought so when she first saw him enter the crowded bar. And he'd come straight to her as she tended bar. Hadn't been interested in the women all around him. Women in their expensive clothes. Women with their own jewels dripping from their skin. Oh, no, he'd been focused on Tonya.

So she'd known that she could work her magic.

The bouncer knew the routine. They'd developed it months ago. They worked it with an idiot who got too flirty with her or with some of their drunker patrons. In an ideal world, the mark was both an idiot *and* drunk. Made things so much easier.

She brought the target outside, made out with him and did her sleight of hand, and then, before the fool could push things too far, the bouncer appeared and scared the guy off. The fool would go running into the night, and she and Mico would split their winnings.

Something sharp pressed into her stomach. "I am going to do far more than kiss you."

Wait, wait, *wait*. That sharpness *hurt*. "Ouch!" Tonya cried. She tried to shove against him, but he was far stronger than she'd expected. Stronger and not nearly as drunk. "Stop it!"

He didn't. She looked down, horrified, as he drove a knife into her stomach. She screamed, but the sound was cut off when he slapped a gloved hand over her mouth.

He'd put the gloves on when they walked out of the bar. She'd thought it a bit odd because it wasn't particularly cold in Shreveport. But she hadn't really cared about the man's fashion choices. She'd just wanted his cash.

But...

This fucker just stabbed me. She lifted her knee, intent on shoving it into his groin as hard as she could.

He yanked the blade to the right. Then to the left. Pain blazed through her.

"I think she already has a scar to match this. But hers didn't go nearly as deep as yours."

Blood poured down her body. Nausea churned in her stomach, and she vomited, choking because his glove was in front of her mouth.

Where was Mico? The bouncer should have been there. Dammit. Where was...

The blade came at her again. Again.

"You've been very bad, Tonya."

She'd never given him her name. They hadn't gotten around to exchanging names. There had been no point in that.

"Guess that evil was just in your blood, huh?"

She hurt so much, and her shirt was soaked with blood.

The blade was deep in her stomach.

"Like father, like daughter..."

What?

"Hey, hey, asshole!" A shout. Mico? Mico?

"Get away from her!" Mico thundered.

The blade was gone. The bastard hurting her was gone. His steps thundered down the alley. And she was falling as her legs gave way. Her hands went to her stomach. So much blood, everywhere. All over her. Soaking her. Terrifying her.

"Sorry I was late," Mico was saying as he huffed and jogged closer. "Dumbass underage frat boys were trying to get inside, and I had to kick their asses down the street and... hey, hey, Tonya? Tonya, what's wrong?"

Like father, like daughter..."H-help..."

"Tonya!"

Her eyes shut, and the last thing she felt was her head hitting the cement of that alley when she fell.

Chapter Seventeen

"HAVE YOU EVER COMMITTED A B&E BEFORE?" ATLAS asked, truly curious because there were depths to Lily that kept surprising him. Delighting him, too.

They were in his parked SUV. One of the many vehicles that had waited in his garage. They were behind Benedict's home, not directly, but near the woods that marked the edge of the property. The better not to be seen.

"Once."

His brows rose at her confession. "Aren't we the naughty one?"

Her head turned toward him. "Sometimes I can be. But since my experience is so limited, let's just treat it like my first time, shall we? I'll follow your lead."

It will be your first time when you put that sweet mouth around my dick. His hands tightened around the steering wheel. Now was not the time to think about her mouth and his dick. Or to think about how fantastic she'd tasted. Or the way she'd come when he'd had his lips and tongue on her.

She'd broken apart beneath him. Shattered and

trembled and all he'd wanted to do was get her to come over and over again.

Definitely on his to-do list.

After the break-in. Work could be such a pain in the ass.

"Atlas?" Lily prompted.

"I've got a bit of experience in this area," he allowed. And by "a bit," well, he meant that he'd been breaking into places he shouldn't be in since he was a teen.

"I hate to be the rain on your parade," she began.

"I enjoy the rain."

"Me, too." She peered through the passenger side window. "But don't you think it will look highly suspicious if you and I are caught here? And won't it basically destroy your reputation if the world finds out you break into other people's homes when the mood strikes you?" Such a very polite tone.

She hadn't been polite when she'd been coming for him. She'd been fierce and hot, and she'd finally let go of her control. He liked uncontrolled Lily.

He was afraid though, that she was scared of uncontrolled Lily. *You fear yourself, don't you, sweets? What you will become?*

It also seemed she feared what would happen to him, if the world learned the truth about who Atlas truly was. He could put her mind at ease. "I've never been particularly worried about my reputation. Besides, when you have as much money as I do, you can buy forgiveness for a lot of things."

"That's...an asshole thing to say."

"Guilty." He forced himself to ease the grip on the wheel. "You should know, though, that I don't intend to get caught. If I thought there was any chance of being caught, I wouldn't have brought you along with me." This part, she needed to fully understand. "I won't jeopardize you." Not ever.

"And how are you so confident?"

"Because the annoying detective..." The dead detective. "He used a security system that was created by my company. I have a back door into it." He also literally had a key to the detective's place, an easy enough item to obtain. "His only neighbors on this dark stretch of road have been in Europe for the last week. They will stay in Europe for two more weeks. There are no patrols, no cops sweeping this area. I suspect your Fed will be here to search tomorrow at an appropriate hour, but for now, the place is all ours. Though, uh, do open the glove box and put on gloves, if you don't mind. No sense advertising our presence." He already had on leather gloves. He'd pulled them on before getting into the vehicle.

"My prints will already be in his house."

His eyes narrowed on her.

"You don't need to get so tense, Atlas."

Not like it was something he could help.

"I wasn't selling you out to him," Lily continued. "Benedict had some research that he wanted me to see, so I came here one night for dinner."

The research was BS. "He wanted to fuck you."

"Perhaps, but that did not happen." A delicate clearing of her throat. "But since I have been here before, I know exactly where to look for the material that might interest you—you *are* looking for additional background intel he'd gathered on you, yes? Intel that was not kept at the police station. You're searching for it because you want to see how many crimes he'd tried to link to you? How much he knew about you?"

He'd confessed to killing two men, just told Lily the

brutal truth. And she was still with him. She hadn't run away, and she hadn't reached for the phone in order to report him to her Fed ex. His instinct to trust her had been dead on target. "I don't strike first." Why did he feel compelled to keep offering her up chunks of his blood-stained soul? "I never have hurt an innocent. They all came at me, Lily. They tried to kill me." But he'd known what they intended. He'd known what they were. Had he set traps for some over the years? Yes.

"I didn't strike first, either," she whispered.

Lily, are you going to tell me about your kill?

"Okay, we should go. In and out, right?" She grabbed gloves. "I'll follow your lead."

He took out his phone. With a few taps, he disabled the security at the ranch-style house. Made sure the cameras went offline. A camera at the front door. A camera at the back door. Then he led the way to the rear of the house. A quiet, unassuming home. The detective had lived there alone for two years.

He put the key in the lock. Opened the door. Stepped inside.

All the blinds were drawn, he'd noticed that as he approached. *No one can see in.* His gloved hand hit the light switch.

And he found chaos. The same chaos that he'd seen at Lily's place, only the destruction at Benedict's wasn't limited to one room. Everywhere he looked—*smashed, destroyed, slashed.*

Lily bumped against him. "Atlas?"

He hadn't reviewed the security feeds from the house. But he sure as hell *would* be reviewing them all, ASAP. If the intruder had come in via a side window, though, the person wouldn't have been caught on the two cameras at the doors.

Obviously, the perp had gotten in without setting off the alarm. He'd just needed to disengage the system. Something any good thief could do. *But this doesn't look like theft. This looks—*

"This is bad," she said.

Yeah, it was.

She darted away from him, and he threw out his hand, grabbing her wrist automatically. When she hissed out a breath, he realized that he'd curled his finger around her bruised wrist, and he immediately eased his grip. "Stay with me."

A nod. "I was just..." Her voice was whisper soft. "The files that Benedict had were in the room to the right."

He went first because if there was a threat waiting, he'd face it. He had a gun tucked into the waistband of his pants. He didn't think she'd even seen him grab it from beneath the driver's seat. He'd grabbed it while she'd been busy putting on her gloves.

But there was no threat waiting. Just like everywhere else in the house, the blinds were drawn in the room Lily had indicated. He turned on a lamp, and the pool of light showed more destruction in what appeared to be a small office. Empty files. A smashed desktop computer. A shredder that had overflowed, and its thin strips of paper had been littered across the floor. A wide, brown cork board hung askew on the wall beside the desk, half torn papers still on it, as if someone had ripped them away.

He eyed the board with vague interest. "Guessing that was his crime board, huh? And was I prominently featured on it?"

"That board wasn't up when I was here before." A soft reply. She pulled open a drawer in a black filing cabinet. The drawer screeched. She peered in the drawer. So did he. No files inside. "Someone took everything." Lily's voice held worry.

Atlas was betting that *someone* hadn't been the friendly local cops. They would have no need for such destruction. "Let's get out of here, now."

"You think...do you think there could be *another bomb?*"

Only if the killer had anticipated that he and Lily would come to that place. And as Lily had said, few would expect him to commit a B&E personally. No, if anything, people would figure that he would send his team to do the dirty work for him. His security personnel.

But there were just some things you liked to handle yourself.

Without another word, he took Lily's hand. Turned off all the lights. They left the house, didn't look back. Tension knifed through him as they used the shadows and the darkness to cover their steps and then they were back at the SUV. He put her in the vehicle first. Atlas shut the door on the passenger side before he stalked around to the driver's side and entered the vehicle.

Quickly, he pulled out his phone and reset the cameras at Benedict's place. He turned the security system back on.

Lily pulled off her gloves and stuffed them into the glove box while Atlas cranked the ride. He did not turn on the SUV's lights, not until they were a bit away from the house. The silence in the SUV was intense.

They traveled a bit more down the road.

And a pair of headlights flashed on behind them.

Lily inhaled and flipped around. "Oh, no, is it—"

"It's Desmond. The guy always has my back." He

forced his jaw to unclench. "I told you before, you would have an army guarding you."

She turned to face the front of the vehicle.

"I mean it, Lily. I will keep you safe."

Her breath shuddered out. "*I'm not worried about myself.* I'm worried about you. You're the target, don't you see that? He's trying to destroy *you.* He has my files. He has Benedict's files. He set the trap with the bomb because he wanted to take out your guards. Your team. Your *friend* Desmond. He knew Desmond would be the first one in the door to save you. Just like Desmond has your back right now. I don't..." Lily stopped.

He kept driving. "Don't leave me in suspense." *Come on, tell me more.* Atlas needed her to keep talking. "You're the expert on killers. You're the one with the degree that lets you get in their minds. Tell me more."

"I think the other kills in the area were practice runs." Softer. "I think he was working up to his real target. And I think that real target is you. I think he wants to punish you..."

They'd reached a red light. Atlas angled his head toward her. He found Lily staring straight back at him.

"He wants to destroy everything that you have. Eliminate the people closest to you. He wants to take everything away, and when nothing is left...that's when he plans the end for you."

His teeth had clenched. With an effort, he eased the tension in his jaw. "I could have died in the blast at that damn cabin, Lily."

"I thought so, too...but now I wonder..." Her voice turned considering. "I wonder if putting us in the basement was part of the plan."

Obviously, it had been part of the plan. *The better to hold us captive.*

Only he didn't think that was what Lily meant.

She confirmed his suspicions when she added, "I think we need to see that crime scene. We need to see if the basement was destroyed or if somehow, it was saved. Because you were right when you once asked me if I knew how to set bombs. I know a great deal about them, thanks to Richard Hawthorne."

The bomber she'd interviewed. Lily and her killers.

"The thing about Richard is that he always directed his explosions. He could stand ten feet behind them, he could watch the destruction, and he would never get hit. He liked to be up close, you see. He liked to feel the heat on his skin but never get burned."

The light had changed. He saw it from the corner of his eye. His head turned toward the front, and he advanced, but he felt Lily's stare on him.

"Richard told me that it was all about the positioning. That if he wanted, he could have an impact that would take out one room of a house but leave everything else untouched."

Sounded to him like Richard had been incredibly cooperative with Lily. *Do you always get your killers to reveal all their secrets to you?* Atlas had certainly revealed all with her, very, very quickly.

Voice still musing, she noted, "The explosion at the cabin looked so big. I thought for certain the whole place was engulfed, but...what if that fire didn't touch the basement?"

"It destroyed everything there, Lily." He could still see the high flames in his mind. "It was so hot the firefighters couldn't even get close. The place was nearly obliterated."

"Appearances can be deceiving. I think we should get back to that cabin."

Yeah, they damn well would be going back. If she had a hunch, an instinct—whatever, he'd listen to her. They'd follow her lead. But not that night. He wasn't going to the scene of their near deaths then. He was taking her home. Locking her inside his house.

Because if she was right...if the killer truly wanted to punish him by taking away the people close to him...

Fuck me. I thought telling the world that she was my fiancée would keep her safe. That she'd be under my protection. Instead, I might have just put an even bigger target on her.

"Don't even think about taking back my ring," Lily said, as if reading his mind. He was starting to wonder if the woman could do just that. "We're a team, remember? We will take him down together."

"He's not going to kill you, Lily." *I won't let him.* "If you leave me, if you go far away, you could be safe. You haven't committed any crimes that he thinks you need to be punished for—"

"You don't think murder is something that requires punishment?" A casual question, but tension beat in her words. "Because most people do. And you see, I murdered a man once upon a time. David Warren. The name that Gage tossed out as a threat to me? I killed him. I killed David Warren. I watched him fight for survival in his last minutes, and I stood there, and I did nothing. I am my mother's daughter. I am as cold and uncaring. And I smiled when he died."

He could not speak.

"But, by all means, please continue thinking that I am some sweet, innocent person who needs protecting. When people think that about me, they underestimate me at their own peril."

Chapter Eighteen

SHE'D CONFESSED TO MURDER. CONFESSED. SHE'D never even told her mother what she did, though Lily knew that her mother certainly suspected the truth.

I murdered a man. She'd smiled when he died. What kind of person did that?

The daughter of a serial killer. Someone who is just as screwed up on the inside as her mother and—

A knock on the guest room door. Because they were back at Atlas's estate. He'd driven with intent focus and very little talking after her confession. Once they'd arrived, all safe and sound, he'd vanished into his study with Desmond. Probably to start a thorough review of the video footage that she'd heard him talking about before that door closed—security footage of Benedict's house.

She'd gone upstairs because a shut door clearly told her she wasn't invited into the chat taking place in the study. And now, she'd closed her own door against him.

Maybe he'd take a hint and move on to his room.

I told you that I killed a man. You said nothing in response.

She'd kept that big confession secret for a very long time, and she'd expected...more, dammit.

Her gaze fell on the closed manila file on her nightstand. His NDA. Idly, she picked it up and began thumbing through the contents. She snorted at some of the stuff she read because no way could that stand up in court.

And...Her eyes narrowed on a particular line. *I will go to the grave before I reveal any secret that Lily Gallo shares with me.*

Definitely didn't sound legal. She swallowed. Not legal, but she did like the intent.

The knock came again. Harder.

"I'm asleep," she said, voice raised.

The door opened. "The hell you are."

She shrugged. She probably should have locked the door. Next time.

He'd yanked open the top two buttons on his dark shirt. His hair was disheveled, as if he'd run his fingers through it. His eyes were intense, extra bright, and that laser stare was locked and loaded on her.

"Finish your meeting?" Lily inquired sweetly as she shut the file and put it back down on the nightstand. "The one you did not invite me to attend?"

"Desmond and I are breaking the law."

She rolled her eyes. Then caught herself.

Lily, get controlled. Get focused. It was hard because... she still felt shattered on the inside. From the orgasm? From letting go? From walking into Benedict's house, knowing he was dead when she'd tried to get him to *leave the cabin?* Seeing all the destruction—seeing...

She drew in a deep breath. "I broke the law with you when we did our B&E." *And when I killed a man. Pretty sure that counts as breaking the law, too.*

"I had to give Desmond new orders."

"Orders you didn't want me to hear?"

He shrugged. "Thought you'd object."

Her stomach clenched. "You told him." That was the only thing that made sense. "You went to him, and you told him what I confessed to you."

He was on her. In a flash. Right in front of her, with his hands *on* her, curling around her shoulders. "I'll take your secrets to my grave. I will never turn on you. Never. But you did say things that caught my attention. See, when you talk, I listen. Intently. If Benedict had done the same, if he'd listened to you, he'd be breathing."

She flinched.

He let her go. "You are the priority. *My* priority. That's what I went over with Desmond first. If you and I should vanish, he finds you first. He gets you out of any dangerous situation...*first*. The team knows they will use any force necessary to protect you. You come before me. They needed to understand that, and, dammit, Lily, stop shaking your head at me. It's my order. I pay them. I can get them to do whatever I want."

She *was* shaking her head. Frantically. "I told you that *you* were the target! You! Not me. You are the primary target! Your team needs to be focused on securing *you!*"

"You said he wanted me to hurt. That he would take away the people close to me. You are the one closest to me."

"That's not true." He was so wrong. "Desmond is. He's like your brother. He has to be the one who matters most." They'd been friends for years.

"I have an engagement ring on your finger."

Yes, and she was very aware of the weight on her hand. "It's pretend."

"No, it's a damn fifty-thousand-dollar ring."

He'd given her a fifty-thousand-dollar ring? Her lips parted.

"You are the closest to me, Lily. You. Fuck, yes, Desmond is like my brother, and that was part of our talk, too. He needs to watch his fucking ass. To put a protective detail on himself. He knows the risks, and he also knows that if anything happens to you..." Atlas's gaze drifted over her face. "I will rip apart the world."

Her breath seemed to freeze in her throat. "Why?"

"Ah, Lily." His head tilted to the side. "You're so smart. So good at figuring out people. How about you tell me *why?"*

She wouldn't have asked the question if she knew the answer. "You don't love me."

"Because I can't love."

No. No. *"I* didn't say you couldn't love." She'd never said that. "You're the one who told me that you couldn't feel emotions. Or that you could shut them on and off at will." Such an interesting talent.

"I can't shut off things with you." Rasped. "I did try. Found out it didn't work so well."

"You just met me."

"Cute. Come on, don't you know? I've been stalking you. I thought that I knew all of your secrets. And, just so we're doing that whole honesty thing that you wanted between us, I already knew about David Warren. Actually, let me clarify, I knew he'd probably been murdered. Did not realize you'd done the deed yourself."

No one realized she'd done it. Though Gage certainly suspected the truth.

"Want to tell me why?" Atlas asked. "Why did you kill him?"

"My mother dated him."

He waited.

But she didn't say more.

"Ah, Lily. I'm sure there is more of a reason. I don't think you just kill the men your mother dates. She seems to do a good enough job of that herself."

Not in the case of David Warren. Magnolia had failed that job. With unfortunate results. "She...she found out that he wasn't the man she thought he was. It, um, doesn't do to disappoint Magnolia."

"So I've heard." His arms crossed over his chest. "How did he disappoint her?"

She looked down at her hands. "He snuck into my bedroom."

"The fucking sonofabitch." Low. Dark. Deadly.

Yes. David Warren had been a sonofabitch. "I was... eighteen. I'd just turned eighteen. My birthday had been a week ago. Magnolia—she'd baked a cake for me." God, that seemed a lifetime ago. "I woke up, and he was right over me. Standing there, watching me. And before I could scream, his hand flew out and slapped over my face. He covered my mouth and my nose. I-I couldn't breathe." That fear still grabbed her late at night. Waking up in the dark. Having a monster leap out at her.

When Atlas had been describing the scene in his dorm room, her muscles had locked down because parts of that terrible scene were so close to her own life.

Tears streaming down my cheeks. His hand over my mouth. Wishing for help to come...

"He...hurt you?" Again, that deadly tone that promised hell would come.

"He thought Magnolia was out of town. Thought I was alone at the house. That I would..." *Be helpless.* "People underestimate me." They always had. Their mistake.

David's mistake. "I fought him. I grabbed my bedside lamp." She flexed her fingers, remembering how she'd desperately stretched her hand to reach it. "I smashed it into his head. I got away from him. I ran like hell. Raced to the neighbor's house." She'd fled down the sidewalk in her nightgown and with bare feet. Her fist had pounded and pounded into Ms. Betty's front door. "I stayed there all night."

"You called the cops."

Bitter laughter slid from her.

His eyelashes flickered. "I will learn what your real laughter sounds like."

She frowned. Those words—they'd sure seemed like a vow to her. "That will be interesting," she told him. "I'd like to learn what it sounds like, too."

He growled.

"I-I didn't call the cops. Calling the cops was something that my mother would never, ever want me to do."

"You knew what *she* was doing. You knew she was a killer."

"I'd found her diary." Soft. So soft. Why were her words so soft? No one was there who would overhear them. "I'd found it a week before, and I knew what she had been doing. And, no, I didn't take that diary to the police. I hid it." The way she still hid it. It was currently tucked under her mattress. "She actually kept a lot of diaries. She was always jotting things down. One book was filled with places that Magnolia had visited and places she *wanted* to see. One was filled with her dreams. One was..." The one currently hidden under Lily's mattress in the guest bedroom. "One was dark." So very dark. "I knew what she'd done, and I couldn't go to the police because—what if they learned the truth? What if they took her away? Locked her up? She was my mother." *I loved my mother.*

Even though Magnolia had done terrible things. *Even though she killed my father.* How could she love Magnolia in spite of that? How could she love her and hate her at the same time?

I do. I just do...

"You told Magnolia what he'd done to you."

Yes. She had. "The next morning. See, my elderly neighbor, Ms. Betty just thought I'd had a nightmare. Ms. Betty told my mother I was scared. That I'd probably watched a horror movie that gave me bad dreams. But my mother knew something was wrong. Even when we got home and I discovered the mess had been cleaned up in my bedroom, even when David smiled at her and told her how much he'd missed her and that he'd been so worried when he couldn't find me in the house...she knew."

"What did Magnolia do?"

"She told him to get the hell out. He left. Didn't even put up a fight. She told me...even as the door shut behind him, that he wouldn't be a problem again. She'd see to it."

"She was going to kill him."

Her eyes closed. "I begged her not to do it. Begged her not to hurt anyone. She told me to calm down. That it was okay." *Mother knows best, my Lily. Now, calm down. Come into the kitchen. I'll make you breakfast and a nice cup of tea. You'll relax and everything will be okay.*

"Lily?"

Her eyes opened. "She cooked for me. I ate her food with no hesitation. I drank the tea with warm honey in it *with no hesitation.* Because this was my mother, and despite what I had learned, I believed with all of me that I was the one person she would never hurt. She loved me."

His lips pressed together.

"Then I was on the floor. I was vomiting. I could feel

my throat burning. My chest burning. My whole body burning as I heaved and struggled, and I knew I was dying."

"*Poison.*"

Yes. "She rushed me to the hospital. They pumped my stomach...I don't even know how many times. The doctors knew I'd been poisoned. They told the cops. The cops got a search warrant. They found the poison at our house. They connected the dots to my mother's previous lovers... husbands..." They'd connected it all. "Everything spiraled when she rushed me to the hospital. When she chose to save *me*. Because I could have died there, in our kitchen, and she could have covered it up. She was good enough with crime scenes that she could have concealed everything."

"But she didn't. She got you help instead."

Lily nodded.

"She loved you."

Yes. "So she saved me, but she got locked away. David Warren went on the press circuit to talk about how lucky he was to have escaped the Poison Princess." Her mother's stupid nickname in the media. "I got better." She hated the memories of that sterile hospital room. The beeping machines. During that time, Lily had come far, far too close to death. *Organ failure.* It hadn't just been a simple matter of pumping her stomach. For days, she'd barely clung to life. But she had recovered. Bit by bit. "I was in the courtroom every single day during her trial. I heard all of her crimes. Saw photos. Heard testimony. I witnessed every gory detail. And I saw my mother look back at me and smile." She had her mother's smile. Was that why she didn't smile very often? *No, no, I never smiled much. My mother used to tell me I was far too serious.* "The DA thought she messed up when she *accidentally* poisoned me. Others believed it was intentional. That she wanted to get rid of her daughter but had a last-minute attack of conscience so she rushed me to the hospital."

"You didn't believe that."

Certainly not. "My mother doesn't have a conscience."

He just watched her. No judgment on his face. Simply hearing. Understanding. Not looking for a way to turn her words against her. Gage had always been looking for a weakness, for something he could use.

Atlas simply waited. He didn't push.

So she told him what she'd told no other person. "My mother didn't poison me. She would never have put poison in my tea. I know that one thing with certainty." She had the proof in the diary that she treasured so much. The diary she would have to burn. The diary that... "David Warren did it."

"Sonofabitch."

"He'd realized what my mother was. Sometimes, I wonder if he knew all along. Some people are truly drawn to darkness. I believe I mentioned that to you before."

"Um, yeah, during our fun conversation with Dr. Owen at the hospital. Hybristophilia." A nod.

"I'm impressed you remember the term."

"I remember everything you say. You're important to me that way." A considering beat. "So David Warren was drawn to your mother because he liked the danger she represented."

"Sometimes, it is a case of like to like. Deviance to deviance."

"Is it?"

"When he understood that he was going to be her next target, I suspect he thought he'd outsmart her."

"And he poisoned you to frame her."

"Yes. She got locked away. He got a book deal." A shrug of one shoulder. "But I didn't get locked away. I was the poor, innocent victim after all. That is what everyone saw when they looked at me. How tragic, to nearly be killed by your murderous mother."

"You *were* a victim. His victim."

She had been a victim. She hadn't liked being one. "I was a victim until the night I slipped into his house. My other breaking and entering experience, by the way. I was a victim until I broke in, and I poured poison into his favorite bottle of whiskey. A very expensive bottle, by the way. There was only a little whiskey left at the bottom of the bottle because he'd been slowly sipping on it. Savoring it before bedtime each night. I knew his routine. I'd made it a point to know. I knew that he'd come in, he'd get the last of that whiskey, he'd drink it in his big chair...and he'd think he was the king of the world." He'd infuriated her. A man pretending to be a victim while he was as evil as they came. "I found other girls," Lily blurted that out. "Girls like me... girls he'd...*hurt* but they had been too afraid to come forward."

She'd gathered her intel. She'd learned every detail that she could about David Warren. Because there were some things you did that could never be taken back. Or never forgiven. "One of those girls was his own daughter. She lived in another state with her mother, and it took some convincing to get her to talk to me. But in the end, she did. She told me how much she wished he was dead."

Wish granted.

Lily was very conscious of each beat of her heart. "He was about to get married again. Did I mention that to you? No?"

Altas shook his head. "No."

"I'm jumping around. I apologize for that."

"Don't apologize for a single fucking thing to me."

That was…

"Be as you are, Lily. That's exactly how I want you. Apologize for nothing."

Her shoulders were tense. Her spine too straight. She just wanted to finish this story. Have it done. "So much time had passed. I'd gone to college. Met Sloane." *Finally had a friend.* "He was engaged. The wife-to-be had a daughter. Thirteen-year-old Taneisha. She had a great smile. Braces. Such a cute, happy kid. Kids should get to stay kids, don't you think?"

He swore. "Yeah, they fucking should."

"My middle name is Oleander."

"I know." Softer. Gentle.

"Oleander poisoning is usually diagnosed partially based on cardiovascular symptoms. The plant has cardiac glycosides." Did that sound too clinical? It felt too clinical.

He raised his brows. "Am I meeting Dr. Lily Gallo? Do tell me more about these cardiac glycosides. I'm fascinated." A beat. "By you."

"They, um, they can cause heart paralysis. I took that idea, heart paralysis, and I found something that would *definitely* get the job done. Not like I wanted to take chances, but I did want his heart to stop." The confession was scary to make. Chilling. And…freeing. "When he was on the floor, grabbing his chest, I walked out of the shadows. My mother had been in prison for over two years by this point. Two years for the circus of her trial to finally conclude. Then two years in prison. I was in my first year of med school. Being in med school allowed me access to all sorts of interesting drugs."

"Lily…"

"I waited. I found my moment. I found my method. And I killed the man who poisoned me."

Done. Confession made.

"His ex-wife and his daughter decided they wanted him cremated. Right away. They took care of the details. The ME ruled it a heart attack without even doing any blood work. No drug scans. Heart attacks happen, you know. There was no investigation. Why would there be? Who would want to kill him? Poison him? Who would even know how? Other than the Poison Princess, of course, and she was locked away. How could she hurt anyone when she was behind bars?"

I learned from my mother. No, I learned so much more than she understood.

Their gazes held. She'd told him everything, and her shoulders sagged as the weight drifted away. "You can walk out," she told him. "You know that I am as twisted as—"

"Me?" Atlas finished.

That hadn't been what she meant. "I don't need protecting."

"Yeah, I think you fucking do." A nod. "For the record, I'm glad he's dead."

"Why?"

"Because it saves me some effort." His dimples flashed at her. "Because know, sweets, *know* that if the bastard who poisoned you was still breathing, I would take great pleasure in eliminating him from this world."

A savage thing to say. Chilling.

But instead of being scared, warmth spread inside of her. "Gage suspected the truth," she admitted. "He asked too many questions, and he...I could see fear when he looked at me."

"Gage Emerick is an idiot. He was using you to profile

his cases and climb up the ranks at the Bureau. If he was afraid of anything, it was that others would find out that he was a poser."

Ah. Her head tipped toward him. "You've been doing your research on him."

"Yeah. I looked into anyone who was close to *you*. Like the good stalker I am. So I will tell you again, he was never worthy of you." A shrug. "I'm not, either, but I'll fight like hell for you. You see my darkness, and you aren't afraid of it. You see it, yet you're still standing right here."

Her hand rose. Pressed to his chest. Over his heart. "So are you."

"Tell me it's not about research, Lily. Tell me I'm not just some new experiment for you."

"I'm the experiment," she whispered back. "I'm something new in your life. A puzzle."

"No, you're not an experiment to me. You're an obsession."

Was that good? Bad? Both? "Obsessions are dangerous."

"Are you going to be dangerous to me?"

She shook her head. Hurting him was not her intent. "You're not an experiment, either."

"Tell me to walk away." A low, rough order.

But Lily shook her head once more. "Why would I do that?"

"Because it's the smart choice."

Was it?

"Tell me to get the fuck out of your bedroom."

She didn't speak a word.

"Tell me our forty-eight hours isn't up." Even harder. Even rougher. "Tell me to back the hell away. Tell me—"

"You're not afraid of me." That was what she told him.

"Actually, I think you might terrify me."

Shock rolled through her.

"You're the one person who will make me lose all control. I know it. The thing that has kept me sane, kept me *focused,* kept me from being like that bastard who gave up his fucking semen for me to be born—it's my control. It holds me back. It stops me from letting go and becoming a full-fledged monster."

Her hand remained against his chest. "That's not what stopped you." She'd wanted to find Atlas. To study him. To...understand him.

And she did.

She understood him better than she did herself.

"I don't want forty-eight hours." She didn't need that time.

A muscle jerked along his jaw.

"When I told you what I'd done, when we were in your SUV, you didn't say a word." This was so important. "Why not?"

"Because I disagreed with you. But that didn't seem like the time to argue." He looked down at the hand that pressed to chest. "This doesn't seem like it, either."

"Disagreed...*why?*" How?

"Sweets."

She always...secretly enjoyed it when he called her that. No one else had ever given her any sort of nickname or even used a term of endearment. Maybe it didn't mean anything to him, but it did to her.

"You will always be protected," Atlas vowed. "I won't underestimate you, no worries on that score, because I'm not an idiot. But you are not evil. You're not going to fly off the rails and hurt people. Even before you told me the rest of your story, I already knew the bastard would deserve what he had coming." He eased closer, his head bending over her. "And the answer to the *why* part on that is easy. I trust you. I can look at you, and I can see good. I can see innocence staring back at me even when you are so sure that your soul is all dark. Maybe that's what you needed all along, Lily. A mirror to stand before you. Well, here I am. Look into me."

A...mirror?

"Born from evil and sin, just like you. A child of a monster. I know what I am, and I know that when I look at you—you are so much more. I want to protect that more. I want to guard you from every threat." His jaw hardened. "I want you to be mine. I'm your broken mirror. Never going to reflect right back for you, not perfectly, but I am ready to cut the world to shreds if it means I can keep you safe."

Her hand was still over his heart. A bruised band around her wrist. A gleaming sapphire and diamond on her ring finger. "I'm not going to tell you to walk away. That is the last thing I want."

"Tell me—"

She knew exactly what to tell him. "I want you to fuck me, Atlas. Right here. Right now."

Chapter Nineteen

Like he had to be told twice.

Lily was in front of him, offering herself to him, and he wasn't going to turn away from her. But she had to understand what would happen next. "I won't walk away after I have you."

"I'm not asking you for any promises."

He had an engagement ring on her finger. How did you make a bigger promise than that? "I'm not talking pretend. This will be real. *We* will be real."

A little furrow appeared between her eyebrows.

"Can a psychopath love?" The question was pulled from him. It was something he'd often wondered about. He didn't believe his father had loved. Didn't think the twisted bastard had ever been capable of loving anyone or anything.

I will not be like him.

"Atlas—"

No. He didn't need an answer. Didn't want to hear one right then. He wanted Lily. She'd chosen him. She'd saved him. He'd tried to keep her away. He'd *ordered* her away, but she just came back. Dammit, Atlas had even gotten the guards at his business to escort her out. She'd come back, and she'd chosen *him*. Saved him.

His mouth swept down onto hers. Soft at first. Caressing. Almost worshipping because he understood that she was something incredibly special to him.

But softness didn't last. He'd been truthful when he said his control would not hold with her. He had to fuck her. To take her.

So the kiss became rougher. More demanding. He curled his hands around her waist, and he dragged her against him. Lifted her up because it was easier to take her mouth and savor her, and when her legs wrapped around his hips, he growled.

She was soft and warm. He was hard and hungry. His dick shoved against her as she rocked against his erection. Teasing and pushing him even more. Oh, such a mistake.

You didn't wave the red flag in front of the bull. Not unless you were ready for him to charge.

Yet he'd already learned so much about his Lily. So much. And the more he learned, the more of an expert he became at just how to handle her...

Lily had to experience pleasure with him. He'd be damned if she ever called his fucking just *fine*. She would need to scream. She would need to claw at him. She would need to shatter beneath him.

Then he'd take her.

He pulled his mouth from hers. She began to kiss his neck as he carried her to the bed. Her legs stayed locked around him, and every step had his dick pushing against her. She gripped his shoulders. He felt the bite of her teeth against his throat. A sensual nip.

Lust flooded through him. *"Lily."*

"Show me what you want. Tell me what you want."

Oh, easy. "You." Wide open. Taking him in deep. Moaning his name and begging for more. He lowered her on the bed. "Strip."

With hands that trembled, she did. He waited, needing her to do this part, to remove the clothing. To show him her scar. To bare herself to him.

She did.

The blouse hit the floor. She kicked away her shoes. Shimmied out of the pants. She crouched in the middle of the bed, wearing only a bra and bikini panties. Her hands pressed to the comforter on either side of her body. He could see her scar, the line that sliced across her stomach.

I would kill the bastard a thousand times for you. And laugh while he begged.

"Take off the bra," he told her even as he yanked off his own shirt and tossed it to the floor. He stripped off his clothes with rough hands, dropping the garments until he was before her just in his boxers.

She reached behind her. Arched her back, and the bra slid away as she unhooked it.

Fuck. She's pretty. She had such pretty, tight nipples. Thrusting toward him. Begging for his mouth. So he just had to take them.

"Flat on the bed, sweets."

She swallowed and lowered down onto the mattress. Her head went onto his pillow.

He climbed on top of her. But, carefully. He kept his body off hers. Not like he wanted to crush her with his weight.

"Are you afraid?" he asked.

She shook her head.

His mouth covered one breast. Licked and sucked the tight nipple.

She gasped and arched toward him.

He sucked harder. His hand snaked between them, going down to touch her through the silk of her panties. He rubbed her, and she was wet. Already wet, he could feel her heat. His fingers eased under the edge of those panties, the better to stroke *in* her, and damn, but she was tight. Tight and so hot, and she was going to feel fantastic when she came around his cock.

But Lily wasn't to that point, not yet. She was too tense. Her body not yielding fully.

"Lily, Lily, Lily," he chided. His control still held, for the moment. "Talk to me. Focus on *me*." He kissed his way to her other breast. Licked and sucked, then used the edge of his teeth.

She moaned.

And got wetter on his fingers.

Down, down he went, his mouth kissing her carefully as he explored her body.

"Atlas...just...just take me. I want you, now. Just come inside—"

His head lifted. "You're not ready."

"I am."

"No." Not for how hard he'd go in her. His mouth pressed to the line that sliced across the silky skin on her stomach. He hated that she'd been hurt. If he could, he would have taken away every moment of pain that Lily had ever felt.

Another kiss against her old wound. His head lifted before he prepared to—

A teardrop slid down her cheek.

"Lily?" Every muscle locked. "What am I doing wrong?"

Tears swam in her gaze. "No one has ever kissed my scar before."

She was crying over that? *Dammit.* But, "Sweets, I am going to kiss all of you. You belong to me."

Her head moved against the pillow. "Does that mean you belong to me?"

Ah... "Yes." He nodded. He did. He felt it. Deep inside. He'd never belonged to another person. No one had fucking wanted him to *belong*. Not any of those foster houses when he'd been a kid and he'd bounced around. Not any of the group homes where the counselors had not-so-secretly feared him. Not the women who'd been too eager to fuck him because they were drawn to his money.

Lily was different.

Did he belong to her? *Yes.*

"Has someone ever kissed your scars?" Lily asked.

He'd had too many lovers. Could barely remember them all. And he—

"I want to kiss your scars, Atlas. I want to kiss all of you."

His whole body jerked. *Do not come until you are inside of her. Do not come...*

But those tempting words from Lily were splintering his control.

"Please," she added in her ever-so-polite tone. Her body shifted. Her hands pushed gently against him. He realized he could probably refuse her nothing in this world. And when the woman was offering to take his dick in her mouth...

Hell, no, not gonna refuse.

So he ditched his boxers and spread out on the bed. Lily climbed over him. Began to kiss his chest. Softly. Tenderly. Hesitantly.

Her mouth pressed to his nipples. Kissed. Licked. Bit him lightly. Turned him the hell on even more.

Then...

Down.

Her soft lips brushed over his chest as she went down. A sensual press of her mouth. Gentle kisses against the old scars that he carried.

No, no. No one has ever kissed my scars. The others avoided them. Were they disgusted? Afraid? Not like I ever asked. Not like I ever cared.

No, they didn't kiss my scars.

But Lily did.

He'd kissed hers. She kissed his. Tender touches that took away pain that had marked them both for far too long.

Only Lily wasn't done.

She eased down his body, positioned herself between his legs. Braced one hand on each of his thighs before she lowered her mouth and put those soft, sexy lips around the head of his cock.

Fuck. He grabbed the bedding. Fisted it.

She took more of him in her mouth. Just an inch. She sucked. Licked. And then took more. Another inch.

He could hear the bedding tear in his grip.

Her head bobbed. She hadn't taken in much of him. One hand now gripped the base of his dick. Holding him. Guiding him. The other still pressed to his thigh as she braced herself. That hot, sweet mouth sucked him, pulled him in a bit deeper. Her movements were careful and slow. Torture and heaven all at the same time.

More. Deeper. She bobbed her head, licked her tongue over the head of his cock, brought her mouth to the tip, and kissed and licked and sucked before she took him in again—

He'd ripped off chunks of the bed covers. His hips flew

up, and his dick surged toward her mouth. She moaned around his dick. He looked down at her. His dick, in her mouth.

He could hear a thunder echoing in his ears. Pounding over and over. His heart? His body was too hard. Too rough. Too big. Need blasted through him. A savage lust that couldn't be contained, not any longer.

He needed her too much.

He let go of the torn bedding and grabbed for Lily. Even as he was grabbing for her, she was yanking off her panties and tossing them to the side. He hauled her up, pulling her over him. Her mouth met his. Her legs spread for him. She straddled him as she bent forward, and her tongue dipped into his mouth.

Fuck, fuck, fuck.

The way she was positioned...right there...

His hands slid between her legs. His cock probed at the entrance to her body. She was wet and warm and so hot, and the head of his cock thrust into her.

Just a bit...

Just a little...

A shudder rocked him.

Hot. Tight. Mine.

She rocked against him, taking in more.

His teeth snapped together.

"You're torturing me!" she cried.

"Never." He rolled them, fast, and pulled out of Lily.

"Atlas!"

His breath heaved. Too hard. Too fast. The thundering in his ears was even stronger. He needed to fuck her. To drive deep and claim her.

Bare. I was in her bare.

He couldn't do that. He climbed from the bed.

"Atlas?"

"Need a condom." Fuck, fuck, fuck.

He marched from the guest room. His hands were fisted, and his dick *hurt*. He wanted in her. Wanted to come far too badly. He made it to his room. He'd left the lamp on in his bedroom, and the soft light spilled toward him. Atlas was far too aware of the fast racing of her footsteps behind him.

Atlas grabbed a condom from the nightstand. When he'd gone into her room, he truly hadn't counted on fucking her. *Or I would have taken a damn condom in with me.*

The forty-eight hours had not been up but...

"Atlas?" Lily had followed him into his bedroom.

He tore open the packet. Rolled it on his dick even as he turned toward her.

She shut the bedroom door behind her. Stood there. Breasts gorgeous, nipples tight. Panties gone. Sex bare.

He took a step toward her. One. Another.

"What are you waiting for?" she asked.

He lunged for her. Pounced. A predator who'd finally gotten the prey he'd wanted all along. She reached for him eagerly, with open arms, with the gold gleaming in her eyes.

His hands curled around her waist. He lifted her up.

Her legs locked around his waist. His dick thrust into her. Again, just an inch, two...

He pinned her to the closed door.

Her eyes began to drift shut.

"*My name,*" he bit out. "*Look at me.*"

Her eyes flew open.

"You will be with me." *Every single moment.* He would not lose her. He knew what she wanted. What she needed.

He would be the only one to give it to her. "My name." One hand snaked between their bodies as he pinned her between him and the door. One hand gripped her waist. One went to mercilessly stroke her clit.

"At-Atlas…" Her eyes were wide. Her cheeks flushed.

"Fuck, yes."

"*Fuck me,*" she fired back.

He did. He drove into her. Pounded into her even as he worked her clit over and over. He kissed her, and he fucked her, and he was relentless. He drove deep, filling her, but he couldn't go in far enough. Not from that angle.

So he carried her away from the door. Lowered her onto the bed. Stood on the side of the big bed, and he hauled her legs over his shoulders. The better to plunge deeper into her. To fuck her harder. To open her completely so he could play all he wanted with her clit even as his dick slammed deep into her.

There was no holding back. Not from him. Not from her. He could see every inch of her. Every beautiful, delectable inch.

Mine.

Her hands grabbed onto his arms. Her nails dug into him.

He smiled and thrust *harder*. "My name…"

"*Atlas!*"

"And what do you want me to do?"

"F-fuck me…" A ragged breath. "Harder."

He was. He did. He drove *harder* as he claimed her. Making sure that she fully understood who was doing the fucking and who would be the one to give her pleasure, always.

Because he wanted to erupt. To pour into her. But she would come first.

He squeezed her clit. Her head tilted back. Her hips slammed up against him, and he watched the pleasure as it flashed across her beautiful face. Her lips parted wide, her breath shuddered, and then she was jerking and arching, and he could feel the inner contractions of her tight, hot core all along his dick. Those contractions maddened him. He thrust harder. Faster.

"Atlas!"

He loved it when she called out his name. Loved it when her hips ground against him, as if she wanted to get closer. As if she wanted more.

He'd be giving her so much more.

He plunged deep, then pulled back, almost withdrawing completely.

"*Atlas...*"

He lowered her legs.

She blinked. Her breath came quickly, making those gorgeous breasts rise and fall. "Wh-what—"

He flipped her over. "Hold tight to the covers." Maybe she'd rip them the way he had done the bedding in her room.

She shifted, crawled forward, putting that gorgeous ass of hers in the air.

He curled his body around hers. Sank into her. One hand gripped her hips. One hand flew around to press to her clit.

"Sensitive," she whispered. "I feel so sensitive!"

"Fucking perfect." He slammed into her.

She pushed back against him.

His mouth went to the curve of her shoulder. Pressed. Kissed. Bit. *Marked.*

His hips pistoned against her, thrusting frantically even as his fingers strummed her clit again and again. Ferocious need blasted through him. A consuming desire that he could not control.

"I will feel you come around me again. I want that. I need it. I love the way you feel when you come around my dick. Do it again. Squeeze me, sweets."

She was moaning and arching, and she was so wet and warm and she was—

Squeezing around my dick. Coming. Begging me to come for her.

She didn't need to beg.

He thrust harder. As deep as he could go, and he erupted inside of her. A blasting release that tore a bellow from him even as he felt the pleasure pour through his entire body. A powerful orgasm that had his jaw clenching, his hips surging, his whole world fucking spinning too fast and realigning.

He came in her. The most powerful release he'd ever had, and she was squeezing his dick every moment with her tight, hot pussy. Still coming for him. Coming around him.

Taking him.

Claiming him.

Even as he claimed her.

Will never let you go now. Can't...

His breath shuddered out. He thrust slowly.

She moaned. He pulled out...

Have to ditch the condom. He stalked away from the bed even as she collapsed against the mattress. He was still aware of the loud, fierce thundering in his ears. Aware that his body felt too tight and too hard.

Aware that he *craved.*

He needed to be in her again. *Feeling her come around me. Coming with her.*

He returned to the bed. Reached into the nightstand once more. Atlas pulled out another condom and rolled it on his dick.

She rolled toward him. "Atlas?"

"I need you again." Guttural. His entire focus had shifted to her. Maybe his entire focus had always been her. "Can you take me again?" Dammit, she had to be sore. He'd been slamming so deep into her. This had to be too much. He had to—

Her legs parted.

He was on her. On the bed. *In* her. Driving deep, and she wrapped her arms and legs around him. A feverish intensity consumed him. There was no holding back, no stopping. The bonds around him had broken. He felt feral as he drove into her again and again.

Need her pleasure. Have to give her pleasure. "Stay with me." He needed her as lost to need and lust and release as he was. "*Stay with me.*" He didn't want to lose her. Not now. Not ever.

Her legs rose. Her knees pressed against his hips. Her breath panted out.

He was beyond restraint. Plunging fiercely. Too lost to her. With her. In her. Unable to hold back. But...

She wasn't speaking. Wasn't saying his name. Wasn't...

Fuck. Fuck. Fuck.

He froze. Body rock hard, Atlas looked down at her.

"Don't you *dare* stop," she snarled. "I'm too close."

Fuck, yes. *Yes.*

He pounded harder and felt her contractions around him. Heard her gasp and moan. Loved the press of her nails into his skin.

Her core squeezed him. His orgasm slammed into him.

He held her hips tightly, sealing them together as he poured out his release.

Can't lose her.

Won't.

No matter what it took, he would not lose Lily.

Chapter Twenty

He ditched the condom. Brought a warm cloth and pressed it carefully between her thighs. Atlas was aware of her gaze on him the entire time, but he didn't speak. Neither did she.

He was too busy trying not to fuck her a third time.

She has to be sore. Show a bit of restraint, you asshole.

And she...why was she so silent? Had he hurt her? Hell, no, he would never want to hurt her, but he'd been so hungry, so lost to need and to the desire that she unleashed within him.

He turned away, still feeling the weight of her stare on him. He ditched the cloth in his bathroom and returned to the bed as quickly as he could. He turned off the lamp, plunging them into darkness.

"What are you doing?"

Not fucking you. I am not fucking you again...yet. "Getting ready to sleep." His eyes adjusted quickly to the darkness, as they always did.

She sat up in bed. "I can't stay here."

His chest ached. "Did I disappoint you?" If she told him the sex had been *fine,* or, worse, if he'd hurt her—

"I can still feel you on the inside."

Atlas stilled.

"I can feel you in me. On my skin. I can still taste you. I feel like every part of me is marked by you."

He froze in place. "I can feel you. Tight and hot around me." Yeah, this was not helping his dick to calm down. Quite the opposite. "I can taste you. I have your sweet scent burned into my memory." Then, to be clear, "There is no part of me that does not belong to you."

"It was...just sex." The rustle of the bedding.

"Is that all it was? Because it felt like more to me. But maybe that's *fine* with you."

She jumped from the bed. Eliminated the space between them. Her hands flew out and wrapped around his arms as she held him in the dark. "You know it could never be just *fine.* I couldn't breathe. I couldn't think. I could only feel, and I've never, ever in my life felt so truly alive as I did...with you. I never knew anything could feel that good. I never wanted the pleasure to stop. I wanted to keep making love with you all night long."

Making love.

He told himself it was just semantics. A word choice. She didn't mean it. They had been fucking. Rough, hard, intense...fucking. Making love—that was supposed to be tender and soft. Careful caresses and gentle kisses.

Not fucking her so hard the bed threatened to break. Not driving into her again and again when she had to be sore from the first time that he'd come inside of her.

But...

Making love. He liked the way those particular words sounded when they came from her.

"I can't stay with you," she said.

Oh, yes, you can. Get ready for forever, sweets.

"I have nightmares. I-I fight sometimes, in my sleep. You don't want to be with me in the dark."

He leaned forward and pressed a kiss to her forehead. "That's exactly where I want to be with you."

"Atlas—"

"I can handle the dark. There is nothing about you that I will not be able to handle." *There is nothing about you that I could not love.*

But...no.

He didn't know love.

Didn't know about any of the emotions most people felt. He faked his way through all the social drama. He charmed. He made light jokes. He bullshitted his way through life so that others would not see the truth. *I'm empty. Cold on the inside. I laugh and I smile and I don't actually feel anything deep inside.*

He'd asked her...

Can a psychopath love? She hadn't answered him. He didn't need her to answer, though, because he'd done plenty of his own research over the years. He'd realized what he was, of course, early on. With his father, how could he not understand the truth?

I heard the screams when I was a child. I ran outside once, to the old shed. But he came out. He caught me. Carried me back inside the house and told me it was just the wind.

The wind didn't scream that way. As if the pain was unbearable and death would be a blessing.

But he'd believed his father.

For a time.

He'd...watched his father. Learned. Realized that he and his father were both so different from others.

Atlas could mimic emotions. He could make sure he did not wind up in a cage, or with a needle in his arm like his father. People wanted to see him happy? Fine. He could show happiness. People wanted to see sadness? Oh, sure, he could muster up a sympathetic expression. Could make his voice thicken and even get a teardrop to appear in his eye.

All of that was just surface.

Masking.

He didn't really love. No matter how much he might want to, no matter how much he might wish—

Atlas shut down the thoughts. He swept Lily into his arms, intent on putting her back in his bed. But then he stopped.

I want to keep her. I want to force her to stay with me.

But if you kept a butterfly prisoner, if you tried to hold it too tightly, didn't you just damage its wings? Didn't you wind up killing the beautiful thing that you wanted to possess so badly?

He'd done that once, as a kid. Not too long after the night that he'd heard the wind screaming. He'd watched a butterfly for days. Seen it flying around his mother's garden. Not some big, fancy garden. Just some wildflowers. They'd planted seeds, throwing them out. Laughing. And...

The wildflowers had bloomed. Butterflies had flown from one colorful bulb to another. He'd chased those butterflies. Been mesmerized by the beautiful flutter of their wings. He'd held out his hand, dirty from playing that morning, from sinking his fingers into the soil, and he'd waited, barely breathing, still as a statue until his muscles ached, until one butterfly—the smallest one there—had finally fluttered over his palm.

Quick as a snake, he'd closed his fingers around his prize. So eager to keep it. To always have it close and watch those wings flutter and flutter. He'd run for his mother, shouting for her, calling out in excitement for her to see what he had. For her to see his most beautiful thing. He'd run to the front of their little house, looking for her. Searching and searching.

She'd been talking to a neighbor. But she'd finally come his way. Smiled at him.

He'd opened his hand. The dirt from his palm had covered the butterfly's wings. The butterfly's still wings.

"Isn't she beautiful?" He'd marveled at the butterfly even as he wondered why the butterfly was so still. *"Watch her fly."* He'd thrown the butterfly into the air. Just to watch her fall back to earth. He'd stared at her, frowning, and the silence around him had grown. Then he'd realized what he'd done.

Too tight. My grip was too tight. I crushed her.

His gaze had swung back to his mother, and for just a moment, he'd caught her staring at him with absolute horror. Fear and horror.

"Atlas?" Lily said his name softly.

He forced his jaw to unclench. He hadn't thought about that damn day in...forever. But now he could see that his mother had already feared he was like his father. His mother had known the truth about his dad way back then. *She covered for him. She knew. She knew...*

Just as she knew that when she looked at her son, she was staring at a monster.

But he hadn't advanced to hurting animals. He'd never done that shit. Hell, he'd made a point of never having pets. Not like they were allowed in the group homes, anyway.

He'd understood what he could become. At fifteen, he'd read about the Macdonald Triad. The three behaviors that could supposedly be the signals that predicted whether or not an individual would be a future serial killer. *Didn't want to turn out like dear old dad.*

He'd had zero of those indicators. No fucking bed wetting. No animal cruelty after the damn butterfly because he'd refused to be around animals, and he hadn't set fires. Hell, there *had* been a fire at one of the group homes, but someone else had started it, not him. He'd been the one to have his meager set of belongings ignited.

Those sonsofbitches in the room there had thought it was funny to watch his faded shirts and pants burn.

No one had been laughing when he'd gotten his payback.

"You have gone somewhere without me," Lily said.

No, he was still holding her. He was just heading for the bedroom door with her and not putting her back in his bed as Atlas had originally intended. He opened the door, not letting her down. She hardly weighed enough. He'd have to be sure that Roland prepared her much bigger meals in the future. Eggs and toast would not cut it.

"Decided you didn't want me with you?" Lily's sigh brushed over his neck. "I understand." Husky. "I warned you, I'm a difficult companion."

He would always want her with him. "You are the only companion I want." He had left her bedroom open. He walked across the threshold as he kept his grip on her. "But I won't crush your wings." With slow steps, he made his way to her bed. His arms wanted to linger around her. He liked the way she felt against him far too much. Yet Atlas forced himself to let her go. He put her in the middle of her bed. Even pulled the mangled covers up over her.

A wise move to cover her naked body and block his temptation.

"I don't have wings," Lily told him.

Didn't she? "You can sleep with me. You can sleep alone. Your choice." He backed up a step. "I'll see you in the morning." *I will not fuck you a third time right now. I will show some restraint. I will not fuck you again right now.*

"Where do *you* want to sleep?" she asked.

With you. With my arms around you so you don't get away. But if I hold you too close, too tightly, I'll crush the one thing I want.

"Atlas?"

"I don't care if you have nightmares. I don't care if you fight in your sleep. I can handle anything you throw at me." A roll of one shoulder. He realized he was stark naked in front of her. His hand reached out and turned off her lamp. They'd left that light on earlier. He turned it off now and plunged them into darkness not because he minded if she saw his naked body or not, but because she needed to sleep. "I have my own nightmares." He'd also started to have his own dreams.

Married to Lily. Her smiling at me. Her eyes lit up.

He turned for the door. Took two steps.

"I'd...like for you to stay with me." Halting. Nervous.

His eyes shut.

"If I cause a problem, you can always leave." A quick rush of words from Lily. "You don't have to stay all night, and if you don't want to be here, I completely understand."

He was already back at the bed. "Scoot over, sweets."

She scooted.

Atlas climbed into the bed with her. He edged closer to her, and, surprising him, she curled her body against his. Soft. Warm.

Home.

His eyes closed. He listened to her breathing. That soft, steady breathing. The most important sound in his world.

"It was...more than just fine for you, wasn't it?" Lily's whispered question.

His head turned toward her. "I fucked you twice, back to back."

"So, you liked it?"

"*Like* isn't the right word. If I didn't think you were going to be too sore, I'd be fucking you again. My main goal in life now is to fuck you as much and as often as I possibly can."

Silence. "I thought we were catching a killer."

"Yes. We will. We are. But...he'll be gone soon."

"Will...I be gone soon, too? Our relationship over?"

Don't hold too tightly... "I want to fuck you as much and as often as I possibly can," he repeated.

The silence grew around them. She snuggled closer. Her soft breaths lulled him. He thought she was going to sleep, but...

"I never felt this way, not with anyone before. It's like I don't have to hide."

You don't. Not with me.

"I could let go with you. I could *feel*."

What do you feel, Lily?

"Thank you, Atlas." She pressed a kiss to his shoulder. Then she snuggled even closer. She put one soft arm over him, over the scars that he carried from an attack long ago. She didn't flinch or pull back. She settled *closer*.

She was soft and warm and precious against him. A gift he'd never expected.

He'd learned a lesson long ago from that beautiful butterfly. You had to be patient to get what you wanted. You had to wait. You had to be still. You had to let the beauty not ever sense the threat.

If you were patient enough, if you played the scene just

right...what you wanted would come to you. You just couldn't let your prey see the threat.

She nestled against him.

I will not damage your wings.

* * *

HE STARED AT THE BUTTERFLY. Golden wings. Sprinkles of darkness. So still. He turned in the bed, the better to see it, to reach it, and his fingers swept out. Clean fingers now. The soft light from the lamp shone on the butterfly as he reached for it.

His bedroom door creaked open.

"Atlas? I—*what are you doing?*"

The door banged into the wall. His mother rushed toward him. He tried to snatch back his hand, but she caught it.

"Oh, God, oh, God. You kept it as a trophy, didn't you? Just like him. Just like him..."

Footsteps pounded. Not soft, rushed steps like hers had been. Harder. Deeper.

His mother sucked in a breath. "Don't do it," she whispered. Begged. "Don't you dare do it, do you hear me, Atlas?"

But he hadn't been doing anything.

Lie. I was...I wanted to bring the butterfly back. Because I didn't mean to hurt it. I would never mean to hurt something so pretty—

"Don't you *ever* hurt something unless it hurts you first. Do you understand me? *Not. Ever.*"

But those heavy, deep, hard footsteps were in his room, and his mother stopped talking. She grabbed the butterfly and swept it into his garbage can.

Too late, though. Because *he'd* heard her.

Dark, rumbling laughter. "That's some bullshit advice. Always strike first. Always attack first. That's how you show the world just how strong you are."

And his head turned once more, but this time, it was so that he could look toward the faded bedroom door and see—

* * *

ATLAS SUCKED in a breath as he woke up.

His eyes flew open, and he stared into the darkness. He was far too conscious of the fast pounding of his heart.

And of the soft hand that pressed over his heart.

Lily.

She didn't stir. He pulled in another breath. Exhaled. Slow. Deep. Again and again.

He didn't keep trophies. He didn't attack first.

"It's all right," Lily's soft voice. And he realized that she had woken up. "Nightmares can't hurt us."

They couldn't. Reality could.

His hand slid over her naked back. Stroked her soft, silken skin. "Sorry I woke you."

"Don't be." She kissed his neck. "I can always go to sleep again."

She'd been afraid for him to sleep with her. Afraid she'd disturb him. Instead, she was the one who gave him comfort in the dark.

He swallowed, twice.

And when she fell asleep again, he kept staring into the darkness.

Chapter Twenty-One

An insistent ringing woke her.

Lily cracked open one eye, glaring at the bedside clock, but when she saw those glowing digits—*What?* She sat upright fast.

The ringing came again. Not a ringtone she recognized —*because it's a new phone. That's your new phone ringing on the nightstand.* Her hand flew out to grab the phone. She swiped her finger over the screen and put the phone to her ear. "Hello?" She'd only called one person with that phone. So only one person should be calling *her* on it since no one else—other than Atlas—would have the number.

Atlas.

She automatically looked over her shoulder. He sat on the edge of the bed, his broad back to her.

"*Lily!*" Sloane's frantic voice in her ear.

But Lily frowned at Atlas. He was...reading something? Her head craned. What was he reading?

"Lily, it's on the news! I'm stuck in the New Orleans airport, and *it's on the news!*"

Lily rose from the bed. She pulled a sheet with her,

wrapping it around her body, and she crept around the edge of the bed to get a better view of Atlas.

He was wearing jeans. When had he gone to put on jeans? And...

That was her diary in his hands. Her open diary.

The diary she'd hid beneath the mattress of the bed. "Atlas?"

His head lifted. Turned toward her. He shut the diary. "I found it on the floor."

"I—"

"*She's dead!*" Sloane cried.

Lily blinked.

"Did you hear me? Because I don't think you did," Sloane huffed. "I am sitting in an airport in New Orleans, watching the news, and the story airing is about Tonya Johnson. The name ringing a bell? Because it did for me. A super loud one. She was murdered outside of the bar where she works in Shreveport."

Lily shook her head.

"Stabbed to death. At least according to the blonde reporter who is talking. This happened sometime yesterday or last night—or, *I don't know*. The blonde isn't really clear on the when part, but I have to tell you, this is making every internal alarm I have *scream* in warning."

Lily's mind was screaming.

"You're taken," Sloane said. "You escape. Your house is broken into. Someone steals your files, and then one of the names on our list—*Tonya Johnson*—happens to be murdered right after that? Tell me you see the waving red flags in this."

"I see them."

Atlas rose. He left the diary on the bed.

Her throat wanted to close on her. Had he been reading the diary, while she slept?

Atlas shook his head. "No."

"It *can't* be a coincidence," Sloane said at the same time, her faint southern accent coming through with her stress. "Because if it is, then that's the worst coincidence in the entire world."

"I wasn't reading it." Atlas stepped toward Lily. "I found it on the floor. I went to my room to get some jeans, and when I came back, I accidentally kicked it. It was on the floor. I picked it up."

Sloane hummed. "Is she—was Tonya—the closest subject to you? No, no, of course not. Atlas Bennett is the one physically the closest."

Atlas was right in front of her, close enough to touch.

"But of the others, she *is*—or, dammit, was—the closest physically to Dallas, Texas, wasn't she? Dallas and Shreveport are like what—three hours away? Two and a half if you drive fast and there is no traffic? I don't like this." Her voice notched up as Sloane repeated, "*I don't like it.*"

Tonya Johnson. The daughter of Meredith and Lyle Johnson. Tonya's father had picked up over a dozen hitchhikers when he'd been working as a big rig hauler across the US. He'd picked them up, and they'd never been seen again. At least, not seen alive. The bodies had all eventually been found...by a group of Boy Scouts out on a hike. Lyle had liked to keep his kills in one central location.

Meredith and his baby girl Tonya had not known of Lyle's crimes. The perfect father had been the devil. And Meredith had spiraled into drugs and booze after his conviction. As for Tonya...

Convictions for petty theft. A brush with prostitution. But Tonya had never physically hurt anyone. She'd gotten out of rehab about six months ago, trying to kick her own drug habit, and she'd seemed to be doing well.

"Who is the next closest one?" Sloane wanted to know. "If this prick got your list, if he's offing the subjects one by one—"

"We don't know that," Lily cut in to say even as her stomach twisted. "We can't jump to that conclusion."

"Yes, well, how about we follow the whole 'better safe than sorry' rule on this one?"

"That's not a rule." Her hair tumbled forward, and she shoved it back with one hand.

"Who is the next closest subject?" Sloane demanded.

"They are not subjects. They are *people*." When had she stopped thinking of them as subjects? *When?*

A beat of silence. "Then we need to find our next *person*. Shit. Forget it, I'm pulling it up on my laptop because no one stole mine—oh, God, that was a bitch statement. I didn't mean it the way it sounded. It's not your fault anything got stolen. *It's that prick's fault.* The one who took it. I didn't mean to be a bitch, you know I didn't. I'm just stressed, and I'm scared, and I am so worried about you." Her words were rapid-fire, as they often were when Sloane was stressed. "I don't want him coming after *you*."

"I'm safe."

A faint line had appeared between Atlas's eyes. "Put it on speaker," he ordered.

She did, swiping her finger over the screen in time for him to hear Sloane say—

"—if this perp killed Tonya Johnson, if he is eliminating the people on our list, then the next person, just in terms of being physically close to you and your location in Dallas, that would be Hatch Davis, in Oklahoma City. That's about three hours away."

Hatch Davis didn't know that his biological father had been the Spring Break Strangler. Another ridiculous moniker because the press liked to sensationalize everything. But, during one long, hot spring twenty years ago, Hatch's father Jeffrey had spent his time along the Florida and Alabama coast. He'd strangled five different women and tossed their bodies into the water. When the first body washed up, with a shark bite on the woman's side, the local authorities hadn't thought of foul play.

But the ME in the area had been damn good at his job, and he'd been very, very thorough.

She was dead before she hit the water.

Then another body had washed up...this one with distinct bruising around her throat.

And another...

And another...

For victim number five, Jeffrey had been caught in the act of dumping the body. He'd been locked away. Given a lethal injection in a Florida prison five years ago. He'd died, and Hatch had never known that when his mother went down to the Gulf Coast for spring break with her sorority sisters so long ago, she fucked a killer.

One who let her walk away even though she looked exactly like all of his other victims.

When Sherry Lee had come back home, she'd immediately married her high school sweetheart. Greg Davis might even believe that Hatch was his son. And Hatch...he'd been the high school valedictorian. He'd gotten a full ride to college. He volunteered with special needs kids. He cooked at a soup kitchen on Saturdays. He'd never even gotten a traffic ticket.

Lily's breath left her in a hard rush. "Hatch isn't guilty of anything. If this is the perp who took me and

Atlas—he wouldn't go after Hatch. Hatch isn't guilty," she repeated.

Atlas's jaw hardened even more. He'd missed the first part of the conversation, and she'd have to fill him in, ASAP.

But for now... "And why would the killer come back here, to Dallas?" Lily asked. "If he wants someone close to Shreveport..." She closed her eyes and envisioned the map she'd made long ago. A map that had been on her laptop. "New Orleans. It's five hours from Shreveport, and Westin Blanchard is down there. He got out of prison for armed robbery three months ago." Westin was well aware that his father was a convicted serial killer. After all, they'd been in Angola together during Westin's recent stay. Father and son had always enjoyed a very close relationship. In and out of prison.

"Two choices." Sloane hummed. She hummed when she was in deep-thought mode. Sometimes, she would literally hum a whole song and not realize she was doing it. "Okay, okay, if this is a punishment-focused killer, then he has to go after Westin. Westin's last victim needed facial reconstruction because of what he did to her in that robbery. Hatch has never hurt anyone a day in his life. So, we need to send the Feds to him. We need to give them a warning, and—dammit. They are calling my flight! Look, I will be there as soon as I can, okay? Call your ex. I know you don't want to do it, but you have to let Gage know what's happening. He'll take credit, like he always does when you solve cases and he gets promotions because he's an asshole like that, but stopping a killer is more important than his bullshit, am I right?"

"Yes," Atlas answered flatly. "You are right. Stopping a killer is more important than bullshit."

Silence. Then. "When you answered the phone, you used your sleepy voice, Lily. Were you in *bed* with Atlas Bennett? Because that is him, speaking, isn't it?"

"Yes," Atlas said.

Just that.

Ahem. Yes, to both of Sloane's questions. "Get on your flight. Stay safe. I'll brief Gage."

"*You* stay safe," Sloane huffed back. "I'm not the one having sex with a potential serial killer and getting engaged to him."

"*Sloane.*"

"Sorry! Sorry! That slipped out! I swear it did. I'm worried, and I'm running through the airport, and everyone is looking at me like I am crazy. Just please, please *stay safe.*"

"I have her," Atlas said.

"*That* is what worries me. Part of it. There are lots of worries right now, honestly."

"She will stay safe," Atlas assured her friend. "I promise you that."

"Sloane." Lily kept her tone calm. Flat. With an effort. "I thought you congratulated me on my engagement before."

"Yes, well, that was when I thought you were finally in love and that he understood you were amazing and would love you forever. You told me that wasn't the case, so now I'm back to being worried." Sloane's rush of breath carried over the line. "I am worried because I care about you, Lily."

She knew that Sloane cared.

"Atlas, you still listening?" Sloane huffed out the words. Probably because she was, in fact, running through the airport.

"I'm here."

269

"If you hurt her, I will make your recent trip to that basement look like a luxury vacation."

She hung up.

His brows rose. "Your friend just threatened to kidnap me...and kill me?"

"She was vague. I don't know if she meant that, specifically." *Though I suspect that is exactly what Sloane meant. Specifically.*

"I missed the first part of your conversation."

He had. "Because you were busy reading my diary." She had a death grip on the phone. Lily forced her fingers to relax. "Did you wait until I went to sleep before you grabbed it?"

A slow, negative shake of his head. "It was on the floor, Lily. I swear it. It was open when I picked it up."

"I left it under the mattress." Not on the floor. Tucked securely beneath the top mattress.

"I did not read it."

She stared hard at him. A muscle flexed along his jaw. Trust had been one of her rules. She'd told him that she wouldn't fuck him unless she trusted him.

She'd fucked him twice during the night.

And...

"I believe you." She did. Though that did create another problem.

One problem at a time, Lily. One at a time.

"It's not secure under a mattress." He stood before her with the jeans hanging low on his hips. Looking sexy and disheveled, and she swore she smelled mint. *The man brushed his teeth.* First thing in the morning—yeah, that was a win.

Him being all shirtless and strong—another win.

Someone finding her diary? Not a win.

"I have a safe in my bedroom. I can put it in there for you," Atlas offered.

She nodded. "Yes, you can do that...after you read it."

"Lily?" His lashes flickered.

"Read it whenever you want. You may not have time to read it now." Probably would not, now that she considered things. "I do think you need to know the part of the conversation that you missed."

His broad shoulders were tense as he waited.

"A woman was killed last night," Lily informed him. "Sloane saw a news story about her death. The victim was someone on my list."

"Your list?"

"Tonya Johnson." Their victim. "Her father was a serial killer."

His stare sharpened on her.

But...

Footsteps. Racing up the stairs. More like thundering up them.

"Fuck," Atlas swore. "Sweets, you need clothes on, now." And he lunged for her bedroom door. He yanked it open, even as she sprang behind him, holding her sheet. She peered over his broad shoulder to see Desmond rushing toward them.

"Company," Desmond snapped. "The Fed is at the door, and he's demanding to see you."

"Gage?" Surprise rolled through her. She'd just been about to call him.

Atlas shifted to the side more, using his body to block her completely from Desmond's view.

"Haven't opened the door to him yet. He used his ID to get past the guards patrolling at the gate. Guy has got his partner with him, the woman," Desmond replied. "Looked at the front door camera on my way to you. Bastard is pissed, shouting to see you *now*, Atlas."

"Then he'll see me." He looked back at Lily. "Get dressed. Then meet us downstairs."

She grabbed the diary and shoved it into his hands. "In your safe. For *your* eyes only."

He nodded. His head bent, and his lips brushed over hers. "You didn't have nightmares with me."

No, she hadn't. "But you did," she whispered back.

"That happens...when you are the nightmare." He nodded toward her. "I'll handle your Fed. After you are dressed, you can come down and tell him about the potential vics." He strode through the doorway. "Desmond, stay up here and guard her. I want her protected at all times."

She poked her head out of the doorway and watched Atlas duck into his room. He came back a moment later, minus the diary. Still shirtless. Still barefoot. Still gorgeous and sexy and with danger seeming to crackle in the air around him.

"Get dressed, Lily," Atlas chided as he bounded down the stairs. "If that prick sees you in a sheet, I will break his jaw, glass or not."

Fine. But first...her gaze slid to Desmond. A Desmond who was not looking directly at her. "Did you enjoy some light reading last night?" Lily inquired sweetly.

He still didn't look her way. "Wouldn't call it light."

"Do you always break into other people's rooms and steal personal items?"

"Returned it, didn't I?"

She'd expected to work harder in order to get his confession. "*Why?*"

Finally, he looked at her. "Because he is my friend. I

will not have someone dangerous slip past my watch again. I will not let him be hurt."

She clutched the sheet tighter to her chest. "You think I would hurt him?"

"I think you have the capacity to hurt a great many people in this world."

Her feet pressed harder to the floor. "I would say you have that same capacity."

"By the time I was ten years old, I had already killed ten men. Child soldiers do not have choices."

She knew his story. The absolute heartbreak and savagery of it. But she had not planned to bring it up to him. You didn't parade around someone else's pain...Yet he'd just laid it bare in front of her. "Why are you telling me about your past?"

"Because I know *your* past. But I have no diary to give you so that you can understand me. I can only tell you who I am. What I am."

"You are his friend." She understood that. A friend who would do anything for Atlas. She could see that so clearly.

Desmond's lips tightened. "He never judged me. Never cared where I had been. Told me it mattered more where I was going. Then he took me with him. Gave me a job and took me with him every step of the way." A pause. "Tell me, Lily Gallo, do you know where you're going?"

"Honestly, no, right at the moment, I'm trying to figure out if I should go to New Orleans or Oklahoma City."

He frowned at her, heavy brows beetling "Are you joking?"

"When you know me better, you'll understand that I am not."

"What the fuck are your intentions with Atlas?"

"My intentions?" Lily repeated, voice rising in a

question. She lifted her hand and stared down at the ring he'd given her. "Are you asking me if I am going to marry him?" Atlas hadn't proposed to her. The engagement was just a ruse.

"I'm asking if you are here to destroy him or here to save him."

Her stare whipped back to his.

"What's it gonna be, Dr. Lily Gallo? Because I think it could go either way." His hands fisted at his sides. "When I was at my worst, he was there. He's walked me through the dark more times than I can count. And every step, every moment, I've known that he is fighting, too. It's so easy to tip those scales, isn't it? To push someone one way or the other."

"No." A shake of her head. "It's not easy."

"Are you going to save him or push him into hell?"

What is he going to do with me? "I would never hurt Atlas."

"Why not?" He took an aggressive step toward her. "Because you're a good person? Because you're trying to help others? To make the world a better place? Bullshit." His eyes glinted. "Tell that to someone who didn't read your diary."

"It's not my diary. It's my mother's."

His expression told her what he thought of that response. Then, "You haven't answered my original question."

"Yes. I have." But she would repeat the answer. "I would never hurt Atlas."

"*Why not?*"

Because...

Because you don't hurt what you love. She licked her lips.

She heard voices rising downstairs. Shouting. "I have to get dressed," Lily said. She began to shut the door.

His hand flew up to block the door from closing. "Why. Not?"

"Because his dimples scare me," she whispered. "But his touch makes me feel safe. Because he kisses my scar, and he sees the chaos in me, and he still says I'm beautiful."

Some of the tension faded from Desmond's face.

"Because nothing with Atlas is ever going to be *fine*." Something she realized with all of her being. "It will be intense. It will be shattering. It will be consuming. I won't ever be able to hold back with him. He won't let me." She considered that. "I won't let him hold back with me, either. I want everything. Good. Bad. The confusing parts that blend them both."

"What if there is no good?"

She tilted her head and sent him a brief smile.

He frowned. Blinked. "What the fuck are you doing? Are you *smiling* right now? You don't usually smile."

No, she did not.

"Shit." A bit disgruntled. "You have a really nice smile. It makes the gold shine in your eyes."

She ignored the compliment. She wasn't looking for compliments. *I have my mother's smile, and she always used it to disarm and charm.* "We both know there is good in Atlas. It's why you fight to defend him so hard. It's why I'm pulled to him. Not for the darkness he carries, but because we can both see the light."

Desmond swallowed. He stepped back. "You can't go downstairs in just a sheet. Atlas would lose his mind." He turned away.

Her hand flew out. Caught his before he could leave. "There isn't just darkness in you, either."

"You don't know…you don't understand…"

"I don't know who you would have been if you hadn't been kidnapped and forced to do terrible things when you were just a child? Unfortunately, no, I don't know that man. None of us will ever know that man. But I see you in front of me. Someone who is so determined to protect a friend. Someone who makes sure to have Atlas's back."

"He pays well." Brisk. "Ask anyone."

"I think you'd be his friend if he didn't have a dime to his name."

No response.

"And *that*," she told him, "is how I know there is far more to you than just the vicious past that you endured. Maybe you need to start looking at yourself a different way. The image you see reflected back when you look in a mirror —sometimes that image is just what we fear, and it's not who we are."

Atlas had said he was her broken mirror.

She'd always thought she was the broken one.

"Fuck." A breath from Desmond. "You are dangerous."

She hadn't been trying to be dangerous. She'd been trying to help.

He pulled away. "Get dressed. Then hurry downstairs so Atlas and your ex don't come to blows."

She stepped out of her bedroom. "Atlas told you that Gage was my ex?"

"Nah." Desmond didn't look back. "Learned it weeks ago when we started digging into your life. Got to know your enemy, understand?"

"I'm not Atlas's enemy."

"I'm getting that…" He darted down the stairs.

She slid back into her guest room. Shut the door. As she crossed the room to get dressed, the sheet trailed behind her.

As quickly as she could, she dressed. Panties. Bra. Long, flowing dress. Lily picked the dress because she could just yank it on and go. Same thing with the flats. She finger-combed her hair, splashed water on her face, brushed her teeth, and hurried back for the door. Even as she yanked it open, she heard the rumble of deep voices.

Her feet flew over the stairs. And as she got closer to the main floor of the home...

"You are a killer, Atlas Bennett. And I'm placing you under arrest."

Oh, no.

Chapter Twenty-Two

Five minutes before...

He opened the front door himself. Yes, yes, he had security. He had staff who could have done the job for him, but Atlas opened the door to the Fed himself. *I know how to open a freaking door.*

FBI Special Agent Gage Emerick glared at him, eyes narrowed, jaw clenched. Fury clear to see in every line of his face. His parter, Sharon Hinkle, shifted nervously behind him, foot to foot, and her head craned so that she could get a look at Atlas. She blinked when she realized he wasn't wearing a shirt. Her green eyes widened.

"Took you long enough to answer the damn door," Gage snapped.

Atlas shrugged. "I was...occupied."

Gage's jaw hardened even more. "Don't you have *people* who could answer the door for you?"

"I do. But in light of recent events, I gave orders that

only I was to determine which visitors were allowed in my home." And, technically, he hadn't allowed the Feds in yet. They were still on the other side of the doorway. "But my *people* did see you through the security feed. I was alerted that you were here, shouting to see me. So, here I am." No sense having the discussion in the doorway, though. "Do come in." He turned away, giving them his back, and he marched across the foyer.

They followed. He heard their quick steps and the slamming of the door. But just as he turned for his study—

"This isn't a social visit," Gage snarled.

"Oh, you mean you didn't come back because you find me incredibly charming and you want to be my new best friend?" He slowly turned back to face the Feds. His arms lifted to cross over his chest. "How disappointing."

Gage huffed out a breath. "I know what you've done."

Highly doubtful. "You know that I gave Lily the most satisfying night of her life?" A deliberate taunt that brought him untold delight. Sue him, he kissed and told. *Because you will never touch her again.*

The Fed surged toward him.

Sharon yelped and grabbed her partner. "No, no! Stop!"

Gage stopped, but his face had mottled with fury.

"I was occupied," Atlas said again. He simply couldn't help himself. Sometimes, he enjoyed being a prick. Especially to this bastard. *You used my Lily.* But...

Fuck.

Time to get down to business. He had assured Lily that he'd handle the Fed, so Atlas supposed he should handle the man. "Tonya Johnson."

Sharon sharply inhaled. A dramatic, loud sound.

They already know about her.

And wasn't that interesting? Either Gage and his partner were a lot better at their job than Atlas had initially realized or...

I'm about to be fucked. And not in the fantastic way that he'd fucked with Lily.

He waited, didn't move. Time for the Feds to put their cards on the table.

"You are *familiar* with Tonya Johnson?" Sharon asked him, voice cautious.

"No. I've never met the woman in my life." True story. "But Lily's friend, ah, Sloane—Sloane Armstrong, I believe is her name." He more than believed it. He had a full report on Sloane in his Lily file. "She called this morning. She'd seen a news story about Tonya." His gaze slid between the two agents. Lingered on Gage. "Sloane was concerned about the woman's death—"

"Her *murder*," Gage bit out.

"Because she recognized Tonya's name."

Gage kept glaring.

Sharon released him. Stepped to his side. "We are aware that Tonya's father was Lyle Johnson. The big rig driver who killed all of those hitchhikers."

Atlas kept his face expressionless.

"Guessing information about Tonya was included in the files taken from Lily's house," Sharon added with a questioning quirk of her brows at Atlas.

"We still haven't been given the all clear to check Lily's house," he returned. "But if we are allowed to go in now, I'm sure we can provide you with a full listing of missing items." He dropped his arms.

"Do you wait for all clears? Is that what you do?" Gage wanted to know. "Or do you just, oh, say break into a place when the mood strikes you?"

Oh, now he's surprising me. But Atlas blinked innocently. "Whatever do you mean?"

"I mean Detective Benedict Swain's house. I'm talking about you, breaking into his place. See, I stopped by there first thing this morning. It was trashed to hell and back."

"And you're accusing *me* of doing that?" He rolled back his shoulders. "Sounds like the same sort of *trashing* that happened at Lily's place. I don't know why you would think I was linked to that type of activity. I'm an upstanding businessman. Ask anyone." Well, except dead Detective Benedict Swain.

"You were there." Gage took an aggressive step toward him.

"At Lily's place? Yes. I was. So were you. You saw me there—"

"Benedict's," Gage bit out.

"When?"

But Gage just stared at him with his furious eyes, and Atlas knew the man was working on conjecture, not truth. Though the fellow's instincts were way better than Atlas had assumed. "How about we get back to the murder victim?" Atlas asked. He thought he sounded polite.

Footsteps were coming down the stairs. A heavy tread. Desmond, frowning.

He should be with Lily. I told him to stay with her.

Atlas lifted a hand, and Desmond stilled half-way down the stairs. A good position to guard Lily *and* to listen to his conversation with the Feds.

Gage glanced toward the stairs. Swept his gaze over Desmond, then returned his attention to Atlas. "Benedict *is* a murder victim. They pulled his remains out of the cabin— what was *left* of the cabin," Gage amended. "His badge was still on his body. Fucking *burned* to him. The poor bastard is unrecognizable."

Atlas did not let his expression change. But he had a flash...a very long ago flash...

A smoke-filled room. Four beds. All bunk beds because that's what they'd had in the group home. The flames had been billowing, eating up the wood and the mattress. His clothes had been scattered on the bottom bunk, and they'd already been burning, and Benedict had been right there, just watching. Laughing. Not even realizing how close he was to the fire.

Atlas had tackled him before the flames could reach Benedict. That time. *That time.*

He kept his pose relaxed. "Tonya Johnson," he said. "She's the victim I was talking about."

"You sure do like saying her name," Gage noted. He edged closer. "Why is that? Is it because you get a little thrill thinking about your victim? Reliving the moment?"

Nope. He'd been wrong. Gage was clueless. Utterly. "She isn't my victim."

"No? Then you didn't get her address from Lily's files? You didn't sneak off in the middle of the night and head to Shreveport? You didn't go into her bar and convince Tonya to walk out with you?"

"No." Easy. Calm. "I didn't." What a crock of BS. How did this man solve any cases for the FBI? Oh, wait, he'd been using Lily to solve the cases. Check.

Gage took another step toward him. "You're telling me that you didn't drive your knife into Tonya's stomach, then yank it to the side—to the right, to the left—to cut her wide open, and then *stab* her until she died?"

Sharon's hand had dropped to her waist, hovering near her holster.

Gage's hand was in the same position. Way too close to his weapon for comfort.

Just what did these two Feds expect him to do? Lose all control because they were asking him a few idiot questions? "Haven't been to Shreveport recently," he retorted. "Been a bit busy. What with getting kidnapped and becoming engaged and all."

"I recognized Tonya's name. I heard the news story, too." Gage's nostrils flared. "I called the Shreveport PD. I interviewed the responding officer. He found some interesting items with the vic."

Based on the smugness in Gage's tone, this was not going to be good news.

"You're a rich man, Atlas."

Desmond still lingered on the stairs. Watching. Listening.

"Rich men buy gold cufflinks, don't they?" Gage wanted to know. "Expensive, distinct cufflinks."

Atlas did not blink.

"They get their initials on their gold cufflinks," Gage continued. "Bet you didn't realize it, but before you killed Tonya, she stole them right off you. See, the bouncer revealed that was what she did. Quick sleight of hand. She'd fleece men in the dark. Make out with them, steal from them, and her bouncer buddy would send them running so that she and Mico could cut profits. She took your cufflinks, even as you killed her. One was found in her pocket. One was still gripped in her blood-stained, dead fingers."

Hell.

Gage smiled at him. "The bouncer chased her attacker off, by the way. Didn't get a look at his face, but he described him. Physically. Your height. Your build. And guess what else?"

He wasn't in the mood to guess.

"I got the cop on scene to send me a pic of the cufflinks. Just another piece of evidence. Another nail in your coffin."

"I don't think I'm dead, so I don't need a coffin. Thanks, though."

"Tonya Johnson is dead. You killed her."

No, he had not.

"You are a killer, Atlas Bennett." Spittle flew from Gage's mouth. "And I'm placing you under arrest."

Oh, this should be fun. "I'd like to see you try—"

"No!" Lily flew down the stairs. "Absolutely not! You are *not* arresting, Atlas!"

He turned his head toward her and smiled. "Ah, there she is. The love of my life. My reason for being. My beautiful and bold protector." He lifted a hand toward her. "Lily, sweets, I am so thrilled that you put on clothing." The dress did look sensational on her. "Well, not thrilled for myself. I do adore you naked, but Gage doesn't get the privilege of seeing you that way...not ever again." He cut his stare toward the Fed. "Not if he wants to keep his eyes."

"What. The. Fuck?" Gage gaped at him.

"You do want to keep them, don't you?"

"She isn't the damn love of your life!"

Why? Just because I can't love? But what if...he could?

"And you don't threaten a Fed!" Gage raged.

"Oh, my lawyer did mention something about that." He let his eyes widen. "I should probably call her, shouldn't I? Hey, Desmond..."

Lily had blasted past Desmond on the stairs.

"Text your girlfriend for me, would you?" Atlas asked Desmond. "Let her know the Feds are trying to pin a murder on me."

"No." Lily jumped between him and Gage. "You have this *wrong*. And, Atlas, stop playing with him."

But it was fun to play. "Don't you want me to have some joy?"

She tossed him an infuriated glare before turning her full focus on Gage.

Atlas smiled over her head at the Fed. "Meet my alibi."

"Fucker," Gage breathed.

"Well, yes, I did fuck her. Truly, the best sex of my life."

Lily elbowed him. "Stop being an ass, Atlas. I know you enjoy toying with others, but now is not the time."

It was second nature to him, though. Especially when he was threatened. Go on the offensive. Disarm your opponent, either physically or mentally. Get them off their game. Go in for the kill.

"Atlas did not kill anyone," Lily snapped.

Oh, she knew that was a lie. Interesting that she could just be all bold and lie right to the Fed's face—

"He did not kill Tonya," Lily amended quickly.

Yep, there was that truthfulness part of her. Precious.

"He was with me last night."

Bam. *That's right, sweets. Tell me him I fucked you and it was so much better than merely fine.*

Sharon grimaced. "All night, ma'am?"

"Yes, all night."

"Bullshit." From Gage. "Bullshit, Lily. I *know* you."

Why did the man harp on that? He'd known her surface, not her soul.

"You might have fucked him. Yeah, fine, I can buy that." Brittle words from the Fed. "But no way you were with him all night. You fucked, and then you probably went to one bedroom while he went to another. There are probably a freaking dozen bedrooms or more in this monstrosity of a house."

"Careful, you're talking about my beloved home," Atlas chided.

Gage ignored him. His full and angry focus was on Lily. "You didn't know when he slipped away because you weren't beside him. You were not with the man every single moment. No lover stays with you, and I'm sorry if that sounds fucking brutal, but it's *your* choice. You don't let them get close. You don't let them stay. You didn't let me stay. So I damn well know the alibi is bullshit. He would have been able to drive to Shreveport and get back...he would have been able to make the trip. But he screwed up, and he left his cufflinks and now we have—*Lily, why are you shaking your head at me?*"

She was. A slow, negative gesture.

Atlas curled his fingers around her shoulders. "You are wrong, Agent Emerick."

The agent's fury pulsed in the air.

"I did not leave Lily last night. I slept in bed with her. Her body was curled around mine. My hands on her. I even had a nightmare once and woke up...probably due to all my recent, traumatic experiences."

A furrow cut between Gage's eyes.

"Lily was at my side. She comforted me. She drifted back to sleep in my arms. When she woke this morning—due to her friend Sloane's phone call—I was in the bed with her." Granted, he'd left to grab jeans and he'd hurried back, but Atlas didn't see why it was relevant to share that information. Not like he could have driven to Shreveport and back in the five minutes it had taken him to grab jeans and brush his teeth.

"Lily...?" What could have been pain flashed across Gage's face. "He...all night?"

"All night," Lily confirmed. "I am his alibi, as I said. There is no way he went to Shreveport without me knowing."

The brief flash of pain vanished as a mask seemed to slide over Gage's face. "The cufflinks..."

"Yeah, about those..." Atlas did not let go of Lily's delicate shoulders. The touch was to say many things...*She's mine. Back the fuck off.*

She's mine...don't ever think of coming after her.

She's mine.

Okay, fine, the touch was basically to say that one thing.

But, regarding the cuff links... "I was wearing a pair of gold, initial cufflinks when I was taken from the parking lot recently. Thought they'd fallen off during the attack. Even mentioned them to the cops who questioned me as the cabin burned." A vague detail that hadn't mattered. Or at least, he hadn't thought it mattered at the time. His cufflinks could have been lost in the parking lot. They could have been lost when he tumbled down the stairs into the basement. Or when he raced from the cabin with Lily. "Check the report, and I'm sure that information can be verified."

Lily looked back at him. "The perp wanted to set you up."

"So it would seem. Guess he didn't count on my ironclad alibi."

"Or he did." Her hair slid over her shoulder. "And he wanted to make sure we fully understood that he was the one doing the killing. He wanted us to give him credit for what he was doing. He used your cufflinks so *you* would know." She whipped her head back toward Gage and

Sharon. "He has my list." Urgency filled her voice. The same urgency that Atlas could feel trembling through her body. "You're standing here, threatening to arrest Atlas, when he's been a victim all along."

"*I am a victim.*" Ah. He'd almost nailed that. Theodora would have been proud.

Lily's voice trembled with urgency as she said, "He used the cufflinks because he wants us to know it's him. He's *punishing.* Don't you see? He was punishing here in Dallas and now, he's—"

"He went after Tonya Johnson because she's a thief?" Sharon cut in to question.

"No, because she's evil. To him. *To him.* She's the product of a serial killer. It's the blood. She's guilty. *To him.*"

But Gage appeared uncertain. "You're losing me, Lily."

"She's not losing me," Atlas fired back. "Could very well be the reason why the bastard came after me in the first place. Because he knew what my father had done. And being that freak's kid was more than enough reason for him to decide I was guilty. At least, guilty in his mind."

"But..." Gage took a step back. "The two other kills in Dallas. Those poor bastards were *not* the kids of serials."

"Killers evolve." Lily's tight voice. "They grow. They develop. This guy—he was too quick. The timing between kills was far too brief. No cooling down period, and that scared me."

"*You* were scared?" Gage asked. He seemed surprised.

She ignored his surprise. "He would want more victims, fast. Because he likes killing. But he thinks what he's doing is *right.* So that means the victims have to be *wrong.*" Her words tumbled out. "The kids of serials—if he believes they were born evil, then he's justified in what he's doing. He's eliminating evil. He's punishing. He has my data. He has my files. Oh, God. *It's my fault.*"

"No." Atlas was adamant. "This is not because of you."

She whirled to face him. "He got the information from me, and now Tonya Johnson is dead."

"You did not kill her."

"No, I just gave him her address."

He would not let her carry this guilt. "*He stole the address.*"

"He has all of their addresses." Breathless. "I worry he is just getting started." And she spun away, whirling toward Gage and Sharon again. "If we don't act, now, he *will* be killing someone else. And it will be *fast.* Not three weeks from now. Not three days. In fact, I think he is hunting right this minute."

Sharon swiped a hand over her forehead. "You...you ever wrong about stuff like this?"

"She knows killers," Gage said. A quiet confidence.

"I am *not* wrong." Lily was adamant. "But...I-I don't know which vic he's going after next. There are two immediate options. *Two.* I figure he has to be going after the one closest but...I don't know if he came back here to Dallas, a spot that I think *is* his home based on the initial kills...or if he went after the vic by driving straight out from Shreveport...which would put him going to New Orleans and—"

"Lily, slow down." Gage rocked forward onto the balls of his feet. "I can't keep up."

She sucked in a deep breath. "Two potential victims are at the top of my list. One is in Oklahoma City. His name is Hatch Davis. Hatch is the son of the Spring Break Strangler."

Sharon's eyes widened. "I remember that vicious bastard. I didn't know he had any kids!"

Desmond climbed silently down the stairs. He stopped when he reached the landing.

"Hatch isn't like his father. He's never hurt anyone in his life. He doesn't even know who his father is." Lily edged away from Atlas. "The second option is Westin Blanchard. He's in New Orleans. The son of—"

Gage swore. "Fuck. Blanchard the Butcher. Yeah, I know about his dad."

"Me, too." Sharon backed up a step.

"Westin was just paroled. He served time for the armed robbery charge, and he's out on good behavior. He'll be walking the streets of the Big Easy." Lily's words still came a bit too quickly, but she had slowed down. Some. "We need protection for both men, but...Hatch really has no idea who his father is. If we reveal it, when he finds out the truth..."

He'll spend the rest of his days wondering if he will become a monster, too.

Yeah, Atlas had been there. Done that for his whole freaking life.

"We need guards on them." Lily was adamant. "They need protection, immediately."

But Gage shook his head. "That's not how it works. I can't send in federal agents when you have a hunch. No way Brass will go for that. Not to just cover random people."

She surged to stand toe to toe with him. "They are *not* random! They are targets! They are potential *victims*. And if you want to stop this killer, if you want to catch him, I am telling you how to do it. He *will* be going after one of these individuals. Catch him before he kills. *Help me to save them.*"

Unless it was already too late. Unless the bastard was already hunting, right then. And, hell, yes, Atlas believed that he was.

But Gage shook his head. "I'll have to pick one as priority for my supervisors, Lily. Tell me, who is he more likely to go after?"

"They are *both* priority! You don't have to pick! That's bullshit!" Lily snapped.

Yes, Atlas rather thought it was.

"That's federal bureaucracy," Gage retorted. "They are already gonna fight me because you are asking me to institute full protection for two individuals in separate states based entirely on a *hunch*."

"It's not a hunch." Ice dripped from her words. "It's years of expertise." Once more, she spun toward Atlas. Lily locked her dark eyes on him. The gold in the depths gleamed. "*You* have pull at the Bureau."

"Who...me?" Atlas modestly touched his chest.

"Atlas, don't. Not with me."

He stared straight at her.

"You could probably blackmail all the top leaders at the Bureau to do whatever you want. You snap your fingers, and people jump."

They did. True story.

"Help me to save these two. Help me to stop him. Help me to catch him."

Ah, but he didn't just want the perp caught. Atlas wanted him dead in the ground.

"Please," Lily added. "Please, for me."

"As if I could refuse you anything." He snapped his fingers. "Let's see how fast they jump." Voice bored, he added, "And if they refuse, then I'll just send in my own security to protect your poor, lost lambs."

"If I'm following along correctly, one of those lambs just got out of prison for armed robbery," Desmond reminded him. The first time his friend had spoken since climbing off the staircase. "Not so sure that one counts as anyone's poor, lost little lamb."

"*He's* gonna be the target," Gage suddenly exclaimed as he whirled and rushed for the door. "Sonofabitch, that makes more sense. You can't pick, Lily, then fine, I will. Westin Blanchard is already guilty as fuck. He's the next target. The killer is going after him." He yanked open the front door.

Sharon raced after him. She darted a few, desperate glances over her shoulder before she hurried outside.

"Thank you for the visit," Atlas called. "A pleasure to see you both. Do come back."

The door slammed closed behind them.

Lily blocked his path. "Help me save them, Atlas."

"Ah, Lily, don't you know…I'd do anything for you?" *Save them…and still kill the bastard who made the mistake of bringing you into this nightmare.* He smiled at her.

"Oh, no," Lily whispered. "Your dimples are out."

He winked at her. "Let's kill the bastard."

"Atlas…"

"Catch," he corrected. "Let's *catch* the bastard. So sorry. Slip of the tongue."

She grabbed his arms. Shot onto her toes even as she yanked him toward her. Stunning him, thrilling him, she pressed a hot, fast kiss to his lips. "No, it wasn't." Her tongue dipped into his mouth. Tasted him. "*That* was a slip of the tongue."

Damn straight, it had been. *I want more.*

"We're catching him," she breathed against his mouth. "We aren't killing him. We are *not* the bad guys."

Oh, she could say that as often as she wanted. "Not the bad guys, check." But...

If he strikes first, he's dead.

Though, technically, the bastard had already struck first. When he had kidnapped Atlas. When he had taken Lily. When he'd tossed them down the stairs and into that basement...

He made the first attack, Lily. I'll make the final one.

But she eased away. "We have to go." Her gaze darted over his chest. "I think it's my turn to say...you need to get dressed."

"You *need* to have breakfast. You didn't eat enough yesterday."

"We have a killer to hunt!"

"You have a breakfast to eat. Roland already has it waiting. Go in the kitchen. I'll dress." Then they'd hunt. Done. "I'll make phone calls. *First.*" Before he dressed. "I'll get the wheels in motion to protect your would-be victims." But first those victims would have to be located. It would take time, a luxury they might not have. He eased past her and headed for the stairs.

His gaze collided with Desmond's. "Didn't see you calling Theodora."

Desmond's head inclined. "I texted her. She said for you to please not confess to any crimes."

He only confessed to Lily. No one else.

"She was coming over," Desmond revealed. "But since the Feds have rushed out..."

"Tell her it's unnecessary. In fact, Lily and I will be leaving soon."

"I want to go back to the crime scene, to the cabin," Lily said.

He'd rather thought that might be one of their stops.

But, before she got her heart set on things, "I doubt the cops are gonna let us get close."

"I need to see it again."

Ah, so determined. He enjoyed her determination. He also understood why she wanted to get back to that crime scene. "Because you want to see if the basement was left standing. Fine. We'll make that a stop." One of many for the day. But before he climbed the stairs, he asked Desmond, "Any luck with the security footage from Benedict's?"

"He's the only one I saw on it. Benedict coming and going before his death. The bastard we are after is a ghost."

A ghost who happened to be very good at breaking and entering. "Keep at it. Go back as far as you can with the footage."

Desmond nodded. "And I'm assuming you want me to start security arrangements for the two would-be vics?"

"Yes." Lily's loud reply. "He does."

Desmond waited.

Atlas smiled. "You heard the lady."

"You always gonna give her everything she wants?"

He headed up the stairs. "I guess it depends on what she wants."

"What if it's your heart?" Desmond called after him.

His steps faltered. "Funny, Desmond. You know I don't have one of those."

* * *

She watched Atlas until he disappeared up the stairs, and only then did Lily glance toward Desmond.

"We both know that was a lie," Desmond said.

She nodded.

"Good. Glad we're clear."

294

Since they were being clear, "He won't always give me what I want. He was exaggerating." Obviously.

Desmond laughed. "Not talking about that." He turned away, hauling out his phone. "The dumbass already gave you his heart."

Lily felt an ache in her own chest.

Atlas doesn't love me. He isn't giving me his heart.

Which was very unfortunate. Because she'd certainly given him hers.

Chapter Twenty-Three

Julia Tutwiler Prison For Women
Wetumpka, Alabama

Present Day...

Sunday afternoons meant tea time at the prison.

Magnolia always enjoyed tea time, though, she had to admit, it wasn't nearly as fun when someone else prepared the tea. The quality was never quite high enough to meet her exacting standards.

The first time that the warden had invited her for tea in his office, she'd been amused. She'd understood his actions, of course. Most men were annoyingly predictable. The warden had wanted to show what an alpha he was. A man brave enough to have tea with the Poison Princess.

He'd smirked at her for most of the time, as if daring her to ask if he'd put something in *her* tea. She hadn't asked. Hadn't hesitated as she daintily lifted the porcelain teacup.

Her pinky finger had been extended because she was a lady after all, and she'd politely sipped the tea.

Now, as a general rule, southern women liked sweet tea. Her own mother had made the most amazing sweet tea in the world. On a hot summer day, there was nothing better, her mother would claim, than some ice cold sweet tea.

However, Magnolia preferred tea of a different variety. Warm tea. With a cube of sugar. A dash of milk. A little habit she'd picked up because it was just so much easier to disguise the taste of poison when you were making a tea that already had so many different ingredients. With warm, flavored tea, you could easily slide a little something extra in the mix. Apple, hibiscus, pomegranate, cinnamon...

Poison.

Yes, her brews were much preferred over her mother's sweet tea. And over the warden's weak blends.

But...

Beggars couldn't be choosers.

She'd been charming during that first tea. After all, she excelled at charm. She'd always told her daughter...*smile more. Draw them to you. Never let them see the threat.*

But Lily wouldn't listen. Sadly. Her smiles had always been few and far between. A pity, that. Because she was sure Lily had her smile.

Physical appeal and charm were two strengths in a woman's arsenal. When would Lily learn to use those strengths?

The warden had enjoyed their initial visit so much that he'd made tea time into a weekly event. He probably thought he'd write a book about the experience one day...

Tea with a Killer.

She'd see about that plan. He'd rather been amusing to

her, breaking up the monotony of prison, so she'd allowed the little visits to continue. But if he pushed her too far...

She might just have to slip a little something into his tea.

Simply because she was in prison, that did not mean she didn't still have enormous power. And fans. *Friends*.

A woman's smile and charm could go a long way in this world. If only Lily would learn that truth.

She sipped the tea. Batted her lashes at the warden. He was ten years her senior, and he'd be more than interested in anything she suggested to him.

But...

Lawrence leaned forward, face all intent. Almost worried. "I need to tell you about a news story..."

She put down the tea. It didn't even clink when she set down the cup. If he'd had something important to tell her, he should have led with that news. Not waited while she sipped.

"It's Lily," he said, voice dramatic.

Magnolia blinked. "She's not due to visit today."

"No, no, she's not coming to visit. It seems...I'm talking about a *news* story." He pressed his hands on the table in front of him, dangerously close to tipping over the teapot. "Lily was taken. Abducted by a killer."

Magnolia was conscious of every single beat of her heart. Every single slow beat.

He watched her like a hawk, looking for a response.

She reached for her tea cup once more. Lifted it. Made sure that pinky finger was extended.

"She was rescued," he added.

"Of course, she was. I'm sure FBI Agent Gage Emerick rushed to the scene. He's quite taken with Lily. Always has been." *Always has been unworthy of her, too. Such a dick. Using my Lily's talents.*

He frowned at her casual response. "Ah, the cops got to her. The place she'd been inside—it exploded right after she got out."

The smallest bit of tea sloshed over the side of her cup, splashing onto her hand. "Oh, dear."

"She is safe," he told her. "I do not want you concerned."

"I've spilled my tea."

"She was taken to a hospital and examined. The reports on the news say that she is safe. There were videos taken of her—her and Atlas Bennett."

Oh, Lily. She stared into the tea. *What are you doing?*

"They're together. Romantically, I mean. I...didn't realize that Lily was involved with him. Atlas Bennett is quite the wealthy individual."

"Quite." She put down the cup. Picked up a napkin and dotted at the small spill on her hand.

"I thought you'd want to know. Seeing as how you and your daughter are so close."

She folded the napkin. "Did they catch the man who took her?"

"Not yet. I'm sure they will. But, uh, about Atlas...I've heard he donates generously to charitable causes, and I was thinking—"

Why start thinking now? But instead of saying that, she nodded in an agreeable, encouraging way. "You were thinking he may contribute to some causes very near and dear to your heart?" Her smile was as sweet as a cube of sugar. "I bet he would. Know what, Lawrence? I have a great idea. Why don't you invite him here? I'll even talk to him for you. Send him straight to me. We'll have a one-on-one chat. I'm sure he will be more than willing to aid you."

The warden beamed at her. "You think so?"

"Oh, I think a private visit with Atlas Bennett is one hundred percent in order." And she thought that the visit needed to be arranged immediately. "Call him. Tell him Lily's mother sends her regards. That I am dying to meet him."

Someone would be dying, all right. It would not be her.

Chapter Twenty-Four

THE DAMN DOORBELL WAS RINGING AGAIN. Now dressed, still pissed, and done with his current batch of phone calls and orders, Atlas bounded down the stairs.

The doorbell pealed again. "Seriously?" Atlas snarled as he reached the landing. "Who the hell is it now?"

"It's the doctor." Desmond waited in the foyer, arms loose at his sides. "Guards at the front gate texted to let me know he was approaching the main entrance."

"Are the guards at the gate just letting everyone through today?" What good were the men out there if they weren't stopping anyone?

Desmond arched one eyebrow. "Not like the guards can stop Feds."

"And they can't stop this guy? They just let some bozo waltz past them?" Maybe some of those guards needed to be fired.

"Not some bozo. He's your doctor."

"What damn doctor?" The only one he wanted in his house was Dr. Lily Gallo. Speaking of Lily... "Where is she?" Only Desmond was waiting in the foyer. No sign of his Lily.

"Lily is in the kitchen, telling Roland that he made the best omelet she'd ever had in her life. And informing him that his French toast is to die for."

Atlas grunted. Good. She'd eaten.

"The *doctor* at the door is the man who checked you and Lily out at the hospital. Now, call me crazy, but I didn't realize Dr. Phillip Owen was the type to make house calls."

Atlas's gaze cut to the door. "Didn't think he was that type, either."

"Interesting that he's here, isn't it?"

Interesting enough. Atlas would handle the man. He rolled back his shoulders. "What the fuck is up with the cufflinks, Desmond?" Something that had been bothering the hell out of him ever since Gage had dropped his little bombshell.

Desmond's body tensed. "The GPS tracker on the cufflinks was deactivated. The last signal I got from them was in that damn cabin. I thought they'd been destroyed in the explosion."

"Apparently, not. Apparently, the cufflinks took a fun little side quest to Shreveport and wound up with a dead woman."

The doorbell rang again.

"He's pissing me off," Atlas said.

"Never a good situation." A grimace from Desmond. "Let me handle him."

"Too late." Atlas was on the way to the door. He put his game face on. Oh, who was he kidding? He always had that face on, and Atlas opened the door.

Dr. Phillip Owen stood there, finger still on the doorbell.

"I am so over uninvited guests." Annoyance filled Atlas's words. "I get why my guards allowed the Feds to rush past them. I do. They're Feds. They flashed badges. Why the hell didn't someone stop *you* before you got to my door?"

Phillip straightened his shoulders. "As I informed them, I am your *doctor*."

Atlas caught sight of the news vans that were stationed down the street. Great. A new day. A new opportunity for reporters to harass him. Not like Atlas was going to tell them shit but...

Maybe someone else is planning for a closeup with the cameras.

Curious, he slanted a stare back at the doctor.

Phillip wasn't wearing scrubs. He had on a suit. His hair was freshly cut. His jaw clean shaven. *Smile for the camera.*

"Everyone wants their five minutes of fame," Atlas muttered.

"I'm here to help you," Phillip told him in what he probably thought was a deeply compassionate tone. It wasn't. It was a little high. Too rushed. Too dramatic. "I need to check on your condition. To make sure that your injuries were not more severe than anticipated." He craned to see around Atlas. "I also have grown increasingly concerned for the well-being of Dr. Gallo. She received a blow to the head, too, but in your haste to leave the hospital, I was not able to thoroughly examine her to my liking."

To your liking, huh? How about this? I do not like you at all. "Lily and I both had imaging done on us during the course of our exams. There were no skull fractures. No brain bleeds. You weren't the only doc on the scene." Just the one in his face the most. The one who seemed to be calling the shots in the ER. "Additional care from you is very much unnecessary."

Phillip cleared his throat. "I thought she'd call to update me on the health status for both of you, but she never did, and, as a doctor, it is my duty to—"

"You're not seeing Lily." Time to cut through the BS.

Phillip's freshly shaved face scrunched. "Excuse me?"

"You're not seeing Lily. I'm really over assholes who are obsessed with her showing up on my doorstep. The routine gets old, believe me. Now, leave my fiancée alone. Go back to your hospital. Do your job, while you still have one."

"*Excuse me?*" Phillip Owen hunched.

"This is a major overstep. You don't show up at a patient's house without an invitation. I'm not even your patient any longer." He pointed toward the news vans. "What are you gonna do? Rush over there to them and act like you're my personal physician? Give yourself a bit more prestige than you have?" He hadn't liked this guy from the first moment they'd met. The man had known far too much about Lily. Phillip had been far too focused on her.

Even as his cheeks reddened, Phillip held his position in front of the door. "I have to make certain of her well-being. I am not leaving until I check in with Dr. Gallo."

Atlas smiled at him. "We'll see about that." He'd been very conscious of several guards edging closer. And because Lily had recently mentioned his handy ability to snap his fingers and make people jump into action...He snapped them.

The guards hurried forward.

"This is your chance to walk away on your own," Atlas said to Phillip. "If you don't go willingly, they can haul you away. Tell me, doctor, which image do you believe will play better for the cameras?"

Phillip spun around and let out a little gasp when he saw the approaching guards. "You would not *dare!*"

Sure, he would. They would. Everyone would.

Phillip whipped back to face him. "I want Lily."

Like that statement wasn't suspicious? And infuriating? "Never gonna happen."

"I-I want to make sure she's safe!" A fast correction. "Why are you hiding her? What have you done to her?"

Oh, for shit's sake. Really? *I fucked her.* Should he just take out a billboard to announce the news?

"I'm fine, Dr. Owen." Lily's calm voice. "Your visit is unnecessary. I am healthy. I am safe. So is Atlas." She was right behind him. Atlas could smell her sweet vanilla scent. Had he made a point of getting her body lotion with that exact scent when he arranged for her clothes and toiletries? Yes. He had.

He arched a brow at the red-faced doc. "You heard the lady. Healthy as can be. Thanks for the visit. Don't come back." He shut the door, knowing the guards would take care of their unwelcome guest.

Atlas turned, putting his back to the door. "What. The. Fuck?"

Desmond still stood nearby. He nodded. "He's suspicious as hell."

An absolute echo of Atlas's own thoughts. Always good to know that he and Desmond were on the same page. Atlas swept his stare over Lily. "I'm sick of idiots getting obsessed with you."

She took a half-step back. "I can assure you, no one is obsessed with me."

"I am." An easy admission. Completely. "That doc knows your whole life story."

"That, uh, doc wanted to be filmed coming to the rescue

here. It's purely a glamour project. Doesn't have anything to do with me." She shifted closer to Atlas. "Did you make your calls when you went upstairs? Do you have protection in place for Hatch Davis and Westin Blanchard?"

"Working on it. Certain powerful individuals at the FBI understand the gravity of the situation. And I've reached out to security agencies in Oklahoma City and New Orleans. The agents will be working to contact and secure your two would-be victims."

Some of the tension left her shoulders. "Thank you."

His hand lifted and skimmed over her jaw. "I am a cold bastard."

A little furrow appeared between her brows.

"But I will *not* be that person to you. You tell me what you want, and I'll always give it to you."

She raised her brows. "Ah, is that because you're obsessed with me?" A light edge that could have been teasing. From another woman, he would have been *sure* it was teasing. But Lily so rarely joked.

So he didn't joke or tease in response, either. Atlas simply gave her the stark truth. "Yes."

She bit her lower lip. Then nodded. "Okay, let's test that."

She wanted to *test* him? Call him intrigued. He'd always been a master at acing tests.

"Take me to the crime scene," Lily directed. "I want to get an up close look at the area. If possible, I want to see that basement. Or what's left of it."

Of course, that would be what she requested. He told her that he was obsessed, that he would give her anything her heart desired—okay, fine that part had been implied, he hadn't technically told her those specific words—and she'd asked for a crime scene tour. That was his Lily, though.

He smiled at her. Because he'd already anticipated this turn of events. *This is how you ace tests.* "Sweets, the limo is ready and waiting."

Desmond cursed. "Is this really wise? Did you *see* those reporters waiting out there? They are gonna follow the limo from the second it leaves here. And a limo just pulling up to a crime scene will be damn noticeable."

Atlas shrugged. "Maybe I'm like Dr. Owen..."

"I have no idea what that means," Desmond threw back.

"It means I like the attention. Or in this case, I want it."

Lily nodded. "Me, too."

Desmond gaped at them both. "Why?"

"Because the perp needs to know that we're looking for him. That we aren't stopping," Atlas said.

Again, Lily nodded. "The killer should understand that we're hunting him."

"Forget being like Dr. Owen. That's bull. You two, though..." Desmond motioned between Atlas and Lily. "You're both just the hell alike," Desmond accused.

Atlas reached for Lily's hand. His fingers curled with hers. "Well, what can I say? She's my soulmate."

Her hand jerked in his. Hard.

He merely tightened his grip. "Keep working on the security footage from Benedict's house, would you, Desmond? And let me know if you find *anything* that rings an alarm for you." Atlas's own internal alarms had been ringing all morning.

But Desmond was shaking his head. "Screw that. I'll delegate the task. Someone else can look through the footage. I'll be the one riding behind you and covering your ass in case the prick you are hunting decides to come after *you.*"

"Didn't you hear?" Atlas kept his hold on Lily. *Why did*

you flinch, sweets? Don't you know what you are to me? "Our perp is either in New Orleans or Oklahoma City. That means I should be completely safe right now."

Desmond's dark eyes narrowed. "That what you really believe?"

"I believe...that I'm going hunting."

* * *

"I'm...NOT wrong about the targets." Lily's halting words as they pulled away from his estate.

He glanced through the window, his gaze drawn to the crowd of reporters. Oh, what shock. Dr. Phillip Owen had paused to speak with them. "Profile him."

"What?"

His legs stretched out in front of him. Carl was driving, the privacy screen was up, and Atlas lounged in the seat across from Lily. "The ER doc who showed up on our doorstep today." The *our* part of that sentence just slipped out. Felt natural as hell to say. "Profile him for me."

She hesitated. "I'm not part of the FBI's Behavioral Analysis Unit."

"Nah. You're probably better than them all. That's why Gage used you, isn't it? The dick." He really did not like that jerk. Then again, he liked few people. *I just dislike him a little bit extra.* "He knew you understood killers, and he used your talent to advance his own career."

Her head turned. As the silence stretched in the back of the limo, she looked at the reporters. At Dr. Phillip Owen. "Do you want to know if I think he could be a threat? If he could be our killer?"

"That guy is no killer. He's a glory hound, a narcissist, but I don't know that he has the killer instinct in him." Atlas

308

scraped a hand over his jaw. He hadn't bothered to shave that morning, unlike Phillip Owen, and the stubble pricked against his fingers. "If he was going to kill, it would be far more subtle, like deliberately screwing up during a surgery. Slicing a patient where and when he shouldn't. Letting them bleed out right in front of him even as he faked trying to save the poor vic."

"Sounds like you're pretty good at profiling, Atlas."

He'd had to learn what made others tick. Learning that helped him to manipulate them better. "Give me your take on him."

"Narcissist. Yes. I agree with you on that one. I would also wager that he has low self-esteem. He wants to be admired by his peers and by women, in particular, but he struggles in that aspect. He didn't achieve his dream of being a psychiatrist, and I think that eats at him. He feels he would have been incredibly successful in that field, if...well, I would suspect he blames others for his life not working out quite as he wanted."

"He's a doctor. Isn't that successful enough for him?" That would certainly be a huge measure of success for a whole lot of people.

"He's currently surrounded by a flock of reporters, and he's grinning from ear to ear. Does that seem like the kind of man who is happy working in a crowded ER? Not sure his current job is the success story he wanted."

So the doc wanted more fawning attention, check. Wanted to be a celebrity. The star of the show. "You didn't say whether or not you thought Phillip Owen could kill."

"I don't think he's a *physical* killer. Not sure that makes sense, but I suppose I mean that I don't really see him dragging you through that cabin. It takes physical strength to do that. Not sure he has that." Her hands pressed to her thighs. "I'd even wondered before if it might have taken *two* people to move you, but I only recalled one attacker."

He snapped to attention. "You didn't mention this important point before." *Two* attackers? Since when?

"I didn't mention it because I have no proof. One person could have done the job. One could drag me, then you. Absolutely, it could be done. Two just would have made the job easier. With the other attacks in Dallas, there was never any indication of a second perpetrator, so that idea is probably wrong."

Probably.

"So, again, I didn't see the point in mentioning it if I was just going to be wrong."

His fingers drummed on the leather seat. "You don't want me to be your soulmate."

She flinched. "Excuse me?"

Atlas allowed a slow, taunting smile to curve his lips. "Soulmate."

She sucked in a breath. "What are you doing? I-I thought we were talking about Dr. Owen."

They had been. Now they were talking about soulmates. They'd left the reporters and the annoying doctor behind. "What am I doing?" He'd be honest. "Playing with you." His head tilted. "Baiting you." *And, oddly enough, hurting myself.* But he kept his smile in place. "Why are you afraid?"

"I'm not afraid of you." Certainty.

"You're afraid that you belong to me. *With me.*" Did she think he didn't see it? "You wanted to study the children of serials because you were trying to figure out how to stop that darkness inside yourself. Only now you're fucking me, and...do you like the dark, Lily?"

"I just told you that I wasn't afraid. Not of you. And, no, I'm not afraid of the dark."

"I didn't ask if you were *afraid* of the dark. I asked if you *liked* the dark."

Her chin inched up. "I don't see the point of these questions."

Oh, there was a point. "You don't want to belong to me."

"Is that what you think?" She wasn't staring directly at him. Her attention was focused on the window near him.

"I think you're scared of yourself, and you're scared of me."

"I told you, *I'm not scared of you.*" Her gaze jumped to collide with his.

"Prove it." A taunt.

"Fine." Then she—she leapt across the small distance that had separated them. Lily jumped toward him. On him. She straddled him as he reclined on the seat, her knees pushing down into the leather on either side of him. Her hands pressed to his cheeks, and her mouth crashed down on his.

Well, well, well...

She wasn't kissing him like she was afraid. She was kissing him like she was hungry, desperate, aroused, and her response was the last thing he'd expected.

His hands curled around her hips. Then, he grabbed the material of her dress—soft fabric, but not as silken as her skin—and he hiked it up. Up, up, and his fingers were sliding over her thighs. Then higher.

Her mouth pulled from his. "I was wrong about you."

He'd touched her panties. He had *not* intended to fuck Lily in the limo. Had not. Had—

"You can't profile for shit, Atlas Bennett."

Atlas opened his eyes. He found Lily staring down at him. Her hands had moved to clamp over his shoulders.

"I'm not afraid of you," she told him. "You're dead wrong on that."

His fingers slid under the edge of her panties. Stroked over her clit.

She sucked in a sharp breath. Her hands clamped harder around his shoulders.

He slid a finger into her. *Tight. So tight.* His thumb played with her clit. "You afraid of yourself, sweets?" She was getting wetter. Hotter.

"I'm afraid...I'm afraid I-I want you too much."

"Too much? Not a thing." He needed her mouth on him again. Needed his dick *in* her.

"I'm scared..." Breathy. Husky.

Ah, there it was...

He pulled his hand away from his perfect heaven. "What are you afraid of? *Tell me.*"

"I'm scared that you'll see all of me, and that you'll turn away. Soulmates aren't real. That doesn't happen. They are a dream. Nothing more. *They aren't real.* Especially not for someone like me." She licked her lips. "Or at least, that's what I thought. I didn't count on you. I didn't think—didn't believe I'd *feel* this way. Ever."

Both of his hands were on her hips now. Holding far too tightly. "Feel what way?"

"I think I'm falling in love with you. It *scares* me because I don't want to feel like I've finally found my home, just to lose it all. To lose *you.*"

His heart drummed too hard. His muscles were too stiff. And his control—*obliterated.*

"Atlas?" Worry.

She could not worry.

Or...maybe she should worry. "I'm fucking you." Guttural.

A fast lick of her tongue over her lower lip. "I was going to fuck *you*."

His breath heaved. His chest burned. "Ditch the panties or I'll yank them off you."

"What?"

Too late. The panties were gone. Yanked away. Tossed on the floor of the limo. Her shoes fell off with them.

He had warned her. As for Lily...

I think I'm falling in love...

He jerked open his pants. Thrust his boxers out of the way, and his thick, eager dick sprang out. Then he was shoving up her dress even more. She still straddled him, and the wide, aching head of his dick pushed into her.

"*Atlas!*" Her fingers were on his shoulders. So tight.

She's tight. Tight and hot and I'm going into her bare. I'm taking her bare.

Bare.

Bare.

His teeth snapped together.

"I'm on birth control," she whispered.

He'd always been afraid of having a child. Afraid the blood in his veins was too tainted. But Lily...his Lily...

What if we did have a kid together? Angel, devil...

Lily's baby...her daughter would be my precious angel. I'd put the world at her feet.

And Lily would love her son. She'd never abandon him. Never cast him out because she feared what he was. Lily...

I think I'm falling in love...

An inhuman growl tore from him, and he drove into her. He lifted her up and down, their bodies slapping together. Need ripping past every other thought. Primal lust consumed and burned away everything else, and he was pounding into her even as he kept that too fierce hold on her waist.

Up and down. Up and down. Frantic. Hard. His jaw locked. His eyes were on her. On her face every single moment.

Pleasure. Give her pleasure.

One hand left her waist. Shoved between their heaving bodies. Mercilessly, he stroked her. She was stretched around his dick. So tight. He strummed her clit. Worked it again and again with his fingers. Faster. Harder.

His hips pounded.

She gave a little shriek, her body collapsing on him.

He wasn't done. Not even close. He twisted, putting her half beneath him on the seat, and he pounded into her with a fury. Bare skin. Hot sex. His Lily.

I think I'm falling in love...

In and out. Deeper. Savage growls. Possessive touches. Hands marking and branding. Mouth on her throat. Her lips.

Falling in love...

His release roared through him.

With you.

Chapter Twenty-Five

"YOU CAN'T BE HERE."

Lily ignored the quaking between her thighs. She had her panties back on, her dress in place, her shoes on her feet, and she hoped—truly hoped—that it was not apparent that she'd just fucked Atlas in the back of his limo.

The fire inspector frowned at her and Atlas. Sebastian Santiago had flashed his ID and blocked their path as they approached the charred remains of the cabin. "This is a closed crime scene," Sebastian informed them. "No way do civilians get to prance up here."

Yes, a closed scene. She got that. But she had not been *prancing*. She'd been walking very carefully. Trying to ignore the fact that aftershocks of pleasure were still going off in her core.

"I'll have to call the Feds if you don't leave," Sebastian continued with a dogged nod.

"Federal Agent Gage Emerick knows that we are here," Atlas assured the man in a bold-faced lie.

He lied so very easily.

And fucks so incredibly well.

315

"He told Dr. Gallo that she could get a quick sweep of the area," Atlas added.

Gage had done no such thing.

"Well, he told her wrong," the inspector snapped back. "It's not safe here, and I'm not going to risk anyone's life. The structure is too weak. The level over the basement was reinforced, yes, but it could still come crashing down, and I don't want anyone getting hurt at my scene. Bad enough that we lost a detective to this freak. We won't lose anyone else. Not on my watch."

She admired his determination. And appreciated the fact that he had just told her something useful. "So the basement *wasn't* destroyed."

"Not destroyed. Not yet. Fire was all in the front, focused mostly near the entrance of the structure." He threw out his hands in a heaving gesture as he explained, "Erupted outward, in a targeted blast. Took out the windows, the front part of the roof." Sebastian's hands stopped shoving forward and dropped to his sides. "That's why the poor bastard died. He was just steps from the entrance door. If he'd been near the basement door—see it's over near the back..." He raised his right hand to jerk his thumb vaguely toward the blackened hull of the cabin. "That would have given him a fighting chance." A shrug as his hand fell again. "Didn't happen. Burns were all over his body."

She stared at the blackened remains that had once been the cabin's front walls.

"What in the hell?" More annoyance from the inspector blocking their path. Only that annoyance was not directed at her and Atlas this time. His glare was focused beyond them as he demanded, "Are those reporters? I already *told* them to stay away."

Yes, but the reporters had probably followed her and Atlas so...

"Everybody needs to stay the hell back!" The inspector marched toward the arriving crews, waving his hands. "*Back!*"

Atlas glanced at Lily. "Discover what you needed to know?"

Yes, she had.

"Then shall we get back in the limo, or do we want to pose for the camera a bit longer?"

She hadn't realized they were posing. But now...

Atlas's body stood protectively near hers. Her dress blew in the faint breeze, and the darkened remains of the cabin were waiting right in front of them. The whole scene probably made for one very dramatic photo. Or video.

"This image will be everywhere," he added. "If you were trying to bait the killer..." A brisk nod. "Congratulations."

They had told Desmond before that they wanted the killer's attention. But...*bait*. The word whispered through her mind. Atlas had used himself as bait before, to draw the killer to him. Atlas had deliberately put himself in a vulnerable position, his guards not close, so the killer would attack.

She didn't want Atlas being bait. Not ever again.

Lily wasn't even sure that their killer would come after him. But...

Will you come after me? "Don't congratulate me yet." Nerves trembled through her. She didn't normally seek out attention. This was far from her realm of comfort. "Hold the thought." And she hurried after the inspector, heading straight toward the small throng of reporters.

"Dr. Gallo!"

"Lily!"

Shouts from the reporters as she drew closer to them.

"Why did you come back to the scene of the crime, Dr. Gallo?"

"Lily, Lily! Is that an engagement ring you're wearing?"

"Dr. Gallo, what do you know about the killer?"

Atlas had followed her. He curled his arm around her, putting it over her upper chest and pulling her back against him. "Sweets..." A breath in her ear. "What are you doing?"

She was going to do what had to be done. She and Atlas both wanted the killer to know they were hunting him. There was certainly one very direct way to do that. *Just tell him. Tell the world.* "I am engaged to Atlas Bennett." Her voice was a little too husky. A bit too breathy. She cleared her throat. "We came back here because we are not going to let the killer get away. We know who he is."

Lots of shouts exploded in the air. Furious exclamations. Demands for more information.

"He is weak, and he is *evil*," she emphasized that point, deliberately. "He is standing in judgment, delivering so-called punishments when he is the one who should be punished. When he is the one with sins tainting his blood. And he is the one who will pay." Her gaze swept over the reporters. She was being filmed. Good. Probably even live-streamed. The better to deliver her message. "Smoke and fire don't fool us. We know who you are targeting. The Feds know. You are the one that is going to be caught. The handcuffs will be on your wrists, and there will be no escape. You're not doing some kind of righteous work, no matter what lies you feed to yourself. You are the monster. And we will stop you."

"Dr. Gallo! Dr. Gallo! Do you have a name for the

suspect? Who is the killer? What does he look like? What does—"

"*Lily is done*," Atlas's voice, cutting through the yells instantly. "And the bastard who took us will soon be begging for mercy." He backed away, pulling her with him, as he guided her to the limo. More shouts followed them. So many more voices.

"When is the wedding?" A quick high-pitched question.

Lily glanced over at the reporter. A woman with short, red hair. "I—"

"As soon as possible," Atlas replied. "Might even fly to Vegas tonight." Then he steered Lily to the waiting limo with even more demand in his touch.

She didn't fight him. She'd said what needed to be said.

She and Atlas ignored the other questions hurled at them. Carl opened the side limo door. "About time we left, sir," Carl noted.

"Yeah, working on it." Atlas gently pushed her in the vehicle first, then he climbed in after her.

Carl slammed the door.

She took a deep breath. One, then another.

"What. The. Fuck, Lily?"

She blinked in surprise. "I...thought that went well." A delicate clearing of her throat. "There is something I need to tell—"

"Are you *fucking* kidding me?"

"You...*we*...talked about getting his attention." The killer's attention. And about the killer—

"Consider his attention *fucking* caught."

She blinked. That was the third *fuck* in a row from Atlas. Not a good sign. "You're angry? With me?" Anxious, confused, she glanced around the limo. *He took me there.*

Right on that seat. Drove into me fast and hard, with barely any foreplay, and I still came for him. Came so easily when I could never let go for others.

Atlas touched her, and she yearned.

Soulmate. That term had pierced straight to her heart. Her mother had mocked her with that same word. Lily had never, ever expected to find someone who could know her so well, who could match her so well, who would make her feel so much.

Until Atlas.

"Hell, yes, I'm angry with you. So angry that I'm tempted to spank that sweet ass."

She frowned. "I'm not into that." The conversation was out of hand. She had to tell him—

"Don't knock it until you try it." Gruff. "Dammit! Don't get me off track!" A muscle jerked along his jaw. "I didn't see it coming. Not until we were standing right there. And it's not going to happen, understand me?"

"No, I do quite not understand you." She wrapped her arms around her stomach. "You're making love to me one moment and yelling at me the next, and frankly, it's quite confusing."

"It wasn't making love. It was fucking."

Pain crashed into her heart. "Sorry. Yes." She looked away, staring through the window. They'd left the crime scene behind. The reporters were far away. But those reporters would do their job. They'd spread the video of her and Atlas far and wide. And in response to that video...*Will you come for me?*

"Lily?"

Her skin felt chilled. They needed to turn on the heat in the limo. "You said it was fucking."

He leaned forward and caught her chin. With a careful

touch, he turned her face back toward him. "Making love is soft. Sweet. Tender. *Fucking* happens when I drive my cock into you before you're ready for me. When I dig my fingers into your waist and pound into you as you're screaming in the back of a limo. Fucking, not making love."

Had she screamed? Lily didn't remember that. Perhaps, though. Possibly. Either way, she should let this discussion go. It would only bring more pain. Just because she felt something, it didn't mean that Atlas shared the emotion. It didn't mean he *could* feel the same way. But...*Why should I pretend that I don't finally feel this way?* "Maybe it's just fucking to you, but it's making love to me."

He let her go at once, as if he'd been burned.

He hadn't been. Benedict had been the one to burn...

Benedict.

She looked down.

"It's making love..." Atlas's rough voice. "Because you've convinced yourself that you're falling in love with me?"

Did the back of the limo smell like sex? Did Carl know what they'd done? Had she looked too tousled when she left the limo? Did the reporters know? Would every person who watched that video footage know?

Did it matter?

"*Lily.*"

"No." Snapped. A bit of surprise rushed through her. She hadn't realized how close her own anger was to the surface. Maybe it was because her control wasn't at its normal level. Normally, she would never, ever *make love* to a man in the back of a limo. But this wasn't normal.

Who are you kidding, Lily? You've never been normal a day in your life. Even her mother had known that.

The diary entries prove it...

A deep breath, then, calmer, she said, "I haven't

convinced myself of anything. I know what I feel. I know what I'm talking about." She looked up, and her gaze collided with his. "Who says that making love has to be soft and gentle? Who decided that rule?"

His lips parted. But he didn't speak.

That was fine. She had plenty to say. "Who says that making love has to be tender? If you love someone, aren't the emotions supposed to consume you? Wouldn't the feeling be raw and savage? Beyond control? Wouldn't you want to take and take and take, to be as greedy and demanding as you could?"

A hard shake of his head. "That's lust."

"Ah, lust." A sage nod. "Love's wicked twin."

"I think that's hate." But his gaze had softened.

And she thought he was wrong. "Maybe lust and love go hand in hand. Maybe our bodies recognize things before our hearts do. Or maybe...maybe love isn't always so gentle and sweet and *easy* for some people." It certainly wasn't that way for her. "Maybe, for some people, it's hard. It's demanding. It's consuming. Maybe it's a feeling that grows and grows inside of you. That takes over and sweeps you under before you realize it. Maybe it slams into place with the force of a freight train, and the way you feel—it won't ever be easy. It will always be hard and fast and frantic." Her chin notched up. "Fucking to one person. Making love to another." And he could laugh in her face. He could tell her that she was wrong. He could say—

"Marry me."

"What?"

"Marry—the fuck—me."

"You...you...no." She shook her head. Her hair slid over her shoulders. "I am not. I don't care what you told the reporters." *The reporters. The crime scene. The killer.* She needed to tell Atlas—

The click of his Adam's apple seemed loud as he swallowed. "Why the hell not? You *love* me."

"I do." Saying the words felt *right*. "I-I love you." She... she smiled. For a moment, she let everything else go. She just focused on him. On how she truly felt.

He shoved back against his seat. "Fuck me. You have a beautiful smile."

"I love you. And I don't care that you don't love me back. I'm not looking to change you or to try and make you feel something that you can't. *I love you.*" Each time she said the words, Lily felt stronger. Better. That was what she'd always wanted. To know...to understand...

I can love. I can love someone. And it's him.

Sometimes, her own emotions were so confusing. So overwhelming. But, not this time. This time, she knew with certainty what she felt.

Love.

"You love me, but you won't marry me." His blue eyes had narrowed. "That's damn cold."

"You..." She still felt chilled. "You just said that part about marriage to the reporters. You knew I was taunting him, and you joined me. Trying to push him over the edge?"

His brow furrowed.

"I think that might do it." Yes, it might be exactly what they'd needed. "Between me baiting him and you adding that bit about the wedding, I hope we pulled his focus."

"Pulled his focus...?" His expression hardened even more. "*And you wonder why I'm angry.*"

He shouldn't be angry. "I want him to come after me. Not you." She did not want to risk Atlas at all. Not ever. "He probably wouldn't go directly after you again anyway, not after last time. And we both know that he has a focus on me already. He went into my house. He showed so much rage there with all of the destruction. Clearly, his fury is directed at me, and because I said I knew who he was to the reporters, because—"

"*You deliberately taunted the sonofabitch so that he'd target you.*" A furious snarl.

She blinked. Yes, she'd done that.

"Lily..."

She wet her lips. "We said... Back at your house, I thought you understood that I wanted his attention."

He leaned toward her once again. Fury poured from him. "And I thought you understood that you were *never, ever* supposed to use yourself as any kind of bait."

"I...don't remember us talking about that."

"It's a fucking given. When you are the only reason I stay sane, then you *don't put your life on the line.*"

"I—" *The only reason you stay sane?* "I'm not. Not the reason you're sane. That's you. You control yourself. Your control is what has kept you going for years. It's what has made you into such a successful businessman. It gave you the empire you have. You—*Atlas!*"

He'd grabbed her, spun her, and had her down on the seat as he loomed over her. His hands pressed into the seat on either side of her body as she half-sprawled there. His head lowered over hers. Bringing their eyes close, their lips nearly touching. "*You don't put your life on the line.*"

"It's my life," she whispered.

"And you're *mine.*"

What did that mean? Her heart raced far too fast in her chest.

"You're *my* life, Lily. The whole damn thing."

"I..." His fury was so much stronger than she'd

expected. She could *feel* it. "I didn't want anyone else to be targeted. If I know he's coming after me, I can be ready." Everyone else would be safe. Couldn't he see that? She'd made the list with the names of the children who belonged to serial killers. Her list. *My fault.* Because her list had been taken, the ones being targeted—they were on her. Their lives. Their deaths.

She didn't want them dying. If she drew the killer's attention back to her, then the others would be safe.

Atlas's fury seemed to swell even more. "The sonofabitch isn't getting you. It will *not* happen."

"We're a team, Atlas. I thought you understood—we were going to the crime scene, we were getting his attention, we were letting him know—"

"You don't know who he is, Lily! You acted like you did, and now he's coming after you." His mouth took hers. So angry and wild and rough. Hard and frantic. Kissing her with a bruising fury because he was...

Scared?

Was Atlas scared?

But he was never scared. Never.

Instead of fighting his kiss, his fury, she kissed him back with desperate passion. Just as rough, just as strong, just as hungry.

And he...

The divider lowered between them and Carl. A hiss of sound. "Am I taking you back home, boss? Or do you have other plans?"

She tensed beneath Atlas.

His head lifted, his mouth moving just an inch away from hers. "Home," Atlas returned, voice gruff. His head lifted a bit more. There was torment on his face. An expression she'd never seen before. "Love...was supposed to be gentle." A whisper, meant for her ears. The divider hadn't risen back into place yet. "It was going to make me a better person."

Why did he need to be better? "I like the person you are."

His eyes squeezed closed. "Lily, you don't know who I really am."

Actually..."Yes, I think I do. I know exactly who you are." But, more than that, there was something she had realized with certainty as she stood in front of that cabin and listened to the inspector...Something that she had intended to tell Atlas as soon as they got back into the limo. Something she would not, could not, hold back any longer. "I know who the killer is, too."

His eyes flew open.

And the car exploded.

Chapter Twenty-Six

THE LIMO FLIPPED, ROLLED. SHE FELT THE LANCING heat of flames burning through the air, heard the shattering of glass. The crunch of metal. Again and again, the limo rolled. The wine and the glasses in the back on the limo's bar slammed into the floorboard, then the roof, sending chunks of glass flying into the air. A piece sliced across her hand, another across her neck, and the slashes happened in an instant. Everything happened in a timeless *instant*. The rolling. The fire. The crash and shatter of glass and metal. Then...

Atlas was roaring her name.

He'd tried to curl his body around hers during the violent upheaval, but they'd been tossed around like dolls, and the fire was raging, coming from the front of the vehicle.

Still. They went still, freezing with a hard shudder while the car was upside down.

Lily found herself on top of Atlas, and blood dripped near her eye, she could feel it. His hands were on her waist, so tight. "Atlas?" Lily pushed up. They were—upside down.

No, no, the car was upside down. The floorboard above them. The roof beneath them.

A growl broke from Atlas.

Smoke poured in from the front of the vehicle. Smoke and flames. The window between the front and the back of the limo had never risen back up fully, and the smoke and flames spilled in from the front. *The front. Carl?* Automatically, she glanced toward the front.

"Get...out," Atlas gasped.

Her stare whipped back to him.

His eyes were open. He had blood on his right cheek. A long slice. His fingers were tight bands around her waist. *"Get...out, Lily."*

She bounded off him. But before she could do more than that, he'd locked an arm around her waist. He shoved at the door to the side. It was jammed, didn't open, and the smoke in the back grew so thick that she started to cough. And the flames—Lily could hear them crackling up front.

What happened? Why is the car on fire?

He kicked harder at the door. Yelled in fury and *shoved* even as he kept a tight hold on her with one arm.

The door opened.

"Atlas!" Desmond was there. Standing just beyond the open door. Wide-eyed. Frantic. He grabbed her. Grabbed for Atlas.

They tumbled away from the vehicle, and she looked back to see that the front of the now upside-down limo was *blazing*. The hood, the engine area—it had ignited. The front seat was full of smoke and flames and—"Carl!" Lily screamed.

Atlas pushed her back. "Get away! Get away from the flames! We'll get him!"

They would *all* get him. She scrambled to help.

Atlas shoved her back once more. "Lily, dammit, *no!* I need you safe! Get to Desmond's car!"

"Left my phone there," Desmond shouted. "Grab it. Call for help!"

He and Desmond barreled toward the front of the limo.

Her breath shuddered out. Fury and fear battled inside of her. They were punching at the glass. The car was upside down, and Atlas was trying to slide *in* the driver's window in order to get Carl while the flames just burned higher.

A bomb? Did the killer set this, too? And if so, there could be another one waiting to explode. One near the gas tank, and if it erupted or if the fire spread, then the car could go up completely, with Atlas inside of it and...

She stumbled back. *Help.* She'd call for help. Her new phone was somewhere in the back of the limo, so she had to use Desmond's. Carl was going to need EMTs. Swiping at the blood on her forehead, the blood that wanted to drip into her eye, she darted for the nearby sedan. Desmond's car. The driver's side door was open. She reached inside.

And she felt a little sting in her side. Just a prick. There one moment. Gone the next. Automatically, she swatted with her hand toward the sting—

Felt a syringe. She glanced down and saw the syringe. The needle. It had gone in her side.

"I think they'll get him out, Lily," a low voice told her. "And we really have to hurry."

The...the hell they did. She grabbed for that open car door, her body slumping toward it even as the man holding her tried to haul her back.

Her strength was waning, a weight settling over her, but even as darkness pulled at her, she grabbed that door...

And hauled it shut on the hand that held her. She

slammed it into him. Trying to crunch his bones. Trying to *hurt* him.

"Fucking bitch..."

You have no idea. Her last thought. When she woke up again—*if* she woke up—then he'd learn that she was truly her mother's daughter.

* * *

FLAMES BIT AT HIS HANDS. Atlas ignored the flash of fire and grabbed tightly to Carl's shoulders. He'd had to break the driver's side window and crawl in to reach the man, and Carl was out cold, no help at all.

The flames had been flying over Carl's shirt, his chest, and Atlas had slapped at them, and now he was going to haul Carl out of there. Dammit, he *was* getting Carl out.

"Pull!" Atlas bellowed.

Desmond had a grip around his waist and his friend hauled back with all of his strength, yanking Atlas out and, since Atlas was not letting go of Carl, pulling the driver out, too.

As soon as they were clear of the car, he and Desmond grabbed Carl. They carried the unconscious man away from the growing flames. Cars were screeching to a halt near them. Reporters jumping from their vehicles. People filming frantically with their phones and camera equipment.

Filming. Not *helping*. "Call nine-one-one!" Atlas shouted at them. Were any of the reporters listening to him?

He spread Carl's body on the ground. A big gash poured blood from the man's forehead, and blisters had already risen on Carl's chest and arms. His pant legs had been eaten away by the flames, but they'd gotten Carl out before those flames raged out of control.

Atlas's gaze cut back to the car. *What in the hell happened?*

"What in the hell happened?" Desmond demanded, voice low, as his question echoed Atlas's thoughts. "I was behind you. Things were normal one moment, and then the limo was flipping the hell over the next minute as flames poured from the front."

The reporters pressed in closer.

"It was an explosion," Atlas said. Then, dammit, because he didn't want one of those jerks with their phones and cameras getting killed right in front of him, he loudly announced, "I think it could have been a bomb." A bomb that had been placed under the front of his limo. "So back the hell away from the vehicle!" Atlas shouted at the reporters. "There could be another one! *And don't you all see the flames? Dammit, get back!*"

They scuttled back. Finally. Atlas yanked off part of his shirt and tried to apply pressure to Carl's head wound. His stare whipped around the crowd again. Lily—had she gone to seek shelter in Desmond's car? He couldn't see her. "I need you to get eyes on her," he said to his friend.

Desmond frowned, then glanced over his shoulder.

"I need you to stay with Lily." No, more than that. "Take her home. Please, man. Get her to safety."

"You coming with us?"

"I can't leave him." Was an ambulance coming? "*Did someone call the fucking police?*"

As if in answer, a siren screamed in the distance.

His breath shuddered out. "Get Lily out of here." Because this place was a circus. Far too dangerous and...

A bomb under my limo?

Desmond rose.

Atlas's hand flew out and curled around Desmond's wrist. "What if there is a bomb on your ride, too?"

"We don't know it was a bomb, not yet."

His instincts screamed that it had been. "You think cars just ignite for shits and giggles? Because this has never happened to me before."

Desmond's expression became even grimmer.

"You keep your car parked in the same garage with my limo." Atlas tried to keep his voice low now, but he feared the reporters were picking up every single word. "Yours could have been tampered with, too." *Fuck me, I sent Lily to Desmond's car!*

"Hell." Desmond's hands fisted.

Yes, the fire made him feel like he was in hell.

Carl groaned.

"It's okay," Atlas told him. "Help is coming."

"What do you want me to do?" Desmond pushed. "Do you want me to drive her out of here or—"

"Just get her. Make sure she's safe." They'd figure it out. The cops were coming. They could get a ride in a patrol car if necessary. But—"*I need eyes on Lily. Now.*"

Desmond bounded off. He shoved through the pack of reporters.

"*What happened, Atlas?*"

"*Are you hurt?*"

"*Who is the injured man?*"

"*Where is Lily Gallo?*"

The questions fired at him, and he ignored them as he focused on Carl. The man's eyes cracked open, and he groaned again, the sound heavy with pain. As he woke up, the pain from his burns had to be careening through him.

"*Lily Gallo was in the limo with you!*"

Yes, he was aware. She'd been in the limo, telling Atlas

that she loved him. Explaining that love wasn't always perfect and sweet. Not soft and gentle.

She'd also been telling him that she knew who the killer was.

"Where is Lily?" A sharp question from one of the reporters.

"She's safe," he snapped back. Lily was safe. Desmond was getting her.

The wail of sirens grew louder. He looked up and saw the flash of lights approaching. An ambulance. A police cruiser. A fire truck.

"She's not here!" Not a reporter's voice—Desmond's voice. He pushed through the crowd even as the ambulance braked nearby. "Atlas, she's not here!"

Atlas felt something rip apart inside of himself. He leapt to his feet even as EMTs barreled toward Carl. They grabbed for Carl.

Two grabbed for Carl. One grabbed for Atlas. "Sir, sir, you're bleeding, and you have burns—"

He broke away from the EMT and raced toward Desmond.

Desmond's eyes were wide. Wild. "She wasn't at my car. Her ring—her ring was on the ground." He lifted his hand and the sapphire and diamond ring rested in his palm.

Lily's engagement ring.

The ring with the tracker so that he could always *find* Lily.

A roar broke from him, and the chaos and shouts from the reporters immediately ceased. All eyes were on him, but he didn't care. He was racing toward the sedan. Desmond and his plain cars. Always saying they helped him to blend in, that they made guarding Atlas easier.

The driver's side door hung open. No sign of Lily. He'd

told her to go to the car just because he'd wanted her away from the flames. He'd wanted her to be safe.

He surged forward, grabbing for that door. Something seemed to snap beneath his foot. He looked down...

A broken syringe.

"No." Atlas shook his head. "Lily?" The car was empty. No Lily. He whirled around. *"Lily!"*

The cameras were rolling. The reporters gaping at him. *"Lily!"*

She was not there.

* * *

"WE'LL FIND HER."

Atlas sat on the couch. His hands were between his knees, his head sagging forward.

"I've got every cop and federal agent in the county searching for Lily," Gage continued as the Fed paced in front of him. "We will *find* her."

Atlas had been taken home by the cops. They'd wanted him to go to the hospital. To get checked out. Screw that. He had no intention of seeing freaking Dr. Phillip Owen again.

Gage had arrived at the scene as the cops and EMTs had been trying to get Atlas in the back of an ambulance. The Fed had needed to physically force Atlas into the back of his government-issued SUV. Atlas had been so desperate to keep searching. To find Lily.

She'd been taken from him. Taken while he'd been busy hauling Carl out of the wreckage. There one moment, and gone the next.

"We're reviewing every bit of footage that the reporters on scene had," Gage continued. He paused near Atlas. His voice was grim but determined, as he added, "Maybe someone picked up something that we can use. Something that will help us."

Lily was gone. The bastard had taken her. And Atlas was *helpless*. "She knew who he was."

"What?"

The doorbell rang. He was so damn tired of that doorbell ringing. Cops and Feds. In and out.

No Lily.

Where would the bastard have taken her? Where would they have gone? He wanted to find Lily. He *would* find Lily.

No tracker. He left her ring behind. I can't trace her. She taunted the freak, dared him, and he saw...the bastard was there. Right there while I was hauling out Carl. So close.

And Lily was gone.

Footsteps rushed across the marble floor. The clatter of high heels. Automatically, his head lifted. His head turned toward the sound. "Lily?" He began to rise.

But it wasn't his Lily.

Lily wore flats, not heels. Flats and the beautiful dress that had fluttered around her.

A woman with strawberry blonde hair and chocolate eyes rushed toward him. She'd been the one at the door. Tear tracks were on her face. Her heels clattered to a halt as she stopped just a few feet from him. "I'm Sloane."

"I know." He'd already recognized her from the pictures he'd obtained...back when he'd been making his Lily file.

Where are you, Lily? He needed the Feds out of his house. He needed to scorch the earth. He needed to crucify the bastard who'd taken her.

"He...has her?" Sloane asked as her lower lip trembled.

They'd known she was coming from the airport.

Desmond had left orders for the guards to allow her access to the house. Unless you had a badge or you were Sloane Armstrong...everyone else was being kept at the edge of the property's perimeter.

Gage turned to confront Sloane. "There was a bomb in the limo. My team thinks it was detonated using a remote, that the bastard was nearby. Watching, waiting..."

And while Atlas had been busy, he'd taken his target. "It wasn't Hatch Davis or Westin Blanchard." As Lily had thought. "They weren't the next targets. He was here, waiting for her. He wanted her." Lily had been the next victim.

Gage glanced back at him. "Hatch Davis has been missing for six days. Found that out right before I got news of Lily's, ah, disappearance." A grimace.

Disappearance? Screw that. Lily had been abducted. Kidnapped. Taken.

"Hatch went on a camping trip, so no one thought anything was even wrong at first. Until he didn't come home. Until the Feds went looking for him—because you pulled more strings than I had and you got them moving in Oklahoma City, helluva fast."

Desmond had been watching silently from his position near the fireplace. He stepped forward. Fast steps. "Is he dead?"

"Probably," Sloane said. She swiped at her cheeks. "If it's been six days, yeah, I'd say the poor bastard is dead by now."

Atlas shook his head. He stood fully, stretching and moving away from the couch. "Lily's files were only *just* taken. *Just* taken," he emphasized. "Not taken six days ago. Hatch can't be dead. The killer shouldn't have him. The kid doesn't even know who his father is. Lily figured that out..." His words trailed off.

The kid couldn't be taken, not unless the killer knew about him before the break-in at Lily's place. And that would mean the killer had seen Lily's files *before* the theft at her home. The killer would have needed to get access to the intel on Hatch Davis at least a week ago.

Atlas's gaze sharpened on Gage. Gage had appeared on the scene of the limo fire so quickly. *As if he'd been close by?*

More than that, though, Gage had been in Dallas very fast, too. Right after Atlas and Lily's abduction, he'd been there. Just *when* had Gage first arrived in Dallas?

Atlas's gaze raked Gage. He really didn't like the bastard. Mostly because he suspected the jerk was still in love with Lily.

Get the fuck in line.

Atlas sucked in a breath. And then—he lunged at the Fed. He slammed his hands around the prick's shoulders and threw Gage against the nearest wall. "If you've hurt Lily—"

"Stop! I didn't! I *wouldn't!*"

Like Atlas was gonna believe that. "She *knew* who the killer was! She'd figured it out, and Lily was about to tell me. She knew, dammit, and he took her! We went back to the scene at the cabin, Lily talked to the inspector, and she —" Atlas broke off.

Gage glared at him. Gage, the Fed who'd let Lily slip through his fingers.

Atlas's head turned.

Sloane stood nearby, another tear sliding down her cheek.

Desmond's hands were clenched at his sides. Fury evident in every tight line of his body.

Atlas felt the same fury. No, not the same. His was so much stronger. So much hotter. It burned. He had no control. All he wanted to do was attack. Destroy. Kill.

And, as he stood there, as the pieces clicked in his mind, as he thought of everything that had happened recently...

The blast at the cabin...

A blast that hadn't touched the basement. But had killed a cop.

The motive of the killer...the violence...

The perp was so determined to punish the guilty. To make them suffer as much as possible for their crimes.

And Atlas thought of Hatch Davis. Potentially killed days before, long before Lily's files had been stolen. But if that was the case, if Hatch was already dead, then the murderer would have needed access to Lily's data sooner. Especially since the info about Hatch being the child of a serial wasn't public knowledge. That was knowledge that Lily had possessed. The killer would have needed to be in Lily's house in order to get the info on Hatch. He would have needed to get close to her...

He would have needed...

"Sonofabitch," Atlas breathed. He let go of Gage. "Get out of here. *Go find my Lily.*"

Gage glared but straightened his shirt. "I will," he snarled back. "This might fucking stun you, but *I* actually care about her. I will get her back. I will save her."

"You think I don't care?" Lethally soft. "*You think I don't care?*"

"Can you?" Gage's nostrils flared. "I'll have police officers and Feds stationed close to your estate." A slant of his gaze toward Desmond. "Seeing as how your guards can't seem to do the job of keeping you and Lily protected."

"Oh, you're a sonofabitch," Desmond noted. "Understood."

"My partner is still at the recent crime scene. She's gathering data and evidence. Know that we *will* track the bastard. We'll check all the video footage. We will find Lily."

"Then go be the hero." *Go the hell now.*

"I will. Because being a hero is something you sure as hell will never be." Gage stormed out. The front door slammed moments later. Atlas stood there, his hands balling into fists as his mind whirled. *So many things to do...*

"Lily never loved him." Sloane's low voice.

His head turned toward her.

"She's so reserved. So controlled. A lot of people get confused about her because of that. They think—they think she doesn't feel anything. That she's cold as ice." A hard shake of her head even as the tears gleamed on her cheeks. "It's the opposite. She feels too much. Too strongly. She keeps her control because she's afraid of all the emotions inside herself."

Atlas had thought he had such great control. *Such a fool.* And to think, he'd boasted to Lily that he could turn on and off his emotions.

Fury blazed through him. Fear choked him. Could he turn them off? No. Dammit, no. "Lily loves me." Something that both gave him comfort and tormented him. He pulled in a breath. The Fed was gone. That meant he could get to work. "She loves me, and I will kill for her." He'd always known that he would. Fuck being the hero. The bad guy was needed more now than anything else.

Desmond stalked closer. "Atlas?"

He flashed his dimples at his old friend. "I know who the killer is, too." More than that, though...He nodded. "I think I can find the bastard." No, correction. "*We can find him.*"

Desmond nodded. "Then let's fucking go."

He was already going. Rushing to his office, grabbing his phone, his laptop. Calling in favors with frantic phone calls even as his fingers flew over the keyboard of his computer. Research and damn development. Yeah, that was what he did. Security research for the government. Medical research for health companies. Computer hacking and data retention. Information was his life.

No, Lily is my life.

He called the right people. He asked the right questions. He demanded his intel.

Lily loves me. I will kill for her.

Because...

I love Lily. "Hold on, sweets. Hold on."

Chapter Twenty-Seven

"You bitch, you nearly broke my wrist!"

Nearly? How unfortunate. She'd hoped that she had succeeded in breaking his bones. Lily slowly opened her eyes. "Better go to the hospital and get that checked out, just in case..." Her voice came out raspy. A little too rough. "And while you're there..." She focused on the jerk in front of her. "You can explain why a dead man is still alive and kicking, Detective Swain." Because the absolute bastard Benedict Swain was standing in front of her. "I've got to say, death has been very kind to you."

"Are you fucking joking right now?"

"Why are people always asking me that? No, I'm not joking. Death was kind. But I can promise you, that kindness will not last much longer." A sad shake of her head that sent some nausea flooding through her. *What had been in that needle?* "You're about to meet hell."

He laughed in her face.

Sort of the reaction she'd expected, but, still, annoying. "Do you think I won't be found?"

The laughter lingered in the air, his amusement so very

heavy. Stifling. "Who's gonna find you?" A smirk. "Your Fed ex? You think FBI Special Agent Gage Emerick is going to rush to the rescue and be your big hero?"

She didn't want a hero.

"Forget it. That dumbass is probably on his way down to New Orleans. Besides, you and I both know he couldn't find his own asshole with a flashlight." More laughter. "He always used you for the hard work. I did my research. I know just how useless he is."

"The man can at least find his own asshole. With or without a flashlight." She shifted in the wooden chair as she tried to take stock of her surroundings. Her hands were cuffed behind her. The cold metal dug into her wrists. "You're underestimating him."

"No, I'm just anticipating his moves. You told Gage that my next vics would be either Hatch Davis or Westin Blanchard." The smug smirk lingered on his lips. "He always follows what you say. Westin is the one with the history of violence, so that means the Fed will figure I am going after him. Gage likes glory, so he'll probably want to swoop down to the Big Easy and try to catch me himself." One hand grabbed her shoulder as he leaned forward and put his mouth to her ear. "But I'm not there."

"Obviously." She didn't let any emotion enter her voice. "How do you know what I told him?"

"I still have a lot of access to police info. Back doors in, if you will. Plenty of chatter went down when Gage was trying to get protection for the vics he thought would be hit next."

"Are you really going to tell me that I was wrong? That you *don't* intend to kill Hatch and Westin?" Where was she? Her gaze darted around. There were fishing poles on the walls. Wooden walls. Faded furniture. A little kitchen to the right. "Are we in yet another cabin? Just how are you finding these places?"

He released her and straightened to his full height as he glared down at her. She knew he wanted her to be afraid. Too bad for him. She was far too angry to be afraid.

"This was my father's place," he snapped at her. "Even has a beautiful fucking lake not too far away. Not that I ever got to see it, not while I was growing up. I didn't exactly fit into my old man's life." His eyes glinted. "That lake is gonna be your final resting place. No one will ever find you. Atlas Bennett will spend the rest of his days searching for you. Think that will rip him apart?"

"I doubt it. Atlas doesn't love me so I don't see why he would be ripped apart by my absence."

Her calm words and certain tone had him blinking...and backing up another step. A holster rested on his hip. A gun inside that holster. She was sure he must have a knife on him, too.

The better to carve me open? She was getting away. She would *not* go out screaming in agony with this sonofabitch.

But he was blinking at her now. Confusion had appeared on his face.

"Is that why you took me?" Lily asked him, voice polite. Curious. "Because you thought it would hurt Atlas?" Her lips tightened. "If so, that annoys me. I'm more than some tool to be used to hurt a man."

"You're a *fucking* killer! Just like your mother!" The smirk was gone. The confusion gone. Spittle flew from his mouth.

Oh, yes, that's the way. Put that DNA everywhere. "What on earth makes you think that? I research killers, I—"

"You fuck them, Lily." His breath huffed out. "You

think I don't know what you did with Atlas? You moved in with him right away. I wasn't even cold in the ground!"

"Hate to point out the obvious, but you are not in the ground. Also, we weren't involved, so I could do whatever I wanted. By the way, I *wanted* Atlas."

"And I wanted to be wrong about you! I *liked* you."

"Did you?" She wasn't so sure about that.

"You rejected me."

Considering that you've kidnapped me, twice, and that you drugged me, I feel that rejection was a good choice. "Yes, I stand by that."

He blinked.

"Who died in your place?" Lily asked him.

He laughed.

Oh, but he was certainly full of himself. So confident. Almost high on his power. That overconfidence could work in her favor.

"You called me that day," he recalled. "Asking for help. I didn't intend for you to be there, you know. Didn't realize you were watching Atlas so closely."

"I called you even as I saw Atlas being attacked. You *answered* my call, so that means you weren't the one who attacked him." She pulled lightly at the cuffs. Not like she could do some Houdini routine out of those. But maybe she could still get *up* with them on her. Her feet pressed into the floor. Her legs weren't secured. Her arms were behind her, but if she shot up quickly, her arms would just slide up and away from the chair. Once she was standing, perhaps she could hurl her whole body at Benedict. Knock him to the floor. *And then what?*

Hmmm.

She truly hated to think this way but...just what would her mother do?

Poison, of course. But not like Lily had some poison right near her. If only.

"Oh, that was a friend…" He eased back another step. "The same friend who taught me how to wire that bomb to explode at the cabin." He raised a clenched hand. A hand with a slightly swollen wrist. "Boom." His fingers spread. "An ex-con who thought I'd go easy on him because he was cooperating with me. Screw that shit. He was going down, too. People have to pay for their crimes. Justice will be served."

"You put your badge on his body. You killed him…" She considered the timeline. "You did that while Atlas and I were in the basement?"

A nod.

"And how did you do it?" *Keep him talking*. If he was talking, he wasn't killing her, and she could keep coming up with options to save her own life.

And to end his.

"You wouldn't have stabbed him," Lily decided. "Or shot him. Not like you could have some sort of injury that didn't match the narrative you were trying to sell."

His hand shoved into his pocket, only to rise a moment later, fingers holding tightly to a clear, glass vial. Liquid was in that vial. Looked like water, but she was sure it wasn't. "Took a page from your playbook, Lily."

Definitely not water. "Poison."

A nod. "Who the hell is gonna run his bloodwork? Do a tox screen? The overtaxed ME? Nah. The poor vic died in a blaze. Burned beyond recognition. Don't even know if they *can* do all those blood tests and tox screens and shit now. Not with the condition of the body they recovered."

She didn't take her gaze off the poison. "It's not my playbook. My mother used poison." But now she was worried. More worried than she'd been before. "What did you give me...at the car?" Was poison already in her blood? Was the clock ticking down and she didn't know it? If so, she really needed to speed this scene along.

"A sedative. Worked like a charm, didn't it? This..." He eyed the vial. "This will put you in the grave fast. Wanted to talk to you first. Needed our one-on-one session. A session with the great Dr. Lily Gallo." Rough laughter. "I had to personally let you know that you didn't see what was right in front of your face."

"I'm not great." He was so wrong on that. "But then, neither are you."

His jaw tightened.

"The evidence pointed to you, and, for the record, I did figure it out. The cuffs were the first tip-off. Police grade handcuffs that you used on me and on Atlas and on the other two kills in Dallas. Guess you just couldn't resist grabbing them from the station and using them on your victims."

His eyes narrowed.

"The killer was punishing his prey, but...you'd had run-ins with both of the victims, hadn't you? With the drug dealer, William Lloyd. With the domestic abuser and accused rapist, Conry Harding."

"The charges wouldn't damn well stick," he snapped. "They kept walking."

"So you punished them on your own. You started with William. Then you went right back for Conry."

"They were dangerous men! They deserved what they got."

She kept hammering at him. "You deleted all the files on your computer. Took as much from your office at the station as you could because you were trying to hide your ties to those men." This was more that she'd figured out. More that made sense to her. "Just as you trashed your own place, didn't you?"

That smug smile spread on his face.

"Your place." She inclined her head toward him. "My place."

"You had a list of killers, Lily. A whole freaking list of people who belonged in the ground. I saw it when I was at your house. You'd gone to answer the phone, talking to your friend Sloane, and I knew, as soon as I saw that info, I knew..."

"You knew you had plenty of people to punish."

A nod. "Yes. *Yes.*"

"But you didn't want anyone to ever suspect you. So you faked your death."

A shrug. "I became the ultimate victim."

You are not a victim. "You went after Tonya Johnson."

"Have you seen the crime scene photos? I gave her a wound to match yours." His gaze fell to her stomach. "Learned about that, you know. Took some doing, but I found out that you were cut open before."

She swallowed. *Am I going to be cut open again?* No, no, that wasn't happening. "You left Atlas's cufflinks at the scene with Tonya. That was a major mistake."

"Was it?"

"Gage thought Atlas was the perp because of those cufflinks. I don't think that was your intention, though. I don't think you wanted Atlas to be the suspect. It wouldn't make sense, not with me right there to alibi him."

"You shouldn't have been with him. I wanted more for you!"

"What is that more?" He still gripped the poison. She had to drag her gaze off the vial.

A gun on his hip. Poison in his hand. *And a knife has to be close by.* While she had nothing but handcuffs on her wrists. Hardly a fair situation.

"I'm more! Me, dammit! You should have been with me!" Fury blazed on his face. In his eyes. In his voice. "But you rejected me, right from the beginning. You were too focused on Atlas Bennett. Atlas and all of his money and his power."

Now that was insulting. "I don't care about his money. Or his power."

"He's an experiment. A test subject, just like the others. You don't care about him at all—"

"Yes, I do. I love him."

His mouth dropped open.

"But he doesn't love me. So you taking me, you trying to hurt him by attacking *me*, it won't do anything to Atlas. I guess, though, it will do plenty for *you*, won't it? Because you enjoy killing so very much." Her body tensed because she knew that she was going to attack. She couldn't risk him dosing her with the poison. Shooting her. Using a knife to slice her open and yank out her—*no*. Lily shut down the thought. Better to do this now, while she could. While she was alert. Aware. If he decided to pump her with more sedatives, she'd be helpless. If he started cutting her and blood loss and pain made her weak, she'd be *helpless.*

Lily didn't intend to be helpless.

Magnolia would not be helpless.

"I...don't enjoy it." A crack in Benedict's voice.

A crack in his armor. "Of course, you do. It's why you killed so quickly after William Lloyd."

"William was trying to stab me! I fought back! That bastard killed three kids with his drugs! I went to question him, and the prick came at me with a knife. What in the hell was I supposed to do?"

"Probably not disembowel him, but you do you."

His teeth snapped together.

"You liked it." She believed this with all of her being. "It's just you and me here. I don't know why you would pretend otherwise when it's just us. I've interviewed dozens of killers. I know what motivates them." She wet her lips. "I know about the darkness that grows and grows inside of you. The need that can get so consuming inside that it threatens to eat you alive. You can't stop it. It's worse than any addiction. It's blinding. It *controls* you."

Sweat appeared on his brow. The lights overhead shone down on him. "There's a rush. A rush that comes because I did the *right thing*."

"You got that rush again when you killed Conry Harding?"

"No one grieved for that bastard. His poor wife wanted him in the ground. He'd hurt her. Bet the woman wanted to give me a medal."

"And Atlas? You came after him because...?"

"He's evil. You fucked true evil, and you got off on it." His hand had fisted around the vial. "Those reporters—they were live streaming you outside the cabin. I heard the things you said about me. I saw the way you *looked*. Messy hair. Wrinkled dress. His hands stayed on you. He touched you like he owned you. You'd probably fucked in the car, and then you stood there, having fucked the devil, and you had the nerve to call me *weak!* I had the bomb in the limo. I'd put it there days ago. I could have made it go off at any time. I did it then, though, because I had to get *you*. I was going to—" Benedict stopped.

She finished, "You were going to punish me because I,

um, fucked evil?" He probably wouldn't appreciate it if she told him that she'd made love with evil.

"You are evil. Born that way. Just like the others."

"The others on my list." Her hands twisted in the cuffs. "Others like...Tonya Johnson."

A nod.

"Westin Blanchard," she stated as she leaned forward a bit, wanting to make sure she'd be able to yank her hands up when she stood.

"I'll get around to him eventually. Got to wait for the Feds to cool the hell down first." He turned away.

"Hatch Davis?"

His shoulders stiffened. "Got him days ago. His body will be found soon enough."

Her heart slammed into her chest. "But Hatch never hurt anyone. If you have my files, you know...*Hatch never hurt anyone*."

"Didn't have all your files at the time. Just had his name. Knew who his prick of a father was." His back was still to her. "Hatch was easy to kill. Dumb kid just walked right up to me when I asked for directions on the walking trail."

"He wasn't evil." She had to blink, quickly, because tears filled her eyes. "He'd never done anything wrong. Not a single thing."

"Evil is in the blood. Your mistake is that you think you can make them better. You think they won't be like their parents, but they were born evil. Eventually, that evil will show. It's just a matter of time. By killing them, I'll save others. I'm doing the right thing."

Was that the lie he told himself? Or did he truly believe those words?

"A lot of names are on your list, Lily. I'll take care of them all. Sooner or—"

She shot to her feet. Yanked her arms up and ignored the ache in her shoulders. If he'd wanted her to stay in the chair, he should have *tied* her to it, not just cuffed her hands behind her back. She lunged forward, even as he began to turn back toward her. Lily slammed her whole body into him. She hit him as hard as she could, and they both fell to the floor. But she scrambled back immediately. She rolled. Twisted. She heaved up to her feet.

"You bitch!"

She drove her foot into his face. Once. Twice. Three—

He let go of the glass vial. Benedict caught her foot, and he yanked her toward him. Lily fell down. She landed on her ass as she slammed onto the wooden floor. Shouting, Benedict jumped on top of her. Blood dripped from his broken nose. His jaw looked twisted. Maybe broken from her kicks? His fist pulled back. "You are going to pay—"

A door flew open. Slammed into a wall with a *crack*.

Both Lily and Benedict whipped their heads toward the sound. And in the doorway, standing there, glaring, shoulders so broad they nearly touched the wood on either side of him...

Atlas.

Atlas...holding a gun. Aiming it straight at Benedict.

"Get away from her!" Atlas bellowed.

Benedict glanced back at her. A smile teased at his lips. "Guess you did matter to him, huh?" Then he yanked the gun from the holster on his hip. He whipped it up, lightning fast, and blasted a shot toward the door. Toward Atlas.

"*No!*" Lily screamed.

Atlas fired, too. A shot exploded from his gun.

But she saw the red bloom on Atlas's shoulder. He'd been hit.

Benedict swore, he jerked, and she knew Atlas's bullet had found its mark, too.

She rolled away as even more bullets blasted. She twisted and contorted, and she brought her cuffed hands under her legs and feet and whipped them up in front of her body. Her gaze fell on the clear glass vial that Benedict had held earlier. The one he'd let go of so that he could grab her kicking foot.

She snatched up the vial of poison. Then she rushed behind the freak.

But Benedict spun toward her. His left hand shoved against his throat where Atlas's bullet must have hit him. Benedict was trying to stop the blood flow with that hand, but blood *poured* from between his fingers. The blood had already soaked his shirt. He weaved before her. His right hand still held his gun, and he was trying to aim it at her.

"Lily!" Atlas's bellow. "*Get away from him!*"

There was no time.

Bam. Bam.

Two more shots from Atlas. They slammed into Benedict's back, and he jerked. Once. Twice. His eyes widened. His mouth dropped open.

She shoved the glass vial between his lips. Her cuffed hands rammed into his face as hard as she could. She heard the glass *crunch* and saw the horror in his eyes even as he began to fall. His legs were giving way, and he fell forward, knocking into her. Taking her down with him to the hard floor.

"Lily! Lily!"

Atlas yanked Benedict off her. Atlas tossed him aside. Blood streaked across the floor. So much blood. Still pouring from the wound in Benedict's neck. Pouring from all his wounds and drenching the floor.

Desmond rushed in. With a quick, angry motion, he kicked away the weapon that Benedict had dropped even as his own gun leveled toward Benedict. A gasping, shuddering Benedict.

Atlas crouched in front of her. "Sweets?"

She smiled at him. "Guess you figured out a ghost was doing the killing, hmm?"

His hands flew over her. "You're not hurt? Tell me you're not hurt." Then, *"You're not hurt."*

"Uh, Atlas? Lily? What is happening here?" Desmond's raised voice.

Lily turned her head.

Benedict's body was jerking. His eyes wide. Wild. A long drop of blood poured from his mouth. His face had twisted into a mask of agony.

Atlas pulled her off the floor. Up and into his arms. He held her in a tight grip. A tremor rushed over his body.

He was warm and strong and solid. He was *hers*. He'd come in that door like an avenging angel, and...she'd known he would. She'd known that he would come for her.

Trust.

Faith.

Love.

Atlas's mouth pressed to her forehead. "Give me just a minute," he rasped to her. "I've got to kill the bastard. Make sure he's good and dead this time." He turned to look at Benedict.

A Benedict whose body twisted as if he were experiencing the worst torture imaginable. His mouth had opened in a silent scream as blood poured now from Benedict's nose and mouth even as the bullet wound in his neck continued to gush blood. All of his wounds were streaming blood.

Good and dead.

"No worries," Lily murmured. "I already did that." Though, technically, Benedict wasn't quite dead yet...but soon.

So soon...

Then a siren screamed in the distance.

"Warned you that they'd follow us," Desmond snapped. "Damn Feds."

Sure enough, the Feds came rushing in a few minutes later. The agents wore bulletproof vests and had their guns at the ready. When the Feds arrived, Atlas still held a cuffed Lily while Desmond stood beside them. She made sure to look traumatized. Because she was, after all. She'd been kidnapped. She'd been drugged. She'd been taken from the man she loved.

But...

She was still alive. She'd survived.

And Benedict was on the floor. Covered in blood. Twisting in agony.

Some poisons could be a real bitch.

Chapter Twenty-Eight

"WHEN DID YOU REALIZE THAT BENEDICT SWAIN WAS the one who'd taken Lily Gallo?"

He didn't have the patience for this bullshit.

Atlas sat at the interrogation room table, with Theodora by his side. Like the good lawyer she was, Theodora had insisted on being present for his interrogation. Though why he was being interrogated, Atlas had no clue.

He wasn't the bad guy.

That would be the dead man.

"Atlas?" Gage prompted, as he leaned forward. He sat across the table from Atlas, and his partner, FBI Agent Sharon Hinkle, hovered at his side. "When did you realize that Benedict Swain had taken Lily? Was it *before* or *after* you attacked me at your house?"

"Did I attack you?" A shake of his head. "I don't remember that." Yes, he did. "Sorry." Nope, not really. "I remember being terrified for my fiancée's well-being. Just...I was not right in the head, emotionally. I was far too desperate to get her back. Everything from that scene is a blur for me." He *had* been desperate. True story. And determined.

As soon as he'd realized that Benedict had to be the one who'd taken her...

The pieces were there. I put them together.

Benedict—his home had been trashed, but video footage showed no one other than Benedict entering or leaving the residence for days before the explosion at the cabin. And no one had gone in *after* until Atlas and Lily had made their little visit. So if no one else had gone inside during that time frame...

Benedict, you tricky bastard, you trashed your own place. An attempt to throw them off the scent. And Benedict had deleted his own files at the police station. He'd hidden as much information as he could...because he'd been afraid people would realize the truth.

The detective was a killer. A monster.

But now he was dead.

Oh, sure, the EMTs and the doctors at the hospital had tried to save him. Dr. Phillip Owen had gone on the news—always eager to talk with reporters—and spoken about how the staff had done everything possible. But...

Some people couldn't be saved.

It wasn't the poison that had killed Benedict. Lily would probably be disappointed when she learned that news. The very *first* shot Atlas had fired—ah, yes, that one had done the trick when it drove into Benedict's carotid artery. The blood had pumped fast and furiously out of him. He'd been bleeding out, dying, right in front of them from the moment that bullet connected.

"*When did you know the truth?*" Gage slammed a fist onto the table.

"I really don't like the tone you are using with my

client," Theodora informed him with a sniff. "He's a *victim.* And he's cooperating with you."

Atlas nodded. "I am a victim."

Beneath the table, Theodora kicked him with her high heel.

Gage exhaled. He seemed to grab for his patience. "Atlas, I need to know exactly when you realized the truth about Benedict Swain—"

"You ever hear of the MacDonald Triad?" Atlas asked as he rubbed a hand along his jaw.

"I've studied psychology, yeah, I damn well know what the MacDonald Triad is!"

So much for grabbing onto his patience.

"What does it have to do with Benedict Swain?" Gage wanted to know.

"Benedict set fires as a kid."

Gage just stared at him.

"Did I tell you that we were in the same group home as kids? No? Yes? Well, whatever. He set fires. That's how he wound up in the same group home as me once upon a time. You see, the rage he felt toward me? That was not new. The man's vendetta against me stretched back for years. Ever since I came in one day and caught him burning the few clothes that I carried from place to place in a damn garbage bag." He could remember that day perfectly. "The fire was burning, he was laughing, and Benedict thought he'd just get away with what he'd done. He didn't, of course." *I used dirty, thin comforters to put out the flames. I hit the flames, over and over again until only smoke remained.* Atlas looked down at his hands. He'd finally gotten bandages on the blisters he'd acquired while hauling Carl from the wreckage. He hadn't even been aware of those blisters. He'd fired his gun just fine with them. If there had been pain, Atlas couldn't remember it.

Or maybe he just would have endured any pain to save Lily.

But...looking at those bandages reminded him of Carl. Carl *would* be fine. The doctors had assured Atlas of that. His burns weren't severe enough to require skin grafting, thankfully. He'd make a full recovery.

Atlas's gaze lingered on his hands. He'd had blisters after the fire at the group home. Benedict had been so smug. So certain that Atlas couldn't touch him.

But I caught you in the middle of the night, didn't I, Benedict? I put a knife to your throat while the others slept nearby. I told you that if you ever touched something that belonged to me again, I'd kill you.

He'd kept that promise.

And...Atlas nodded as he shifted his attention back to the Feds. "I believe bedwetting is another part of that triad. I do recall that supervisors at the group home found Benedict with soaked sheets on one occasion." That occasion had been *after* Atlas put a knife to the guy's throat. "That would be two elements from the triad. The third element would have been hurting animals, and I just figured Benedict had done that, too. The guy probably had all three elements going for him, and when I added in the fact that the bastard has always hated me, always wanted to destroy me..." A shrug. A long exhale. "When I stopped and thought about all of that stuff, the signs sure pointed to Benedict as being the killer."

Gage's face had gone stone hard. "You didn't say a word to me about this at your house. And how the hell do you know so much about the Macdonald Triad?"

"I believe in being well read. Is that a crime?"

Another kick under the table from Theodora.

"As for not telling you, I do apologize, but you left too quickly. Ran out. So determined to save the day."

"*You* wanted to find Lily yourself. You wanted to save her."

"Absolutely, I wanted to save her. She's mine." Wait. Had that sounded too primitive? "My fiancée." A slight correction. But the truth was...*She is mine. Will always be mine.*

"You wanted to *kill* Benedict Swain."

Theodora tapped her well-manicured nails on the table. "That's not a question. That's a statement. Do you have actual questions for my client? Or can he go? Because he wants to reunite with his fiancée. They've both been through enough trauma."

"Fine. I'll rephrase." A vein bulged near Gage's right temple. "Did you *intend* to kill Benedict Swain?"

Yes. But instead of saying that, Atlas replied, "I intended to rescue Lily. Once I realized Benedict had to be alive, I dug deep and fast and looked for any property connected to him. I realized there was a fishing cabin not too far away. The place belonged to Benedict's father—the same father who gave him up years ago. Jason Swain died three years ago, and no one was using that property. It was isolated. Abandoned. Or, it should have been abandoned. But someone was paying for the power to stay on at that abandoned spot. That looked like a red flag to me."

"You figured Benedict was there."

He'd figured correctly. "With the perfect body dumping spot—the nearby lake—yeah, I figured that would be where he'd take Lily."

The vein bulged a little harder. "Instead of sharing that news with the authorities, you went off on your own. With a gun."

"I have been stalked and kidnapped recently. I was certainly within my rights to have a gun for protection."

"You used the gun to *kill*."

Theodora's nails had stopped tapping. "My client *saved* his fiancée! My client—"

"I think he fired first," Atlas recalled. "Everything happened so fast when I kicked in that door. He whirled toward me. His hand was flying toward his holster." Atlas winced as he looked down at his shoulder. His bandaged shoulder. The bullet had just grazed him, but he knew how to play up an injury. *Benedict couldn't shoot for shit. His bullet barely skimmed me.* "When the door flew in, he was on top of Lily. He was hurting her. I stopped thinking. He fired, I fired and..." An exhale. "I guess he won't be hurting anyone else, will he?"

Beside Gage, Sharon shook her head. "No, he won't." Sympathy filled her gaze as she stared at Atlas. "I'm very sorry for all you endured."

"Thank you." He exhaled and inclined his head toward her. "Any news on Hatch Davis?"

"His body was found," Sharon revealed. "It was...um, a pretty gory scene."

Dammit. Poor kid. "Benedict Swain was an exceedingly disturbed individual."

"Yes, I believe that he was." Sharon closed the file in front of her. "Thank you for your time." She nudged Gage. "I believe we are done here?"

Gage kept glaring at Atlas.

Sharon leaned closer to him. "You know what Brass said. *Time to go.*"

Ah, had Gage been given orders to stand down?

Atlas snapped his fingers.

Gage's eyes narrowed.

"I forgot," Atlas said smoothly. "How did you get to the fishing cabin so quickly? Were you...following me?"

"I was given orders to stay close," Sharon revealed. "To keep you safe. When you left so quickly, I called Gage."

Atlas lifted his brows at Gage. "Is that what it was about? Keeping me safe?"

"What else would it have been about?" Gage finally rose to his feet. "We have some statements for you to sign. Then you're...free to go." It almost sounded as if he had to choke out those last words.

Atlas smiled. "How fantastic. And my fiancée, she's free, too?"

Gage's lips pressed together. "Yes. Not like Lily has committed any crime."

"Of course, not. She's the victim." His phone rang. A loud, insistent chime. Atlas pulled out his phone, glancing at the screen. Odd. This was his personal line, and the call was from a number that he didn't recognize. Spam calls weren't typically a problem for him.

"You're really gonna get that?" Gage demanded, as Atlas swiped his finger over the screen. "Now?"

"We're done here, aren't we?" Atlas asked politely.

Gage whirled away.

Atlas put the phone to his ear. "Who the hell is this?"

Gage looked back.

"Atlas Bennett?" A man's voice. "This is Warden Lawrence McHurley, from the Julia Tutwiler Prison For Women. I believe we need to talk."

Gage was still watching him.

"This isn't the best time. How about I call you back? Very, very soon."

* * *

She wanted to see Atlas. She needed to see Atlas. And if she had to stay in that little office at the FBI's Dallas field office for another moment—

The door opened.

Lily surged toward it but quickly caught herself. That wasn't Atlas in the doorway. It was Gage.

A Gage who looked...

Tired. Grim.

Apologetic.

"I'm sorry, Lily."

She didn't move.

"Sorry you were taken." He took a step toward her. "Sorry you were hurt. Sorry that...hell, sorry that I ever doubted you."

What was this about? Unease settled like a knot in the pit of her stomach.

"I know you didn't kill David Warren."

Uh, she *had* killed him. She'd planned out his murder in meticulous detail. Executed it. Gotten rid of the evidence.

"It was Magnolia. I..." A rush of breath from Gage. "You might want to sit down, Lily. I know you've already been through a lot today."

Yes, she had. And she wanted to get out of there and find Atlas. *Where is Atlas?*

But she sat down in the nearby chair. Gage crouched in front of her. He took her hand.

She immediately wanted to snatch her hand away from him.

"I thought it was you. I doubted *you*."

She was more than aware that he thought she was a killer. *Guilty.*

"I didn't see how it could have possibly been Magnolia. She was locked up. You had to have done it. You had to be the one to kill David Warren."

"I'm really tired," Lily began. *And David Warren's death was attributed to natural causes. Why can't you just let this go?*

"But the doctor is dead, too. Dr. Francis Locke."

Lily shook her head.

"Do you know him? Even recognize the name?"

Yes, she recognized it.

Gage must have thought she didn't, though, because he explained, "He's a doctor from Baton Rouge who was exchanging messages with your mother. A lot of messages. He even went to her prison in order to visit with her. He wanted to marry Magnolia." His hold tightened on her hand. "He's dead. I suspect poison."

"That's...unfortunate."

"I've checked this out. I've investigated thoroughly. You were in Dallas when he died. You didn't kill him. I know that she got to him. Magnolia. She did it. Or she arranged for it to be done. I talked to a guard at the prison...he said she has so many fans—followers—who do what she wants."

"Friends. Magnolia has a lot of friends."

"Lily, I think your mother got someone to kill Dr. Locke. And to kill David Warren. And I'm so sorry that I suspected you. I see the truth now. You aren't like her. You aren't a killer. I was wrong." He leaned closer. "I want another chance with you. You don't belong with someone like Atlas Bennett. He will never understand you. He will always try to pull you down into the dark with him. He won't—"

"Knock, knock," Atlas said from the doorway.

Lily's stare jumped to him.

Gage didn't move.

"FBI Special Agent Emerick, please tell me that you are not *proposing* to my Lily. To *my* fiancée. Because it looks as if you are down on one knee in front of her..." Silky. Menacing. "And you're holding her hand with a very pleading look on your face."

Lily pulled her hand away from Gage. "He isn't proposing. He's apologizing."

Atlas leaned against the doorframe, arms crossing over his chest. Acting as if he didn't have a large bandage on his shoulder from where he'd been *shot*. "Do tell," he encouraged. "Why is he apologizing to you? Is it because he used you to advance his career? Because he was an ass to you?"

She rose.

So did Gage.

"Gage doesn't think I'm a killer any longer," she informed Atlas. "Seems my mother has been pulling strings from prison."

Atlas's thick eyelashes flickered. "How interesting."

"Gage believes she murdered David Warren and a doctor named Dr. Francis Locke. I'm no longer under suspicion in his mind. I'm not some evil murderess." She tried to step around Gage.

But he blocked her path. Blocked her from seeing Atlas.

"Lily..." Emotion—desperation—deepened Gage's voice. "You need to make the right choice. I'm a Fed. My job is to hunt criminals. To stop predators. We can hunt them together. We can be on the right side of the law. I love you. I can say that. Say it without hesitation because I know how I feel."

Oh, really? And he'd loved her when he'd thought she was a killer?

I am a killer. Right.

"Can he say the same?" Gage wanted to know. "Has Atlas Bennett ever said he loves you? Do you think he ever *will* love you?"

A low growl came from Atlas. Then the floor was creaking as he approached. "*Move*, Agent Emerick. Now."

Jaw tight, Gage stepped to the side.

Atlas was now in front of Lily. Tall. Strong. With those brilliant blue eyes blazing at her. No sign of his dimples. No taunting smile. Just...

"What do you want, Lily?" Atlas asked her. "Because I will give you anything in this world. Even if what you want...isn't me."

He was telling her that she could walk away.

"Ask him if he loves you," Gage snapped.

Ah. Gage. Thinking he had such insight into Atlas. Thinking that he knew a psychopath and a psychopath's capabilities...and limitations. But Atlas wasn't like that. Gage was wrong.

So many people were wrong.

"I don't have to ask him," Lily said, completely certain. She reached out for Atlas.

He caught her hand. There were bandages on his fingers. Bandages to cover the wounds he'd gotten while *saving* Carl, so she touched him very carefully.

"I know how he feels." She did.

Despite the bandages, his grip tightened on her. "Lily..." Atlas said her name like it was a prayer.

"I'm ready to go home, Atlas. Take me home?"

A jerky nod. Then he was pulling her close, tucking her against his side, holding her so tightly, as if he'd never, ever let go. They were almost to the exit at the FBI office when—

"Lily!" Gage's choked voice. "Why?"

She glanced back. He'd followed them.

"Why?" Gage asked again.

Because Atlas takes me as I am. All of me. He always has. And because he risked his life to save me. He would do that, again and again. And if that's not love...

Then she didn't know what was. She opened her mouth to reply—

"Because I love her, dumbass. Every single part of her. And don't go expecting an invitation to the wedding. You will not get one."

Shocked, she looked back at Atlas. He was staring at her, jaw locked, appearing disgruntled, and he'd just said that he loved her. He'd called Gage a dumbass, but Atlas had said he loved her and—

Lily laughed. Joy just surged inside of her, and light laughter rang out. Warm. Free. Happy.

Benedict Swain was gone. She and Atlas were safe. He loved her. He understood her. He accepted her.

"That's the most beautiful sound I've ever heard," Atlas whispered.

No, it wasn't. But she'd just heard some beautiful words from him...

I love her, dumbass.

"Take me home." She needed to get away with him. But, the truth was, even as they left the station, even as they entered the dark SUV that was waiting—with Atlas's guards on the side, with Desmond watching protectively— she knew that Atlas was her home.

With him, she'd finally found a place to belong. She'd found a protector. A safe haven.

A partner who would treasure her. Accept her.

Love her.

A lover who would kill for her and show no hesitation.

That was fair because she would certainly do the same for him. Protect him. Fight for him. Kill for him.

With no hesitation.

Epilogue 1

Julia Tutwiler Prison For Women
Wetumpka, Alabama

THREE WEEKS LATER...

"I HEAR that you might have murdered another man, Mother." Lily sat at the little table in the visiting room with Magnolia, aware of the guard's eyes on them. His eyes. His ears. His whole focus.

Magnolia cast a teasing grin toward the guard. "Oh, Jesse, can you imagine? Little old me...killing someone... while I'm locked away in here?"

Jesse shook his blond head. "I just can't imagine that," he rumbled as he pushed back his slightly rounded shoulders.

She winked at Jesse, then looked back at Lily. "Who have I killed? And who told you such a terrible story?"

"FBI Special Agent Gage Emerick told me the story."

"Well, we've both agreed before that the man is a fool. Just who is it that he believes I've killed now?"

"Dr. Francis Locke."

Magnolia cut her gaze toward the guard once more. Lily realized that her mother looked far too pleased. The guard looked smug, too.

Oh, no. "Mother, what have you done?"

Magnolia blinked, all innocence. "A mother always looks after the child she loves. Protecting is a mother's job."

"I wasn't in any danger from Dr. Locke. I didn't even know the man. I didn't need protecting from him."

Magnolia widened her eyes. "Yet I'm believed to have killed him? While locked up in here? What a silly story. Isn't that silly, Jesse?"

"Yes, ma'am," he agreed. His arms remained crossed over his chest.

There seemed to be silent communication going on between Magnolia and the guard. Another *friend* to her mother?

"But...if little old me could exert my influence and get Dr. Locke killed...perhaps I'm also the one who killed say... David Warren?"

"David Warren's death was attributed to natural causes."

"Yes, but some people—some federal agents—just stubbornly thought otherwise, yes?" A smile played at Magnolia's lips. "But, given the events with Francis, I would think a new theory may be circulating."

A new theory was, indeed, circulating.

"I suppose Agent Emerick thinks that I am so wickedly guilty? Responsible somehow for the deaths of David and Francis?" A soft exhale. "He's wrong, as usual. But at least the man will stop baselessly suspecting you. I mean, honestly, we both know that David died of a heart attack. Sometimes, people just die. I bet that's what happened to Dr. Locke, too. He just died. Such a shame. So terrible..."

"He was poisoned, Mother. I've read his tox screen."

Sympathy instantly flashed on Magnolia's face. "He *was* always far too interested in poison. Oh, my. Oh, dear. When I rejected his last proposal of marriage, do you think he killed himself? Do you think my rejection was just too much for him to handle?"

Highly doubtful.

"Goodness. I just had the most dreadful thought." Magnolia's eyes were so wide. "What if Francis has been obsessed with me for *years*? What if...what if he killed David so long ago? How about that theory?"

Yes, how about it.

"Perhaps the guilt just ate and ate at him...and Francis had to take his own life." A despondent sigh from Magnolia. "Such a tragedy. Oh, well, I will grieve. Then, somehow, I will find the strength to go on."

"I am sure that you will." Lily pushed back a lock of hair that had slid against her cheek. "You always find that strength."

"That's a lovely ring," her mother murmured as her gaze sharpened on the hand Lily had raised. "Sapphires and diamonds. Sapphires...they're a symbol of loyalty, aren't they?"

Lily stilled. She hadn't taken off the ring when she came into the prison, mostly because Atlas had made her promise to never, ever take off the new engagement ring that he'd given to her.

She hadn't wanted to break a promise to him.

"Where is your fiancé?" Magnolia asked. "I would very much like to meet him."

Yes, she knew that. Knew that her mother had used the warden to call Atlas in for a meeting. Though they still weren't quite sure how the warden had obtained Atlas's private number. When Atlas had pressed him, the warden had told him that Magnolia supplied the number.

How on earth did you get that number, mother? She would save that question, for later. For now, Lily asked, "What do you want him to do? Donate to the warden? Pay him off so you get cushy treatment before your execution?"

"Oh, darling, my lawyer says I shall be getting a new trial any day. And things are quite cushy enough for me." Her smile came and went. "No, I just want to...meet the man who is taking my daughter away from me."

Not good. "Magnolia..."

"He's here with you, isn't he? I bet he is. I bet he watches over you very closely and..."

The door opened behind Lily. She *felt* Atlas. Didn't even glance back.

Magnolia's gaze rose. Assessed. And what could have been a flash of fear came and went in her eyes. Ridiculous, of course. Magnolia didn't fear anyone.

Or anything.

No, that's not true. She was afraid once. When she thought I was dying.

Magnolia rose, resplendent in her prison orange. And she offered one cuffed hand to Atlas. "Magnolia Calhoun, so pleased to meet you."

Slow steps. Atlas extended his hand. Took hers. "Atlas Bennett."

Magnolia's head tilted to the left. "You *think* you're going to marry my daughter?"

"I think—correction, I *know* that I'm going to love your daughter for the rest of my days."

"Love?" Magnolia pounced. Her grip on his hand seemed to tighten.

"Yes." No hesitation. Then, "Lily has a beautiful laugh."

Magnolia sucked in a breath. She snatched her hand from Atlas. Then that hand pressed to her chest as her stunned gaze flew to Lily. "She...does?"

A nod from Atlas. "I intend to hear that laugh a great deal."

"Lily doesn't laugh easily." She seemed uncertain. The first time Lily could remember her mother being that way.

"I know." Softer, from Atlas. "But I'm a patient man."

"Patient," Magnolia repeated, as if tasting the word. "And what else? What kind of man are you?"

"The kind who will always put Lily first. The kind who doesn't hesitate to protect what he values most in this world."

Lily could not take her gaze off them. They seemed like two predators, sizing each other up. Perhaps...even reaching some sort of truce?

"What do you value most?" Magnolia wanted to know.

"Lily."

A broad smile curved Magnolia's face. "Tell me, do you believe in soulmates?"

Atlas turned his head toward Lily. His eyes were on her. His entire focus, seemingly only on her. "I believe in Lily."

Those words sank into her. Filled her. The ice inside wasn't there. No more hollow aches. She felt warmth and joy and hope.

Hope that her life could be so much more than it had been before. That she could be accepted. Fully. Always. That she would love—and be loved in return.

"You don't think..." Magnolia's considering voice. "You don't think that's she's broken? That she needs to be fixed?"

"There's nothing broken about her. Never has been. Never will be."

A pleased laugh spilled from Magnolia. "Well, aren't you just delightful? Just...delightful."

He glanced back at her mother.

Just in time to catch the deliberate flutter of Magnolia's lashes. "And here I thought you were some big, bad monster..."

"I am."

If possible, her smile stretched even more. "I am going to *like* you."

"That thrills me to no end," Atlas told her. "Because I hear that when you don't like men, bad things happen to them."

Magnolia laughed again.

And Lily realized...

She and her mother had the same laugh.

Epilogue 2

Epilogue Two – The Diary

Dear Diary,

Is it silly to start my entry this way? Dear Diary...as if I am a teenage girl, no, a pre-teen, scribbling away all my secrets to you. But I don't know how else to start, and it's my diary, after all, so...I'll write whatever I want. And today I want to say...

I don't know what it means to be happy. Everyone else seems so happy. All the time. I can smile like them. I can laugh. But I don't feel happy. In fact...

I feel quite the opposite.

* * *

Dear Diary,

I was molested when I was sixteen. Molested. That's a

legal, cold term for something ugly and dark. Don't worry. I took care of him. Had a nice cup of tea. He had tea, too...

The right cup of tea can always make things better in this world.

* * *

DEAR DIARY,

Men lie. They make promises. They don't keep those promises. I hate when people lie to me. Disappointment—again and again. Did I tell you that John hit me? Me? Not a slap. A hit with his fist. I smiled at him after he hit me, and I prepared him a very nice cup of tea. Not my mother's sweet tea. My blend. My fancy tea in my grandmother's teapot.

He drank every drop.

But I just don't think that tea sat well with him.

He shouldn't have hit me.

* * *

DEAR DIARY,

I never put dates in you. Should I be doing that? Time just slips past so quickly. The years flow. You blink, and time is gone.

I'm married now. Found a man who treats me well. So well. Like a princess. I should love him. He does everything right. And yet...

Why don't I love him? I will try. I will try very, very hard to love Dustin Gallo.

I will try.

* * *

DEAR DIARY,

I've had a baby. A little girl with eyes just like mine. Dustin—he adores her. Loves her more than I think he loves me. I suspect...Dustin may know that I don't return his affections. That I've just been faking. I...

My daughter is named Lily. Lily Oleander. She has never been used by a man. Never been lied to. Deceived. Molested. Oh, that dreaded word. She has never had the world abuse her, and she never will.

I don't love my husband. I tried, but I can't. I can't force a feeling that just isn't there. And yet...

Yet when I look at my Lily...

I do feel something stir inside of me.

Is this love?

* * *

DEAR DIARY,

Dustin is dead. He was screwing his secretary. Told me that he wanted a divorce. I offered him a nice cup of tea. Important discussions are always conducted best with a cup of tea.

Lily is sad. So quiet. She loved him. He loved her. I feel...

Never mind. What's done is done. Can't change the past. Can only go forward. Besides, it's not like Lily knows. Who would know? It will be better with just the two of us. Lily is so smart. What a sharp mind. And I think she looks like me...

Maybe when she grows up, she will be just like me.

Or...maybe she will be better. I hope...

I hope she will be.

Be better, my Lily. Please.

* * *

Dear Diary,

Something is wrong with Lily. She doesn't smile like the other children. Doesn't laugh. At first, I thought it was grief because of Dustin. But...

Is it something more? Is it...because of me?

Did I mark my daughter before she was even born? I...

I am sorry. I have never said those words out loud. Not to anyone. I don't regret the things that I do. There is no point in regrets but...if I made Lily like me, if I did this...

I am sorry, my darling.

My beautiful, serious Lily.

* * *

Dear Diary,

Time rolls past. It won't slow down. Lily has grown up—a beautiful teen now. Still, far too serious. No dating for her. No silly parties. Hardly any friends. I ache for her. For the life she should've had, and I know...I see the way she watches me.

She realizes what I've done. She must. Does she think I'm a monster? Is she afraid of me?

She shouldn't be. Not ever. Lily is the only person in this world I would never, ever hurt. She is my daughter. She is my light.

She is the one good thing I have in my life.

I...love my Lily. Love. Maybe I don't love her the way other mothers love their kids. So easily. So freely. But I love her my way.

I would do anything for her. I <u>will</u> do anything. I am going to marry again. David. David Warren. He dotes on Lily. Watches her so closely. Is so very interested in her life. He will make a great father to her. He will be perfect.

I will be perfect...just you wait and see...

* * *

ATLAS CLOSED THE DIARY. He stared into the flames of the fireplace. Lily sat in the nearby chair, silent. She'd been silent as he read the entries. "David wasn't perfect."

"No." Quiet.

He watched those flames. "Do you want the diary back?"

"I want to burn it. It's time to let the past go."

He offered her the diary. She rose, came to him with soft steps, and she took the diary from him. Their fingers brushed, and he felt the surge through his whole body.

My Lily.

She tossed the diary into the fire. The flames bent, then danced. Ashes flew into the air. "She loved me. Magnolia wrote the words in her diary, where she thought no one would ever see them. True words. She wrote down her confessions about her crimes. Her truth about loving me... even as she feared something was wrong with me."

"There is nothing wrong with you." He caught her hands in his. Pulled her closer. "You are going to marry me. We are going to have a great life together."

She seemed to be holding her breath. "And what about children, Atlas? Do you want them? With me? Or are you afraid of—"

"Hell, yes, I want children with you. You will be an incredible mother. Protective, kind, *loving*." How could she not see this? "You have so much love to give, Lily. I am not my father. You are not your mother. We are different. We will have a family. *Our* family. I will spend my life protecting you and our children." Giving them every single thing they wanted.

You are my life, Lily.

An obsession? Yes, but so much more. So very much *more.*

He'd turned off his emotions for most of his life. Turned them off, turned them on.

But with Lily, there was no turning off or on. There was simply just being. Loving her. As basic as breathing.

She'd been right before, when she told him that *making love* wasn't about gentleness. Being in love wasn't, either. It wasn't some sweet, tender rush of emotion. He'd been wrong to think that it was. Being in love—for him—was dark and consuming. A feverish intensity that consumed and compelled. That drove him to be better, to do better, to prove that he could be worthy of her.

To prove...

That you matter, Lily. That you will always matter to me.

Feverish. Binding. So powerful that he knew he'd break any law, take any risk—for her. That was his love for Lily. A love that would tie him to her. That would fill his mind and his heart. Always.

She was his addiction. She was his obsession. She was his world.

His Lily.

His love.

The diary burned, and he brought his mouth to hers. Her hand pressed over his heart. The heart she owned.

Maybe evil did run in his veins. But so what? He could love. He *did* love. He could do what was right. He could be with Lily. They could have a wonderful life.

And if anyone ever tried to hurt her...tried to hurt the family they would have...

Well, Atlas certainly knew how to protect the people who belonged to him in this world.

And he would never, ever be afraid to get his hands dirty.

Some people were just worth killing for...

Lily was one of those people.

THE END

Darkness.

"You just woke up, didn't you? I can tell. Your body went all tense and extra hard."

A woman. Her voice—soft and husky in the darkness. She was…on top of him? He could feel her curves pressed against him. Could smell her scent. Strawberries.

"I'm going to need you not to panic. Panicking will not help us in this situation."

Who the fuck was she? Where the fuck was he?

She was on top of him, he was below her, his body spread on something *hard*. Felt like a damn board.

"You don't know me, but my name is Sloane."

Sloane.

"And it's going to be all right," she assured him.

He liked her voice. He didn't like the cobwebs in his mind.

"Try to keep your breathing nice and slow," she encouraged him. "Because we *are* going to make it out of here. I, um, don't know how much air we have and how long it will last so I'm just trying to—"

"What. The. Fuck?" How much *air* they had?

Her breath blew lightly across his cheek.

His hands lifted to curl around her waist. He was gonna move her *off* him. But, when his hands moved, his knuckles slammed into something hard. As hard as the board beneath him.

Wait a damn minute…

A board below him.

Boards on the side of him.

Darkness all around.

"I'm afraid I can't get off you," she said, sounding apologetic. "There's just nowhere for me to go."

Rage twisted inside of him. "What is happening?"

A soft sigh. "I'm afraid...that we've been buried alive. Together."

He opened his mouth.

And she kissed him.

Author's Note

Thank you very, very much for taking the time to read COMPULSION. I've been wanting to write this book for a long time, and I am so happy that I finally had the chance to tell Lily and Atlas's tale.

I will confess—I'm a true crime addict. I often curl up on the couch with popcorn and true crime, and I get lost in the shows. The shows inspired COMPULSION. In the true crime tales, in the news, we always hear about the killers... but what about their families? What happens to the people who grow up, living with monsters? Those questions led me to COMPULSION...and the "Poison In My Veins" series. I do have another book planned—Sloane's story will be coming your way very soon!

If you have time, please consider leaving a review for COMPULSION. Reviews help readers to discover new books—and authors are definitely grateful for them! (I am super grateful!)

If you'd like to stay updated on my releases and sales, please join my newsletter list. Did I mention that when you sign up, you get a FREE Cynthia Eden book? Because you do!

By the way, I'm also active on social media. You can find me chatting away on Instagram and Facebook.

Again, thank you for reading COMPULSION. Books are my favorite escape, and I hope that they allow you to slip away and destress for a while, too.

Best,

Cynthia Eden

cynthiaeden.com

More Books By Cynthia Eden

Protector & Defender Romance
- When He Protects
- When He Hunts
- When He Fights
- When He Defends
- When He Guards

Ice Breaker Cold Case Romance
- Frozen In Ice (Book 1)
- Falling For The Ice Queen (Book 2)
- Ice Cold Saint (Book 3)
- Touched By Ice (Book 4)
- Trapped In Ice (Book 5)
- Forged From Ice (Book 6)
- Buried Under Ice (Book 7)
- Ice Cold Kiss (Book 8)
- Locked In Ice (Book 9)
- Savage Ice (Book 10)
- Brutal Ice (Book 11)
- Cruel Ice (Book 12)

- Forbidden Ice (Book 13)
- Ice Cold Liar (Book 14)
- Ice Cold Christmas (Book 15)

Wilde Ways
- Protecting Piper (Book 1)
- Guarding Gwen (Book 2)
- Before Ben (Book 3)
- The Heart You Break (Book 4)
- Fighting For Her (Book 5)
- Ghost Of A Chance (Book 6)
- Crossing The Line (Book 7)
- Counting On Cole (Book 8)
- Chase After Me (Book 9)
- Say I Do (Book 10)
- Roman Will Fall (Book 11)
- The One Who Got Away (Book 12)
- Pretend You Want Me (Book 13)
- Cross My Heart (Book 14)
- The Bodyguard Next Door (Book 15)
- Ex Marks The Perfect Spot (Book 16)
- The Thief Who Loved Me (Book 17)

The Fallen Series
- Angel Of Darkness (Book 1)
- Angel Betrayed (Book 2)
- Angel In Chains (Book 3)
- Avenging Angel (Book 4)

Wilde Ways: Gone Rogue
- How To Protect A Princess (Book 1)
- How To Heal A Heartbreak (Book 2)
- How To Con A Crime Boss (Book 3)

Night Watch Paranormal Romance
- Hunt Me Down (Book 1)
- Slay My Name (Book 2)
- Face Your Demon (Book 3)

Trouble For Hire
- No Escape From War (Book 1)
- Don't Play With Odin (Book 2)
- Jinx, You're It (Book 3)
- Remember Ramsey (Book 4)

Death and Moonlight Mystery
- Step Into My Web (Book 1)
- Save Me From The Dark (Book 2)

Phoenix Fury
- Hot Enough To Burn (Book 1)
- Slow Burn (Book 2)
- Burn It Down (Book 3)

Dark Sins
- Don't Trust A Killer (Book 1)
- Don't Love A Liar (Book 2)

Lazarus Rising
- Never Let Go (Book One)
- Keep Me Close (Book Two)
- Stay With Me (Book Three)
- Run To Me (Book Four)
- Lie Close To Me (Book Five)
- Hold On Tight (Book Six)

Bad Things

- The Devil In Disguise (Book 1)
- On The Prowl (Book 2)
- Undead Or Alive (Book 3)
- Broken Angel (Book 4)
- Heart Of Stone (Book 5)
- Tempted By Fate (Book 6)
- Wicked And Wild (Book 7)
- Saint Or Sinner (Book 8)

Bite Series
- Forbidden Bite (Bite Book 1)
- Mating Bite (Bite Book 2)

Blood and Moonlight Series
- Bite The Dust (Book 1)
- Better Off Undead (Book 2)
- Bitter Blood (Book 3)

Mine Series
- Mine To Take (Book 1)
- Mine To Keep (Book 2)
- Mine To Hold (Book 3)
- Mine To Crave (Book 4)
- Mine To Have (Book 5)
- Mine To Protect (Book 6)

Dark Obsession Series
- Watch Me (Book 1)
- Want Me (Book 2)
- Need Me (Book 3)
- Beware Of Me (Book 4)

Purgatory Series

- The Wolf Within (Book 1)
- Marked By The Vampire (Book 2)
- Charming The Beast (Book 3)
- Deal with the Devil (Book 4)

Bound Series
- Bound By Blood (Book 1)
- Bound In Darkness (Book 2)
- Bound In Sin (Book 3)
- Bound By The Night (Book 4)
- Bound in Death (Book 5)

Stand-Alone
- Waiting For Christmas
- Monster Without Mercy
- Kiss Me This Christmas
- It's A Wonderful Werewolf
- Never Cry Werewolf
- Immortal Danger
- Deck The Halls
- Come Back To Me
- Put A Spell On Me
- Never Gonna Happen
- One Hot Holiday
- Slay All Day
- Midnight Bite
- Secret Admirer
- Christmas With A Spy
- Femme Fatale
- Until Death
- Sinful Secrets
- First Taste of Darkness
- A Vampire's Christmas Carol

About the Author

Cynthia Eden loves romance books, chocolate, and going on semi-lazy adventures. She is a *New York Times*, *USA Today*, *Digital Book World*, and *IndieReader* best-seller. She writes romantic suspense, paranormal romance, and fun contemporary novels. You can find out more about her work at www.cynthiaeden.com.

If you want to stay updated on her new releases and books deals, be sure to join her newsletter group: cynthiaeden. com/newsletter.